"I ABSOLUTELY ADORE this series and was so EXCITED to see another book released (which I PROMPTLY bought and devoured in the space of 5 hours...And to top it off, it features an UNDER-GROUND FIGHTER (in a historical setting). What else, can I say, except...I LOVED IT!!!" -Sheryl, *Goodreads*

"I thoroughly enjoyed this story. Grace Callaway is a remarkable writer." -*Love Romance Passion*

"This one is definitely my favorite of the series...I wasn't a big fan of Paul in Her Wanton Wager because he really screwed up and Percy had to deal with the consequences but I really liked him in this one. He actually was trying to change and be a good husband for Charity which was incredibly sweet and romantic. I also love how I got more of Helena, Nicholas, Percy, Gavin, Marianne, and Ambrose because my favorite thing about this series is the characters. I love how each relationship is so different from one another. I also love how all of the characters develop and helped each other out in the many difficult situations they got themselves in. This is definitely one of my favorite romance novels I have read." -Michelle, *Goodreads*

"A refreshing change from most historical romances, and a peek at the lives of the emerging middle class in England. I liked both main characters, and the sex was pretty hot!" -Rhiannon, *Goodreads*

"This book was a surprise. Charity is such a nice person and deserves someone to love her. She has been in love with Paul for a long time and of course it was unrequited. At the beginning of the book Paul is his typical self, drunk, no job, and a wastrel. When they are forced into marriage they both fight to make it work and Paul grows up and steps up and becomes the man he was meant to be for Charity. Their love story is beautiful. Definitely worth reading again." -Angela, *Goodreads*

"I loved Paul and Charity. They were a cute couple. I liked their connection they both thought they were lost souls. It was a fun read. I loved knowing what was going on with the other couple from previous books. Great ending to a really good series." -Yolonda, *Goodreads*

"I love this series, and this installment was no exception." -Karen, *Goodreads*

"I love Paul and Charity! I think they are absolutely perfect together! I love that she had the unrequited love for many years and was a total wallflower that no one ever noticed.... The angst had me literally aching in my chest! The self improvement that both of them had to work through was quite inspiring to witness!" -Kelly, *BookBub*

"Without doubt, this is a very brilliant, dark and beautiful series. The passion and love between all the characters were so intense I could get burned. Sigh* This author is a genius in delivering us a wild and heartmelting adventure with this series. TRULY, A MUST READ." -Greselley, *Goodreads*

Olivia and the Masked Duke

Pippa and the Prince of Secrets

Fiona and the Enigmatic Earl

Mrs. Peabody and the Unexpected Duke (Holiday Novelette)

Glory and the Master of Shadows

Charlotte and the Seductive Spymaster (2024)

HER
Prodigal
PASSION

Mayhem
IN MAYFAIR
BOOK FOUR

GRACE
CALLAWAY
USA TODAY BESTSELLING AUTHOR

Cover Art: EDH Graphics

Cover Image: Period Images

Typography & Book Design: KM Designs

Formatting: Colchester & Page

Chapter One

SPITALFIELDS, LONDON

It was the worst and best thing she'd ever done.

Miss Charity Sparkler was not one to break rules, and yet here she was in the Spitalfields slum, a place no proper middling class miss had any business being. She paid the indifferent hackney driver, her heart thumping as she approached the squalid tenement. For once, she was grateful for her invisibility. Being plain, small, and quiet by nature, she blended unnoticed into most any landscape, and it proved no different here than anywhere else.

As out of place as she was, no one paid her any mind. She walked by weary-faced women toting laundry on one hip and a babe on the other. She squeezed past jug-bitten men playing cards on an overturned crate. Her face shielded by the brim of her bonnet, she clutched her small basket and ascended a rickety flight of steps, recalling her bosom chum Persephone Fines' instructions:

My brother has the room on the top floor at the end of the hallway. You can't miss it—one more step and you'd sail straight off the building where the railing is rotted away. But, Charity—worry had flashed in Percy's blue eyes—*are you certain you wish to do this? I would check on Paul myself, but the cutthroat who holds his vowels is having me followed. I cannot risk giving away my brother's hiding place.*

Charity had insisted on taking the mission for Percy was her very best friend in the world. Despite their differences—Percy was an uncommonly pretty and spirited girl whereas Charity possessed modest looks and a sensible nature—the two of them had gotten on like peas and carrots since their days at Mrs. Southbridge's Finishing School. Yet Charity had to admit to herself that loyalty to her chum was not the only reason she'd agreed to embark on the risky undertaking.

Like a caged bird, the truth fluttered within her breast. As far as she was concerned, it would remain there, forever and anon, for there was no point in releasing that foolish creature from captivity. Why set something free, only to have its wings clipped at first flight?

You're nothing to look at, Father's stern voice reminded her, *but we Sparklers take no stock in vanity. Prudence and self-discipline are what matter. Keep your head down and do as you're told—that's how you'll get by in life, daughter.*

For the first time in her two-and-twenty years, Charity was defying her papa's rules. Guilt and fear shivered over her. She knew her current actions were reckless, highly improper, and if her father found out, he would never forgive her. Uriah Sparkler was a man who did not suffer fools lightly, and everyone—from the employees of his jewelry shop to his only daughter—knew better than to incur his wrath.

But it was too late to turn back now—and she didn't want to.

Because she loved Paul Fines. She'd do anything to help him.

At least she'd had the wisdom to keep her unrequited feelings locked within the deepest chambers of her heart. She'd never confessed her secret to a single soul—not even Percy, though she was certain her friend suspected her wayward infatuation. It was far too embarrassing for Charity to admit aloud so impossible a *tendre*: the object of her yearnings was as handsome and virile as Apollo, the bright, shining god for which he'd been aptly named whereas she ...

She climbed the steps, the boards silent beneath her slight gravity. *I'm invisible. Or at least exceedingly easy to overlook.*

Stopping before the appointed door, she told herself she would be content to admire Mr. Fines from afar. And if, from time to time, she could be of service to him, a friend when he needed one ... Throat cinching, she tamped down her deeper longing.

Don't be foolish. Friendship is all you can hope for.

Straightening her sturdy grey skirts, she took a breath and knocked. When she received no reply, she looked this way and that before reaching for the knob. The door swung open, its rusty hinges heralding her arrival.

Venturing into the windowless chamber, she said in a hushed voice, "Mr. Fines? Are you there? 'Tis me, Charity Sparkler—Percy's friend."

A rustling noise drew her eyes to the far corner of the room. As her vision adjusted to the gloom, she saw a pallet on the floor and upon it ... Pulse thrumming, she quickly shut the door behind her and headed straight for the makeshift bed. Paul Fines lay on his side facing the wall, huddled beneath his greatcoat. As she knelt beside his prone figure, her heart lurched.

A bruise darkened one of his perfect cheekbones. Dried blood clung to his upper lip.

"Mr. Fines," she whispered, "are you alright?"

He mumbled something unintelligible. Stripping off her gloves, she smoothed away a gilded forelock and found his brow clammy, but thankfully not feverish to the touch. His long eyelashes lay in shadowed crescents against his pale skin, and dark gold stubble covered his jaw. He'd fallen asleep in his shirtsleeves, his laces undone and throat bare. A faintly sweet odor drifted up.

It didn't take a physician to diagnose Mr. Fines' ailment: he was utterly tap-hackled.

"Oh, dear. We must set you to rights," she murmured.

She left his side to gather supplies. Using a towel and water from a cracked ewer, she cleaned him up as best she could. Her heart squeezed at his disgraceful state, a far cry from his former impeccable self. In her eyes, however, he remained the most splendid being of God's creation. She cleaned up the dried blood and was relieved to find no cut beneath. She guessed that he'd gotten into a brawl, incurring a temporary nosebleed as well as the bruise on his face. With tender care, she wiped the towel over his damaged cheekbone, patrician nose, and lean jaw, experiencing a *frisson* of guilty pleasure as she did so.

At the same time, worry flooded her: was there no way to halt Mr. Fines' cycle of self-destruction? According to Percy, he had wagered away his fortune and was now hiding from the gaming hell owner to whom he owed money. For how long could he continue to evade his debtor? He couldn't run from his problems forever, and his drinking was definitely not helping matters. There had to be a better solution.

"Thirsty ... water."

Her heart leapt at his hoarse request. "Yes, of course," she said quickly.

Reaching into the basket, she located the bottle of barley water she'd brewed earlier. Flavored with citrus, mint, and a touch of honey, the beverage was a remedy for everything from indigestion to megrims. She poured out a cup. Mr. Fines appeared to have fallen into a stupor again, and when he would not rouse, she eased his head onto her lap.

"Here you go." She held the drink to his lips. "Try to take a few small sips. Slowly now."

Eyes closed, he drank greedily. "More," he rasped.

She refilled the cup and again he downed the liquid. When he was finished, his lashes lifted; even the dimness could not obscure the brilliance of his regard. His pupils were bluer than the heavens, their vivid purity contained by rims of midnight. From years of discreet observation, she'd learned to read his mood from the balance of bright and dark and the gradations of opacity in his eyes. Clear azure reflected amusement and playfulness. Deeper, cloudier shades forecasted darker feelings. At present, his gaze smoldered with smoky intensity.

"You came to me," he said huskily.

His rich, smooth voice never failed to stir her. Her skin prickled as if caressed by a silky feather. Her heart thumped faster when he reached out a hand. His palm, roughened by hours spent sparring at Gentleman Jackson's, cupped her cheek with startling intimacy.

"Your sister ... she sent me, sir," Charity blurted. "I came to ascertain your safety."

"My own guardian angel," he murmured.

His heavy-lidded eyes made her pulse skitter like a spilled basket of buttons. In truth, he'd always been kind and charming toward her and never more so than during the years when she'd been afflicted by spots. One time, as she'd stood planted in her usual position against the back wall of a ballroom, her hands clutching her lilac skirts and the hateful blemishes burning upon her cheeks, he'd approached and swept her a gallant bow.

"*A violet by a mossy stone, half-hidden to the eye.*" His smile had spurred her heart into a wild and ungoverned rhythm. "My dear Miss Sparkler, would you honor me with a dance?"

She'd been certain that Percy had put him up to it. Even so, Charity had floated through that set with him and purchased a copy of Mr. Wordsworth's poems the very next morning. She'd read the ballad that Mr. Fines had quoted to her until the verses were branded upon her soul. To this day, "She Dwelt Among the Untrodden Ways" remained her favorite work of poetry.

Yet despite his many kindnesses, Paul Fines had never gazed at her in the way he was doing so now. As if he was truly ... seeing her.

"Angel of mercy," he whispered. "I have waited so long for this moment, my love."

Shock and joy collided, exploding with the glory of the famed Vauxhall fireworks. It was as if her innermost dreams had been illuminated and brought to vivid life. Disoriented, dazed, she couldn't think, couldn't breathe as her suppressed longing spread its wings. Before she could react, Mr. Fines sat up and brought his mouth to hers.

The astonishing sensation rendered her immobile. She'd had vague notions of what a first kiss might be like, and this was nothing like the peck she'd imagined. For one, his lips lingered, warm and firm, the pressure gentle yet drugging. For another, she found herself kissing him back. Her mouth molded to his like wax yielding to a flame. Her lungs pulled for air, her insides blooming with heat.

Heavens, what is happening?

Dimly, she noted the faint thud of her bonnet hitting the ground, her thoughts growing foggier as the kiss continued. It was so sweet and fantastic that surely this had to be a dream. If so, she *never* wanted to awaken. Her blissful sigh turned into a gasp when she felt a nudge against her lower lip. Goodness, surely he didn't mean to put his tongue *there* ... But he licked again at the seam, the caress coaxing her lips to part. Another sound escaped her as his tongue swept boldly inside her mouth. The taste of honey, mint, and male made her senses spin.

"Devil and damn, I've wanted you for so long," he said roughly.

Fire rushed over her, rendering her thoughts to ashes, leaving nothing but the hot, urgent magic of the moment. *He wants me,* her heart rejoiced. His hands drove into her hair, holding her steady, angling her for his deep exploration. She kissed him back with all of her pent-up longing, all of her trembling heart and soul. He groaned and the world tilted, taking her with it. Her spine arched against the pallet as his kisses blazed along her neck.

Her blood turned to honey, her entire being suffused with sweetness and heat. She clutched at his shoulders, helpless, whimpering in the wake of the exhilarating sensations. So many of them, layer upon layer of delight. He caught her earlobe between his teeth, suckling it, making her squirm and pant. Her breath hitched when his hand covered her breast, his fingers finding the straining peak beneath the layers of fabric. He strummed her nipple, and stars flashed.

"Please," she heard herself whimper.

"Yes, love." Rolling and pinching the sensitive bud, he breathed, "You make a man burn."

She was the one burning, her skin itching with desperate heat. For so long, she'd watched him from afar; now she couldn't get close enough. He muttered an endearment and then his thigh wedged shockingly between her legs. Even through all the barriers of clothing, the heat and hardness of him set off sparks at the core of her being. With sudden panic, she registered how far things had gone, but then his leg ground against her and the wicked, exquisite sensation obliterated all reason, all thoughts save ... *more*.

"Will you come for me, my darling?" he rasped.

What does he mean ...?

His leg left her, and she wanted to weep. Fabric rustled, layers pushed up and away. She couldn't even think to protest as his hand traveled up her stocking-clad leg, past her garter, over her bare thigh, and then—dear God, *then*.

A moan escaped her; her thighs locked together on instinct.

"Poor little puss is weeping," he whispered. "I know just what it needs to feel better."

Only then did she register how wet she was ... down *there*. Mortified, she tried to close her legs again, but he kept stroking her with skillful fingers, showering her with guttural praise.

"Never hide from me, darling. I love how lush and wet you are —it makes me want to pet your sweet cunny all the more. And here especially ..."

Fiery pleasure streaked through her as he touched a transcendent place. Her lips parted on a soundless cry. Her hips bucked helplessly.

"You *like* that," he breathed. "How about this?"

Merciful heavens. Her eyes squeezed shut as the unfamiliar thrills intensified with each circling stroke, each flicking caress. *Too much.*

"Oh, please, I can't ..." she gasped.

"Yes, you can." His eyes were dark, glazed with passion. "Let go, my love. Fly for me."

The chains of caution and self-doubt fell away. She soared, climbing higher and higher, incoherent words spilling from her lips. *I love you. I always have and always will* ... She hit the sun, and the blinding brilliance made her cry out. Heat shimmered through every nerve, searing and cleansing, leaving nothing but her shining adoration—

"Rosalind, my only love, don't ever leave me again," he groaned.

Charity lay there, dazed. Tremors of delight still coursed through her body as her heart crumbled. Not into pieces, but ashes. The deadening weight settled in her chest. As the mix of pain and pleasure grew too intense to bear, numbness spread through her. An eerie calm. In the silence, she could hear her disordered breaths and feel his steadier ones striking rhythmically against her neck.

Rosalind Drummond, she thought dully. *Of course he loves her —he always has. How could I be such a fool?*

Moments passed—she didn't know how long—before she came to her senses. Her mind took note of the fact that she was lying wantonly beneath the man of her shattered dreams whilst he ... The faint snore snapped her fully back to reality.

Dear God ... he'd fallen *asleep*?

Humiliation and panic imbued her with stealth. With care, she eased from under him; he remained lying upon his stomach as if he'd been passed out the entire time and she'd never been there at all. As if this had all been a terrible dream ... With shaking hands, she attempted to straighten her rumpled gown. She gathered up her things and tiptoed toward the door, freezing at the sound of his voice.

"Sick of hiding."

Turning, she saw with relief that his eyes remained closed—he was mumbling in his stupor. But his next words chilled her.

"Bastard can have my vowels." His head rocked against the pallet, his face contorted. "Don't care—nothing matters anymore. Failure ... all I am. March over and hand 'em over myself first thing ..."

Breath held, Charity waited until he quieted. Only then did she slip out the door. She hurried down the steps, making her way back as she'd come ... unnoticed.

Chapter Two

COUNTRY SEAT OF THE MARQUESS OF HARTEFORD

NINE MONTHS LATER

Reclined against cushions in the guest chamber, Paul Fines reflected that house parties were a deuced bore. Then again, that was the case with life in general, and it was only the alternative to living that made boredom more palatable. *Tedium over death* ... that could be his motto. It was a pragmatic philosophy: for while he knew of no antidotes to the sweet hereafter, he was well acquainted with those for *ennui*.

"You were *splendid*," a female voice breathed in his ear.

His attention returned to Lady Augusta Beaumont, who lay naked next to him in bed. From her profusion of red curls to her bountiful curves, everything about her was excessive. Subtlety had never been his strong point.

"I must return the compliment," he said.

She traced a coy circle on his chest. "I daresay your prowess in bed exceeds even your abilities in the boxing ring."

Last month, Paul had participated in a series of exhibition matches sponsored by Gentleman Jackson's Boxing Academy. The tournament had paired students with seasoned prizefighters to show how gentlemen could benefit physically and mentally from training in the "sweet science." Despite his status as a gentleman student, Paul had won all five of his bouts. The papers had capitalized on the crowd-pleasing outcome, hailing him as a symbol of The Fighting British Male (clearly, they knew nothing about him). Overnight, he'd become a sensation and all the rage amongst the *ton*.

And, in particular, amongst the upper class ladies. Although he'd never lacked for female companionship, Paul now found himself plagued by fashionable females. Not that he was complaining. He never looked a gift horse in the mouth or an attractive bed partner in the ... well, no need to extend *that* particular analogy. The point was that sex provided only a temporary remedy; already he could feel the restlessness creeping back.

As if she sensed his withdrawal, Augusta rubbed her cherry-tipped breasts against his arm. "Ready for another round, lover?"

"You wore me out, pet." His hand squeezed her plush bottom; his mind worked on a polite exit strategy.

"Well, it *was* a challenge." She fluttered her lashes. "I don't believe I've ever sported with such a well-endowed partner before."

Though the jaded part of him doubted the flummery—she hadn't had the least bit of trouble handling him, no matter his size —he gave her an easy smile. "You flatter me."

"And *you* were well worth the wait," she purred. "With so many ladies vying for a fuck, I despaired of ever having my turn."

"You've never been good at sharing, sister dear," another voice chimed in.

Turning his head on the pillow, Paul met the limpid gaze of Lady Louisa Parkington, who lay on his other side. The wife of a conveniently absent earl, she was Augusta's twin sister, and, arguably, the more voracious of the two. Which was saying something.

"That is untrue," Augusta protested. "You had your turn."

Louisa's plump lips formed a pout. "But you received his *prime* attentions. As usual, I received an inferior seat at the table."

Inferior? Paul's brows inched upward. Being a gentleman, he always saw to his partners' satisfaction before his own. Pleasuring two ladies simultaneously had been no simple business: he'd expended more effort than usual. And unless he'd been mistaken—which he doubted, given his level of expertise in the matter—the sounds that Louisa had made as she'd perched over him had hardly been complaints.

"There's no need to be a spoil sport. Look at him." Augusta's gaze roved downward over his person, and she licked her lips. He had the unsettling sensation of being eyed like a meaty bone by a ravenous mongrel. "Clearly there's *plenty* to go around."

"I don't care. I'm getting first dibs," Louisa said, "for I deserve to make the most of my lord's absence. I mean to have my fun whilst Parkington is off dallying with his string of whores."

"At least *your* lord can cock up something other than his toes," Augusta shot back. "The only stick that old Beaumont is capable of using is the one that helps him walk. *I* definitely deserve first choice next time."

As the sisters bickered, Paul felt faint stirrings of alarm. *Next* time? Devil and damn, he'd already gone several rounds with the insatiable wenches. In truth, he was beginning to regret choosing bed sport over the honest trading of blows. His host and close friend, Nicholas Morgan, the Marquess of Harteford, had an excellent sparring chamber next to the study, and a few rounds would have battled monotony just as well as sex.

Being a man of sizeable appetites, some means, and no purpose whatsoever, Paul found that his greatest enemy in life was restlessness. Fending off boredom was like fighting the Hydra of legend:

each time he managed to lop off one head, two sprung back in its place. It seemed that nothing could defeat that monstrous sense of ... emptiness.

Although his papa Jeremiah had resided with the angels for some years, Paul could still see the look of befuddled disappointment on the old man's face. He could hear his sire's lecturing refrain as well.

What is the matter with you, Apollo? No Fines has ever lacked in fortitude and purpose. If you fail, you must buck up and try again.

Without a doubt, Jeremiah, esteemed founder of Fines & Company Shipping, had been the most industrious and determined fellow who'd ever lived. He'd built an empire from nothing but blood, sweat, and ambition. Yet the poor sod had somehow managed to produce the ultimate prodigal offspring.

Shame clamped Paul's insides. He thanked the Gods that his father had not been around to witness his ultimate disgrace. A year ago, he'd taken leave of his senses or, more accurately, pickled them in spirits. His drinking and gambling had spiraled out of control, and at his lowest point, he'd wagered his shares of Fines & Company—his papa's *legacy*—on a round of hazard.

That wasn't even the worst part. Drunk and desperate, he'd resorted to hiding like the veriest coward from the cutthroat who'd held his vowels. Only the intervention of his sister Percy and Nicholas had saved him from the abyss of ignominy.

When it came to personal virtues, Paul could claim only one: he had the ability to see his own faults clearly. Like Cassandra, he could forecast his own doom, and his biggest flaw lay in his neck-or-nothing personality. He was incapable of doing anything in half-measure. Either he couldn't lift a finger toward it—as in the case of his father's company—or he threw himself into the endeavor with such abandon that he lost himself entirely.

As had been the case with Rosalind Drummond.

Heartbreak had been the beginning of the end for him; even

now, two years after losing Rosalind to another man, he tasted the bitterness of regret. The pain had dulled, however, to the point where he no longer had to mask it with spirits or gaming, vices that had turned his situation from bad to worse. A lack of self-discipline was a despicable weakness, but it was his. To retain what remained of his self-respect—and it wasn't much—his only choice was to avoid temptations of the heart, bottle, and wallet entirely.

This, unfortunately, left few options with which to slay time. Thus, he'd turned to pugilism, spending his days training at Gentleman Jackson's Saloon. And since his unexpected triumph at the exhibition, an opportunity had recently presented itself. For the first time in a long time, anticipation stirred in him as he contemplated the future.

If properly executed, his new plan could provide a means to rebuild his fortune. For though he'd recovered his shares of Fines & Co., he'd gambled away what savings he'd had. Now he would have a shot at redemption. Not only at getting his money back, but at proving, for once, that he could get things right. That he was a *winner*.

But first, he wanted to discuss this new development with Nicholas. Perhaps he should go now to hunt the other down for conversation and a few rounds. But now that Nick was a husband and father—and amusingly devoted to the roles—the old chap probably had better things to do than to talk and spar into the wee hours of the morning.

"We are agreed then, Augusta?" Louisa was saying. "We'll toss to see who rides where."

Paul stifled a sigh. Like cheap gilt, the novelty of the twins had worn off. Besides, he had a suspicion that if he didn't make his exit soon, he might not make it out alive.

Thus, he said in an appropriately regretful tone, "Ladies, as lovely as you both are, I must admit that you have humbled me. How can a mere mortal keep up with goddesses ... and a pair of them at that?" Patting the voluptuous hips on either side of him, he sat up. "It has been a true pleasure, but now I must bid *adieu*."

He blinked as two pairs of hands pushed him back against the pillows.

"We are not yet finished with you, sir," Louisa said.

Good God. "But I'm afraid *I* am finished. Done in. Tapped out."

"I doubt it. Your stamina is legendary," Augusta said. "Lady Eugenie claimed that at the Yardleys' hunting party you did not leave her bedchamber for the *entire* weekend."

Damn his own libidinous ways. The trouble was that he liked women, their perfumed company and plush embraces. He'd learned to choose lovers who sought the same things as he did: pleasure, a few moments of forgetfulness.

Love was a vice he couldn't afford.

"There was only one of Lady Eugenie,"—he pried Augusta's fingers off of his chest—"and I was a younger man back then, pet."

"But the Yardleys' party was only two weeks ago," Louisa said, frowning.

He swung his legs over the edge of the bed. "Nevertheless, a man needs time to recover. Along with my sex's other failings," he said, "we haven't the endurance of ladies—"

Determined hands clamped onto his shoulders and yanked him backward onto the bed. His back met the mattress, and, giggling, the wenches pinned him, each sitting atop one of his arms. Mildly entertained by their antics, he allowed it.

"Nonsense. All you need is a restorative." So saying, Augusta applied her mouth to his torso. Despite his mind's flagging interest, her practiced licks caused the bands of his abdomen to tauten. "And I do so enjoy a challenge."

"Me, too," Louisa said.

Her breasts brushed against his thigh as her explorations took her southward. Egad, she had an adept mouth. Paul exhaled slowly.

"Oh, goody. You're rising to the occasion already." With a cat-got-into-the-cream smile, Augusta nudged her sister. "Make room for me as well, Louisa. Let's see if our combined efforts can hasten the process."

Louisa made a noise which seemed to indicate agreement—he couldn't be sure as her mouth was rather occupied. Augusta joined the fray, and his thoughts began to blur. Mindlessness beckoned ... and he had nothing better to do at present anyway.

Staring up at the ceiling, he lay back and endeavored to think of England.

Chapter Three

Sometime later, Paul left the satiated pair. At one in the morning, the darkened hallway had as much traffic as Rotten Row on a weekday afternoon. He exchanged nods with gentlemen returning from a night of frolicking and avoided the frankly inviting gazes of several ladies draped in the latest boudoir fashions. Devil and damn, what he wouldn't do for a brandy. But he'd sworn off liquor and getting cup-shot would do nothing to improve his disposition on the morrow.

He heaved a sigh. Might as well get a book and try to bore himself to sleep.

Too lazy to trek to the library downstairs, he stopped by the parlor on the present floor. His hostess was a bit of a bluestocking, so books could be found in most public areas. Wandering in, he saw that a fire lit the large stone hearth at the center of the room, and a few lamps burned at a low flicker. Wingchairs and couches were scattered throughout in cozy configurations.

Ah, excellent: bookshelves claimed the entire back wall.

Paul browsed indifferently through the shelves. Socrates, Plato, Aristotle ... all the old boys from his Cambridge days were present and accounted for and no livelier a bunch now than they'd been back then. He stifled a yawn. Ye Gods, his plan was working already.

A quiet rustle made him spin around. He blinked: a female had materialized, seemingly out of nowhere. A second passed before he recognized her. Charity Sparkler, his sister's bosom chum from finishing school.

He bent at the waist. "Beg pardon. I didn't notice you, Miss Sparkler."

"I know," she said.

He must have imagined the wry edge to her reply. From their past interactions, he knew her to be a retiring little mouse. A marked contrast to his hoyden of a sister, yet the two were as thick as thieves. Indeed, a few Seasons ago Percy had begged him to dance attendance upon Miss Sparkler during the latter's unfortunate episode of spots. Feeling sorry for the chit, he'd done his part and squired her through a few ballrooms. In truth, he had only a hazy memory of those instances: his mind had been engaged elsewhere.

Back then, all his thoughts had centered on Rosalind. An image of shining midnight hair and violet eyes crowded him even now. Beautiful, passionate Rosalind. He could still picture that vivacious smile she'd worn for all her suitors even as her gaze smoldered only for him. His throat tightened as he remembered their trysts and stolen moments—if only he'd acted on his heart's desires rather than made a game of them. By the time he'd discovered his courage, it had been too late.

He'd lost the love of his life. Worse yet, he knew that she had chosen the better man. It was another failure to add to all the rest.

He pushed aside the bitter regret and watched as Miss Sparkler returned his courtesy. With some surprise, he saw that she had ... changed. The past year had been good to her. Free of blemishes, her skin glowed like porcelain in the lamplight, and she'd subtly blossomed. Though she'd never be a classical beauty, her small, neat features and uncommonly large eyes possessed a delicate charm. She put him in mind of a wood nymph, actually—though a rather stern and Quakerish one.

If Miss Sparkler wanted for admirers now, it was not because of looks but style. Specifically, the lack thereof. Her scraped-back coiffure would pass muster in a convent; her dull brown topknot was so tightly wound that *his* temples throbbed just looking at it. Her ill-fitting gown dwarfed her waifish figure and, for the daughter of a jeweler, she had precious little to show for it. A plain silver locket appeared to be her sole bauble.

The most peculiar thing about her, however, wasn't her appearance but her manner. Her stillness and the perspicacity in her gaze would discomfit any man. He had the disconcerting thought that although Miss Sparkler might escape the observation of others, she did plenty of observing of her own.

He became acutely aware that he was standing there in a state of undress; after leaving the twins' company, he hadn't bothered tying on a cravat or throwing on his jacket. His throat was bare above his shirt laces, his hair mussed, and the faint musk of sex clung to his skin. In Miss Sparkler's quiet presence, he suddenly felt ... dirty. Embarrassed, though as a hot-blooded and unattached male he had no reason to be. Besides, it wasn't as if the prim miss would pick up on the post-coital clues. She probably didn't even know what fornication was.

Hell, she'd probably never even been kissed.

Which brought to the forefront of his mind that she *was* an innocent girl—precisely the kind he avoided—and here they were standing unchaperoned in the parlor past midnight. He'd best exchange a few niceties and beg off for propriety's sake.

For lack of anything better, he asked, "Did you arrive after supper?" Then he had the alarming thought that perhaps she *had* been there—and he'd overlooked her yet again.

"My journey was delayed. I arrived just an hour ago," she said. *Thank God.*

"I'm sure you must be peaked." He hoped she'd get the hint.

"I sent my maid to bed," she replied. "But then I couldn't sleep so I thought to find something to read."

"Find anything good?" He glanced politely at the volume in her hands.

She blinked ... and then she did the *oddest* thing. She shoved the book behind her back.

"No," she said. "Not really."

Oh ho. Why was the chit prevaricating?

Surprised and a bit intrigued, he studied her more closely, trying to discern the reason for her little covert action. She returned his stare, her long, curly eyelashes fanning rapidly. Her irises were a shade of jade and shale that ought to have been dull ... and yet he saw now that they produced a rare, subtly opalescent gaze. As the lamplight flickered, shards of amber and emerald flashed with sudden fire.

With a jolt, he wondered why he'd never noticed Charity Sparkler's exceptional eyes before. Probably because in the past she'd kept them fixed in the vicinity of his chest or upon her tiny slippers. And he, himself, had admittedly been preoccupied by other matters. But now she had his attention because *nothing* piqued his curiosity more than a secret.

"If I promise not to make a grab for your evening's pleasure," he said in genial tones, "will you tell me what you've got there?"

"It's nothing, really I ..." Her throat worked. "It wouldn't interest you."

He was startled to discover that it did.

"We'll only know if you show it to me," he coaxed.

Her straight, fine brows drew together. "I'd rather not."

She had more gumption than he'd expected. Another tactic was called for. "If you won't tell me," he said, raising his brows,

"I'll have to assume it's because you've got your hands on something improper. Material a young miss has no business reading."

"Such as what ... exactly?" Her grey-green gaze gave nothing away.

Devil and damn, she'd outmaneuvered him. Had she done so intentionally or was she so innocent that she didn't understand he was teasing her? At any rate, he couldn't very well accuse her outright of filching a naughty book.

Raking a hand through his hair, he gave her an amused glance. "You win, Miss Sparkler. I have no argument left except a claim to friendship. We are old friends, are we not? As such, surely you would not leave a man dying of curiosity?"

"I do not think it possible to expire from curiosity, Mr. Fines."

"I could be the first," he said, "and then you would have to live with the guilt."

"I'll manage to survive."

Hearing the dry edge to her tone, he realized that Charity Sparkler was not as placid as she first appeared. Beneath that calm surface, an agile mind shimmered. If there was anything he enjoyed, it was a duel of wits.

"As a personal favor to me,"—he gave her his best cajoling look, one that had reaped countless female favors (and all of them a great deal more intimate than the current request)—"will you please tell me what you have behind your back?"

It was overkill, and he knew it. But now he was *burning* to know.

Her lips pursed, and then he was struck by the comeliness of her mouth. The top lip had a pretty bow shape that made him think of hearts and angels, the bottom a pouty fullness that made him think of the exact opposite. As if that heady balance of innocence and sin weren't tempting enough, it seemed nature wanted to tip the scales: a tiny beauty mark floated just beneath her lower lip, the most wanton little speck ...

He caught himself. What the devil was he about? Was he actually lusting over *Miss Sparkler's* mouth? He shuddered. All the carnal overindulgence must be affecting his brain, making him see sex everywhere. Yet it seemed that the more one looked, the more one discovered with this odd little mouse.

So stop looking, you coxcomb.

Just as he was about to let her off the hook, she drew her hands from behind her back.

"Alright." Her fingers clasping the leather volume as if it were a prized treasure, she held it out. "If you must."

He couldn't help peering at the cover.

"*The Lyrical Ballads* by Wordsworth," he said in bemusement.

"Yes." Her chin angled upward, her eyes searching his.

Why the deuce did she feel compelled to hide a volume of harmless poetry? And why was she gazing at him in that ... *expectant* way? As if she'd just disclosed an extraordinary piece of information—like she'd been a spy for Bonaparte or some such thing—and was waiting for him to react accordingly.

Curious gel, no doubt about it.

Silence stretched between them. The ticking of the longcase clock grew louder in his ears.

"I've read it myself," he said in pleasant tones to offset the awkwardness, "and, if you ask me, the verse is overrated. For its soporific qualities, however, I daresay the poems are first-rate. If you're trying to fall asleep, Wordsworth should do the trick as well as laudanum."

Silence greeted his witticism. As the tension grew, he let out a quiet laugh to emphasize that he was trying to be amusing. But her stricken expression—like a crack spreading through a fine Limoges plate—killed the sound in his throat. He had that incontrovertible feeling one got the instant one's boot made contact with a steaming pile on the street. He felt an overwhelming urge to ... apologize? Before he could open his mouth—to say what, he had no idea—she drew a sharp breath.

"I must go. It is late." Her composure was back, and the only sign that he'd ruffled her was the faint quivering of her bottom lip. "Good night, Mr. Fines."

Her eyes remained trained on the carpet.

"Er, the pleasure was mine, Miss Sparkler." Baffled, discomfited, he bowed low.

By the time he raised his head, she was gone.

Chapter Four

Charity stifled her impatience as Sarah halted again on the pebbled path leading to the picnic. Sarah was the Sparklers' housemaid, but as Charity had no proper lady's maid and needed a companion for the house party, Sarah had accompanied her. The housemaid was clearly enjoying her temporary role. Peering over a manicured hedge, she let out yet another excited squeal.

"Lord above, miss! Do you know who that *is*?"

A rhetorical question. Because while Sarah obviously spent her spare time memorizing the society pages, Charity did not. Consequently, she hadn't recognized anyone who Sarah had stopped to gawk at, which was just as well. She was here for one reason only: to see her bosom chum Percy.

Don't fool yourself: you wanted to see him *too.*

She exhaled. And so she had. She'd seen Mr. Fines, spoken with him, and their exchange had driven the last nail into the coffin that held her dreams. If she'd ever required proof that she meant nothing to him, she'd gotten it last night. She'd known from their past interactions that he remembered nothing of Spitalfields: his inebriated state had taken care of that. But to learn that he didn't even recall quoting Wordsworth to her ...

That had wrung the final drop of hope from her heart.

She'd hoarded that poem as if it were a precious jewel when, in reality, it had been a compliment made of paste. Disposable, meaningless, and without worth ... the kind of nonsense a gentleman would utter to a chit he felt sorry for. Her throat thickened.

"Look quickly, Miss Charity, or you'll miss her!" Sarah exclaimed.

Sighing, Charity aimed her gaze in the direction of the maid's finger. She saw an immaculate lawn sprouted with yellow canopies. Guests dressed to the nines strolled or lolled languidly on blankets. Like an army of ants, sweating footmen delivered refreshments, their movements efficient and unceasing in spite of the day's heat. A string quartet played, notes mingling with the laughter of frolicking children.

Scanning the crowd, she said, "Am I supposed to be looking at someone specific?"

"You don't see her, the lady in the lavender lace gown?"

"That describes half the party," Charity said in exasperation.

"With the lovely auburn hair and ruby necklace the size of an egg? The one with the three strapping footmen? The one *everyone* is trying to get a word with?"

Ah. Charity located the object of Sarah's interest standing several yards away. A handsome, slight woman who carried herself as if she were a queen. Which might very well be possible, given that the party's guest list included the *crème de la crème*, from aristocrats to foreign dignitaries to the celebrated artists of the day.

"Who is she?" Charity asked.

"Your father really ought to let you out more, miss." Sarah sighed. "That's Marietta Stone. The famous actress?"

Even Charity had heard about Mrs. Stone, who'd gained a reputation for playing heroines disguised as males. Some said that Mrs. Stone's portrayal of Viola in *The Twelfth Night* was legendary; others claimed the sight of the actress' pantaloon-clad legs filled theatres night after night.

Charity herself had never attended the theatre for Father prohibited frivolous activities. She'd never been to a country house party either, but she'd pleaded with uncharacteristic tenacity until her papa had finally relented and let her come. She'd received an invitation because of Percy, whose family had a long and close history with the hosts, the Marquess and Marchioness of Harteford.

Charity desperately wished to see her friend. Now that Percy was married and busy with her new life, the girls' time together had become increasingly rare. Percy would be arriving at the party fresh from a six-week-long wedding trip with her new husband, and Charity was anxious to know how the other was doing.

She had her own news to share as well. Anxiety mounted as she thought of the parting conversation with her father.

"I'm counting on you, daughter," he'd said, his thin face aged by worry. "You need a husband, and I need a son-in-law to help with Sparkler's. Business isn't what it used to be. You must do your duty if the shop is to survive."

"But surely there are other ways I can help—" she'd said desperately.

"This is the only option. I am sorry, Charity." Her father had given her an awkward pat on the shoulder, but his tone had brooked no refusal. "While you're away, I will make all the arrangements."

Thus, Charity's fate was sealed. The shop meant everything to her father, and she would never let him down. When she returned to London, she would greet the future he had planned for her. She released a breath. If she had only precious days left of freedom, she would not waste them. She wanted to spend that time with her best friend in the world.

"Miss Sparkler, over here! Do come join us."

The melodious tones dispelled her reverie, and she looked over to see her hostess, Lady Helena Harteford, waving from a table shaded by a canopy. Beside her sat Mrs. Anna Fines, mama to Percy and Mr. Fines. Heading over, Charity made her curtsy and took one of the empty chairs. Sarah went off to join the gaggle of maids supervising the children's games.

"You're in fine looks today, Miss Charity," Lady Helena said, smiling.

"Thank you, my lady."

While Charity appreciated the other's kindness, she knew she was unremarkable in her high-necked fawn muslin. *Never gild a lily—or a weed*, Papa oft said. *The weed that draws attention gets plucked. We Sparklers may not possess beauty, but we have the wisdom of modesty.*

Out of habit, she touched the silver locket he'd given her for her twelfth birthday; though it was small and plain—what he'd deemed suitable for her—she cherished the gift. She took her father's advice to heart as well, sticking to simple fashions in unobtrusive shades. The only cosmetic she used was a pomade to keep her unruly hair in place. She had no wish to draw attention to herself or her flaws.

Though if she were beautiful, Charity thought with a wistful pang, she might wear dashing clothes like the marchioness. The lady's warm chestnut beauty was perfectly set off in a frothy, yolk-colored silk embroidered with primroses.

"'Tis you who looks well, my lady," Charity said earnestly.

"Nothing flatters more than a good night's rest." Lady Helena cast a fond glance at the wicker bassinet on the chair next to her. Charity glimpsed the adorable lump of the Hartefords' new infant beneath the white blanket. "Unlike his older brothers, little George actually sleeps. The nurses don't know what to do with the free time."

"The younger siblings have softer temperaments ... or so I've been told. I wouldn't know personally," Mrs. Fines said, with a shake of her downy grey curls, "as *both* my children were hellions and never slept a wink."

Charity hid a grin. Despite the good lady's wry (and rather deserved) complaints, Anna Fines was entirely devoted to her offspring. Familiar tendrils of yearning crept over Charity. She'd never known a mother's love for her own mama had succumbed to fever shortly after her birth.

"You're enjoying yourself, Charity, I hope?" Lady Helena said. "I am sorry you missed Mrs. Stone's performance last night. Her rendition of Julia from *Two Gentlemen of Verona* was riveting. But never fear: we have an array of brilliant artists scheduled for the week."

"You're too kind, my lady." While the entertainment would no doubt be impressive, what Charity really wanted was a heart-to-heart with her best friend. "Have you heard from Percy, Mrs. Fines?" she blurted. "I thought she and Mr. Hunt were scheduled to arrive by midday."

"Lord above, you know Percy. Always getting distracted by one adventure or another. Now that she is a published author,"—behind her spectacles, Mrs. Fines' gaze aimed heavenward—"she finds even more excuses to get into scrapes. Research for her novels, she says. Thank goodness she married someone with good sense." She let out a sigh. "Now if only my *other* child would do the same."

"Mr. Fines seems in good spirits," Lady Helena remarked. "And he was so impressive in that boxing exhibition. Everyone is still agog over his performance."

"It is a relief that Paul has found something to keep him busy —and away from drinking and gaming. The devil makes work for idle hands, I've always said. Now if he would only cease the skirt-chasing as well," Mrs. Fines said, "he'd really be onto something."

"Anna," Lady Helena said with a smothered laugh, "you'll embarrass poor Charity."

"I'm not embarrassed," Charity said.

How could she be, when for one brief, glorious moment she'd been one of the skirts he'd not only chased but caught? The memory of Spitalfields flooded her with yearning and agony in equal measure. Like a weary desert traveler stumbling upon an oasis, she'd gulped down handfuls of the sparkling water ... only to choke on sand. Mr. Fines' desire for her had been a mirage, nothing more.

Which is why you must forget him, avoid him at all costs.

"There you all are. We've been looking all over for you!"

Charity spun in the chair to see her bosom chum approaching in coltish strides. Gladness disbanded her gloomy thoughts. The other girl looked so *well*. A hat with a floppy cornflower-strewn brim topped Percy's sunny curls, and her lithe figure was clad in a smart, lace-trimmed muslin. She carried a matching parasol, although she needn't have bothered: her husband, Mr. Hunt, provided ample shade.

Gavin Hunt was built as solidly as an oak, and the jagged scar on his right cheek was a memento of his former career as an infamous gaming hell owner. After his marriage, he'd sold his club and bought into partnership with Fines & Company. He now worked with the Marquess of Harteford, who presided over the business.

At one time, Charity had doubted Mr. Hunt's suitability for Percy, but she was relieved to be proved wrong. Percy radiated happiness. Mr. Hunt's steadying influence seemed exactly what the spirited girl needed, and the reverse seemed true as well: Percy's liveliness relieved some of her husband's brooding intensity.

Mr. Hunt bowed to the group. "Good afternoon, ladies," he said in his deep voice.

"And to you, Mr. Hunt." As Mrs. Fines received Percy's kiss on the cheek, she gave her son-in-law a look of approval. "Survived a trip with my girl, have you? And looking none the worse for wear, I see."

A quicksilver grin crossed Mr. Hunt's features. "I hide the scars well, madam."

"Harteford says you are the bravest man he knows," Lady Helena said with a twinkle.

Percy wrinkled her nose. "Back in England not three days and the teasing begins. At least I know I have *one* friend amongst you all." Her round blue eyes found Charity, who'd been standing to the side, not wanting to intrude on the family scene. Percy held out her arms. "Dear Charity, it's been ages!"

Charity couldn't hold back her trembling smile. "Oh Percy,"—she returned her friend's enthusiastic embrace—"I have missed you."

"And I you. We must have a long chat, just the two of us." Drawing back, Percy gave her an oddly abashed look before addressing the group at large. "But, um, before we do, Mr. Hunt and I have some news that we'd like to share with everyone."

Charity's heart thumped faster.

Mrs. Fines' hands flew to her mouth. "Oh, my dears, are you ...?"

Percy nodded, roses in her cheeks. "Come autumn, you'll be a grandmama."

The announcement led to congratulations and another round of hugs. Charity clasped her chum's hands. "Oh, Percy, I am so very glad for you. You will be the best of mamas, I know it."

"I wouldn't be so sure." Percy shot a mischievous glance at her spouse. "Mr. Hunt is convinced that if we have a daughter, she will turn out a hoyden just like me."

"Are you worried, sir?" Mrs. Fines said, blotting her eyes with a handkerchief.

"Not at all. I like a challenge," Mr. Hunt said.

"Do you have an intuition about the baby's sex, Percy?" Lady Helena said. "Not that a mother's sense is necessarily accurate. I was certain our latest was going to be a girl." The marchioness cast an exasperated look at her rambunctious twin boys who'd just won a three-legged race and were now whooping their triumph in the other contestants' faces. "Obviously," she said dryly, "that was wishful thinking."

"I think we'll have a boy," Percy said, "but Mr. Hunt predicts a daughter. We have a wager on it."

Her husband's tawny eyes gleamed. "One of your finer qualities, buttercup, is that you've always been a gracious loser."

At that rather cryptic remark, Percy's cheeks turned even pinker. "I did *not* lose that—oh, never mind. I shan't waste my breath arguing. You're as stubborn as a bull when you've made your mind up."

"That makes us a perfect match." With a smile that softened his harsh features, Mr. Hunt said, "Now shall I make myself scarce so that you ladies may gossip in earnest?"

"We do not gossip. We have important female conversations," Percy informed him. "But, yes, do find Nick and Paul and break the news to them. Then you may attend to the vital male business of pummeling one another and smoking smelly cigars."

"When you put it that way, how can I resist?" Mr. Hunt cupped his wife's cheek, his thumb brushing over her lower lip with a tenderness that made Charity's throat constrict and Mrs. Fines blow noisily into her handkerchief. "Remember what the doctor said and don't overdo, alright?"

"We'll keep an eye on her," Lady Helena assured him.

With a bow, Mr. Hunt strode off.

"Come, Percy, you must sit. In your condition—" Mrs. Fines began.

"Oh heavens, Mama, you're worse than Mr. Hunt." Percy went over to the bassinet to admire the babe whilst Lady Helena watched on, beaming. "You know I've always had the constitution of an ox, and pregnancy hasn't changed that one whit. Now what have I missed?"

"We were just talking about your brother," Mrs. Fines said.

Percy's head jerked up. "Is something amiss with Paul?"

"Nothing new. He's just drifting," her mama said. "All he does is box and dally with women."

"Well, he *is* a rake," Percy said. "That's what rakes do."

"Your brother is *not* a rake."

Lady Helena cleared her throat. "Are you quite certain of that, Anna?"

"Paul may *act* like a rake, but he isn't one," Mrs. Fines insisted.

"Um ... what is the difference?" Percy said.

A notch formed between Mrs. Fines' brows. "He may fool others with his devil-may-care attitude, but I know my boy. He's only engaging in tomfoolery because he hasn't found something better to do."

"Paul is bored. Most rakes are," Percy said. "I still don't see the difference."

"The difference is character," Charity said quietly.

Mrs. Fines gave a triumphant nod. "I've always said that you're an astute girl, Charity."

"Then I must be dull-witted because I still don't get the difference," Percy muttered.

At Mrs. Fines' urging look, Charity said hesitantly, "Mr. Fines is not careless ... at heart. To the contrary, he has a sensitive, compassionate disposition. Unlike a true rake, he cares about others—deeply, I should say. And his family most of all."

She felt a pang of bittersweet yearning. One of the qualities she most admired in Mr. Fines was his intense loyalty toward the ones he loved. Toward his family ... and Rosalind Drummond.

"Exactly so." Mrs. Fines reached over and patted her hand. "You understand my son's nature completely. As a boy, he brought his mama flowers, protected his sister, and always had a kind word and a helping hand for everyone. I've never known a soul so capable of joy. He may believe himself a disappointment at the moment,"—sadness ghosted through her faded blue eyes—"but a hero lives within him yet."

"A hero needs but a cause," Lady Helena murmured. "There

are many suitable young ladies present, Anna. Shall I make introductions?"

Mrs. Fines sighed. "One can lead a horse to water."

The two ladies began to discuss a list of candidates. Charity wanted to tell them that it was useless: Mr. Fines had given his heart to the one lady he could not have, and despite his rakish facade, his *was* a faithful heart. Whoever he married would be fated for misery if she hoped for his love.

She told herself she was lucky that he didn't notice her. She might not possess looks or charms, but she did have good sense. She must put Mr. Fines out of her mind and focus on the future laid out for her. To do anything else would inevitably lead to heartbreak, and once was quite enough.

Chapter Five

The punch caught Paul in the midsection. Though he grunted, he welcomed the cleansing jolt of pain and retreated, bouncing lightly on the balls of his feet, his arms up in guard position once more. Gentleman Jackson had drilled the importance of keeping one's fists in the correct posture, ready to attack or defend as the situation warranted. From the looks of it, attack would be Paul's next move. Though Nicholas Morgan was the larger man, he was showing signs of fatigue, his dark hair drenched with perspiration, his broad chest heaving as he and Paul circled each other in the ring.

Paul pressed his advantage. As the quicker of the two, he advanced his attack, letting his fists fly in a jab-jab-hook combination. He stayed light on his feet, ducking blows and landing his own in a fierce, rhythmic staccato. He punched with the entirety of his being, sweet concentration emptying his mind. His muscles took over; his blood sang.

Punch. Duck. Feign to the left.

Right jab. Right jab.

Left uppercut.

"Bloody hell, Fines. Stop. I give."

It took an instant for the other's words to sink in. Swiping the sweat from his eyes, Paul saw that Nicholas was leaning against the ropes. The marquess stripped off his practice gloves and touched a hand to his jaw, wincing.

"Alright, old boy?" Paul said.

"Hell of a facer. No wonder you won those exhibition matches," Nicholas said ruefully. "And you're not even winded, damn your hide."

"The Gentleman keeps his students in excellent condition. If you'd come to the saloon once in a while, you'd be in better fighting shape yourself."

"I've been busy." Stepping through the ropes, Nicholas said in a pointed tone, "Fines & Co. doesn't run itself you know."

"With you at the helm, it nearly does," Paul said smoothly.

He was all too familiar with the direction the conversation was heading. For years, his mother and Nicholas had been on him to assume what they considered his rightful position in the company his father had founded. Nicholas had been Jeremiah's protégé and had worked his way up to partnership. After his mentor's passing, Nick had taken over the helm.

As a lad, Paul had initially resented Nick, who, in truth, had been the son Jeremiah had always wanted—the one Paul could never be. At the same time, he'd been too honest to envy another for something he himself had no intention of working for. Had he longed for his father's approval? Yes. Had he wished that he and his father might meet on some common ground? Certainly. But did he intend to slave away at the company and sacrifice everything else in his life?

No. Bloody. Way.

As a boy, he'd witnessed the aftermath of his father's work ethic. Night after night, he'd glimpsed the lonely tears his mama tried to hide. He'd watched his baby sister post herself at the parlor window, the hope in her eyes fading as the figure she waited for didn't materialize. Though Paul doubted their sire had kept a mistress, Jeremiah had betrayed his women nonetheless. The warehouse had been as demanding as a harem of doxies.

When it came to gaining Jeremiah's attention, Paul hadn't fared any better. He'd never had a head for numbers or business, and his father's constant lectures hadn't made him all that keen to acquire the skills. The things that Paul did have a natural affinity for—gentlemanly pursuits such as sporting and the arts—frustrated and bewildered Jeremiah to no end.

What is the point of boxing, lad? You're wasting time and energy that could be spent on serious endeavors. When will you mature and face your responsibilities?

If being mature meant giving up everything and everyone he loved, then he supposed the answer to Papa's question was ... *never*. He fought off the familiar mix of resentment and shame.

"Anna's fondest wish is for you to have a place at the company," Nicholas began.

Paul grimly stripped off his shirt and toweled himself off. "At this point, the mater's accustomed to being disappointed by me. Why confuse her now?"

Frowning, Nicholas donned a fresh shirt and waistcoat. He dressed himself with a facility foreign to most gentlemen for he hadn't always lived the life of a lord. Many years ago, when they were changing after one of their first sparring matches, Paul had inadvertently seen the grotesque scars crisscrossing Nick's back: souvenirs of a childhood spent surviving the stews. Any jealousy Paul had harbored had vaporized, replaced by ... compassion.

From that moment on, he'd figured that Nicholas Morgan deserved all the affection that the Fines family could provide—his own included.

Nick had paid their loyalty back in spades. He'd helped Jeremiah to expand the business to its current empire and, after the latter's death, continued to run the company and provide for the Fineses. Paul's yearly income of five thousand pounds came from a share of the profits. And when Nick had unexpectedly inherited a title, he hadn't turned his back on them; he'd continued to treat the middling class Fineses as he would his own kin. In truth, he'd long been an older brother to Paul and Percy.

Like any older sibling, Nicholas had the annoying habit of thinking he knew best. He began to pace the length of the exercise room. A bad sign, for it indicated that he meant to go on awhile.

"'Tis no laughing matter, Fines. Your mother is concerned about your future, and frankly, so am I. It's been nearly a year since ..."—Nick cleared his throat—"the setback. Now that you've recovered, 'tis high time you set your life's purpose."

Leave it to Nick to call nearly losing one's fortune and becoming a gin sot a *setback*.

"You're seven-and-twenty, with excellent prospects. All you need is structure and discipline. You must decide upon your goals and work diligently toward them," Nick continued in an imperious manner worthy of any marquess.

It was as good a time as any to share his plan, Paul supposed. He'd woken up this afternoon both spent and dull-hearted from yet another evening of debauchery. The strange interaction with Charity Sparkler hadn't helped matters: she'd made him feel like a cad ... and he didn't even know *why*. If an encounter with a mousy miss could throw him off-kilter, then he obviously needed something—anything—to anchor his drifting existence.

He mentally reviewed the best way to share his new goal. He told himself his plan was sound, yet the pitiful truth was that his past mistakes had made him doubt his own judgment. He needed to air his ideas, to get advice—and if there was anything Nick could be relied upon to supply, it was the latter.

"As it happens, I agree with you," Paul said.

Nick's dark brows came together. "You ... do?"

"I've become aware that it is time for me to pursue some defined purpose in life."

"Exactly. That is clear thinking, Fines."

"In order to do so, however, I believe that one must find a balance between one's, er, passions and gainful activity."

"Do you speak of marriage? A wife certainly can provide balance to a man's life." Nicholas' grey eyes warmed, and it wasn't difficult to guess why. Nick's marchioness was a prime article, though Paul would probably lose his teeth if he were to mention it. "Mean to shop the marriage mart at last, do you, Fines? That would please your mama to no end."

"Actually, that isn't what I—"

The opening of the door cut Paul short. Two men entered, as opposite from one another as day and night. Ambrose Kent, the taller and lankier of the pair, was an upstanding member of the Thames River Police. He spent his days chasing down criminals, and several months ago he'd managed to catch the ultimate prize. For the life of him, Paul didn't understand how an earnest policeman with only pennies to rub together had managed to capture the heart of the stunning—and stunningly wealthy—Lady Marianne Draven.

Which went to show, Paul mused, how little he understood about love.

Then there was the other fellow. The strapping one with the pronounced scar and ruthless air, whose mere presence made Paul's muscles bunch with instinctive apprehension. Not so long ago, Gavin Hunt had been the cutthroat who'd held Paul's vowels ransom. But destiny had taken an unexpected turn, and now the blackguard was his bloody brother-in-law.

The Fates did indeed have a twisted sense of humor. Yet Paul had to grudgingly admit that he'd never seen Percy happier—and Hunt seemed as fiercely devoted to her as a wolfhound. 'Twas a small consolation, Paul supposed, to see his former enemy and lord of the underworld panting after his sister like a damned canine. But it didn't mean that he had to like the man.

He rose and inclined his head stiffly. "Good day, gentlemen."

"Fines." Hunt's mouth had a derisive bent. "Getting knocked around, are you?"

"Step into the ring and we'll see who gets knocked about," Paul challenged.

"I'd sit this one out if I were you, Hunt," Nicholas said. "There's a reason the lad bested those prizefighters. Just now I was the unfortunate recipient of his prowess."

Hunt looked unimpressed. "There's Bond Street boxing, and then there's real fighting. I can handle myself."

"Before this ends in bloodshed," Ambrose Kent said mildly, "I was promised a cigar. Mrs. Kent dispatched me to smoke with you fellows so that she could find your ladies and gossip with them."

"According to Percy, it isn't gossip," Hunt said with a know-it-all air. "They talk about important female matters."

"So speaks the newlywed. I propose we retreat to the study whilst we still have the chance," Nick said dryly.

Soon they were all ensconced in the wingchairs of the male refuge, the rich scent of leather and cigar smoke curling in the air. A view of the picnic was framed by the tall windows. By some tacit agreement—Paul was both embarrassed and relieved to note—the others did not partake of spirits, sticking instead to the fortifying pots of coffee and tea.

"Have to hand it to you, Harteford,"—Hunt blew out a smoke ring—"you know how to live."

"Don't get the wrong idea. This sort of peaceful interlude happens in this household only during the eclipse," Nick said, "and perhaps the full moon. Any moment now the twins will come charging in, tossing their new brother between them like a ball."

Knowing the Hartefords' high-spirited boys, this scenario was not farfetched.

"Has your fair lady forgiven you for saddling her with yet another male?" Paul said.

Nick's grin flashed white against his swarthy complexion. "I'm working on it."

"There's always the next time," Paul drawled.

"Which shan't be for a while. We have our hands full with three scamps," the marquess said. "We'll leave the breeding to the other married fellows present."

Silence descended upon the study. Hunt rubbed the back of his neck and put out his cigar with undue concentration. Kent's face turned a ruddy shade.

"Good God, the *both* of you?" Paul said.

"Percy wanted me to share the news." Hunt's gruff tones did not hide the pride in his voice. "The babe's due in autumn."

His hoyden of a sister was going to be a *mama*. Paul could scarce comprehend it. Despite the wholehearted gladness he felt for Percy, the winds of change stirred his nape. He experienced a moment's panic—like that of a child lost in a crowd. Everyone and everything was changing around him; if he didn't find his way soon, he'd be left alone and far behind.

"And ours soon thereafter," Kent said.

"Welcome to the club, gentlemen." Grinning, Nicholas rose to exchange hearty back slaps.

Paul went and offered his hand to his brother-in-law. "Congratulations, Hunt."

Hunt returned his firm shake, muttering, "If the babe's a boy, Percy's got a bee in her bonnet about naming him after you."

"*Apollo* Hunt—is she mad?" Paul said, aghast. "With a name like that, my nephew's head will be intimately acquainted with every chamber pot in Eton—*if* he survives to school age. I'll have to teach him to box just so he can protect himself."

Hunt grunted in agreement.

Once they were settled in their chairs again, Nicholas said, "We old fellows shouldn't hog all the attention. We must hear from the younger set as well." He turned an expectant gaze to Paul. "Before you gentlemen arrived, Fines was about to tell me his own good news."

Kent's dark brows shot up. "Has our young rake been bitten by the matrimonial bug at last?"

"Percy hasn't breathed a word about this." Hunt looked puzzled, as if he couldn't fathom his wife not telling him everything. "Have you told her or your mother as yet?"

"Lord Almighty, I am *not* getting leg-shackled. Being around you love-addled fools is enough to turn any man off the idea of marriage." Paul shook his head in exasperation. "What I was trying to tell his lordship is that I'm going into business for myself."

"Business?" Nick frowned. "Of what sort?"

In for a penny.

"Prizefighting," Paul said succinctly.

A pause.

Nicholas said, "Be serious. You said you had a purpose in mind."

"I am serious. I plan to rebuild my fortune through boxing." When silence met his words, Paul took a breath and plunged on. "After the exhibition matches, Viscount Traymore approached me. He thinks that I have the potential to be a champion. He wants to back me in a tournament the Fancy is organizing."

The Fancy was a powerful group of men who financed, organized, and wagered on sporting events. The ultimate men's men, the members of the Fancy came from all walks of life and shared one common goal: they thrived on risk and danger. The prizefights they sponsored were illegal, arranged in semi-secrecy, and attracted thousands of spectators. Hundreds of thousands of pounds traded hands at a single match. The riots and bloodshed that oft occurred were part of the thrill.

"I know prizefighting falls outside a gentleman's domain, but given the dishonor I've heaped upon myself, I've nothing to lose, have I?" Paul gave a self-deprecating shrug. "And perhaps much to gain. Two months from now, matches will be held across England to determine the Fancy's next Champion, and Traymore wants to be my patron. He's got a bottle man and knee man lined up," Paul said, referring to the duo that assisted a boxer during matches, "and he'll cover the expenses of the training and accommodations. All I have to do is put in the hard work. So what do you think?"

"You don't want to know," Nicholas said grimly.

Paul felt his hackles rise. "You might consider my plan for more than a second."

"I don't need a second to know that this is an idiotic, harebrained scheme."

"Because it doesn't fit your narrow definition of gainful enterprise?" Just *once*, why couldn't anyone take him seriously? Jaw clenched, Paul said, "Many would argue that trade isn't fit for a marquess and yet you toddle off merrily to a warehouse every day."

Nicholas' brows lowered. "That's hardly the same—"

"Is it sport or true enterprise that you're after?" Hunt cut in. "Because no one gives a damn what you do for leisure, Fines. God knows you top-o'-the-trees gents got plenty of free time."

"I *said* business and I meant it," Paul snapped.

"Where's the blunt to come from, then? Because business involves money." Hunt spoke with the emphasis one might use when explaining matters to a small, slightly daft child. "So far I ain't heard a word about how you intend to profit from dancing pretty around the ring."

Patronizing ass. "The purse for the tournament is five thousand pounds, and I'll split the winnings with Traymore fifty-fifty," Paul said through gritted teeth. "Which is only fair, given that he will put up the stake."

"Five thousand quid ain't sizeable enough for Traymore to invest his time and effort. I've been to fights hosted by the Fancy; the true profit comes from all the wagering that goes on. And I was under the impression that you'd sworn off gaming," Hunt said pointedly, "having nearly lost your fortune at it before."

"Only because you laid a trap for me, you holier-than-thou

bastard!" Paul's face heated, his chest straining beneath his waist-coat. "This is different!"

"The situation may not be as different as you believe." Though Ambrose Kent had remained quiet up until now, his measured words commanded attention. "These matches attract all manner of riffraff—er, no offense, Hunt ..."

"None taken," Hunt said.

"... including cutthroats, percents, and bookmakers looking to make an easy mark. These are not the sort of men you wish to get involved with."

"I won't get involved with the wagering," Paul protested. "What Traymore does with his money is none of my business. *My* goal is to win the title. As Champion, I can open my own boxing saloon like Jackson or Richmond before him. *That* is how I intend to rebuild my fortune."

"And if you don't win? What then?" Nicholas said.

Anger scorched like acid in Paul's chest. "Why must you assume the worst of me? Why can't anyone, just once, clap me on the back and support my decision?"

"Because this is an asinine plan," the other snapped, "and I don't want to see you make any more mistakes than you already have."

The blow could not have been aimed any lower. Paul had no defense against the leveler; how could he, when he had indeed made a hash of his entire past and was a failure through and through? Jeremiah's voice, raspy and faint, echoed in Paul's ears.

You could have been more, my dear boy. Far more. That is my greatest disappointment.

He shut out the words, the last he'd heard at his father's bedside. Yet, sensing blood, all the demons roused within him. Rosalind's tear-stained face surfaced. *It's too late, Paul. My father has promised me to Lord Monteith.* He saw himself imbibing bottle after bottle of ruin to wash away the pain. And at the clubs, throwing his money away, brawling over the slightest provocation ... hiding, desperate and despicable, in that hovel in Spitalfields ...

Paul pushed to his feet, needing to escape from his failures. From the hiss and snap of his bedeviled past. "Since there's to be no discussion," he said tightly, "I'll take my leave."

"Damnit, Fines, have some bloody sense—" Nicholas began.

"I do. And you're right—I *am* a feckless fool." He paused at the door, his lips twisting. "Damn me for thinking I could ever be more than that."

Chapter Six

"You cannot be serious. You're not truly considering marrying a man you don't love!"

"Please lower your voice, Percy. I don't wish for everyone at the picnic to know my private affairs," Charity said.

Casting a glance about, she was relieved to note that none of the other guests were looking in their direction. She and Percy had excused themselves to take a stroll around the perimeter of the garden. Finally alone with her friend, Charity had shared the news of her soon-to-be arranged nuptials.

"But this is *madness*. You don't even know this man," Percy said in a furious whisper.

"Mr. Garrity is my father's business associate. He's come to the shop on several occasions." Three, to be exact. "Father likes him very much."

Percy narrowed her eyes. "And what do *you* think of him?"

Charity bit her lip. Mr. Garrity was a tall, dark, and elegant gentleman in his thirties. Many would consider him handsome. Yet there was something about his eyes—cold and dark as onyx—that stirred her unease. As she'd gone about her duties, he'd watched her the way a predator might watch its small, furry supper.

"I think that he will be a boon to Sparkler's," she said truthfully.

"Then Mr. Sparkler should take him on as a business partner, not a son-in-law!"

"You know how Papa is about the shop. He doesn't trust anyone but family."

"Well, that's easy enough for him to say. He doesn't have to marry ... oh *God*." Percy stopped in her tracks, pained horror spreading across her face.

"What's the matter?" Charity said with instant alarm. "Is it the babe? Are you—"

"*I'm* fine. But, Lord, it just occurred to me. If you wed this man, you'd be ..."—Percy's blue eyes widened—"*Charity Garrity.*"

An awkward name, admittedly.

Charity cleared her throat. "Marriage is about more than a name."

"Exactly. It ought to be about love and passion." Percy's skirts swished against the carpet of grass, her pace in rhythm with the rapid-fire cadence of her words. "Marriage should be about the mating of two *souls*—not the joining of business interests."

Charity smiled wryly at her friend's incurable optimism. "Most marriages *are* based on practical considerations. Yours is the outlier, dear."

"Better to be an outlier than the unhappy norm," Percy said decisively.

"We can't all be outliers, can we?" Charity said in reasonable tones. "Besides, I would be content knowing that I'm doing my duty. Father is getting older, and his constitution is frail."

A chill crept over her. Over the past few months, her papa had become increasingly grey and tired. He'd had several spells; the physician had diagnosed him with a weakening heart. Yet neither the good doctor nor she could dissuade her father from working his grueling hours.

"Between us, sales have fallen. Papa needs someone to help

turn things around," she said tightly. "He can't do everything by himself any longer."

"Why doesn't he let *you* take over the shop? Lord knows you could run the place if you put your mind to it." The cornflowers on Percy's hat fluttered as she said with emphasis, "You know Sparkler's inside and out, *and* you're the most organized, efficient person I know."

Percy's words stirred a dangerous accord in Charity. That secret, wayward part of her that believed that she could run Sparkler's—if Father would entrust her with responsibilities beyond what he deemed proper for a young woman. It wasn't that she minded keeping the shop tidy or helping customers when needed; it was that she suspected that she could do far more.

When she'd gathered the courage to suggest this to her father, he'd given her an incredulous look. *A girl—managing a business like Sparkler's? Don't be ridiculous. Get back to your duties, Charity, and don't waste any more time on this nonsense.*

A hot feeling flared beneath Charity's breast bone; she tamped it down, told herself it was immodest to assume that she could run the shop. Such vanity would only anger Father, and he might bar her from the shop entirely. Then where would she be? She couldn't risk losing her role at Sparkler's; she'd *earned* her place there.

All her life, she'd worked hard for the privilege of accompanying her papa to work. For it was there that she could share a few moments alone with him, just the two of them. After the store closed for the night, she'd help him unpack the new inventory, and he'd take the time to show her the beauty of each piece.

Look at this pearl. It isn't flashy like a diamond, but its value is in its purity and substance. His grey eyes would focus on her. *Be wise, my girl, and don't be fooled by glitter.*

She felt a pang. She couldn't bear to disappoint her father.

Clearing her throat, she said, "Whoever heard of a woman running a business as large as Sparkler's? It simply isn't done."

"You could be the first," her friend replied stoutly. "Remember all those late nights we spent talking about our deepest, most innermost dreams? You said you wanted to have your own shop—and now you have the opportunity."

"Dreams aren't the same as reality."

"You've always supported me in *my* dreams." Percy's blond curls tipped to the side. "Now I'm married to Mr. Hunt and writing novels. If I can find the ultimate happiness, why can't you?"

Because Percy was pretty and spirited, deserving of everything good. Whilst Charity was ... *Never gild a lily or a weed. Keep your head down. Do as you're told.* She chased a rock away with the tip of her kid boot.

"Picture a new sign on the storefront." Percy waved her hands with dramatic flair, as if unveiling a grand masterpiece. *"Sparkler & Sparkler: Purveyors of the Extraordinary.* It has a ring to it, don't you agree?"

"Only because you've a way with fiction." Tucking away her longing, Charity said, "The reality is I have suggested it before, and Father wouldn't even hear of it. Marriage to Mr. Garrity is the only way to help the business *and* make my papa happy."

"But what about *your* happiness?"

"I'll be happy knowing that I've acted prudently and in the best interests of everyone."

They walked on in uncharacteristic silence. Charity was struck by unease, justified when her friend said, "What about ... Paul?"

The sounds of the garden melded into a loud buzz. Charity's heart raced; her skin tingled. All at the mere mention of his name.

"I know you have feelings for my brother," Percy said quietly, "and if he weren't such a numskull, he'd recognize it too. But I think he is finally ready for love, Charity. And if you'd let me tell him what you did for him—"

"*No.*" Charity clutched her friend's arm. "You *promised*, Percy.

You gave me your word on our friendship that you would never disclose my visit to Spitalfields."

"I know I did, which is why I haven't breathed a word of it to anyone. But, Charity," Percy said with obvious frustration, "don't you think my bacon-brained brother ought to know the truth? You risked your reputation, your very *life*, to nurse him when I couldn't do so. You were as brave as any heroine, and I wish you'd let me tell him so."

Charity shook her head, in desperation and ... guilt. For she'd kept the truth of what had transpired between her and Mr. Fines a secret, even from her best friend. The humiliation of being kissed by mistake was already too much: she couldn't bear Mr. Fines finding out and offering for her out of obligation. *Pity*, for God's sake.

Embers smoldered in her chest. She could endure many things —but never that.

"What would that accomplish?" Charity said as calmly as she could, "The truth is I count it a blessing that Mr. Fines was too inebriated to take note of my presence. Going to him was an act of folly rather than heroism, and as for my feelings for him ..."— mentally, she crossed her fingers—"they were naught but a passing infatuation. I've grown up, Percy, and I'm quite done with that foolishness."

"But that was only nine months ago. And you're the most constant person I know."

"Done," Charity repeated.

"I just think that if Paul had any inkling—"

"If you divulge my actions now, you'll only ruin my reputation and my chances of marrying Mr. Garrity. He will help Papa and save the business. Ergo, he is the man I must wed."

This was exactly the sort of sensible, practical argument she ought to be making. Yet the words felt as dry as sawdust in Charity's mouth.

"My brother might not seem to possess business savvy, but I

assure you he can do anything he puts his mind to." Her expression troubled, Percy said, "In retrospect, I think Papa erred in trying to browbeat Paul into working at Fines & Co. My brother is as stubborn as a mule: the more you push him, the harder he plants his heels. He and my father had endless rows over it."

Charity recalled some of these arguments. Several times, when she'd been over visiting with Percy, she'd overheard the raised voices coming from Jeremiah Fines' study. Words like "irresponsible" and "reckless" had seeped through the walls.

Empathy had filled her. Living up to a parent's expectations was never easy. She'd tried to please her father all her life.

Mr. Fines, on the other hand, had seemed inclined to employ the opposite strategy.

"My brother *is* a capable fellow, however," Percy went on, "and when he decides upon a thing, he's utterly dedicated. Look at his success at boxing. And he's loyal too: even at his lowest point last year, he risked life and limb to defend my honor." Her eyes shimmered. "I've always looked up to him."

"I know," Charity said gently. "But the fact remains that Mr. Fines would have no interest in Sparkler's. Or, more importantly, me. I'm not the sort of girl your brother fancies."

I'm no Rosalind Drummond.

"*You* are an absolute gem, and my brother would be lucky to have you." Percy chewed on her lower lip. "Oh, I just wish he would grow up!"

"Keep your promise to me. You'll say nothing to your brother —to anyone—about my trip to Spitalfields. Swear it, Percy."

Charity held out her gloved pinkie. Her friend hesitated before doing the same. Their fingers caught and held in the most solemn of vows.

"For a girl who's supposedly quiet and reserved, you argue like a bloody barrister, you know," Percy grumbled.

A half hour later, Charity parted with Percy, who was ready for a nap after all. Not wanting to waste the lovely afternoon, Charity continued the walk alone. She saw Sarah in the distance chatting with the other maids and decided not to disturb their conversation. In truth, she wished for time alone with her thoughts. Spying a path in the woods that bordered the gardens, she made her way over, letting out a sigh of pleasure as the cool, leafy shade enveloped her.

Here, her worries abated. The country idyll was a rare escape from the bustling, smoke-choked bosom of London. Here, she took in buzzing dragonflies and chirping birds rather than clattering carriage wheels and raucous street mongers pitching their wares. Even the splendors of Hyde Park paled in comparison to this verdant, untamed paradise.

Surrounded by towering oaks, overgrown bushes, and glittering streams of sunlight, Charity felt removed from the troubles of the world. There was only the spongy squish of her kid boots against the forest floor and the humid air bathing her senses. A pair of squirrels darted across her path, their bushy grey tails swishing as their game of chase took them high into the leafy boughs. Through perforations in the forest canopy, she spied birds winging through the sky.

What would it be like to be so ... free?

She wasn't accustomed to such idle thoughts. Her ordinary life was organized around gainful activity: an unending list of tasks to be completed at the shop and another list when she returned home. She enjoyed keeping busy. It prevented her from the devil's work—from thinking too much. And from futile ... longing.

For the attention of her father, who already had too many burdens upon his shoulders. For the care of her mother, who she wished she might have known. And for ...

A love that can't be mine.

She caught herself. Solitude was making for a poor companion indeed, if it encouraged her to indulge in such foolish thoughts.

"What is the matter with you, Charity Sparkler?" she said aloud. "You're carrying on like the heroine of a maudlin opera. Next thing you know, the violins will start playing and you'll be tossing yourself over a bridge."

Regaining her practical senses, she took another step—and lost her footing. Her boot encountered a hole hidden beneath the carpet of moss, and she yelped as her ankle went over. She lost her balance, tumbling into the shallow gully next to the path.

Lying on her back, breathing rapidly, she blinked up at the leaves and glittering patches of light. She became aware of an odd buzzing noise and thought, at first, that her ears were ringing because of the fall. But the sound grew louder and darkness swarmed her vision, obliterating leaves and light, covering all in a vortex of black, swirling frenzy.

Wasps. *Thousands* of them.

Panicked, she scrambled to get up, but her skirts were caught in the brambles. She yanked at them as the insects roared. She managed to stumble to her feet, only to fall with a cry as her wrenched ankle gave out. The wasps descended in a humming shroud. She curled into a ball, shielding her head with her arms, her heart hammering with helpless fear.

The ground shook beneath her. The rhythmic vibration jolted her to her senses. The pounding of hooves, a horse ...?

She cried out, "Help! Over here, help me, please!"

Heartbeats passed. Powerful arms reached through the veil of death and swept her up.

Chapter Seven

J ust beyond the woods, Paul drew his horse to a stop at the folly. It was the closest place he could think to go. He lifted Charity Sparkler into his arms, ignoring her protests, and carried her through the gothic arches into the gazebo. With care, he placed her down on a stone bench, surprised to realize that his heart was pounding.

"Are you hurt?" he said tersely.

"I didn't get stung." She peered up at him with worried eyes. "What about you?"

"I'm fine." He exhaled. "We'll have to wait here until the blasted things clear from the path."

He thought it was a miracle that she'd escaped unscathed. With the exception of the dirt smudged on the tip of her little *retroussé* nose and the leafy bits clinging to her gown, she appeared much as she usually did. Most ladies he knew turned into watering pots in the presence of one buzzing insect, never mind thousands. But not Charity Sparkler. Her expression was as composed as a sonata.

His mouth twitched as he noted that although she'd lost her bonnet, only a single lock of hair had escaped her topknot. The strand had an unexpected wave and clung with gentle sensuality to her cheekbone. She brushed it away, and, as she did so, the tendril caught the light. The burnished glimmer made him blink.

Frowning, he scrutinized her coiffure. Whatever she used on her hair—some sort of waxy substance?—obscured its natural brilliance. Up close he glimpsed hints of shimmering gold and bronze twined with rich hazelnut. Why would she hide such an asset with pomade and pins? His palms prickled with a sudden memory of silken waves, grasping them as he plundered the softest, sweetest mouth—

He rubbed his hands over his thighs, shaking off the queer sensations. Where the devil had that come from? Was he hallucinating now? The aftermath of danger must have unbalanced him. Or mayhap her hair reminded him of a past lover's, some spontaneous and inexplicable association ... yes, that must be it.

Yet he couldn't recall bedding anyone who resembled Miss Sparkler. He made it a point to stay away prim and proper types. Not to mention virgins.

"Thank you ... for saving my life," she said softly.

It had been a long while since anyone had looked at him this way. As if he were wearing a coronet of stars. His chest expanded, even as he replied with his usual wit.

"Happy to oblige. I know you adventurous types thrive on risk," he drawled, "but in the future I must remind you of that old adage: never stir a hornet's nest."

"I didn't do it on *purpose*, sir. And I'm not adventurous—not at all."

She sounded so appalled that he almost chuckled. What an earnest little mouse she was. He couldn't resist teasing her a little more.

"*The lady doth protest too much, methinks.*" He tapped his chin. "As I recall, the last time we met you were marauding in the parlor at midnight. Now you're wandering about the woods alone."

Pink spilled over Miss Sparkler's cheekbones, emphasizing

their unique slant and the fey shape of her little face. "I know I ought to have summoned my maid. But I ..."—she hesitated and then her shoulders hitched in a rather forlorn movement—"I wished for some solitude."

"Tired of the company, are you? House parties *are* a dreadful bore."

"Oh no, it's not that. Everyone has been most kind. And it is an honor to be invited at all. It's just that ... well, I'm not sure I can explain."

"Try," he said.

Because he *was* curious. Why had the little chit hailed off on her own? Given the rarefied guest list, any middling class miss worth her salt would be angling to make the best matrimonial catch.

Her gaze on her lap, Miss Sparkler said, "I suppose being surrounded by people made me feel more alone." She fiddled with the beige folds of her skirt. "Sounds silly, doesn't it?"

Actually ... it didn't.

"It's the happy ones in particular," he said with feeling, "that really make one miserable. And we two seem to be surrounded by a surfeit of lovey-dovey couples, don't we? It's like a disease, and it's spreading."

"I wouldn't worry for your health, sir. I'm certain the condition is not contagious."

There it was again: that sly wit of hers. He hadn't imagined it last night. Her mouth tipped up at the corners, and it was a charming expression for her.

"You misunderstand, I'm not worried about *me*," he said. "We hardened rakes have a natural immunity against the softer sentiments. 'Tis young innocents such as you who had better have a care. From what I hear, quite a few eligible bachelors at the party are looking to get leg-shackled."

"With my slight stature, I fear I would make a poor ball and chain."

A laugh rustled from his chest. "But your stature is quite charming and I daresay no barrier to any gentleman's pursuit. In fact, I'm surprised you're not already spoken for."

The laughter in her eyes faded. Her smile, too.

His chest inexplicably tightened, and he masked it by quirking a brow. "Or, perhaps, you are? I apologize for assuming otherwise. I hadn't heard anything from Percy."

"I'm not. Spoken for, that is. At least, not definitively."

For the first time, Miss Sparkler sounded flustered. Interesting. A horde of wasps didn't disquiet her, but a possible attachment did? Having his own aversion to marriage, he experienced a surge of empathy. Perhaps he and she had more in common than he realized.

Gently, he said, "Do you wish to talk about it?"

Her lashes fluttered like butterfly wings. She bit her lip—the plump bottom one. The one right above that wicked little beauty mark ...

"I don't think so," she said.

He cleared his throat. Tried to get his thoughts on track. "You can trust me. After all, you and Percy are sisters in every way but blood, which makes us practically related. Old friends, at the very least."

"We're friends?" Miss Sparkler said.

He was discovering many admirable qualities about Charity Sparkler. Beneath her unassuming demeanor lay honesty and wit, a steadiness of character. She was refreshingly different from the usual array of giggling debs and sultry matrons.

"I'd like to think so. One can never have too many friends," he said with an easy smile.

"If I may be frank?" she said.

He nodded.

"You don't seem to lack for companionship, Mr. Fines. Particularly the female kind."

The back of his neck heated, and he rubbed it. "That's plain talking, ain't it?"

"I'm afraid that is my tendency."

"And a refreshing one it is," he said ruefully. Her calm countenance made it strangely easy to speak the truth. "In a nutshell, Miss Sparkler? I grow tired of my habits. Of their lack of substance."

"Then why not find more meaningful pursuits?" she asked.

It must be the way she phrased things, Paul mused, that made all the difference. When Nicholas or his mama harangued him on the topic, his defenses rallied immediately. He *hated* being told what to do. Yet when this chit spoke, he heard no judgment, merely an observation.

He decided to test the waters. "Actually, I have. I'm going to compete as a prizefighter. Not in an exhibition—in a real tournament."

Her brow puckered. "Won't that be dangerous?"

"Not if I'm prepared. Before the tournament, I'm going to train in earnest. I've a patron, Viscount Traymore, and he's offered up a place in the country where I can practice in seclusion and without distractions. I'm willing to do whatever it takes to become a Champion," he said fiercely.

I'm going to show them all that I'm a winner.

Her head tipped to one side. "Prizefighting is an unusual pursuit for a gentleman. Why does it interest you?"

Not *are you daft?* Or *how could you be so bloody irresponsible?* Simply ... *why?*

He experienced a wild urge to *hug* Charity Sparkler.

"Because I love being in the ring. I have a talent for it. Winning those exhibition rounds wasn't even that difficult—I could beat better fighters, I know it." Words rushed from him like water from a dam. "It would be hard work and a great challenge, but I think ... nay, I *believe* that I could be a Champion. That I could win the title and use that fame to start my own academy."

"It sounds like you have given the matter some thought," she said.

"I have."

"Are there any downsides to your plan?"

"I told Harteford and the other men. They think I've bacon for brains," he said flatly.

She smoothed her skirts. "You agree with them?"

He frowned. "Of course not."

"Yet you're allowing their opinion to color your own."

He mulled over her observation. Was he *afraid* that Nicholas was right? Was that fear making him doubt his own dreams? Had he so little faith in himself—was that his true problem?

"You are terrifyingly astute, Miss Sparkler," he said in wonder.

"Not really. I'm just acquainted with the Fines temperament." Her cheeks curved, and her beauty mark seemed to wink at him. "Once Percy makes up her mind, nothing can get in her way—except, perhaps, herself."

"My sister is fortunate indeed to call you her friend." He bowed. "May I also have that pleasure?"

To his surprise, silence greeted his request. She bit her lip. His breath stuttered as opalescent sparks glimmered in her eyes.

"We should go," she blurted. "The others will be looking for us."

Before he could question her non sequitur, she jumped up ... and a cry escaped her as her left leg buckled. He caught her before she hit the ground. Sweeping her off her feet, he set her back on the bench and knelt on one knee beside her.

"Why didn't you say anything? Did you hurt your ankle?" he demanded.

"I ... I might have turned it a little."

He reached for the hem of her skirt; her hand clamped onto his.

"It isn't proper," she said in a small voice.

"Is it proper to let you writhe in pain?" he said grimly. "We can't ride back if you've broken something. I have to take a look."

Her grip on his hand slowly eased. Thank God she was a practical chit.

"Tell me if anything hurts," he said.

He removed her kid boot with care. Encased in sturdy white silk, her foot was exceedingly dainty and feminine—shapely with little toes and the prettiest arch ... with a jolt, he realized the direction of his thoughts.

Devil and damn, what is the matter with you? Get your mind out of the gutter.

He concentrated on examining her right ankle. Although he detected no broken bones, he could feel a slight swelling beneath the stocking. He'd have to remove the layer to truly assess the injury. He decided to sin first and repent later. Without further ado, he reached higher up her skirts.

Her hand slapped down on his. Though hers rested atop her muslin skirt and petticoats and his beneath, her grip was viselike.

"What are you doing?" she gasped.

He swallowed. Somehow she'd managed to trap his hand above her garter, his palm smooshed against the softest, silkiest thigh he'd ever touched. His temperature shot up. His cock as well. Thank God his riding jacket hid the rapidly burgeoning bulge.

"I was trying to undo your stocking," he said hoarsely. "To have a closer look at your ankle."

"Is that ... necessary?"

Her breathy voice tickled his ear, made all his muscles stiffen. Had she leaned closer? He couldn't tell; her eyes were mesmerizing, disorienting, drawing him in ... He tried to tear his gaze away, only to have it land on her mouth. Her lips were parted, that naughty bottom ledge jutting out. Was she this plump and pink everywhere?

Sweat glazed him. He tried to regain his senses. Tried to resist the pull of her fresh scent, like a newly made bed he wanted to roll around in. His heart thumped with unrivaled force. His fingers shook against her satiny thigh. Her tongue suddenly darted out, moistening her lips ... and his self-control snapped.

He yanked his hand from her skirts. Hooking her by the nape, he dragged her mouth to his.

She was sweeter than anything he'd ever tasted. Honey and heat ... intoxicating. His mind blurred. He wanted more, delving with his tongue, and a fresh wave of lust crashed over him when she let him inside. Mmm, so silky and *hot*. His tongue slid against hers, urging her to play, and the shy, sensual brush of her little tongue shot straight to his groin. His balls drew up, his cock throbbing like a second heartbeat.

He tore his mouth from hers to nuzzle hungrily at her throat. Her unique, linen-fresh scent pervaded his senses, and he couldn't get enough: of her smell, her taste, her smooth white skin beneath his lips. He licked the pulse near the base of her throat, and she trembled against him. He groaned when her fingers ruffled his hair and slid against his scalp, holding him closer to her arched neck.

He lowered her to the bench. His mouth captured hers once more, their tongues tangling, his hand fitting over the most exquisite little breast—

The thundering of hooves pierced his haze of lust.

His head jerked up at the same time that she stiffened beneath him.

He jumped off her. Backed away.

"Holy hell," he said hoarsely.

She sat up, blinking at him. A wide-eyed innocent whose bloody topknot remained almost entirely intact. His sister's best friend ... whom he'd nearly *debauched*. What was the matter with him? Where was his sense of honor? How could he bungle things up so badly *yet again*?

His mind reeled in panic.

"I'm sorry. I—I don't know what came over me," he stammered. "I don't do this. That is, not with girls like you. Bloody hell, it was a mistake ..."

"A mistake," she said in a faint voice.

He could hear their names being called. Any minute now they would be discovered. His cravat seemed to tighten like a noose as he tried to summon the honorable words.

"I'm sorry," he said again. "Don't worry, I'll do the right thing if I have to—"

Footsteps sounded. Seconds later, Nicholas and Hunt ducked through the archway.

"There you are, Miss Sparkler." After a frowning glance in Paul's direction, the marquess said, "My wife was worried that you might have gotten lost in the woods. Hunt and I encountered the wasps along the path—you are well, I hope?"

"Yes, my lord," Miss Sparkler said in a calm voice. "I stumbled upon the nest by accident. Mr. Fines found me and brought me here to recover."

Hunt's brows lifted. "A hero are you, Fines?"

Paul ignored the jibe. He was too busy experiencing chest palpitations. "There's something I have to say ..." he choked out. "Miss Sparkler and I ... we ..."

"We escaped unscathed." She cut him off with the quiet precision of shears snipping an annoying thread.

"What?" he said, confused.

"Let us not make a mountain out of a molehill, sir."

He stared at her. "A ... molehill?"

"It's certainly not the first unfortunate incident I've experienced. And it's not even the most memorable." Her eyes were as cool as moss. "I can only hope it will be the last."

Two opposing emotions warred within Paul. Relief ... and sudden, irrational anger.

Not the first incident? Who was the bloody bastard who kissed her before me?

"Just in case, we'll have a physician examine your injury, Miss

Sparkler," Nicholas said. "Are you able to ride? We've brought an extra mount."

"I'm ready to go," she said.

Taking the marquess' arm, Miss Sparkler departed without a backward glance.

Chapter Eight

The following afternoon, Percy returned to the guest bedchamber with her husband at her heels. One look from Gavin and her lady's maid scurried from the room. Peeling off her gloves and tossing them onto the vanity, Percy said excitedly, "Did you *feel* the undercurrents during tea?"

Gavin gave her a blank look. "What undercurrents?"

"You didn't notice *anything* out of the ordinary just now? No tension of any sort?"

"I suppose Miss Sparkler looked tense." Her spouse sat at the end of the bed, stretching his long legs in front of him. "But she's always wound tighter than a spool of thread."

"I wasn't talking about Charity—who, by the by, is not half as severe as you paint her. If I had to live under her father's tyranny, I'd be *twice* as tense."

"You've never done well with authority, buttercup." With obvious satisfaction, Gavin added, "Except mine, of course."

Percy decided to let him labor under the husbandly delusion.

"Charity can barely breathe without Mr. Sparkler's permission. He underestimates her dreadfully," she said with indignation. "And now he wants to force her into a loveless marriage!"

"Is that her opinion or yours?"

"Mine ... but it's the *truth*. Charity's blinded by her loyalty to her father. His word is gospel, and there's nothing I can say to convince her otherwise."

That didn't mean that Percy wouldn't *try*.

"Best not to meddle," Gavin advised.

"I'm not meddling. I just plan to"—inspiration struck her—"fan the flames of latent passion." It was an excellent phrase; she ought to jot it down for her next novel.

Her husband looked puzzled. "What are you talking about?"

"You didn't notice the undeniable chemistry? The crackling, unspoken awareness between my brother and Charity?"

"Fines? And *Miss Sparkler*?"

"Why is that so amusing?" Astonished, Percy watched as her husband's broad shoulders shook with laughter. "It would be an excellent match," she insisted. "Charity is exactly what my numskull of a brother needs—"

"A bridle may give a stallion direction, but he's not going to welcome it." Still chuckling, Gavin said, "Fines has no interest in your little friend. Trust me. If there are any fireworks going on, they're between him and one of those red-headed twins." Gavin snorted. "Or both of 'em. Randy cull, your brother."

Percy had to admit that the lascivious sisters *had* flirted shamelessly with Paul over supper last night. They'd batted their eyelashes and taken every opportunity to give him—and every other male present—an eyeful of their overblown charms.

Percy wrinkled her nose. "I suppose you *would* notice Lady Augusta and Louisa—"

The rest of her words were lost in a yelp as her husband yanked her onto his lap. His ore-flecked eyes gleamed into hers. "Notice, yes. Tawdry wares are hard to miss, especially when they're displayed for all and sundry." He nuzzled her ear, sending a familiar quiver up her spine. "But those high-kick tarts can't hold a candle to you."

"I'm not fishing for compliments," she said, looping her arms around his neck.

"You don't have to fish." With a wicked grin, he brought her bottom flush against his groin; even through the layers of their clothing, she felt the unmistakable evidence of his arousal. "You've already landed the biggest one."

"Is this the kind that gets bigger with every telling?" she teased.

"Why don't you find out?"

He set her onto the mattress beside him. Capturing her hand, he brought it to the placket of his trousers. His rock-hard virility quickened her breath. She gave him a squeeze, and he growled his approval. She'd always been responsive to her husband, but oddly enough pregnancy had made her even more wanton ... a fact that Gavin took full advantage of.

His hands planted on the mattress behind him, he ground his rampant cock against her hand, his eyes smoldering and heavy-lidded. "You know just how to handle me, buttercup."

She *loved* touching him and was tempted to give into the desire he always roused in her. But in all good conscience, she couldn't—not until she'd aired her concerns. The happiness of her best friend and her brother lay in the balance.

"Can we talk first?" she said.

"I have a better idea. Why don't you keep doing what you're doing, and I'll lend a hand as well ..."

His proprietary caress up her leg made Percy tremble, yet she said, "Please, darling. I'm ever so worried about Charity and Paul. And you always give the best advice."

"Bloody hell." Gavin let out a long-suffering sigh, but his hand stilled on her thigh. "What is it that you want to talk about?"

Percy flashed him a grateful smile. "Did you notice how Paul and Charity kept looking at one another during tea and tried to appear as if they weren't doing so?"

Gavin's tawny brows drew together. "I'll grant that there *may* have been some awkwardness between the two." Just as Percy was about to cheer, he said, "But that doesn't mean they're attracted to one another. Fines seemed antsy to me; mayhap he was itching to be elsewhere."

Drat. Paul *had* seemed fidgety. Could it be that he'd wanted to simply get away? Yet the way he'd snuck glances at Charity ... Percy had never seen him do that before. He either looked at a girl or he didn't; what was this dithering about?

"Paul didn't seem himself. Something was bothering him," she insisted.

"I know the answer to that, and you're not going to like it."

"What is it?" she said in surprise.

When Gavin told her about the men's conversation in the study, she burst out, "Mama will *murder* him if she catches wind of this. Who ever heard of a gentleman prizefighting?"

"Conventionality doesn't exactly run in your family." Her spouse grinned when she made a face at him. "We tried to talk Fines out of it. The betting is steep at events hosted by the Fancy, and the cutthroats and bookmakers find the easy marks. There's no saying what your brother could get mixed up in."

Percy chewed on her lip. Since the debacle last year, Paul had given up his more dangerous vices, and yet she knew he had not fully recovered. Despite the carefree front he put up for the world, she sensed he was hurting inside. He hadn't been himself since he'd had his heart broken two years ago.

"Blast that Rosalind Drummond. This is all *her* fault, you know." Percy's fists clenched in her lap. "She was a beautiful, shallow flirt and had all the gentlemen dangling after her that Season. Even my brother was hopelessly infatuated. In fact, I think he was on the verge of declaring for her."

"Your brother never mentions this Drummond chit."

"That's just Paul's way. The more something matters, the less inclined he is to talk about it. He was entirely tight-lipped about the affair. But his troubles all started after Rosalind upped and married that Scottish earl."

"There now, love," Gavin murmured. "Don't get overset. It isn't good for the babe."

Pregnancy did have the disconcerting tendency to make her emotions more volatile. Just remembering her brother as he'd once been made her eyes swim with sudden tears. Like his namesake, Paul had been a golden boy, one who'd drawn everyone into his orbit. Whilst he clearly continued to draw the attention of ladies, his charisma back then had been of a purer sort. One rooted in a true zest for life rather than hard-edged cynicism.

Percy blinked back moisture. "I just wish I could do something for him. After all, he's looked after me my entire life."

"You've got me now. You don't need him or anyone else."

Her husband's possessiveness sent a primitive thrill over Percy's nape. Having lived most of his life in the stews fighting for his very survival, Gavin had a need for control greater than most men.

She touched his lean cheek. "I know that, darling. But do you think it possible for a heart to break and never recover?"

"Once, I would have said no. But then I met you." Beneath her palm, Gavin's scar drew taut. "I don't know what I would do if I lost you, Persephone."

Seeing the stark look in his eyes, knowing he was recalling the night that had almost ended them both, Percy snuggled closer. "You'll never have to worry about that again, I promise."

"Love can make—or break—a man." His arms tightened like steel bands around her, one big hand coming to rest upon the slight swell of her belly. "That I can vouch for."

"So you believe that love can heal a broken heart?"

He drew back to look at her. Tracing her lips with a blunt finger, he said, "If you're thinking about your brother and your friend, it's not going to work. They're too different."

"*We're* different. And look how well we turned out."

"We had an attraction from the start, buttercup. I couldn't keep my hands off you. Still can't, as a matter of fact."

The next instant, Percy found herself on her back on the

mattress. She fought back giggles as her husband crawled over her, his expression wolfish.

"Paul likes Charity," Percy said in a breathy voice. "They've conversed and danced."

"There's making chitchat with a female ... and then there's wondering what it'd be like to tumble her." Gavin purposefully spread her thighs, heating her blood. "I'd wager a string of thoroughbreds that Fines has never thought about Miss Sparkler the way I'm thinking about you right this minute."

"What are you thinking—"

Her bantering words turned into a moan at her husband's masterful touch. With unerring precision, he played with her, rubbing and stroking and fingering until her hips arched in helpless surrender. As her mind glazed over, she made a mental promise to discuss matters with Helena and Marianne at first opportunity. If the three of them put their heads together, surely they could devise a plan to—Percy gasped as her spouse tickled an exquisite spot.

"Christ Almighty, you're wet for me. You're drenching my palm," Gavin said reverently.

The rest of her thoughts evaporated in a hot rush. In that moment, only her husband existed, the hunger and adoration blazing in his tawny gaze.

"You have that effect on me," she whispered. "Being married to you is the most exciting adventure I've ever had."

"That's good to hear, love. Makes me think you're ready for what I have planned next ..."

And her husband set about proving his point: there was, indeed, no end to his wickedly inventive ways.

Chapter Nine

That night, Charity waited until the last possible moment to go down to supper. Her dove grey skirts whispered against the polished parquet as she followed the sounds of gaiety to the main drawing room where preprandial refreshments were being served. With each step, she reminded herself of her plan.

If you see Mr. Fines, continue to act as if nothing happened. Avoid him if you can. Whatever you do, don't let him see your true feelings.

As she slipped into the crowded room, she fought for composure despite the vise clamping around her heart. The dazzling chandeliers and sparkling finery of the guests blurred for an instant before she blinked away the sheen of moisture. She'd believed that there couldn't be anything as painful as being made love to by accident and then promptly forgotten. Yesterday, Paul Fines had proven her wrong.

He was sorry he'd kissed her. He'd called it a *mistake*.

She drew a shaky breath. Forced her shoulders back.

She would not humiliate herself further. If she was meant to be Charity Garrity, then so be it. She'd embrace her destiny with dignity. She'd stop pining over someone who would, as he so charmingly put it, do the right thing—if he *had* to.

She was done tormenting herself over Paul Fines.

Speaking of the devil ... her gaze caught on his gleaming golden head by the fireplace. As usual, Mr. Fines was surrounded by a bevy of beauties. With one arm braced against the mantel and his lean virility emphasized by the stark formality of evening dress, he was the epitome of the stylish buck. He took in the scene with heavy-lidded eyes, his expression one of boredom. Rather than putting off his admirers, his jaded air stirred them into a frenzy of competitive giggling and eyelash batting.

As his eyes latched onto Charity's, she saw a flare of brilliant blue and, for an instant, forgot to breathe. Then she caught herself.

Done.

She turned away ... and nearly collided with another guest.

"I b-beg your pardon," she stammered. "I should have looked—"

"No harm done, my dear." The lady regarded her with a faint smile. Dressed in a bold coquelicot gown that complimented her auburn coronet, the woman was perhaps in her early forties and radiated confident femininity. Something seemed familiar about her slender figure and hazel eyes, but Charity couldn't imagine where she would have met such a dashing personage.

The lady's elegant fingers brushed her large ruby pendant—and Charity remembered. Sarah had pointed this woman out at the picnic.

"You're Mrs. Stone. The famous actress," she blurted.

"Indeed. And you are ...?"

"Charity Sparkler." An awkward moment passed in which she debated praising the other's art. Having never seen Mrs. Stone perform, however, she didn't wish to pay a false compliment. So instead she said, "I'm honored to meet you."

"And I you, Miss Sparkler," Mrs. Stone said in amused tones. "A word to the wise, if I may?"

Charity blinked. "Yes?"

Mrs. Stone leaned toward her. "You seem to have acquired an admirer."

"An admirer? Me?"

"That handsome blond gentleman by the fireplace has been watching you since you entered the room. In fact, his eyes are on you right this moment." With a wink, the actress glided off.

Astonished, Charity was debating whether to risk a glance in Mr. Fines' direction when she heard Lady Helena call her name.

The sea of guests parted for the marchioness, who was radiant in topaz silk. Flanking her were Percy and Mrs. Marianne Kent. The former looked fresh and fetching in sky blue satin that matched her vivid eyes, the latter stunning in an *au courant* gown of silver-shot gauze that had other ladies casting jealous glances her way. Gentlemen, too, were staring at Mrs. Kent; a few tried to approach her, only to be shooed away like pesky insects.

In truth, Charity had always felt a tad intimidated by Marianne Kent. Not only was the lady an Incomparable with her ice-blonde beauty and willowy figure, but she was clever and sophisticated to boot.

Charity dipped a curtsy. "Good evening."

Percy took her by the arm, and the four of them headed over to an alcove shielded by an Oriental screen. In the quasi-private space, her chum said, "Feeling more the thing, dear?"

"I'm fully recovered from the accident," Charity assured her.

"Excellent. We have plans for you, Miss Sparkler," Mrs. Kent said.

"Plans?"

"Percy tells us you have changes ahead and could use a bit of guidance." Mrs. Kent's emerald gaze ran expertly over Charity's ensemble, and her lips pulled into a slight grimace. "More than a bit, I should say."

Charity shot Percy an annoyed look, but her bosom chum said innocently, "I only mentioned it because if your betrothal goes through, you'll have wedding preparations to make. Since you don't have a mama to oversee things, I thought the three of us could pitch in."

"I should love to lend a hand," Lady Helena said, "and offer any advice that I can."

"I shouldn't look that gift horse in the mouth. When it comes to winning over a husband," Mrs. Kent drawled, "Lady Harteford is our resident expert."

Lady Helena's porcelain cheeks turned pink. "You're no less qualified than I am, Marianne. Mr. Kent is positively devoted to you."

"A fact that never ceases to amaze me." Wonder softened Mrs. Kent's eyes. "After all, I did little enough to deserve it."

"Nonsense. We all deserve devoted husbands," Percy said cheerfully, "and this includes you, Charity. If you're bent on marrying this Mr. Garrity, then we'll just have to make sure he adores you, too."

Looking at the circle of smiling faces, Charity understood Paris' dilemma when he was asked to choose the fairest of three goddesses. Lady Helena, Mrs. Kent, and Percy were all so beautiful, each in their unique way; it was no wonder their spouses worshipped the ground they trod on.

But she, Charity, was no goddess.

"I'm not the sort a gentleman notices, let alone adores," she said quietly.

Mrs. Kent startled her with a husky laugh. "My dear girl, is that what you believe?"

"It is the truth," she said. "I know my personal charms are in short supply."

"Charity—may we forgo tiresome formality?"

Charity gave a quick nod.

"Men are, as a whole, unobservant creatures," Marianne went

on. "They don't notice much at all, unless it's waved like a red flag in front of their noses and even then they might miss the mark. In short, they simply perceive what we *want* them to perceive, and you, my dear, do an exceptional job of remaining invisible."

Charity's jaw slackened.

"What Marianne is trying to say is that you are ever so lovely, Charity," Percy chimed in, "and all it would take is a little embellishment to draw the attention of my—um, Mr. Garrity, I mean. Or anyone else for that matter."

Charity knew her friend was only being loyal in calling her lovely. Yet she couldn't help but ask, "Embellishment?"

"Actually, in your case, *less* is more." Crossing her arms beneath her faultless bosom, Marianne declared, "At least two inches less at the neckline and we must do away with those dreadful sleeves altogether. As for your hair, there's simply too much of it, and the army of pins you use to keep it in place does not help matters. And do not let me get started on that *substance* polluting your coiffure. Beeswax?"

"And egg whites," Charity said in a small voice. "It's a recipe concocted by my housekeeper."

"It's a recipe for *disaster*." Marianne gave a visible shudder. "But never mind, this is where I come in: I am to fashion what Helena is to wifely virtue. With help from the two of us, you'll have gentlemen falling at your feet."

Charity's hands went instinctively to her bodice and her hair. Panic beat in her throat. *I'll be exposed. Everyone will see me ... for the weed that I am ...*

"Oh dear, now you've gone and frightened her." Helena gave her friend a chiding look before saying gently, "I know that our proposal must seem overwhelming, Charity, and believe me when I say I understand. I was once a wallflower, you know."

Charity looked into the marchioness' smiling countenance and blurted, "But that's impossible. You're *beautiful*."

"No more than you. I'll let you in on a secret, shall I?" Hazel eyes twinkled at her, so inviting of confidence that Charity leaned in. "The most difficult thing to overcome is not the perceptions of others, but those of *oneself*."

As Charity attempted to digest that notion, Percy said, "Don't forget about me. I'm going to help, too. Whilst I don't have a knack for fashion and admittedly fall short in the virtue department,"—she flashed an unabashed grin—"I do have one indispensable skill."

"Yes?" Charity said.

"No one hatches a plot like I do," Percy said with relish.

Now during the years at Mrs. Southbridge's, Charity had had considerable experience with her friend's high-spirited capers. More oft than not, she'd been the one to bail Percy out. Be it Chinese firecrackers released at inopportune moments or skipping etiquette class to visit a traveling gypsy caravan, Percy's ideas had invariably led to trouble.

"Er, why would I need a plot?" Charity said warily.

"Because romance takes planning and creativity. If we want Mr. Garrity—or, um, anyone else—to fall in love with you, we must devise a course of action," Percy declared.

At that, Charity stifled a grin. Percy was the dearest girl, but planning was not exactly her forte. She let her cook design the menus because she enjoyed surprises. Her idea of household management consisted of stuffing things in cupboards before the guests arrived. Not to mention the fact that she'd won her husband's heart in an impulsive wager.

Evidently, the other ladies shared similar thoughts. Helena was trying to hide a smile, and Marianne failed entirely, letting out a smothered laugh.

Rolling her eyes, Percy said, "My actions might not appear deliberate in the *traditional* sense of the word—"

"Or in any sense," Marianne said.

" ... but I assure you that I can think ahead. As a novelist, I arrange all sorts of romantic adventures for my heroines. What is that, if not planning?"

"Truthfully, I'd prefer not to get locked up in a catacomb. Or caught in a runaway hackney or kidnapped by a dastardly villain." Softening her words with a smile, Charity said sincerely, "Thank you—all of you—for your generous offer. I appreciate your kindness, but I am content to go on as I am. Truly."

She touched her locket, her father's voice drilling in her head. *Modesty is its own protection, daughter. Don't forget that.*

Percy looked like she wanted to argue, but the supper bell rang.

"Goodness, it's time already," Helena said. "With this crowd, it takes forever to sort out precedence and supper partners."

"You go attend to the sticklers," Marianne said. "We ragtag bunch will sort ourselves out."

"I shall see you all after supper then. And Charity?"

"Yes, my lady?"

"I have a surprise planned for the evening's entertainment, one you won't want to miss out on. Do promise you'll come to the Ivy Room after supper?"

"I'll be there," Charity said.

With a wink, Lady Helena melted into the melee.

Marianne said, "Perfect. Here come our supper partners now."

Charity's corset suddenly felt too tight, her lungs straining for air as three gentlemen strode toward them. Though Mr. Fines hadn't Mr. Kent's height or Mr. Hunt's brawn, she thought he was the most handsome—which was saying something, given the dazzling masculinity of the trio. He made an elegant leg, and his sapphire gaze locked on her.

"Miss Sparkler, I was hoping to see you. How are you feeling?" he said.

For some reason, his apparent concern chafed at her. Why did his voice have to have such a pleasant rasp to it, his eyes so sincere a gleam? What did he care how she was feeling when kissing her had supposedly been nothing more than a gross misjudgment on his part? And most irritating of all: why did her kneecaps wobble at his mere proximity?

She lifted her chin. "Your concern is unnecessary, sir."

His expression fell.

"Gentlemen," Marianne said, "you've arrived at an opportune moment. We are in need of supper partners."

"Are you, love? That would be a first," Mr. Kent said dryly.

He narrowed his amber eyes at the pack of gentlemen gathered in waiting behind his wife. Beneath his stare, they disbanded like mongrels with their tails between their legs.

"*Desirable* partners, I mean." Marianne smiled at him, and the policeman looked as moonstruck as all her other admirers. "Luckily, with you three," she said, "we are evenly matched and delightful company all around. So, darling, why don't you escort Percy, and I'll accompany Mr. Hunt. Mr. Fines, you'll take Miss Sparkler in?"

"Delighted," Mr. Fines said.

With no other choice, Charity placed her fingertips on his proffered arm—then jerked away when shock crackled from the point of contact.

His lips twitched. "Beg pardon. Sparks are literally flying between us, it seems."

Her cheeks grew hot. She reminded herself that flirtation was as natural to him as breathing, and he didn't mean anything by it. Especially not when it came to her. *I don't do this*, he'd said. *Not with girls like you.*

Pressure swelled beneath her breastbone. Blood pulsed in her ears.

"I believe it is called static, not sparks," she heard herself say. "The Hartefords have an electrifying machine in the library that replicates the phenomena. As I recall, static occurs when objects repel."

Silence ensued, the only movement being that of eyebrows shooting up. Over her pounding heart, she registered with shock that she—quiet, sensible Charity Sparkler—had delivered her first public set-down. What had come over her? She resisted the urge to clamp a hand over her mouth.

"Touché, Miss Sparkler. I deserved that and more."

Her shock deepened to see that the target of her barb was *smiling*.

He murmured, "So the mouse can roar."

"I am not a mouse," she managed to say.

"You tell him, Charity," Percy said.

"Only a fool would mistake a lion for a lamb," Marianne drawled.

Mr. Fines held up his hands in mock defense. "Fellows, I could use a second here. Being overrun by females, can't you see?"

Mr. Hunt snorted. "You've never complained about that before."

"The wisest man is the one who knows he knows nothing." Lines of humor fanned from Mr. Kent's eyes. "Sometimes an apology is the best defense, lad."

"Fat lot of help you chaps are." Nonetheless, Mr. Fines swept a bow and said, "I have a tendency to act rashly, but I vow I meant no disrespect. Will you forgive me, Miss Sparkler?"

She understood that his apology was for the kiss as well as for calling her a mouse. She steeled herself against his boyishly hopeful expression. He held out his arm—a gallant gesture.

Should she make peace?

She placed the tips of her fingers on his sleeve and said, "All is forgotten."

As they followed the others in, he bent his head toward her, and his quiet words caused her heart to somersault in her chest.

"Just so we're clear, sweeting, I asked to be forgiven ... not forgotten."

Chapter Ten

Supper was proving a disaster.

Paul found himself sandwiched between a baron's wife, who couldn't keep her hands to herself, and Charity Sparkler, who couldn't bother to give him the time of day. All through supper, he hardly tasted any of the courses. Lobster patties, roasted peahen, turbot in saffron sauce ... none of the decadent dishes piqued his appetite because he was being fed a steady diet of frustration by the recalcitrant miss sitting to his right.

Being ignored by a female was a novel experience. He couldn't say that he liked it, only because the female in question was Miss Sparkler. How could she be so indifferent after what had passed between them? Yet there she was sitting with her back to him and chatting up a storm with Kent, who sat on her other side.

Paul gritted his teeth. He couldn't make out their conversation, but the attentive tilt of her head conveyed her absorption in the exchange. Damnit, shouldn't she be talking to *him*? After what had transpired at the gazebo, they had plenty to discuss.

He remained appalled at his lack of self-control. At the same time, he reckoned that the kiss they'd shared would throw any man off-kilter. By God, in all his years he'd never experienced anything so ... consuming. So sweetly erotic. And the shock of discovering the passionate creature beneath that prim little exterior?

His spine tingled; his groin stirred.

Staring at the slender length of Miss Sparkler's back, all he could think about was how supple she'd felt in his arms. How beneath that bland grey frock lay the softest, silkiest skin. And her unique scent—he had the wild urge to nuzzle the curve of her neck to search out that elusive blend of linen and clean woman again. He hardened at the thought of smelling her, tasting her, losing himself in her honey and fire ...

Focus, man. You're supposed to make amends, not debauch her all over again.

The arrival of the final dessert course interrupted his brooding. As the poached pear in wine sauce was placed in front of him, Paul felt a slipper wandering up his calf. Unfortunately, it came from the wrong side. He jerked his leg away and cast the baroness a scathing glance.

She giggled, her darkened eyelashes lowering in an unmistakable wink.

For God's sake. Heat crept up his neck as he saw the knowing glances exchanged around the table. Sitting across from him, Marianne Kent sipped her wine, but he knew she didn't miss a thing. Through the silver bars of the candelabra, he could see the faint lift to her fair brows, and he knew that she—and the other guests— were judging him. As if getting molested by a randy matron was somehow *his* fault.

Anger smoldered. Along with embers of embarrassment.

Deuce take it, he was tired of the lewd affairs. The meaningless sexual games. Drowning one's sorrows with sex was no different than doing it with whiskey: the mindless oblivion was inevitably followed by regret and self-recrimination in the morning. When the baroness' slipper crept up his leg again, his hold on his temper slipped. Gentlemanly manners be damned.

"Desist, madam." Though he spoke under his breath, the steel in his tone was unmistakable.

Finally, she got the message. She gave him an uncertain glance—and removed her foot. Her curls bobbed as she quickly turned to the gentleman on her other side.

Paul returned his attention to Charity, only to find that she was *still* absorbed in her conversation with Kent. What was so captivating about the blasted policeman? Just because Kent spent his days protecting society and chasing down criminals ... if he, Paul, wanted to do something useful, he could too.

Probably. Maybe.

Picking up his spoon, he stabbed at his pear. Vexing chit. She was confusing him *on purpose*. She'd lured him in with her unexpected depths and quiet empathy, that fascinating mix of propriety and sensuality and then—*bam*.

She was giving him the cold shoulder. The coldest, in fact, that he'd ever gotten.

"Stewing has never been my preference," Marianne Kent drawled from across the table.

The amusement in her eyes made him cringe. He put on a debonair smile. "I suppose it depends on whether one likes one's fruit soft or"—he waggled his brows—"with more of a bite."

"Oh. Were we talking about the dessert?"

Paul felt himself turn as red as the wine sauce. "What else would we be discussing?"

"Your unusually meditative state." Leaning forward, Mrs. Kent said in an undertone, "She's lovely and original, you know. Mr. Kent is quite taken with her."

"That doesn't bother you?"

Mrs. Kent's lips curved. "I trust my husband."

Though this was simply stated, Paul had to wonder at the change in this once infamous widow. Before her marriage, she'd been his match and more when it came to jaded sophistication. But since pledging her troth to Kent, she'd shed that world-weary mantle, revealing, of all things, an honest woman in love with her own spouse.

"Easy for you to say. Kent has eyes for no one but you—poor bastard's been sneaking glances at you all evening long," Paul said.

"I know." Her smile reached her eyes. "Now will you admit the same?"

"That I've been admiring you, too? Guilty as charged."

"You know what I meant." She sipped from her wine glass. "I've never known you to be a coward, Mr. Fines."

Then obviously you don't know me very well.

He'd nearly gotten Percy killed because he hadn't had the bollocks to face his gaming debts. He'd almost destroyed Fines & Co. because he couldn't handle a broken heart. And he'd lost Rosalind because he hadn't been man enough to convince her that he was a risk worth taking.

Rosalind ... With a twinge, he saw again her shimmering violet eyes, the tears coursing down her alabaster cheeks.

I love you, Paul, but what kind of future can you offer me? Earl Monteith has promised to pay off my father's debts, to bring my sisters out into Society. And Mama has always wanted a title for me. If I don't marry Monteith, my family will disown me, and I'll be disgraced forever. Is that what you wish?

He'd failed to come up with a convincing argument. *I love you* hadn't been enough. And it'd been true that he lacked the things her family wanted. Worse yet, he hadn't even been able to find a single flaw with his rival: Monteith was known to be an upstanding peer, the rare lord who didn't drink or game and took his responsibilities seriously.

Compared to such a paragon, how could Paul compete?

Hell, he'd *deserved* to lose Rosalind.

'Twas a reminder of why he'd avoided marriageable ladies since then. He didn't need to have his gut wrenched to pieces again. He slid a look at Charity—*still* jawing away with Kent—and his mouth tightened. He ought to be relieved that things hadn't progressed much beyond a kiss. And even more so that she'd headed his honorable offer off at the pass. What kind of husband would he make?

"Oh, fie." A familiar, sultry voice penetrated his ear. "I dropped my reticule, and it seems to have rolled beneath your chair, sir."

Just bloody *perfect*.

His jaw set, he rose and turned to face Lady Augusta. She wore a low-cut gown and a smirking expression. He'd spent all of last evening deflecting her and Louisa's advances. What would it take to be rid of the wenches?

"Allow me to fetch it for you, my lady," he said curtly.

As he bent to retrieve the object, his gaze collided with Charity's. Jeweled fire blazed in her eyes ... and then she turned away. Staring at the rigid back of her topknot, he was swept up in a bewildering gust of rage and shame. He hadn't invited Augusta to drop her bag beneath his chair; it wasn't *his* fault that she was employing the most transparent ploy imaginable to get his attention. A ploy that was, unfortunately, inviting more than a few raised brows and knowing looks.

Wanting to get the business over with, he bent down on one knee to complete the fool's errand. On the pretense of helping, Augusta squatted beside him.

"Come to my room tonight," she said *sotto voce*. "It'll just be you and me this time—Louisa's got her hands full with her lord's sudden appearance." Glee lit her eyes. "When he's not off gallivanting, Parkington keeps her on a short chain."

Paul could give a fig about Louisa's marital affairs. In truth, he wished he'd never bedded either of the sisters. Why did the paths he chose always end up being the rockiest ones? What was supposed to be a casual tumble was fast turning into a sticky situation; he needed to extricate himself from the twins' web posthaste.

"Thank you, but I must decline." He groped in the darkness. Where was that blasted bag?

"Decline? You're turning *me* down? Surely you jest."

Catching the strings of the beaded purse at last, he pushed it at her. "As you'll recall, we agreed to share a night's diversion," he said in low tones, "and nothing more. Let us not taint that pleasant memory."

"Taint it? *Au contraire*, lover, I wish to *add* to it. I haven't yet had my fill of you."

"I, however, am done." He swatted away her grasping hands. "I hope you'll enjoy the rest of your visit. I shan't be a part of it."

Flags of color stood out on her face.

"Rest assured, I shall not lack for company," she hissed.

"Your servant." Rising, he offered his hand.

Ignoring his assistance, Augusta jumped to her feet and stormed off in a swish of red. Jaw taut, Paul looked to Charity's seat: its emptiness was as glaring as a judge. Snickers emerged around the table, fans beating the air in a titillated rhythm. Not wanting to provide further fodder for gossip, he sat down, his shoulders stiff.

Why the devil was he always mired in disaster? Why couldn't he do anything right? The answer blazed in his brain: *Because you're a failure through and through.*

He found himself staring at his wineglass. He hadn't touched it all evening—and now the ruby depths winked at him. He could almost taste the oaky spice upon his tongue, feel the smooth slide over his insides, the numbing warmth. It was just wine, after all. Not heavy spirits, so it would only be bending, not breaking, the rules.

Kent's low voice reached him just as his fingers circled the stem. "I think you've been down that road before, lad, and decided it wasn't a trip worth repeating."

Paul clenched the crystal.

"What's done is done," Kent said quietly. "The only thing a man can control is the present."

Paul's grip on the glass tightened ... and then he let go.

Hell's teeth, Kent was right. He *had* been down this particular path before, and it had led him straight to hell. He had no intention of going there again.

He blew out a breath. "I seem to have lost my thirst."

Kent's chin lowered in approval.

"In that case," Mrs. Kent said, "I suggest we make our way out. There's to be a lecture in the Ivy Room, and indeed"—she paused delicately—"I believe Miss Sparkler was headed in that direction."

Normally, he couldn't give a damn what others thought of him, but with Miss Sparkler, it was ... different. Maybe, in this instance, different was good. Sudden energy buzzed through him, a feeling not unlike the rush he experienced during a boxing match. He'd just stared down one of his demons; surely he could take on a stubborn miss.

He made his decision.

He would speak to Charity, try to fix the animosity between them.

"Lead the way," he said.

Chapter Eleven

Charity followed the trail of guests to the Ivy Room, a high-ceilinged chamber with a leafy trellis stenciled over the mint green walls. The rows of chairs had filled up quickly, leaving only a few empty seats near the back. Charity considered abandoning the enterprise, yet she had promised to attend and wasn't one to go back on her word. Neither was she a coward. She refused to flee to her chamber and give into an unprecedented bout of tears.

She was *done* crying over Paul Fines.

"Please take your seats everyone."

Lady Helena's clear tones came from the front of the room. Beside the marchioness stood a gentleman with silver spectacles and a stern, schoolmasterish bearing that made Charity hastily slide into one of the remaining seats.

"I have the great pleasure of introducing our speaker for this evening," Lady Helena said. "Dr. Ernst Frankel is renowned for his work in the science of cranioscopy, and tonight he will be lecturing on the diagnosis of temperaments from the shape of the human skull. Please join me in welcoming our distinguished guest."

Excited murmurs and applause swirled through the room.

"Thank you," the doctor said in a heavy German accent. "To begin, I draw your attention to the map of the human brain."

His pointing stick whipped against the poster on the stand behind him, so sharply that several members of the audience gasped and twitched in their seats.

Dr. Frankel's lecture proved a welcome distraction. Charity found herself fascinated by the notion that one's personality could be derived from the profile of one's skull. She followed along as Dr. Frankel mapped out the locations of various faculties: *acquisitiveness* (the tendency to amass and hoard riches, located at the lower temple), *secretiveness* (the capacity for cunning, seated near the top of the head), and *ideality* (the pursuit of perfection, which could be read from the width of the temples).

"You don't really believe this claptrap, do you?" With nonchalant grace, Paul Fines took the seat beside her. "The bumps on a skull no more determine one's disposition and future than a gypsy's cards."

Charity's hands balled in her lap. Why did he persist in interfering with her peace? Clearly he had no shortage of females to go bother—why was he pestering her?

She kept her eyes forward, saying repressively, "You're interrupting the lecture, sir."

"Didn't know you were a bluestocking."

"There's a lot you don't know about me."

"Each time we meet, I'm discovering that more." She made the mistake of glancing over; his slow smile made her heart flip-flop as haplessly as a fish washed ashore. "You surprise me at every turn, and never more so than at our last encounter."

"I don't want to talk about it," she said.

"But I do. If only to apologize."

"Fine, you've apologized. Now will you leave me be?" she said curtly. "I'm sure you have many friends to get back to."

"Why, Miss Sparkler, I didn't know that you noticed or cared about the company I keep."

"I *don't*." Feeling the heat of censorious glances, Charity tamped her voice down. "What you do and whom you do it with is none of my business, Mr. Fines."

For an instant, she thought she'd quieted him.

Then he murmured, "You're wrong, you know."

Hearing the annoyed grumbling around them, she kept her eyes fixed on Dr. Frankel as he pointed out areas of the brain. The scholar could have been speaking Greek for all she knew. Mr. Fines, blast him, had hooked her attention.

Unable to help herself, she muttered, "Wrong? About what?"

"I don't have many friends." This startling assertion made her turn her head. His smile was crooked and boyish, devoid of its usual urbanity. The effect battered at her defenses. "Not many with whom I could share a heartfelt conversation, at any rate. And not any I could talk to ... the way I find myself talking to you."

Don't give in. He regrets kissing you. He called it a mistake.

She swallowed. "I'm not interested in being your friend."

"Maybe that's not what I want from you either."

He looked as surprised by his words as she was.

Her pulse raced. *Don't get fooled again by his charm.*

"I don't care what you want," she said.

His brow furrowed. "For a slip of a thing, you're remarkably stubborn."

The reference to her insignificance made her patience snap. "First I'm a mouse, now I'm a *slip*? Well, I may be small, but *you* have an overly large head," she said in a furious undertone. "Especially when it comes to your own countenance."

Mr. Fines' lips pressed together. Before she could savor the triumph of putting him in his place, a muscle twitched alongside his mouth. His eyes danced. He was silently *laughing* at her!

All pretense of listening to the lecture fled.

She spun in her chair to face him. "I fail to see what is so amusing."

He shook his head, his wide shoulders shaking.

"*Ahem.* Am I interrupting anything?"

The heavily accented words directed Charity's gaze toward the stage. Dr. Frankel's grey brows formed a stern line, his wooden stick directed at them like an accusing finger. "The gentleman and lady at the back. Do you have something you'd care to share with the rest of the audience?"

"N-no," Charity stammered. She felt like an errant miss caught in a prank, a sensation as novel as it was mortifying. Her cheeks pulsed as every pair of eyes turned in her direction. "B-beg pardon, sir. We were just—"

The doctor gestured impatiently with his stick. "Since you have captured the audience's attention, I will use the pair of you for my demonstration."

"No, really, I—"

"Glad to lend a hand, Dr. Frankel. Fascinating stuff, your lecture." Mr. Fines' insouciant tones cut her off. He pulled her to her feet, murmuring, "Come on, this will be fun."

"No, it won't." She tried to pull her arm free.

But his grip didn't budge from her elbow, and he steered her down the aisle. "When one is called to the carpet," he said under his breath, "resisting is futile. Doing so will result in satisfaction for him and rug burn for you. Best to play along—trust me on this."

"*You* would know," she said through her teeth.

He flashed an unrepentant grin. "Getting into hot water is a Fines trait, I'm afraid. If you think Percy has a talent for it, wait until you see her older brother at work."

It was too late to argue further; they'd arrived at the stage.

"Take a seat facing one another," Dr. Frankel instructed.

Fuming, she took the chair on the right. Mr. Fines took the opposite one, which was placed so close to hers that their knees touched. She pulled away as if burned.

"Who will conduct the examination first?" the doctor asked.

Charity's hands grew clammy. All her life, she'd followed rules and done what was expected of her. Yet thanks to Mr. Fines, she had no clue how to proceed.

The cad had the gall to offer her a bland smile. "Shall I have a go first, Miss Sparkler?"

Torn between relief and annoyance, she gave a curt nod. He reached over, and her pulse leapt at his nearness. As he ran his hands gently over her hair, his subtle cologne teased her senses. The masculine combination of cedar and musk warmed her insides, made them quiver.

In desperation, she tried to concentrate on something else. She counted the grey stripes on his waistcoat. One stripe, two, three ... when he moved, the fabric stretched over his chest, molding perfectly to the rigid musculature. Perspiration bloomed on her skin as she recalled the sensation of that virile form crushing her body, her breasts pressing against unyielding sinew—

"Well?" Dr. Frankel's voice jolted her.

To her mortification, she realized her nipples were puckered and stiff beneath her bodice. Gulping, she slanted a glance downward: thank goodness nothing showed through the layers of her unmentionables! But she'd been so distracted that once again she'd lost track of what the doctor was asking.

Mr. Fines spoke up. "Can't feel a thing, I'm afraid. Too much hair. Beg pardon, Miss Sparkler," he said, "but know that your sacrifice is in the interest of science."

Before she could register the meaning of his words, a brown lock fell into her eyes. Then another. Mr. Fines was *plucking out* her pins! Her hands flew to her head in panic, but it was too late: her topknot toppled, waves tumbling madly over her shoulders.

She heard a collective titter rise from the crowd and wanted the ground to open up and swallow her whole. Her cheeks blazed with embarrassment ... and *anger.* How could the bounder humiliate her so? What had she ever done to him? As heat prickled her eyes, she aimed her gaze at the ground.

Hold it together. Don't let him see you cry.

"So that's what you've been hiding. But ... why?"

The note of wonder in his voice permeated her disgrace. She peered up through her lashes. What she saw lodged her breath in her throat. His vivid gaze was admiring, his expression impossibly sincere.

Dazed, she heard him murmur, "How fetching you are, sweeting. Quite the prettiest little thing I've ever laid eyes on. That disguise of yours is criminal."

Disguise? Criminal? Her head spun at the implication of his words—*Thwack.* She jerked as Dr. Frankel's pointer connected with the podium.

"Proceed," the doctor said sternly. "No time for shilly-shallying."

"Right-o." Mr. Fines gave her a tender—tender!—smile. "Shall we, Miss Sparkler?"

Before she could reply, his hands slid into the loose mass of her hair. His touch sent shocks over her scalp, down her neck and arms. She pressed her lips together for fear that she might moan aloud with pleasure. With each fettered breath, the taut tips of her breasts chafed against her corset; petals of heat unfurled in her belly. All too aware of observing eyes, she squirmed, praying her stimulated state did not show.

"Describe for us the general landscape of her skull," Dr. Frankel instructed. "Note any asymmetry or imbalances between the left and right sides."

Mr. Fines brushed the curve of her ear, and that sensation amplified the illicit tingling at her breasts, the dampening between her legs. Shivering, she restrained herself from nudging against his hand like an eager kitten.

"I can detect no imbalances. Her head is exceptionally smooth ... and lovely," he said in a husky tone, eliciting a ripple of laughter from the audience.

"*Lovely* is not a term employed in craniology, sir. Focus." The doctor aimed an austere gaze over his spectacles. "How would you describe the subject's orbital-parietal region?"

"Perfectly formed."

Pleasure suffused her as Mr. Fines gently massaged her scalp. Her neck muscles grew so warm and lax that she could scarcely keep her head up.

"And the shape of the protuberances? Rounded or flat?" Dr. Frankel inquired.

"Rounded."

"Size—full or scant?"

"Somewhere in between, I'd say." Mr. Fines' gaze dipped to her bodice, wicked heat flaring in those blue depths. "The perfect size."

"With that information, I shall now interpret the subject's profile," Dr. Frankel announced to the audience in peremptory tones. "Taken together, this is the profile of a cautious individual. The lady is apt to think before she acts and is given more to reason than impulse."

Charity blinked at the accuracy of his assessment.

"In addition, she forms lasting attachments and shows unwavering loyalty to her loved ones."

Right again, Charity mused. *What a fascinating science.*

"And last, but not least, the prominence of the anterior skull demonstrates a prideful bent. Despite her modest demeanor, this is a lady of strong will. I would think twice before crossing swords with her," Dr. Frankel concluded.

Charity's cheeks heated as laughter erupted.

"I take back what I said earlier," Mr. Fines said in an undertone. "There may be more to this craniology business than I believed."

She narrowed her eyes at him.

"Time to switch roles," Dr. Frankel said.

With no means of escape, Charity reached reluctantly for Mr. Fines' head. His hair had a naturally windswept quality, springing up between her fingers like gilded wheat. The thick, silky friction sent a sensual hum through her. Trying to ignore it, she explored his scalp with tentative strokes. He watched her all the while, the rim of his pupils darkening. His neck arched slightly to her touch, and an answering tremor traveled up her arms.

"Describe what you feel," Dr. Frankel said.

She wet her dry lips. "The front of the skull seems, um, prominent and equally developed on both sides. And the section above the ears is, perhaps, more pronounced than the surrounding areas?"

She had no idea was she was saying, but the doctor gave a vigorous nod. "And the posterior of the skull?"

She could not reach the back of Mr. Fines' head whilst sitting. Rising, she leaned over him, running her fingers behind his ears, then sweeping them up and down the back of his head. She became aware of the hot, quick beat of his breath against her bosom, and her own blood seemed to pulse in rhythm.

"The area behind the ears," she said in a husky voice she hardly recognized, "is, um, well developed." She tried to remember the terminology used earlier. "His protuberance is large and rather hard."

For some reason, her observation led to tittering and muffled laughter from the crowd. Mr. Fines tilted his head back, and she lost track of the world around her, his blazing eyes engulfing her entirely. Her heartbeat skittered; her blood turned to honey. In that liquid moment, no others existed but the two of them. Her lips parted, and she swayed closer—

"Based on that reading, I will now decipher the gentleman's character." The doctor's words brought Charity back to reality. She yanked her hands from Mr. Fines' hair and stumbled back into her seat. "His center of *mirthfulness* is well developed. He has a propensity toward wit and irreverence: style over substance, as you English say."

Charity frowned at that conclusion. To her mind, Mr. Fines

possessed both style *and* substance, but he looked amused by the doctor's interpretation.

"Touché, Dr. Frankel," he said. "Do tell me more about myself."

The doctor obliged. "The pronounced areas above the ears indicate that *ideality*—the love of beauty—is also a significant aspect of the subject's personality."

"On that we agree. I am drawn to beauty,"—Mr. Fines' gaze locked on her face—"particularly when it is rare and unaffected."

Charity's lungs pulled for air. Surely, he couldn't be referring to her. Couldn't mean that he found *her* beautiful ...

"Finally, there is the protuberance at the back of the skull." Dr. Frankel straightened his cravat before saying, "The quality of *amativeness* appears to be prominent. Exceedingly so."

To Charity's amazement, raucous cheers and whistles exploded in the room. Looking at Mr. Fines, she saw that ruddy color stained his high cheekbones. He rubbed the back of his neck, the gesture one of embarrassment. What was this *amativeness* the doctor spoke of?

Lady Helena came to the rescue. "Thank you, my dears. You are hereby relieved of your duties." To the audience, she said, "Now the rest of you will have the opportunity to practice what you just saw. Please raise your hands if you wish to participate."

Every hand in the room shot up.

As Lady Helena and Dr. Frankel went to organize the guests into pairs, Percy and Mr. Hunt came up to the stage.

"Well, that was quite the performance," Percy said brightly. "You two were brilliant!"

"Stuff it, sis," Mr. Fines muttered. Inclining his head to Charity, he said, "If you'll excuse me, I have matters to attend to. We'll talk again soon, I hope. Your servant, etcetera."

Bemused, Charity watched his retreating back. "Percy?" she said.

"Yes, dear?"

"Why was everyone laughing near the end?"

A muffled sound came from Mr. Hunt; Percy nudged him with her elbow.

"Do you know what *amativeness* is?" Charity persisted.

"It's the organ that supposedly governs physical appetite." Her cheeks pink, Percy said, "For, er, amorous pursuits and the like."

It took a second for the information to sink in. "Then I just said in front of everyone that ... that ..."—blood pounded in Charity's ears—"that your brother has excessive ...?"

"I wouldn't worry, Miss Sparkler," Mr. Hunt said with a grin. "You just called a rake a rake."

Chapter Twelve

Paul worked out his frustrations in the sparring room. Practicing his combinations, he pounded a punching bag until sand leaked from its seams. By midnight, he was soaked with sweat, his muscles aching and knuckles smarting. The physical exhaustion, however, did little to alleviate the desire clawing at his belly.

Devil take it, whose idea had it been to instigate a night of public groping? Craniology? Another name for *foreplay* as far as he was concerned. His blood stirred at the memory of Charity's touch. The way her fingers had tunneled through his hair, caressing him ... it had taken all his willpower not to drag her onto his lap and take up where they'd left off at the gazebo.

Apparently, he had a sensitive head—make that *two* of them. If he hadn't left, he might have tossed Miss Sparkler onto the nearest surface and had his way with her. As it was, his jacket had barely hidden the fact that he'd been sporting a huge, pulsing cockstand.

A large and hard protuberance, indeed.

But what hot-blooded man wouldn't be drawn to Charity Sparkler? With her hair free, her eyes vibrant, and her mouth ripe and trembling, she'd been enticing beyond words. And his instincts told him he'd only scratched the surface. She was like a rare opal: her milk-smooth surface hid fiery depths, facets of untold brilliance—

Snap out of it, man. Finally, his voice of reason took up the fight. *That's your bollocks doing the thinking, and you know they aren't the brightest of fellows. Consider the matter carefully: are you really ready to go down this path again?*

Scowling, he shrugged into his jacket and headed back toward his chambers. Was this yet another instance of rash judgment? If he actually used the organ between his ears for once, he had to admit that he and Charity were as mismatched as two left shoes. They had little in common: she was responsible, sensible, and self-disciplined whereas he was ... not. Though he couldn't quite put his finger on the source of it, some ineffable tension seemed to charge their interactions.

He wasn't even certain that Charity *liked* him.

A memory hit him: back at the gazebo, hadn't she mentioned some vague attachment? Did she have some fellow waiting for her in London? Was that the bounder whose kiss had made Paul's a *molehill* in comparison?

Paul stalked down the hallway, wanting to plant a facer on the sod. He didn't like the way he was feeling, on edge and ... jealous? Had he *ever* felt this possessive before? Probably not. Not even over Rosalind, oddly enough. She'd been surrounded by a constant throng of admirers, so perhaps he'd gotten used to all the competition.

But Charity was different. Her beauty didn't hit a man with the force of a tempest; no, her attractions unfolded gently, softly, like the blossoming after a spring rain. In fact, it took an observant man to notice the extent and depth of her loveliness, but once he did, he wanted it all to himself ...

Paul frowned at the direction of his thoughts. Charity confused the hell out of him, and he wasn't a man who needed more confusion in his life. He told himself not to rush his fences. He ought to calm down, think things through.

What he needed was a cold bath. A calming cup of tea.

Or ... he *could* frig himself to high heaven, fantasizing about all the ways he wished to debauch the delicious Miss Sparkler.

The notion sent a sizzle up his spine. He hadn't had to resort to self-pleasure since he was a greenling with an overabundance of animal energy and no skill to put it to better use. Since becoming a man, he'd been too lazy to do for himself what others would willingly do for him. Tonight, however, he would have to make an exception. Because he was randier than a sailor on leave and the fantasy of Charity Sparkler was far safer than the reality. Better to let off steam than get burned by it.

Frig first, think later—definitely the way to go.

Breathing heavily, he entered his room. He was surprised by the darkness that greeted him—his valet usually left the lamps lit— but at present moment obscurity suited his purposes just fine. He stripped off his clothes and boots and made his way over to the bed. He tossed aside the covers, got in, and—

"*What the bloody hell?*"

A giggle greeted his startled exclamation. "Surprise," a sultry female voice said. "I thought you might like some company."

Devil take it.

He fumbled to light the bedside lamp. Seeing the familiar face, he bit back an oath. Hell's teeth, what would it take for the doxy to get the message?

"I told you, Augusta. I'm not in the mood tonight," he said shortly.

"It's *Louisa.*" The woman in his bed pouted, tossing red curls over her bare shoulder. "And you're *always* in the mood."

Goddamnit, he wasn't some bloody stud to be ridden at any female's whim.

"Not tonight," he repeated.

She switched tactics. "But you seem so happy to see me," she said coyly.

He pried her questing fingers off his erection and got out of bed. He was sorely tempted to tell her his aroused state had nothing to do with her. Ye Gods, he was tired of the man he'd become. The sort who fell into bed with any available trollop—simply because he had nothing better to do. It struck him that he wanted more. He wanted ... Charity. To explore what could happen between them.

Mad as the notion might be, it was also true.

"I'm not interested, Louisa," he said. "Please leave."

Her eyes squinted, her mouth turning hard and petulant. "But I just got here."

"Get out of my bed," he said grimly. "Now."

She crossed her arms over her breasts. "Make me."

Before he could contemplate his next move, a male voice sounded in the distance, the rage behind the words unmistakable. "I know you're with that bastard, Louisa—your maid has confessed everything. I'll not be cuckolded! Show your face, sirrah—or I'll knock down every bloody door until I find you!"

Blood pounding in his veins, Paul shot a look at Louisa. She didn't seem worried, and, in fact, appeared rather ... *smug*. The realization pelted him like a cascade of bricks.

"You *want* your husband to find you in my bed?" he bit out.

Her smile could have sliced diamonds. "Why shouldn't Parkington have a taste of his own medicine? He keeps a string of whores, so why shouldn't I have my fun?"

With an oath, Paul dragged on his robe and shoved his feet into slippers. No way in hell would he be a pawn in her manipulative games. If Louisa wanted her lord's attention, she could damn well get it another way.

He threw her dressing gown at her. "You're getting out of here."

"If I step foot in the hallway, Parkington will see me." Her eyes glinted with twisted delight. "I can hear him tromping down the hallway now."

Deuce take it, she was right. Paul's eyes circled the room in panic, latching onto the armoire. Given her abundant figure, there wasn't a chance of Louisa fitting inside ... or beneath the bed. That left only ... He raced over to the balcony doors. Throwing them open, he stepped onto the small ledge. Identical stone balconies stood in a row like stepping stones across the velvet night. The balustrades were close together, separated by mere centimeters; one could cross from ledge to ledge without fear of tumbling to the ground below.

He counted three balconies between his and the largest one, that of the first floor parlor. An easy enough escape route—and from the increasingly loud bellows in the hallway, one that would have to be embarked upon immediately.

He strode back to the bed and grabbed Louisa's arm. "You're getting out of here. You can take the balconies to the parlor."

"A countess scrambling away like a thief in the night?" She stuck her nose in the air. "I will do no such thing. 'Tis ungentlemanly for you to even suggest it."

"I wouldn't have to suggest it if you hadn't shown up uninvited to my room," he bit out, yanking her out of the bed. "Now *get going*."

She grabbed onto one of the bed posts and gave him a triumphant look. "I'll scream if you make me."

Fuck, fuck, fuck.

"Louisa!" Parkington's voice boomed—he was nearly at the door. "Where the hell are you?"

Desperation clawed Paul's insides. Any minute now the enraged earl would barge into the room, and Paul would have no way to prove his innocence. He'd be forced to fight a duel; he'd be damned if he had to shed another man's blood over a scheming wench.

She wouldn't leave? Fine.

He would.

He sprinted out onto the balcony, ignoring Louisa's protest. With a smooth motion, he leapt over the first set of balustrades onto the neighboring balcony. One down. As he ran toward the next set of railings, he heard a door slam and Parkington shouting Louisa's name. Breath burning in his lungs, Paul kept going, his slippered feet skidding as he landed on the second terrace. *Almost there.* If he could get to the parlor without Parkington seeing him, nothing could be proven. He'd say that he'd never been in his room; if Louisa had wandered in ... it was her mistake and not his problem. Worse come to worse, it'd be her word against his.

He jumped over the last balustrade, his feet touching safety at last. He grasped the door knob to the parlor ... and it was locked. *Goddamnit.*

"Fines! Is that you?" Parkington's voice pierced the night like a shot.

On instinct, Paul dropped to his knees behind the balcony railing. Bloody hell, had the earl spotted him? It was dark and unless the man had the eyes of an eagle—

"I see you, you bastard." The earl's voice rang from the balcony of Paul's bedchamber. "I'm coming to string you up!"

Fuck again.

As the earl charged off, shouting for blood, Paul jumped to his feet. He had to get in and out of the parlor before Parkington found him. Bracing, he charged shoulder first into the door. Instead of a hard impact, he encountered thin air as the door opened at the last second. He barreled into softness, heard a startled whoosh of breath, and had the presence of mind to grab onto his rescuer, rolling her atop him so that he took the brunt of the fall, his head smacking against the parlor floor.

When the dots cleared, he saw Charity's face hovering just inches above his.

"Sorry—sorry," he managed to breathe. "Are you alright?"

She gave him a wide-eyed nod.

He understood in that moment that she'd overheard everything. Hell, by now the entire household had. He heard the footsteps approaching the parlor, and a desperate urge surged through him: he needed to make her understand.

"I wasn't with Louisa tonight. 'Pon my honor, I wasn't," he said hoarsely. "She set this up ... some sick game to get her husband's goat."

He didn't know why he even bothered trying to explain. Why Charity's opinion mattered so much. He couldn't expect her to believe him, not with his libertine history and, goddamnit, his behavior toward *her* didn't exactly inspire confidence. In her shoes, he'd probably assume he was guilty.

She continued to stare at him, was probably thinking that he was the biggest bastard alive. His throat closed. It was too late. He couldn't sway her, would fail in this as he had so many things in his life ...

The door swung open. Parkington charged in. "I've got you now, you bastard—"

The earl stopped in his tracks. Belatedly, Paul realized how compromising the scene appeared: Charity was draped over him, escaped tendrils of her hair brushing his jaw. And he was wearing nothing more than a dressing gown. With an oath, he shot to his feet, taking her with him. He pushed her to stand behind him and felt the quiver that passed through her slight frame. Bloody hell, he'd do pistols at dawn if necessary, but he wasn't going to allow any of this to harm Charity or her reputation.

"What do you want?" he said to the earl.

Stocky to begin with, Parkington was breathing so heavily that the gold buttons of his waistcoat threatened to pop off. His sideburns bristled as he jabbed a meaty finger at Paul. "You were with my wife, you scoundrel! I'll not be cuckolded—"

"He wasn't with your wife, my lord," Charity said from behind him.

Her assertion was calm, quiet, and yet it set off a cataclysm in

Paul's chest. Made it expand with ... hope. Despite all the evidence to the contrary, she believed him at his word, believed in his honor, in *him*. Though he kept his gaze trained on the irate earl, he could feel the support of her presence—like an angel at his shoulder—and it infused him with strength.

"Of course he was! She was in his bedchamber," Parkington spat, "and though he might have run off like a coward before I arrived, he'll still answer for the insult, sirrah!"

"How is it my fault if your wife wandered into my room with me not present?" Paul said through gritted teeth. "As her husband, it's your job to keep tabs on her, not mine."

"Why you insolent cad! I know you were there—"

"He wasn't." Charity poked her head from behind him.

Paul tried to keep her back.

"Keep your mouth shut in front of your betters. Common chit," Parkington sneered, "what do you know about anything?"

"*That's enough.*" Paul's fists balled. "Apologize to Miss Sparkler this instant or name your second."

"There's no need." Before he knew what she intended, Charity darted forward, inserting herself between him and the earl. At the same instant, Paul glimpsed the audience gathered just beyond the door. Bloodthirsty onlookers angling to get a better view of the kill.

Seemingly oblivious to the danger, Charity continued, "No duel is necessary over my honor or Lady Parkington's. My lord, this has all been a simple misunderstanding."

"A misunderstanding?" Parkington barked.

Paul took hold of her arm, intending to pull her out of the line of fire, but she resisted with unexpected strength, saying, "I have proof that Mr. Fines was not with your wife this evening."

"Proof?" the earl spat. "What proof?"

"Me." Charity's calm declaration detonated like a grenade in the sudden silence. "I can vouch for Mr. Fines. You see, I was with him this entire time."

Chapter Thirteen

"No need to fret, dear. Everything will turn out fine." Sitting next to Charity in the luxurious carriage, Mrs. Fines issued a smile that didn't quite disguise the worry in her eyes. "In my heart, I know there is nothing to worry about."

Charity managed a weak smile.

Mrs. Fines had been making such predictions since the debacle of two nights ago. Charity thought the other lady's optimism was remarkable, considering the fact that all hell had broken loose the moment she'd stepped between Mr. Fines and the maddened earl.

What was I thinking? For the umpteenth time, Charity berated herself for her recklessness. The truth was that she hadn't been thinking—had acted instead on pure, ungoverned instinct. Her first impulse had been to defend Mr. Fines from the danger of a duel, and she hadn't thought through the consequences of her actions.

Those consequences, however, now had her on a jostling carriage ride back to London. Thwarted from his role as the righteous husband, Parkington had wasted no time in finding another outlet: like a volcano, he'd spewed vile tales of ruination—hers, to be precise—to all and sundry at the house party. The lies included lurid details of her and Mr. Fines being caught *in flagrante*. The gossip had spread like wildfire and with such ferocity that not even the Hartefords could put a stop to it.

By breakfast, everyone from the duke down to the scullery maids had heard about her so-called debauchery with Mr. Fines. Charity had gone from being the party's most invisible guest to its pariah. She had kept her chin high, outwardly ignoring the smirks and cut directs, while inside she'd curled into a numb, quivering ball. And the humiliation was not going to stop there. Yesterday, the Parkingtons had packed up and left for town before dawn— which meant that news of her shame would soon be circulating in London.

Disaster awaited her return.

Her hands clenched in her lap as she revisited yesterday's meeting in Lady Helena's drawing room. The Hartefords, Hunts, and Kents had sat around the coffee table, discussing the situation from every angle, debating various means of silencing Parkington. Mr. Fines, who'd been pacing before the fire, suddenly stalked over to her. His eyes captured hers, and the regret and rage in those blue depths stormed through her.

In a firm voice, he said, "Despite what our friends may think, Miss Sparkler, the truth is you have no option save one. Unfortunately for you, that option involves being married to me. I regret to say that that is the only way to salvage your reputation."

His words hammered at her temples. All she could think was that this second attempt at a proposal was even worse than the first. *Regret to say? Unfortunately?* In all the years she'd spent pining over Paul Fines, in all the countless stupid fantasies she'd woven about him, never *ever* had she imagined that it would come to this: a half-baked offer issued with keen reluctance.

"Thank you, but I decline," she said with admirable restraint.

His brow knit ... as if he was *confused*. Why, because she was not falling over with gratitude at his offer? Or, perhaps, performing somersaults of joy?

"I don't think you understand," he said in terse tones. "I've ruined you. There's no other choice but for us to tie the knot. Now I know you've hinted at other plans for your future—and frankly, I wasn't exactly expecting this disaster myself—but that's done with now. We have to make the best of a bad situation."

Wisely, Charity did not reply. If she opened her mouth, there was no telling what might come out. One possibility being, *Do you actually think I'll say yes to that daft proposal, you giant lummox?*

"Really, Paul," Mrs. Fines interjected from an adjacent wingchair, "is that any way to make an offer? After all, poor Charity is in this muddle because of you. What she did—"

"I am perfectly aware of what Miss Sparkler did and why, Mama."

The quiet vehemence of his words sliced through the room. Then Charity noticed that his hands were balled at his sides, the knuckles white. The muscle alongside his jaw ticked like a clock. It struck her: he was furious.

At *her*?

An answering swell rose in her breast. Did he have the gall to blame *her* for this situation? If he dared to—

"She was trying to save my hide," he said, "and now I am attempting to return the favor. It would help if I didn't have to do so in front of a cursed audience."

Lady Helena spoke up from the divan she shared with the marquess. "I'm afraid that's not possible," she said. "I blame myself for allowing this to happen,"—at that, her husband's arm tightened protectively around her shoulders—"and I will do my utmost to ensure no further harm comes to Charity's reputation. She will remain under my watch for the remainder of her visit."

"No use shutting the stable now. Horses have long bolted," Mr. Hunt muttered.

Percy chewed on her lip.

Mr. Fines raked his hair in frustration. "All I require is a few moments of privacy ..."

"It isn't necessary." Charity was surprised at how calm she sounded, given the tempest roiling inside her. Once again, her father had been proven right: a girl like her had to get by on good sense—it was all that she could rely on.

Thus, she continued in brisk tones, "None of this is, although I do appreciate all of your efforts on my behalf. The truth is nothing happened last night. I know it, Mr. Fines knows it ... even the Earl of Parkington knows it, though for some reason he persists in saying otherwise. The fact is that I've done nothing wrong, and, thus, I have nothing to be ashamed of. I cannot control, nor do I care, what others think."

"A noble sentiment, Miss Sparkler," Mr. Kent said. "Quite sensible."

"Quite stupid, more like." Mr. Fines had the temerity to glare at her. "You have no idea what it's like to be ruined, and, upon my honor, I'll not allow you the experience. I landed you in this mess, and I'm getting you out of it. End of story."

The pressure at her temples intensified. Her self-restraint slipped a notch. "You do not have a right to tell me what to do, sir."

"Since we're to be married, I believe the law disagrees with you."

"We're *not* getting married."

"We are." He crossed his arms over his broad chest, his chin jutting at an implacable angle. "The sooner you get used to the idea, the better."

Breathe in, breathe out. Do not lose control.

Percy intervened. "Charity, may I say something?"

Charity took another calming breath. "Yes, of course."

"I know this must all be very shocking," her chum said

earnestly. "But once you have time to think it over, you'll see that my brother is right."

Mr. Fines gave a righteous nod. Charity narrowed her eyes at her bosom friend; it was the look Caesar gave Brutus just as the blade struck home.

Percy went on, "Although Paul is going about the business in the most ham-handed manner imaginable,"—at this, Mr. Fines' smug expression faded—"he is correct in that you do *not* deserve to suffer public disgrace. Think of it, Charity: you won't be welcomed in polite society any longer." Anxiety shone in her friend's eyes. "It will destroy your chances of future happiness."

Swallowing her own panic, Charity said, "My future is my own to decide—you said so yourself. And I will not trade one bad bargain for another." Out of the corner of her eye, she saw Mr. Fines jerk at her words. She straightened her shoulders. "I'll find a way to manage."

"But your papa—" Percy began.

"Once I explain the situation, I'm certain he'll understand."

This, unfortunately, was a lie: Charity was quite certain her father was *not* going to understand. But she could only deal with one fiasco at a time, and the more pressing matter was to hang on to the last shreds of her pride.

"I spend my days in a shop, not the drawing rooms of the *ton*. I doubt that anything will change for me," she said.

"Doubt anything will *change*?" Mr. Fines stared at her as if she'd grown two heads. "Are you mad?"

"No," she said. "Are you?"

His eyes flashed. "You obstinate creature, *everything* will change. Parkington is going to spew his vitriol far and wide. The scandal sheets will feed off this for months. Everyone from the top ten thousand down to the lowliest chambermaid will know of this. There will be no safe place for you to hide: not in society, your shop, or even your own damned bedchamber!"

"Language, Paul," Mrs. Fines scolded. "That's no way to speak to Charity."

"She best get used to it, Mama," he said, his jaw clenched, "for she'll be getting far worse from the wagging tongues if she doesn't get it through her thick skull that she has to marry me. She has no choice."

Before Charity could argue that she did have a choice, that she would live a hermit's life before getting married out of pity, Marianne Kent spoke up.

"He's right, I'm afraid. Society is unforgiving, Charity," she said, "and never more so than toward middling class misses who haven't centuries of blue blood to justify their bad behavior."

"I don't care what Society thinks."

"But you do care about your father's business," Marianne said.

Chill seeped into Charity's blood. "What ... what do you mean?"

"Simply this: I am familiar with men like Parkington." The other's eyes turned icy, reminding Charity of the rumors that Marianne's first marriage had not been an easy one. Mr. Kent claimed his wife's hand, and her fingers clung to his as she said, "Bastards like him will trample anyone just for the satisfaction of doing so—and the more defenseless his victim, the better."

"But I didn't do anything to him!" Charity protested.

"You got in between him and Mr. Fines. I doubt Parkington truly wished to meet at dawn, and now he has a convenient—not to mention safer—alternative: he can vent his fury at *you*. In his mind, he can blame you for foiling his revenge, for humiliating him because you're an easy target," Marianne said bluntly. "Why do you think he's shredding your reputation? My guess is that he'll move on to Sparkler's next. When he's done, it'll be a den of iniquity that polite society will not step foot inside."

The air squeezed from Charity's lungs, making her dizzy. "He wouldn't. Can't. My papa ... Sparkler's is everything to him!"

Dear God, had she unintentionally put her father's life's work at risk?

Marianne exchanged grim looks with the marchioness, and the latter said, "Parkington *is* a vile man, I'm afraid, and a powerful one. He's capable of anything."

"There must be a way to stop him," Charity said through dry lips.

"There is."

Her gaze went to Mr. Fines, who stood hands on hips, his features hard and set. He watched her with singular focus. Any trace of gentlemanly torpor had vanished; he was a fighter, fierce and unyielding, determined to win the match. In spite of the situation, a betraying thrill coursed up her spine.

"We're getting engaged," he told her in a tone that brooked no refusal. "We'll battle Parkington's muckraking with the story that he mistook an innocent moment between a betrothed, albeit unchaperoned, couple. It won't stop the damage entirely, but it will at least contain the fire."

No. Not this way.

Even as her mind rebelled at the idea, her throat cinched with panic. What if she had compromised the future of the shop? Papa would never forgive her.

"That is an excellent plan, Mr. Fines," Lady Helena said. "Harteford and I will back your story by saying that we allowed you such a moment to celebrate your engagement." She turned to her husband. "Darling, you'll spread the word at the clubs, won't you? No one gossips more than gentlemen."

"Of course, my love." The marquess' grey eyes landed on Charity. He was an austere man, one she found rather intimidating, but his gravelly voice was kind as he said, "Miss Sparkler, know that you have our full support. Despite the regrettable circumstances, you have nothing to fear. Fines is a man of honor, and you must allow him to do what is right."

She didn't know what to say. For once, neither did Mr. Fines, who shot the marquess a glance she couldn't quite interpret. She fidgeted as the silence lengthened. She knew everyone was waiting for her answer, but her mind was whirling.

What would Father want me to do? Have I truly destroyed the shop?

How can I marry Mr. Fines, knowing he's only offered out of obligation?

"I need to speak with my father," she blurted. "I cannot make any decisions until then."

Hence, the present journey back to London. Mr. Fines was traveling in a separate carriage with Lord Harteford. As she couldn't abandon her own party, Lady Helena had stayed behind, with the Kents remaining to help her.

From the opposite bench, Percy said, "We're almost there, Charity. Have you thought of what you will say to Mr. Sparkler?"

Charity's heart palpitated. In truth, she'd considered and discarded countless explanations, none of which were going to appease her papa.

As if reading her thoughts, Percy prompted, "Perhaps you'd care to run through a few scenarios? I've always found it helpful to rehearse before giving bad news."

"Trust her on this," Mrs. Fines said. "When it comes to giving bad news, my daughter is the expert."

Seated next to Percy, Mr. Hunt let out a chuckle.

Undeterred, Percy said, "I'll play the role of your papa, and I'll respond as he might. You just be you."

Charity slid a self-conscious look at the carriage's other occupants. "I don't know about this."

"Trust me, this method works. I use it all the time, even when I don't have a person to practice with. Sometimes I just pretend that the hat stand is Mr. Hunt," Percy said.

Her husband's brows shot up.

"Well ... alright." Charity paused. "How do we begin?"

"I'll start." Her voice lowered to a gruff, masculine octave,

Percy said, "Well, daughter, how was your visit with the Hartefords?"

"Um, fine," Charity said.

When she said nothing more, Percy/Papa said, "Is there anything you wish to tell me?"

Charity expelled a breath. "As a matter of fact, yes. Father, I ... you see, there was a bit of a problem. A misunderstanding, really—"

"Spit it out, girl. I haven't all day to jaw—the shop doesn't run itself, you know," Percy/Papa grumbled with startling accuracy.

"Right." Pulse quickening, Charity said, "Well, I was helping, um, a friend to avoid an unfortunate situation and, unfortunately, the situation was misinterpreted—"

"Who is this friend you speak of?"

"Percy's brother. Mr. Fines," Charity said haltingly.

"Never did like that Fines chit. Nothing but trouble. Her brother can't be much better."

"But it wasn't Mr. Fines' fault. He was being falsely accused of ... of ..." Charity wracked her brain for a euphemism.

"Prevarication is a stepping stone to sin," Percy/Papa warned.

" ... keeping company," Charity rushed on. "With, um, a married lady."

"The bounder! Discovered *in flagrante*, was he?"

"But he wasn't ... that is, the lady *was* in his bedchamber, but he didn't invite her there—"

"Egad, are you *defending* this philanderer?"

Hands clammy, Charity stammered, "N-no. I mean, yes, I did, because he didn't do it. The philandering, I mean." With spiraling panic, she blurted, "Her husband got it wrong."

"*He* was there too? What sort of depraved gathering was this?" Papa bellowed. "I knew I should have never allowed you out of the house. From here on in, girl, you're to stay away from that Fines lot, you hear me?"

Charity felt the blood drain from her face. "Please, Father, I—"

"Do you hear me?"

She shrank back, whispering, "Yes, I hear you."

The next moment, she was once again back in the carriage, staring into her friend's rounded blue eyes. Percy was chewing upon her lip, her brow pleated. Mrs. Fines and Mr. Hunt watched on with somber expressions.

"Well," Percy said, "it appears we have some work to do."

Letting out an unsteady breath, Charity gave a slight nod.

"Right then. Let's start with the married lady in the bedchamber bit ..."

The carriage rolled on, and Charity gathered up the pieces of her courage—and her story.

Chapter Fourteen

"We're almost at Sparkler's," Nicholas said.

Stirred from his brooding, Paul lifted the curtain. As they wound their way into the heart of London, he saw streets crammed with people and horses, vendors hawking their wares before the great dome of St. Paul's. Despite the early afternoon hour, the ubiquitous haze from the chimney stacks darkened the sky. The mingled scents of kitchen fires, rubbish, and the murky Thames wafted into the cabin.

"Nothing like the sweet smell of home," he said.

Nicholas cleared his throat. "Before we arrive, is there, er, anything you'd care to discuss?"

Not an order or demand, but a question. This was a first.

Paul quirked a brow. "Is this your attempt at being tactful?"

"I'm trying to be helpful." After a pause, the marquess muttered, "It has come to my attention that in past conversations I may have been perhaps too ... hasty."

It was the closest to an apology Paul had ever gotten from the other man. There could only be one reason for it. He drawled, "Your lady talked some sense into you, did she?"

"Helena thought that I was too hard on you. About the

boxing, I mean." Nicholas frowned. "She said that I ought to have listened to your plan before jumping to conclusions."

"This is why I adore your marchioness. Not only is she beautiful, she's always right."

Nicholas gave him a look that told him not to push his luck.

Being himself, he pushed his luck. "I accept your apology, old chap," he said graciously.

"I'm not apologizing," his lordship said between his teeth. "I'm merely saying that I am willing to listen if there's anything you care to discuss. About present circumstances."

"There's nothing to discuss. I'm marrying the chit," Paul said.

In the end, the decision had been surprisingly simple. His honor demanded that he wed Charity Sparkler. Though marriage hadn't ranked high on his list of priorities—being slightly more preferable than, say, getting a tooth drawn—marriage to Charity didn't seem so ... terrible.

He already knew that he enjoyed her company. She was steady and sensible, undoubtedly the sort of influence he needed in his life. And the way she'd defended him against Parkington? Her sweet loyalty would warm him for the rest of his days. And as he thought of the marital *nights* that awaited him, certain parts of his anatomy heated even further ...

"I gathered as much from your, ahem, proposal," Nicholas said.

Paul winced. In hindsight, his offer had been fumbling at best. But he'd been so furious at *himself* for putting Charity in harm's way that he hadn't been thinking clearly. And she hadn't exactly helped matters. He found her streak of willfulness both annoying ... and strangely arousing. There were so many facets to her, so much to discover beneath the surface. In truth, he'd been fascinated with her since their first encounter in the parlor.

A notion struck to him: could this latest fiasco be Fate's way of giving him a shove in the right direction?

Still ... "It would have gone better had she cooperated," he muttered.

"Welcome to marriage," Nicholas said with a faint smile. "Take my advice, Fines, and go gentler in the future. Lure with honey rather than vinegar, if you take my meaning."

Given Paul's rather infamous success with the ladies, 'twas the height of irony to be told this by the taciturn marquess. For some reason, Paul's charisma and confidence seemed to evaporate around Charity. She made him feel awkward, like a bumbling schoolboy.

Face heating, he said, "Don't worry, I've got things in hand."

For once, he was going to do things right. He even had a three-part plan. First, he would woo Charity, use every charm at his disposal to convince her to marry him. Once wed, he'd treat her with the affection and respect she deserved. When it came to bedroom matters, he would certainly see to her and his own enjoyment, but he would always keep his head. Which led to the third and most critical point of all: none of this neck-or-nothing business. From here on in, he was going to be the master of himself. To be a worthy and respectable husband to Charity.

"Have you planned what you'll say to Sparkler?" Nicholas asked.

"You know me: I've a talent for being extemporaneous." The truth was Paul hadn't a clue what he was going to say. "If that doesn't work, I'll use my natural charm."

The carriage came to a halt. When the door opened, Paul stepped down first. Scanning the row of crowded storefronts, his gaze latched onto the shop in the middle.

His jaw slackened. "*That's* Sparkler's?"

Beside him on the walk, Nicholas said neutrally, "It appears so."

Though Paul knew of Sparkler's, he'd never shopped there. He patronized the more fashionable establishment of Rundell, Bridge, and Rundell, located a few blocks away on Ludgate Hill. Compared to this other shop, Sparkler's was a *dump*.

The store was a plain box, without any decoration, not even a planter, to relieve its severity. The weathered grey exterior could have used a new coat of paint—about a decade ago. The sole indication that this was indeed an emporium that offered priceless jewels was the small sign hanging above the entryway, and its modest lettering did not inspire confidence.

"I thought *your* office could use refurbishment," Paul said under his breath. "Holy hell, who runs a jewelry business in this fashion?"

"If that's a sample of your natural charm, I predict trouble ahead," Nick said.

At that moment, the Hunts' carriage rolled up behind them. Hunt exited first, handing down Percy and then Mama. Anticipation made Paul stride over.

"I've got Miss Sparkler," he said.

Looking amused, his brother-in-law stepped aside.

Paul found himself looking up into Charity's surprised eyes, which widened further when he reached up and caught her gently by the waist. Egad, he could almost span that narrow expanse with his two hands. He lifted her from the carriage, absorbing her delicious little tremor. Her lashes beat rapidly as did the pulse just visible above the demure ruffle of her neckline.

"How was your journey, my sweet?" he said.

In the next blink, she recovered. "We've arrived at a good hour," she said briskly. "There's usually a lull in customers in the early afternoon, so Father should be free to speak with us."

Paul thought the lull at Sparkler's likely wasn't limited to the present hour. Wisely, he withheld that comment, offering instead, "I look forward to meeting with your father."

"That makes one of us," she said, and his lips twitched at the honesty of her words. "But there's no sense in delaying matters. Come along, then."

She led the way through the narrow entryway of the shop. Paul had to duck to pass through. As his eyes adjusted to the gloom, he saw that the interior was as shabby as the exterior. The dreary beige room was lined with utilitarian display cases, a few worn lamps flickering on the counters. The main redeeming quality of the place was its tidiness. Not a speck of dust could be found, and the merchandise was arranged in neat rows behind glass.

He peered into one of the cabinets. To his surprise, he saw that the goods—in this case, gentlemen's accoutrements—were of premium quality, as fine as anything he'd seen at Rundell's and so much more the pity. A jeweler ought to know that a fine gem required a matching setting to display its true brilliance. With his shop's lack of style, Sparkler was cheapening his wares.

"Miss Charity, we weren't expecting you back so soon." A clerk as old as Methuselah hobbled from behind the counter. His wide smile boasted a remarkable absence of teeth. "Thought you'd be awhile rubbing shoulders with the carriage set."

"There was a change of plans, Mr. Jameson," Charity said. "Is Father available? We've a matter to discuss with him."

"Mr. Sparkler's occupied." Jameson's rheumy gaze darted to the back. "He's with a business associate in his office, and the fellow didn't look too happy."

Charity's face drained of color. "Which associate is it?"

The sound of voices preempted Jameson's reply. A moment later, a door swung open at the back of the shop. Paul knew straightaway that the thin, grey-haired gentleman leading the way was Uriah Sparkler. Though the man's demeanor was pinched and stern, his ascetic features held a shadow of Charity's delicate beauty. Following him was a more robust fellow in his thirties, dark-haired and with an elegant, ruthless air about him. This last observation was reinforced when the man's gaze cut to his.

Paul flashed to a performance he'd seen at Vauxhall. An Indian snake charmer had played a flute whilst a cobra had woven back and forth, staring into the audience with unblinking black orbs identical to the ones boring into Paul now. His muscles bunched; his hands clenched on instinct.

"Charity?" Sparkler came toward them. From the incredulity and anger stamped on the man's features, it didn't take a genius to guess that Parkington had wasted no time in spreading his dirty lies. The bastard.

"Hello, Father. Mr. Garrity." Charity did a quick curtsy. "These are my friends—"

"I don't care who they are," Sparkler said in a voice that shook. "What is going on? Mr. Garrity here has informed me that rumors of your behavior are circulating around London."

Charity's lower lip quivered, but she said bravely, "Father, it's not what it sounds like—"

"Were you or were you not caught alone with some *blackguard*?"

Seeing Charity's cowed expression and shimmering eyes, Paul could hold silent no longer.

"The blackguard you are referring to is me." He stepped forward and bowed. "Paul Fines at your service, sir. And let me assure you that Miss Sparkler is an innocent victim here. She has done nothing wrong," he said with emphasis. "She was attempting to defend me, and in doing so, got caught in the crossfire."

Irate color replaced Sparkler's pallor. "A *Fines* is involved. I might have known." His glare shifted from Paul to Percy, who gave him a weak wave of her fingers.

"Please, Father. Nothing happened. It was a misunderstanding —" Charity pleaded.

"According to the Earl of Parkington, you were caught *in flagrante*, Miss Sparkler." Though Garrity spoke quietly, his words dripped with venom nonetheless. "I would not call that nothing. The whole Town is abuzz over your unbecoming conduct."

Charity shrank back as if slapped.

Anger sizzled through Paul's veins. "Who are you to judge her, you bounder?"

Garrity's stare remained hard, unwavering. "I *was* her fiancé, according to the marriage contract Sparkler and I signed three days ago. But now I must reconsider: a man such as I will not take on soiled goods."

This revelation took Paul aback—Charity *Garrity?*—but only for a second. "She is not soiled goods, damn your eyes," he growled. "She's an angel. Not that it matters: you're not marrying her—I am."

"What?" Sparkler choked out.

"I am marrying your daughter," Paul said through his teeth—probably not the best way to speak to one's future in-law, but his back was up at the other's mistreatment of Charity.

Why wasn't Sparkler defending his daughter, giving her the benefit of the doubt? Anyone with eyes could see that she was a sweet, innocent girl incapable of such misdeeds. But the old man wasn't even listening to her. Paul suddenly flashed to his troubles with his own father, which seemed pale in comparison. At least Jeremiah had tried to understand him.

"Over my dead body!" Sparkler's sparse frame vibrated within his ill-fitting clothes. "Mr. Garrity and I have an agreement."

"*Had* an agreement," Garrity said in cold tones. "You promised me a maiden of unblemished virtue. Not this"—his eyes flicked to Charity—"disgrace."

A gasp broke from Charity's lips; Paul saw red. Before he knew what he was doing, he was heading straight for the bastard. Hands pulled him back, restrained him.

"Let me go," he grated out, struggling.

"Cull ain't worth it," Hunt said from one side.

"A brawl won't help anything," Nicholas said from the other. "Keep your wits about you, Fines. There are matters to sort out, the most important being Miss Sparkler's future."

Chest heaving, Paul fought for control.

Lines of displeasure bracketed Garrity's mouth. Donning his

hat, he said, "I don't suffer fools, Mr. Fines, nor insults. You have inconvenienced me, and I shan't forget it."

Paul returned the other's glare measure for measure. "We can settle it now or at dawn, if you wish. You've only to name the place."

Garrity's smile was not a smile. "You're not worth dirtying my hands over."

"Mr. Garrity, wait!" Sparkler stumbled after his associate. "We had a deal, you and I—"

"Your daughter violated the terms." Garrity spoke without turning. "The deal is off."

In a last ditch effort, Sparkler flung himself in the other's path, blocking access to the door. "We can come to an understanding. Perhaps my daughter is not at fault, I've raised her to be a good girl—"

"Out of my way, Sparkler." Garrity's tone dripped with menace.

After a few seconds, Sparkler drew in a shaky breath and moved aside.

Garrity slammed the door behind him.

In the aftermath of stunned silence, a calm voice inserted itself. "Well, thank goodness that is over. What a dreadful man. I'm sure you must be relieved, Mr. Sparkler."

Sparkler, who remained slumped against the doorframe, raised an unfocused gaze to Paul's mama. "Relieved?" he said in a dazed voice.

"That Garrity fellow is clearly not deserving of dear Miss Sparkler," Anna Fines said. "And all the better to discover that before it was too late. Thus, despite the unfortunate circumstances, I do believe things have worked out for the best, don't you?"

Though framed as a question, it was not. Having had years of experience dealing with his mother's brand of velvet-covered steel, Paul was aware of this. Sparkler was not.

"Best?" the jeweler sputtered. "Everything is ruined! All because of—"

"A *mistake*," Mama said in a tone that few would dare to contradict. "All of us are here today to bear witness to the fact that no misconduct occurred between my son and Miss Sparkler. That said, Paul has offered for your daughter, and I hope you will find joy in the fact as I and others have. Our children have many supporters, you see, including the Marquess of Harteford."

She nodded to Nicholas, who bowed. Looking confounded, Sparkler returned the courtesy.

"The marquess will assist in procuring a special license," Mama informed Sparkler. "Our children's nuptials can occur within a sennight, which gives us little time to prepare, but I'm certain you agree that expediency is key to minimize any disruption"—her gaze pointedly encompassed the store—"to business as usual?"

Again, not a question.

"I am ruined. This is the end," Sparkler whispered.

"Please, Father, don't say that—"

"My life's work, gone. Because of your reckless behavior." Sparkler turned stark grey eyes to his daughter. "How could you?"

The bastard might as well have stuck a blade in her chest—it might have been kinder. Rage rushed through Paul's veins as a single droplet trickled down Charity's cheek.

"Miss Sparkler is not to blame," he said fiercely, "but 'pon my honor, I shall do what is necessary to ensure Sparkler's survival and success."

As soon as the words left him, his mind reeled. *Dear Lord, did I just sign up to ... work? And how in bloody hell am I going to straighten out this dump* and *prepare for the tournament—less than two months away?*

Before he could backpedal or at least clarify his time schedule, he glimpsed Charity's face. His breath caught. Through the veil of her tears, she was gazing at him with ... wonder. As if he'd just hung the sun back in her sky. His chest pounded with the sudden desire to have her always look at him thus.

"You? What are you going to do, unless ..." Sparkler wet his lips. "How much did you say you are worth, sir?"

"Father," Charity mumbled.

"He wishes to marry you. I have the right to know his financial situation." Sparkler drew himself up. "If he hadn't compromised you in the first place—"

"I'm recouping from some losses." Paul saw no point in beating around the bush. "But while I haven't a nest egg now, my income from my father's company is five thousand a year." He decided that now was not the time to disclose his plans vis-à-vis prizefighting. Instead, he said confidently, "I shall be back on my feet by year's end."

His prospects were considerable. To his surprise, Sparkler's face fell.

"I'm done for," the man said in a bleak voice.

Holy hell, how much trouble was the shop in?

Nicholas' imperious tones cut in. "Paul is the son of Jeremiah Fines, and mercantile talent runs in his blood. Once he sets his mind to a thing, he is steadfast. You can ask for no better help than his."

Seeing no trace of irony in the other's expression, Paul felt a surge of gratitude.

A moment passed before Sparkler said tonelessly, "Everything's ruined. What difference does anything make? Do as you will." Shoulders slumped, he headed to his office like a man off to the gallows.

Paul's gaze went to Charity, who was clutching Percy's hand, looking so young and lost that all his protective instincts roused. He wanted to cross over and haul her into his arms. To hold her close and tell her everything was going to be alright.

Instead, he waited. They had her father's permission of sorts. Now it was time for Charity to make her own decision.

"Charity, dear, you don't mind rushing things along?" his mama said gently. "We'll all pitch in with the preparations. You won't have to worry about a thing."

"Thank you, Mrs. Fines," Charity said quietly.

Paul expelled a breath that he hadn't known he'd been holding.

"It is my greatest pleasure, dear girl, to welcome you to our family," his mama said, smiling.

Percy flung her arms around Charity. "We're to be true sisters at last!"

With a feeling of triumph, Paul went over and tapped his sister on the shoulder.

"May I cut in?" he said dryly.

Releasing her friend, Percy grinned at him. "I suppose." Then she surprised him with a hug, whispering in his ear, "I *knew* this would happen. You're going to be so happy, my dearest brother!"

"I'm your only brother," he said with a catch in his voice.

Smiling, Percy went to join their mama.

Paul took his bride-to-be's hand. Within his grip, her delicate, chilled fingers fluttered like a hummingbird's wings.

"You do me a great honor," he said softly, "and I'll endeavor to return the favor by seeing to your happiness."

Though her lips trembled, she didn't pull away.

Chapter Fifteen

Ensconced in Mrs. Fines' cozy parlor the next morning, Charity battled a sense of unreality. It wasn't the room itself that was odd or unfamiliar; over the years, she'd spent hours here with Percy, the two of them curled up on the chintz sofa framed by matching curtains. Likewise, the occupants gathered around the tulipwood coffee table were no strangers. Thus, what imbued the scene with a surreal feeling must be the topic of conversation: a wedding.

Her wedding ... to Paul Fines.

As she sipped her tea, she snuck a glance at the gentleman she would be marrying in five days. He was at the sideboard perusing the breakfast offerings. His hair gleamed; his tobacco brown jacket and buff trousers clung lovingly to his physique. He appeared rested, his chiseled features showing none of the strain that might be expected when a man had to marry out of necessity. He remained the Apollo of Master Bernini's imagination, a study in masculine grace and beauty.

As if he sensed her regard, his vivid blue eyes locked on her.

She quickly looked away. Even on her best day, she was no Daphne, the elusive nymph Apollo sought to claim. And since she hadn't slept a wink last night, she knew that shadows hung beneath her eyes and her cheeks lacked any color at all. She didn't need to see disappointment darken his gaze. For despite his gentlemanly courtesy—and he'd been kindness itself during yesterday's hideous scene at the shop—she knew that his true reaction to all of this must be regret.

Now that Charity's indignation—and, yes, wounded pride—had faded, she could see the situation through a clearer lens. Not only had Mr. Fines lost the incomparable Miss Drummond, but now he was to be saddled with *her*. A girl he did not love. A girl he was marrying out of honor, obligation, and, worst of all, pity.

She hadn't missed the disgust on Mr. Fines' face at her papa's reaction, and her humiliation had deepened. She'd wanted to explain that it wasn't Father's fault: he was under a great deal of financial pressure, and she'd pulled the rug from beneath his plans with Mr. Garrity.

Of course Father had been irate. And if anyone was to blame, it was she.

She gripped the saucer of her teacup. The other culprit was, of course, Parkington. The earl continued to carry out his diabolical revenge. The *Times* had devoted an entire column to the scandal involving a certain jeweler's daughter and the scion of a shipping empire. Thanks to the earl, they were being made into an example of Moral Mayhem amongst the middling class. Mr. Fines' dire prediction had come to pass: marriage *was* the only hope now for controlling the damage.

"Nicholas is taking care of the license as we speak, so the most critical item is covered," Mrs. Fines was saying to Percy. "As for the remaining tasks, I took the liberty of making a list."

She withdrew a small roll of parchment. Charity's eyes rounded as the paper unwound onto the lady's lap, curled over her knees, and came to a stop at the hem of her skirts.

"Mama, the wedding is going to take place in *five days*," Percy said. "There's no time for elaborate plans."

"Which is why I've distilled this list down to the essentials."

Percy peered over her mother's shoulder. "*Doves* are essential?"

So the conversation went. Charity didn't contribute much for none of the preparations seemed real to her. She didn't feel a bride's giddy excitement. Instead, she was distracted by the questions that had kept sleep at bay.

What sort of marriage will ours be? What will be the rules and expectations?

And most panic-inducing of all: *How on earth can I marry the man I love ... knowing he loves another?*

Her hands trembled, rattling the cup. For in the midst of yesterday's terrible scene, a truth had blazed, incinerating the layers of denial and self-protection. She loved Paul Fines. She always had and always would. She adored his noble nature, his willingness to forfeit his own happiness in order to protect her reputation.

The way he'd defended her against Mr. Garrity and offered to help her papa made him a hero in her eyes.

She ought to be grateful just to have the protection of Mr. Fines' name: it was more than a girl like her could hope for. Yet while she knew that expediency and honor had prompted his offer, she couldn't extinguish a little spark within her. She recalled the energy that had seemed to crackle between them during the craniology demonstration and that kiss in the folly. He'd seemed as absorbed in their exchanges as she had been ...

She shook away her foolish longings. More likely than not, she was just imagining things. And, at any rate, whatever energy she'd sensed was hardly the same as love. Thus, for the sake of marital harmony, she would have to find a way to keep her true feelings locked away. She would strive to be a dutiful wife ... and not get in his way.

Her heart ached at the thought. Yet it was the only way to survive a marriage of convenience to the man she loved.

The cushions beside her sank. The subtle scent of spice and

masculine musk made her heart hammer, as did Mr. Fines' sudden close proximity.

"Your cup's half empty," he said.

He didn't know the half of it.

"I've had enough tea, thank you," she said.

"You haven't eaten anything," he remarked.

He'd noticed her lack of appetite?

"Here, try this." To her further astonishment, he tore a piece off the bun on his plate and offered it to her. "Lisbett's rolls will tempt anyone's appetite."

Heat climbed in her cheeks. "No, really. Thank you. I'm ... I'm not hungry."

"Go on, eat it. By now, you should know better than to argue with a Fines." His teasing smile made it difficult to think, let alone come up with a response. "It's best just to give in and let us have our way."

"No one can have their way all the time," she said.

His smile deepened. He waggled the piece of roll at her. Not wishing to attract the others' notice, she sighed and held her palm out for the morsel.

"Alright, but I'm truly not hungry—" Her eyes widened as buttery, apricot-studded pastry muffled the rest of her sentence.

"Not eating, not sleeping—you have to take better care of yourself," he murmured.

She focused on chewing and not choking with surprise.

In his regular drawl, he said, "Mama, if you're quite done with Miss Sparkler, I'd like to take her for a tour of the roses."

Charity's hands went clammy at the notion of being alone with him. Which was ridiculous given that they would be man and wife at week's end. But here, in the comfort of his family's presence, she could almost pretend that theirs would be a union based on something other than necessity. Alone, just the two of them, reality would have to be addressed. She knew that he was too much of a gentleman to go back on his word, but he was also too much of a gentleman not to be honest with her. Surely he wished to spell out the terms of their arrangement.

Gulping, she made a last ditch effort to forestall the inevitable—which wasn't like her at all. She was a sensible girl, one who looked reality in the eye and did not falter. Until now.

"I must stay and help," she said. "You've all taken on such a burden—"

"Nonsense, dear girl. 'Tis my *pleasure* to plan my child's wedding." Behind her spectacles, Mrs. Fines' eyes grew misty, and her lace cap trembled upon her salt and pepper curls. "If your mama were here, I'm certain she'd feel the same way. But as she isn't ... I hope you don't mind my saying that I already consider you a part of the family, which doubles my joy in the preparations."

Charity's throat thickened. "You are too good to me."

Mrs. Fines smiled. "Now the bride-to-be's job is to remain calm and collected, and a turn through my roses would accomplish that nicely. So go on, enjoy yourself."

"Don't worry about a thing. We've got everything well in hand," Percy added.

"You heard them." Mr. Fines stood and offered his hand. "No more stalling, sweeting. The roses await."

Chapter Sixteen

Although not large, the garden was his mama's pride and joy, especially now when her prized roses were in bloom. But, for him, the showy flowers were eclipsed by the quiet charm of the girl who walked next to the hedges. Charity had left her bonnet off, and whilst her hair was in its habitual knot, the sun picked out fiery strands and made them glimmer. Her fingers trailed over the lush, velvety heads as she strolled; recalling the delicate sensuality of her touch, he envied the blossoms.

Time for that later, he told himself. What he needed to do first was clear the air and forge an understanding with his fiancée. They had much to discuss.

Clasping his hands behind his back, he said, "I'm glad to have a minute alone."

"Yes."

He couldn't read her expression; her moss-green eyes gave so little away. Aware of the building tension, he plunged on. "The thing of it is ... I should begin by apologizing."

Her brows lifted; she looked surprised. "For what?"

Where should he *begin*?

"For dragging you into this fiasco. Exposing you to the

condemnation of others. And then," he said grimly, "there's the way I botched my offer to you."

She looked at him as if he had bats in the belfry. Perhaps he wasn't making himself clear?

"I haven't yet thanked you for intervening with Parkington, though I wish you hadn't." Devil take it, he sounded awkward to his own ears. "I mean to say, I'm sorry that you've had to suffer for it. That is my biggest regret: that harm has come to you because of my actions."

She slid him a glance as they strolled along. "That's what you're sorry for?"

"Well, it's not the only thing. I'm sure I could add to the afore-mentioned list of wrongs."

Her cheeks turned pink, and he wondered if she was thinking about the kiss he'd stolen at the gazebo. Or maybe she was recalling his rakish reputation. Or his stupid entanglement with Louisa, which had led to this mess. He wanted to smack himself in the head.

Way to get your future wife to cogitate about what a bastard you are.

"I'm not usually so maladroit. You seem to bring it out in me," he muttered.

"I make you ... clumsy?"

Inspiration hit him. "Your beauty unravels me, I'm afraid."

Thank God for *that* recovery. That was the direction to head in.

"Hmm," she said. "Your tongue, at least, doesn't suffer from knots."

Her sly witticism startled a laugh from him. Some of the tightness in his chest eased.

"Minx," he said appreciatively. "So despite my bumbling apology, will you accept it? Knowing that it is heartfelt and offered sincerely?"

She hesitated, then said, "Yes."

The relief was exhilarating. He had the urge to seize her in his arms and thank her with a kiss ... but he told himself to hold the reins, stay in control for once. So he took out a pocket knife and clipped off a brilliant pink bloom. Shaving off the thorns, he offered her the flower.

She rewarded him with a tremulous smile. "Thank you."

"Thank *you*, sweeting," he said huskily. "Now that the slate is clean, perhaps we should discuss the future." He liked how mature and rational he sounded; he was definitely turning a new page. "Though this marriage has come as a surprise, we should approach it with our eyes open, I think."

Some of the softness fled her eyes. "I agree that clarity is important."

"Exactly. You're a sensible sort and—let's face it—far more sensible than I could ever hope to be," he said ruefully. "It is one of the qualities I most admire about you."

He'd meant that as a compliment, yet her shoulders tensed.

"I mean to say, we're different, you and I," he said quickly.

She said nothing.

"Given our differences, I think it's important we discuss our expectations of marriage," he went on uneasily. "Have you given thought to what you wish from our union?"

In truth, he wanted to know what she wanted. The kind of husband she imagined for herself. Lord knew he could use a few pointers.

The path had taken them to the majestic willow at the back corner of the garden. Beneath the shade of the trailing branches, Charity drew herself up the way one did when something unpleasant had to be said.

"You needn't worry about my expectations, sir." Her gaze remained on the pink rose in her hands. "I am grateful for the protection of your name, and I will endeavor to make our marriage as convenient as possible for you."

"Convenient?" He frowned, not understanding.

Still not looking at him, she dipped her chin. "I won't get in your way. You must carry on as before."

"Carry on ... doing what, exactly?"

"Whatever you choose to do and with"—her voice hitched—"whomever."

Comprehension struck him. "With *whomever* ... are you saying what I think you're saying?"

"I understand your wish for a marriage of convenience," she whispered to the ground.

He stared at her bent head, anger rising inside him. "Well, that's utter bollocks, isn't it?"

Finally, her gaze flew to his. "P-pardon?"

"Has the word convenient ever passed my lips in conjunction with our marriage?"

"W-well ..." she stammered, "no."

"There's good reason for it. Frankly, no marriage is ever convenient and never more so than bachelorhood. I do, however, recall proposing to you and you accepting. Which means in five days we will be vowing—before no less than God, mind you—our fidelity to each other." He could actually feel his temperature escalating. "And you're telling me you *expect* me to have extramarital affairs? What kind of man do you take me for?"

She stared at him.

"If you believe me so lacking in honor, I wonder that you'd consent to marry me in the first place." His hands balled as a thought punched him in the gut. "Or perhaps it is *you* who wishes for ... freedom in marriage?"

That would happen over his dead body. Or, more accurately, the other man's—because he would murder anyone who dared to touch Charity. She was *his*.

"That's not it." She sounded appalled. "Not it at all."

"What about that fellow who kissed you?" he demanded.

Her brow furrowed. "Um, what fellow?"

"At the gazebo, you implied that you'd had previous, more memorable *incidents*."

"Oh, that." She bit her lip. "I believe I said that because I was angry."

"So no one has kissed you before me?" he persisted.

Her lashes flickered. With a sigh, she said, "No, you're the only one."

Relief poured through him. "I trust you'll keep it that way," he said sternly. "In the past when I was *carrying on*, as you so delicately put it, I wasn't married. When I am, I will stay true to my vows."

"You mean that? Truly?"

He gave a gruff nod.

A slow smile lit her face, made it as radiant as dawn. "That ... that would be lovely."

Unable to help himself, he cupped her cheek. Her tremor of awareness made the blood rush in his veins. "Now that that's settled, what else do you want from this marriage, sweet?"

"I don't know. You've already given me far more than I expected."

By Jove, she was sweet.

"And I want to thank you especially for offering to help my father. That means the world to me," she said earnestly.

Right. Time to clarify his schedule. He dropped his hand, bracing himself. "About that ..."

"Yes?"

He cleared his throat. "Do you recall that I have a tournament coming up?"

She nodded.

"I mentioned this in one of our earlier conversations, but given the recent brouhaha, it may have slipped your mind," he said with a nervous laugh.

Her head tipped to one side.

"The thing is, I have to leave for training soon. Straight after our wedding trip, I'm afraid. My patron Traymore has a place set up for me in the country. He thinks that practicing in seclusion for a month—focusing on nothing but boxing—will improve my chances of winning."

She seemed to digest his words. "That ... makes sense. And I can help my father while you're away."

His tension subsided. Yet another bonus to marrying a sensible girl: Charity wasn't prone to hysterics. She was rational, calm ... unlike Rosalind, who'd possessed a far more tempestuous nature. The latter had *expected* things to go her way, probably since there'd been so many suitors ready to leap at her slightest whim. She'd once refused to receive Paul when he arrived fifteen minutes late for their drive in the park ...

Why am I even thinking about Rosalind? he chided himself. The past was done, and it was time to move on. Especially now, when he had the luck to be engaged to a woman as sweet and understanding as Charity.

"After the tournament, I'm all yours," he said with gratitude. "I'll devote my entire attention to Sparkler's."

She smiled. "Thank you. For that and for your honesty."

"Between honesty and commitment to our vows, we'll have more than most marriages," he said with satisfaction. "So called love matches included."

Her sudden stillness gave him pause.

His worries were justified when she drew in a breath and said, "On the topic, there is something I feel I should ask. It has to do with ... Lady Monteith."

Had he inadvertently signaled that he'd been thinking about his past love? Guilt and unease tightened his chest.

"What about her?" he said.

"Do you ... have feelings for her still?"

He wasn't surprised that Charity knew about him and Rosalind. After all, she was best friends with his sister, and she'd probably observed herself the way he'd trailed after Rosalind back then. Scanning Charity's face, he saw no judgment there. Only curiosity and acceptance, which made it possible to broach a painful subject. A topic that he'd never spoken of—to anyone.

"I was in love with Rosalind, and I was disappointed," he said. "As you know, she is married now. The mother of two, I believe."

Charity nodded.

"Love's a messy emotion, and I've learned my lesson," he said with feeling. "No more of that nonsense for me. You see, I'm the sort for whom sentiment ... lingers. Not prettily, I'm afraid. But the feelings I have for Rosalind are less than what they once were." As he said it aloud, he realized the truth of his assertion. "And I can assure you that those feelings will not interfere with our marriage. Do you believe me?"

"I believe you," she said.

Tenderness swelled within him. "God love you for it. I do think we have a fair shot at making a go of things, don't you?"

She gave a shy nod. She was so pretty, a nymph beneath the bower of a willow. He couldn't resist the temptation any longer.

"There is, of course, a marital topic we've yet to address," he said huskily. "Though, in this, I'd prefer a demonstration to a discussion. May I kiss you, my sweet?"

Above her fichu, her pulse fluttered. "Oh. Yes."

He meant for this to be a gentlemanly kiss. A sealing of the promises they'd made one another. Yet from the moment he touched his mouth to hers, fire sparked between them. Her lips molded to his, and she was even hotter and more delicious than he remembered. The sparks burst into a blaze, and when her knees weakened, he caught her against him.

Before he knew what he was doing, he was backing her against the trunk of the tree.

He explored her mouth some more, groaning as her little tongue rubbed against his. So *good*, this kissing. What harm would it do to take things a bit further? He wouldn't take her here in his mama's garden; he had more self-control than that.

But he *could* pleasure her, give her a preview of the delights ahead.

Hungrily, he tasted her jaw, the smooth curve of her neck. Her primly fresh scent made him giddy. As did the little moan she made when he plucked off her fichu to reveal more of her downy skin. Her hands planted against his shoulders.

"What if someone sees us?" she said breathlessly.

"Hang 'em. We're engaged. How much more trouble can we get ourselves into?"

She bit her lip. He wasn't going to let her ponder the matter, not with his blood pounding and his cock jutting like a steel pike between his legs. So he took matters into his own hands: two small yet enticingly perky matters. Her eyes grew unfocused as he squeezed her tits, rubbing the excited peaks through the lilac muslin.

"Like that?" he growled.

"Mmm."

He'd take that as a yes. "What about this?"

He trailed his tongue across her décolletage, around her silver locket. Her fingers grasped his hair, pulling him close. Groaning, he obliged, licking more of her fragrant skin. When she squirmed restlessly against him, he gave her a gentle bite just above her modest neckline. Her sigh traveled straight to his erection. Lost in her sweet wantonness, he wedged his leg between her skirts. Lifted her so that her sex rode his thigh. He rocked her against him.

Her eyes squeezed shut, her fingers tightening in his hair.

"God, you're beautiful. Keep going," he urged.

Lungs burning, he continued to grind his thigh against her, kissing her ear, her neck. She wriggled desperately against him, panting and whimpering and making him mad with lust. Somehow doing this fully clothed made it all the more erotic, their bodies restrained by layers, straining and heaving to get closer. His imagination fired: what would this be like naked, skin against skin, his prick driving not against his trousers, but inside her tight, wet little pussy ...

With a groan, he drove his tongue deep, taking what he could. She shivered and shook, and when her crisis hit, he swallowed her abandoned cry, triumph raging through him. He felt a hot spurt against his smalls ... and realized that he was a hairsbreadth from losing his seed. From coming in his trousers like a green lad with his first wench.

All from a fully clothed kiss.

Devil and damn.

He dragged in breaths, holding her until they both calmed. When she lifted her head from his shoulder, the dazed expression in her eyes made his lungs expand once more. His cock, too. To distract himself, he straightened her dress and replaced her fichu. His finger brushed the small love mark he'd left on the slope above her right breast ... and he quickly tucked the linen over it.

"I take it back," he said abruptly.

She blinked. "Take what back?"

He bent to retrieve the rose that she'd dropped in the throes of passion. As he handed it to her, he said with a rakish grin, "We've more than a *fair* shot, my sweet. You and I—we're going to rub along famously."

She blushed, fairer than the blossom she held, and gladness unfurled within him.

Chapter Seventeen

On Thursday, two days before the wedding, Charity found herself in one of the changing rooms at the back of Madame Rousseau's exclusive establishment. Left to her own devices, she wouldn't have dreamed of seeking the services of the famed modiste, but Percy had insisted.

"Where else are you going to get a stylish trousseau?" her friend had demanded.

"I thought I might make over my white muslin. I've hardly worn it, and with the addition of a few tucks and a bit of trim—"

Percy's eyes had rounded with horror. "Charity Sparkler, this is your *wedding* we're talking about. And you're marrying my brother, *the* most fashionable buck in Town. Do you really want to march down the aisle toward him wearing last season's frock with ribbons you've tacked on?"

Presented in that manner, Charity had reconsidered her initial plan. Ever since the passionate embrace with Mr. Fines in the garden, she'd been giddy with newfound hope. He'd kissed her— and he hadn't apologized! He'd called her *beautiful* whilst he was sober. He'd touched her with heat and hunger and need, and it hadn't been for Rosalind.

This time, it had all been for *her*.

A tingle worked up Charity's spine. At the same time, her practical mind set in. Mr. Fines had been clear that there was to be no possibility of love ... but one couldn't wish for the moon. She'd already planned to keep her feelings to herself anyway. If she felt a twinge of guilt for not telling him about their kiss at Spitalfields, she pushed it aside. That incident was too revealing of her love for him, and he'd told her that he was done with that "nonsense". Yet the things he had wanted—loyalty, honesty, respect—well, if they could have those, it would be enough.

More than she'd dared to hope for.

Thus, she was determined to not let him down, to be the bride he wanted. That included not looking like the veriest dowd. Yet she'd balked at the idea of incurring such expense for the sake of vanity.

"Father won't pay for a trousseau," she'd said, "and my allowance won't cover much."

Though her papa now seemed resigned to the marriage, it didn't mean that he approved of it. He'd hardly spoken to her since her return, a fact that filled her with anxious guilt. In the shop, over supper, he seemed so preoccupied that he barely noticed her presence. She prayed there was some way she could earn his forgiveness and resolved to work twice as hard to ensure Sparkler's survival.

"Don't worry about the cost," Percy had said. "'Tis my gift to you."

"Oh no, I can't allow you to—"

Percy had clasped her hands. "You are my bosom chum, Charity Sparkler, my sister in every way but blood—and now we're going to have that too." Her friend had looked at her with teary joy, and Charity's own eyes had dampened. "You've seen me through thick and thin, and now you're going to make my brother so happy—the *least* I can do is give you a small gift. I won't take no for an answer."

That had been that.

Now Charity stood on a dais before a full-length looking glass as Madame Rousseau fussed over the final fitting. Percy, Helena, and Marianne—the latter two having just arrived from Hertford-shire—watched on from ivory curricle chairs. Normally, Charity avoided mirrors, but now she couldn't tear her gaze from her own reflection.

"And there she is: the true Charity Sparkler," Marianne said.

"My brother is going to expire from shock when he sees you," Percy said gleefully.

"You put me in mind of a faerie creature," Helena said, smiling. "Positively radiant."

Dazed, Charity mumbled her thanks, her eyes still riveted on the image. Though she was no arbiter of fashion, even she knew magic when she saw it. Madame Rousseau's creation was *extraordinary*. The lacey bodice gave the appearance of flowers and leaves clinging to her bosom; beneath, the eggshell muslin cascaded like a fall of water, skimming over her hips to swirl at her ankles. Subtle lace inserts along the hem completed the masterpiece.

"*C'est parfait*." Dressed in chic black, the French dressmaker gave the skirt a final twitch and stepped back. Satisfaction gleamed in her dark eyes. "One detail more and it would be gaudy. One less, dull."

"Thank you, Madame. You've managed a miracle," Charity said in wonder.

"My talent is undeniable, *oui*, but the true miracle is what *mademoiselle* has managed to hide." The modiste gave the gown Charity had arrived in the look one might a dead animal at the side of the road.

"On that, we are agreed," Marianne said, "which brings us onto the next item on the list. This afternoon, we consult Signore Antonio."

"*Bien sûr*. He is the best," Madame Rousseau agreed.

"At what?" Charity asked.

"Dressing the hair." At Charity's horrified look, the modiste said with a frown, "Surely you are not considering pairing my creation with"—she waved her hand at Charity's topknot—"*that*. It would be like serving English wine with French cuisine: an absolute insult to art."

"It'll just be a snip here and there," Helena said in a reassuring tone. "Don't worry, we won't let the signore get carried away."

Charity gave a hesitant nod. In for a penny, she supposed.

Madame Rousseau snapped her fingers at an assistant, who helped Charity back into her regular clothes. Another assistant gathered up the bridal gown, traveling dress, and unmentionables that made up Charity's trousseau. Looking at the pile, Charity bit her lip; Percy had been far too generous. As if sensing her disquiet, Percy winked, placed a finger to her lips, and followed the modiste out of the dressing room before Charity could say anything.

"Come have a seat," Marianne said. "Helena and I wish to have a little chat with you."

Charity did as she was asked. "What would you like to discuss?"

Marianne smoothed the skirts of her white and green striped carriage dress. "It's not so much what *we'd* like to discuss, but what questions *you* might have for us."

Charity blinked. "Er, questions?"

Helena leaned forward. "The thing of it is, dear, you've grown up without a mama. And mamas are typically a young lady's source of advice concerning ... marital matters." The marchioness paused as understanding caused Charity's cheeks to warm. "Marianne and I would like to give you the opportunity to express any concerns and curiosities you might have. Being married ladies, we have some, er, information that you might find useful on your wedding night."

"There's no aphrodisiac like knowledge," Marianne said.

"What's an aphrodisiac?" Charity said.

Marianne slid Helena an amused look. "She has a lot to learn."

Over the next half an hour, Charity discovered that truer words were never spoken. Being a sensible sort, she listened with keen concentration as the facts of married life were described to her. By the end of the lecture, all three of them were pink-cheeked.

"Well," Marianne said, fanning herself, "I do believe you're now the most informed virgin in all of Christendom. Any last questions?"

Charity's head was spinning. Yet she couldn't deny that her newfound knowledge did lessen her anxiety ... and provided her with greater confidence to greet the intimacies ahead. She'd already been determined to be the best wife she could; now she had some specific strategies with which to do so.

One can never have too many tools in one's sewing box, she thought prosaically.

"Thank you," she said. "I've got it all down, I think."

Lady Helena laughed. "Poor Mr. Fines. He won't know what hit him."

"Case of the jitters?" Nicholas said in a low voice. "Don't worry —'tis perfectly natural."

"I'm not nervous," Paul muttered.

"In that case, I'd suggest not tapping your foot like a debutante waiting for her first dance."

Devil and damn. Paul stilled his foot. His nerves, however, refused to quiet. Who could blame them, given that his own wedding ceremony was about to take place?

Morning light filtered into the elegantly appointed drawing room of the Harteford's townhouse. The place had been done up for the occasion, festooned with flowers and swaths of white gauze.

The intimate gathering included family and friends, all seated facing the front of the room where he, Nicholas, and the minister stood. His mother and Percy waved at him from the first row, and he managed a nod back.

Next to him, the rotund minister was dressed in ceremonial robes, smiling beatifically—and well the chap ought, given the king's ransom Paul had paid for the special license. He'd insisted on reimbursing Nick, for the use of the Harteford title to obtain said hasty license was favor enough.

Hasty. License.

Out of nowhere, a voice whispered in his head, *Act in haste, repent in leisure.*

Blast it, when had his inner monologue started spouting aphorisms? The restless feeling in him grew. His stomach, empty except for the carafe of coffee he'd downed earlier, churned uneasily.

"Easy, lad. Fellows get married every day," Nicholas said in an undertone.

Yes, but it wasn't some deuced fool standing there at the moment—it was *him.* He, Paul Fines, who'd never done anything right in his life, was going to plead his troth to a young, innocent girl who obviously didn't know what she was getting herself into. So what if he'd saved her once or twice? He'd landed her in trouble just as often. So what if they got along and enjoyed each other's company? He'd irked her more than once and was bound to annoy her again in the future; he seemed to have a talent for it.

And so what if kissing her was the hottest, most sensual experience of his entire life?

He was supposed to stay in check, wasn't he? Wasn't that his plan? Convince her to marry him (check), be a good husband (likelihood debatable), and, above all, stay in control (in serious question at present moment). The realization slapped him in the face: he'd been so intent upon wooing Charity that he'd only focused on the first item on his list. Now the other two requirements loomed.

What if he bollixed this up? He'd never been a husband before.

Worse yet, what if his neck-or-nothing self raised its ugly head again? The business with Rosalind had nearly killed him; he couldn't go through being a lunatic again. Nor did he wish to expose Charity to his true demented self.

And what if he failed to keep Sparkler's in business? What if he failed at boxing? What if, at the end of the day, he proved ... unworthy of her?

Once they were married, she would be stuck with him. This wasn't some casual affair they could put an end to—this was *until death do us part.*

Bloody, deuced, buggering *hell*. He had to resist the urge to drag his hands though hair that his valet had slaved over for the occasion. That and bolting straight out the double doors. Toward freedom and then ... what? The question stopped him in his tracks.

Where would he go? What all important business did he have to attend to?

What better place did he have to be ... than here?

Here, facing his responsibilities and his future as a man.

Here, surrounded by his family and friends.

Here, waiting for the girl—no, *woman,* for surely their embraces had proved her as such—whose quiet charm and sweet loyalty held the promise of purpose and stability, and, aye, mayhap even happiness.

Beneath his dove grey morning coat, his heartbeat suddenly calmed. The urge to flee subsided. Two simultaneous facts struck him: he did indeed have the deuced jitters ... and he'd just faced them down like any rational man would. He, Paul Fines, had acted *sensibly*. The relief was sharp, cooling. Mayhap his problems weren't as incurable as he believed. Mayhap with Charity's steady influence, he could change for the better.

He would work to keep Sparkler's afloat. He would train hard, win the Fancy's Championship. He would prove to everyone—

himself included—that he wasn't an imposter, but the genuine article. A winner in every respect.

The doors parted, and Paul's breathing hitched. Not from panic this time, but ... wonder.

Christ above, what had happened to Charity?

A collective murmur rose from the audience as she entered the room. He blinked, yet the enchanted creature did not vanish, though she seemed fully capable of doing so being made of moonbeams and flowers, her eyes sparkling with all the shades of magic. This nymph of forest and stream ambled toward him, her lustrous, wavy hair threaded with gilded leaves, her complexion as dewy as a snowdrop at dawn. Her gown swirled with gentle sensuality around her sylph-like form, and his heart began to drum in a wild, primitive rhythm.

Was this truly his bride?

She arrived at his side. "Hello, Mr. Fines."

At her greeting, tinged with the sweetest uncertainty, he knew that she *was* his Charity. For all that he'd been fascinated and aroused by her hidden depths, he'd never envisioned her quite like this. It wasn't a transformation, precisely—more a revelation of who she was. A peeling away of layers. She still wasn't classically beautiful ... she was so much more.

Radiant, inside and out.

"Hello, sweeting," he said in awe.

Hearing a grumble, he wrenched his gaze from his bride to the man on whose arm she'd floated in. If he needed further proof that this faerie princess was indeed Charity, then the troll at her side confirmed it. Uriah Sparkler's expression was as black as his ill-fitting coat. He looked prepared for doomsday rather than the happy occasion of his daughter's marriage.

"Are we ready to proceed?" the minister asked.

Paul's eyes returned to Charity, and her shy nod banished the rest of his concerns. Whatever future they faced, they would face it together. He took her hand, and her fingers linked with his.

Clearing his throat, the minister opened his leather-bound Common Book and recited the fateful words.

"Dearly beloved, we are gathered together here in the sight of God, and in the face of these witnesses, to join together this Man and this Woman in holy Matrimony ..."

Chapter Eighteen

The wedding ceremony and breakfast passed in a heady blur for Charity. Though her habit was to avoid attention, for once she didn't mind the felicitations and compliments on her good looks. Partly this was because these were offered by her dearest friends, but mostly it was because she didn't occupy center stage alone. Her husband stood at her side. At times, she was tempted to pinch herself to make sure that it wasn't a dream.

But, no, she didn't imagine the warmth of his hand at her waist as they stood together receiving the guests. Or the way he'd leaned halfway through the breakfast to whisper in her ear, "Have I told you how beautiful you are, Mrs. Fines?" Any lady less sensible than she might have swooned and landed face first in the asparagus soufflé. As it was, her cheeks flushed to the degree that Mr. Bellinger, one of her husband's rakehell friends, cried out, "Demme, the bride's blushing, and it ain't even the wedding night yet! Always said you were a lucky dog, Fines! A toast—to your good fortune!"

With so many toasts and farewells—including a tearful hug from her bosom chum and a stiff nod from her father—it was past noon by the time she and Mr. Fines changed into their traveling clothes and boarded his carriage for their weeklong wedding trip. Luckily, their destination was only a few hours away; as a wedding gift, the Kents had offered up a stay at their cottage located in the picturesque Berkshire countryside.

Charity barely noticed the passage of time for Mr. Fines entertained her the entire way with his clever wit and amusing anecdotes. He seemed to take special delight in bantering with her. He managed to tease blushes and giggles out of her as well as a daring riposte or two. Where had the awkward, sensible Charity Sparkler gone? But she wasn't Charity Sparkler any longer, was she? She was Charity Fines.

Mrs. Paul Fines.

Her joy was the sweet pain of a lanced boil. Years of desperate longing had finally come to a head. Well, *almost* to a head. The fact that had been hovering in her awareness the entire journey— that they were alone, married, and heading toward their wedding night—took front and center in her thoughts. And mayhap in his as well, for a sudden tension descended upon the cabin. She couldn't distinguish the galloping of the horses from that of her heart.

The wedding night advice she'd been given echoed in her head.

"Be yourself," Helena had said. "Be honest, and don't hide your desires."

"Gentleman want to be wanted," Marianne had said, "and here's a simple rule of thumb: whatever feels good to you will feel good to him."

Charity had never been missish, and the talk had reinforced her belief that the act of physical love could deepen the marital bond. And she yearned to be as close to Mr. Fines as possible. Though Miss Drummond claimed the love of his heart and soul, she, Charity, had a shot at the rest of him. *More* than a fair shot, he'd said. She peered upward through her lashes at him, all virile lines and masculine grace. So handsome that her heart ached.

"Penny for your thoughts, sweeting," he said with a lazy smile. "Or have I worn you out with all my chatter?"

"I'll never tire of listening to you," she said.

"Then I'm a lucky man, indeed." The husky timbre of his voice made her shiver. "But have a care, sweeting: your honeyed words may go to my head—and then there'll be no stopping this talented tongue of mine."

Heavens. The cabin turned sweltering. She wet her lips.

His eyes followed the movement and grew heavy-lidded.

At that instant, the carriage slowed.

"Just when things were getting interesting," he said with a wicked wink.

Indeed.

The driver opened the door, and Mr. Fines exited first and handed her down. As her half-boots touched the pebbled walk, she looked around her, let out a gasp of delight.

"How beautiful," she exclaimed.

"Yes," he said, his gaze on her face.

All too aware of the driver's presence, she ducked her head and walked on. Mr. Fines reached the garden gate before she did, unlatching it for her, and as she stepped through the trellised arch covered in yellow roses, her senses drank in the magic of the Kents' cottage. Blanketed in ivy, the snug abode possessed a rustic, tumbledown charm. Its cheerful windows overlooked overgrown hedgerows, and a symphony of crickets and birds accompanied the deepening pink of dusk.

As Mr. Fines instructed the groom on where to set their things, Charity investigated the premises and found the interior just as cozy and welcoming. Besides the kitchen, the cottage boasted a front parlor with overstuffed furniture that invited one to sit back and relax, a small dining area, and three bedchambers. The sight of the large tester bed in the master suite made her tummy flutter.

Everything in good time, she told herself.

She removed her gloves, her plain gold band catching the last rays of the day. It gleamed softly, a promise of things to come. Mr. Fines wore a matching, thicker version of the ring. With a wistful smile, she set her reticule on the vanity before returning to the main room. Her husband stood next to the dining table, examining the large wicker hamper on its surface. He handed her a folded note.

"Found it on the dining room table," he said by way of explanation.

"*Dear Mr. and Mrs. Fines,*" she read aloud and with secret thrill, "*I hope you find everything to your satisfaction. Mr. Kent and I have spent many happy hours here, and it is our most sincere wish that you, too, will experience the enchantment of Chudleigh Crest. I've arranged for a girl from the village to bring your meals and take care of the household tasks. Newlyweds have no need to bother with anything but each other.*"

Pausing, she slanted a quick look at Mr. Fines, whose lips curved in amusement.

She read on. "*If you should bore of the cottage, the shops down the lane boast a delicious rose-petal jam and a surprisingly good milliner (I never leave without a half-dozen hats.) Mr. Kent adds that since there is more to life than shopping—being a man, he would think that—you might like to explore the nearby parks and a stream where the locals go to fish. With that, we bid you adieu and fond wishes for your stay. Yours, The Kents.*"

"How thoughtful of them," Charity murmured.

"I'll say," Mr. Fines said, peering into the hamper. "There's food enough here to feed an army. Hungry?"

She shook her head. "The wedding breakfast was rather elaborate."

"I'm not wanting for food either." Reaching out, he cupped her cheek, his touch awakening every nerve ending. "What would you like to do, darling? We could stay up and chat some more. Or perhaps given the long journey you are ready," he murmured, "to retire?"

He was giving her a choice.

Heart hammering, she whispered, "I think I'm ready to retire."

He took up her hand as casually as if they went off to bed together every night. "Good. I'll come along and play lady's maid then, shall I?"

Chapter Nineteen

Closing the door to the bedchamber, Paul felt the simmering anticipation in his blood rise another notch. All day, Charity's closeness had teased his senses —her clean scent in his nostrils, her supple waist beneath his hand. And alone with her in that carriage? His ceaseless babble had served not only the purpose of putting her at ease but also that of keeping himself in check. To prevent himself from doing what he had truly wished to do.

For he had plans and they didn't involve tossing up his new bride's skirts and having his way with her in a carriage. He had more finesse than that.

Catching the way Charity's glance darted to the bed, he hid a smile. Poor chit must be a bundle of nerves. He couldn't blame her. Even he experienced a small twinge of unease, which was patently ridiculous. Though he hadn't much experience with virgins—alright, *any*—he knew all about female pleasure. Bedding his wife was the one husbandly activity he could approach with confidence. Thus far, Charity had experienced only fully clothed, vertical pleasure with him; she hadn't an inkling of his skill under more ideal circumstances. What he could do to her once she was naked and horizontal beneath him ...

His blood got even hotter. An eager pulse took up in his groin.

All in good time.

"Nervous, darling?" he asked softly.

"A little. I'm not used to being alone with a gentleman in a bedchamber."

"Just in libraries and follies," he said with a smile.

"Only with you, sir."

"I am glad to hear it." He wound a finger around one of her loose curls, tugging gently. "We're eons past formality at this point. Call me Paul, will you?"

"Paul," she said tremulously.

"Charity," he whispered back. "Now be a love and turn around so I can help you with your frock."

Cheeks rosy, she obeyed, and he began to work on the hooks at the back of her dress. His knuckles brushed against the elegant curve of her spine, and satisfaction rolled through him when she shivered. He *adored* her response to him. Tonight, he meant to ease away her mantle of maidenly modesty and fan her inner flames even higher.

A sudden image penetrated his mind's eye: Charity, her gleaming hair spread over the coverlet, her slender white back arching as he feasted on her pussy, licking her until she spent against his mouth ... He had to bite back a groan.

Don't rush your fences, man. Remember she's an innocent. Go slow.

Breathing in, he concentrated on the task of undoing her gown and corset and not scaring his new wife witless with the more advanced aspects of lovemaking. The initiation was very important, he reasoned, and this first night was to be about tender consideration. Later on, mayhap in a few months, he could ease her into more adventurous pursuits. But for now: the basics.

When he loosened the last string, she turned, clutching the garments to her front.

"I can, um, do the rest myself," she said.

"Call if you need me," he said.

She nodded and darted toward her dressing screen. He made his way toward the partition on the other side of the room. He inspected his portmanteau; rarely did he travel without a valet, but Bromley would have proven a fifth wheel on this particular excursion. Thus, sacrifices had to be made. After Paul shed his clothes, he paused to contemplate his wardrobe choices.

His habit was to just throw on a dressing gown to lounge in until bedtime. Then he'd take that off, too, for he slept in the buff. But now he had Charity's sensibilities to consider. He was quite certain that gentlemen did not carry out their wedding night activities stark naked. A glance down at his bobbing equipment confirmed his hunch: the old boy's enthusiasm might be off-putting to a gently bred virgin.

With a martyred sigh, he pulled a billowing nightshirt over his head before donning his robe.

He returned to the center of the room—and halted as if he'd hit an invisible wall. Which would have been no less shocking than the sight before his eyes.

"Holy Mother of God," he breathed.

His blushing bride said, "Do I look, um, alright?"

For once in his life, he was incapable of speech. It was as if she'd delivered him a swift uppercut. He saw stars and when those cleared, the vision remained: a sensual nymph, her hair a wild, free mass around her piquant face, her lithe form clad in a slip of leaf-green silk. A cherry satin bow rested like a butterfly upon each bare shoulder; those ribbons appeared to be the only thing holding up the sleeveless, backless scrap of scandal.

"The dressmaker said these were all the rage in Paris," she said, her face now as rosy as the bows, "and Percy insisted that I have one. But I packed my old night rail. I'll just go change—"

He was there in a second, his hand cupping her nape to prevent her from fleeing. "Like hell you will, sweetheart. And for God's sake, don't mention my sister at a time like this. Not when the sight of you has me as wound as a clock, and I ache just to look at you."

Her long curly lashes swept up. "Ache ... in a good way?"

"I've never known a sweeter pain," he said with feeling. "By Jove, *look* at you."

Unable to help himself, he skimmed his hand down her neck and the smooth line of her spine left bare by the negligee, God love it. Her skin, he marveled, was softer than anything he'd ever touched. His fingers splayed at the alluring dip of her back, and, in an easy movement, he swept her into his arms and laid her on the bed.

Then he stared at her in awe.

Her wavy, hazelnut tresses fanned over the bedspread. Her bosom rose and fell beneath the deep V of her neckline, her taut nipples poking out against the thin silk. At that erotic sight, his cock, already hard, burgeoned to new proportions. Hell, he'd hardly even touched her yet.

Stay in control of the match. Don't get knocked out in the first bloody round.

"Don't be frightened, love." Leaning over, he brushed his lips against the thrumming pulse of her throat, the irresistible hollows above her collar bones. At her hitched breath, he murmured, "We'll go slow. We have all night."

"Actually ... would it be possible to, um, pick up the pace?"

His head jerked up. Make that both of them.

"The truth is ... I've been waiting all day for you to kiss me again," his wife said shyly.

With that utterance, she ripped the reins from his grasp. Wild horses couldn't stop him now. With a growl, he took what was rightfully his.

Her mouth met his, open and hot. Delicious. Only their third kiss, yet they fit together like they had done this a hundred times. A thousand. He would never tire of her taste, as hot and pure as a drink of sunshine. Her fingers threaded in his hair, and her sweetly eager touch aroused him more than all the practiced caresses he'd known before. The past faded. There was only here and now. Only Charity, his wife, her honest fire burning him up alive.

He broke away to drag kisses down her throat. He licked her exposed décolleté and heard that little hitch again, the sound that told him he was doing everything right. He curved his palm around one silk-covered breast, his blood rushing at the delicate heft. When his thumb grazed the not-so-subtle tip, she made a little sound that was a moan, a sigh, music to his ears. So he did it again. And again, until she arched into the caress and he knew she was ready for more.

He bent and suckled her through the silk.

"Goodness," she gasped.

"Like that, love? How about this?" He traced the stiff little peak with his tongue.

Her fingers dug into his scalp; her head fell back against the pillows.

Good answer. He untied first one and then the other cherry bow. It was like unwrapping a present ... and *what* a present. He tossed the green silk aside, feasting his eyes upon every sensuous detail. Her milky skin, delicately flushed. The pretty, modest curve of her breasts contrasted by the proud jut of her pink nipples. Her tiny waist and gentle hips. And just below ...

His blood pulsed in his veins. As if sensing its target, his cock thrust like a steel lance against his nightshirt. Devil and damn, she had the *prettiest* pussy, nutmeg curls glossy against her pale thighs. His mouth watered.

Running a hand along her hip, he said, "You're gorgeous."

"I'm relieved you think so," was her breathy reply. "Now that you've looked your fill ... might I do the same?"

Hell, yes.

Her curiosity inflamed him. Rising to his knees beside her, he made short work of his robe and yanked the infernal nightshirt over his head. Wide-eyed, she studied his naked form, her scrutiny like a touch. Her gaze swept from his face to his shoulders and chest, down the quivering ridges of his stomach, all the way to his cock. Her eyes got even bigger, and he could see why: the randy monster was prodigiously large at the moment, the shaft thick and pulsing, the dark head mottled—and, damn, weeping with arousal.

To an experienced female, his ready-for-action member would have elicited anticipation, but for a virgin on her wedding night? What the bloody hell was he *thinking*?

"Oh, Paul." Her wobbly voice made him fumble for his robe. "You're so ... so ..."—his fingers closed over the damned garment— "... *magnificent.*"

His hand stilled.

"Like a sculpture," she said. "Only finer for although you're made of flesh and blood, you have none of its imperfections."

Well. His chest puffed.

Then he fell upon her like a ravaging wolf.

His lips closed over her nipple, this time taking it deep into his mouth. Her grip tightened on his shoulders as he flicked the sweet bud with his tongue then suckled it some more. Her moan told him she liked that, and, by God, so did he. He kissed her delicate breast all over before licking his way over to the other side, where its delightful twin awaited him.

With a happy sigh, he lavished similar attention on this tit while his fingers plucked and played with the nipple he'd left behind. When she moved restlessly against him, he knew she was ready for more. So he kissed her hot and deep as his fingers trailed over the fine grooves of her ribcage and the smooth valley of her belly. He dipped his finger into her silky nest and groaned at what he found.

Her cunny was already wet, drenched, and hotter than the fires of hell itself.

Maidenly instinct must have kicked in, then, for her thighs locked together. He didn't mind. Trapped between those smooth silken limbs, his hand was exactly where he wanted it to be.

"This won't hurt, sweeting," he murmured. "In fact, if you let me, I can make you feel so very good. Believe me?"

Her eyes looked so trustingly into his.

"Yes," she whispered, and her legs slackened.

"Good girl. I don't ever want you to be afraid of what happens between us." He found her pearl, and when he slowly diddled the plump bud, her breath made a hitching sound. "That's nice, isn't it? 'Tis your pearl and what a lovely jewel it is. How does it feel when I stroke it this way?"

Her throaty sigh sent a quiver up his cockstand.

"How about this?"

Her hips wriggled, her pussy pressing against his hand. "Oh, Paul ..."

"Christ, that's good," he breathed. "I think you're ready for more."

He slid a finger down her folds and between her shy, moist lips. When he found the entrance to her grotto, his heart thumped, more moisture leaking from his cockhead. Ye Gods, she was tight. Perspiration dotted his brow as he ventured forward, breaching her with the tip of his middle finger. When she stiffened, he bent to suckle her nipples again. Within moments, she relaxed enough for him to sink his digit inside.

Pulsing heat gripped him.

Holding onto his self-control, he rasped, "Alright, darling?"

"Yes ... I think so." Her eyes had a glazed look.

With tender care, he fingered her. Her flowing dew eased the way and made his lungs burn with anticipation. When he saw no signs of discomfort, he drove deeper and added another finger. His excitement soared as her hips began to move, her pussy taking his penetration so thoroughly, with such sweet, lush abandon, that he knew she was ready for his cock.

First, he wanted to watch as she took her initial flight over pleasure's precipice.

Stroking her bold pearl, he continued to plunge into her hole.

"Oh ... oh *my* ..." she panted.

"Come for me, darling," he said.

Her eyes shut as she obeyed. Her cries—the sweetest he'd ever heard—erupted with passion worthy of an opera. In the next heartbeat, he was between her thighs. He shuddered as he dragged his bulging tip along her slick folds. With his cock coated in her cream, he notched it to her slit and drove forward. Past the initial resistance, her snug sheath gave way, her aftermath rippling over his shaft, the luscious squeeze wringing a groan from him. Soon he was buried to the balls, wrapped in the hottest, most generous embrace of his life.

He was inside his wife. His. Wife.

Pleasure deepened, rooting in his chest. Triumph and possessiveness rolled through him. Taking his weight on his arms, he rasped, "Love, look at me."

Her lashes lifted, and then he was drowning in the limpid depths of her eyes. In the amazing ardor he saw there, so natural and real. Before he could ascertain her comfort, she lifted her palm to his jaw; with that tender permission he knew that everything was alright. More than alright. His sweet nymph wanted him as much as he wanted her.

His control, so tightly held, unraveled, and then he was moving, plunging deeper and deeper into her welcoming depths. Arousal poured over him when she began to take up the movement. Her hips learned his rhythm, lifting in sweet synchrony. So perfect, so natural, he was dazed by the easy joy of it. He saw the desire building again in her eyes, and he gritted his teeth, trying to hold on. She was so wet, so tight. The pressure in his bollocks grew, and he fought to hold back, to give her another climax before he found his own.

He grasped her knee, hitching it high against his hip.

Each thrust of his cock grazed her pearl, and her head flung back on a cry. He wanted to kiss the sweet sounds from her lips. So he did, swallowing her moans as she came for him once more, then pouring his own groans right back as his crisis raged over him. His seed boiled up his shaft, shooting out with such force that his teeth clattered, his hips grinding desperately as he gave her everything he had ...

He collapsed atop his wife, breathing hard.

Her breath puffed softly against his jaw, her fingers brushing his nape. Time suspended; he could have stayed that way forever. For even as pleasure began to ebb, peace took its place and a satisfaction he'd never felt before.

Even better than winning a match, he thought drowsily.

His eyes grew heavy, and he barely had the wherewithal to roll off her. He tucked her against him and dragged the coverlet over them both.

She made a soft sound, snuggling deeper into him.

A perfect fit, came the hazy thought. *My wife ... mine.*

His eyelids closed, and he swirled and vanished into the sweet fog.

Chapter Twenty

Charity awakened sometime later to a flickering fire in the hearth and an even warmer presence next to her in bed. *My husband*, she thought in wonder. Mr. Fines—no, *Paul*—lay on his side, head propped up on his left hand where his wedding band gleamed. When their gazes met, his mouth tipped up, and an answering smile formed on hers.

They'd done it. They were well and truly married.

"Hello, sleepyhead. Didn't know if you were done in until the morning." His thumb swept over her bottom lip. The casual intimacy made her heart skip a beat.

"I must have dozed off. But I'm feeling quite awake now," she said. It was true. Being with him like this, snug in their intimate cocoon, she didn't want to miss a thing.

"Good. Because there's something I forgot to do earlier," he said.

Thinking of his thorough lovemaking, she couldn't imagine *anything* he'd missed.

He must have read her thoughts because he laughed. "What a wicked little baggage I've married, to be sure."

Flushing with sudden embarrassment, she averted her gaze.

Had she been too wanton? Helena and Marianne had said husbands preferred honesty, and so she hadn't tried to hide her response to him. In truth, she thought with growing worry, she wasn't certain she *could* conceal her desire for him.

He tipped up her chin. "What's going on in that head of yours?"

"Nothing," she said quickly.

She couldn't bring herself to admit her concerns. To ask Paul what he'd thought of her ... in bed. For her, their lovemaking had been magical, but she wasn't experienced like he was. By reputation, he was a connoisseur in these matters, and she'd seen for herself the kind of women who'd attracted his attention. Ladies far more beautiful and worldly than she ...

"On to your wedding present, then," he said.

This took her from her worries.

"You ... you have something for me?" she said.

With a wink, he got out of bed, treating her to a spectacular view of his backside. *Now that*, she thought wistfully, *is the only present I need*. But she had her own surprise and went to fetch it. By the time he returned, she was back in bed wearing her robe and holding out a small package she'd painstakingly wrapped in paper and twine.

"I have a gift for you, too," she said.

Climbing in next to her, he said with a grin, "You shouldn't have"—and snatched it from her.

Charity watched with amusement as he proceeded to tear off the wrapping with the glee of a boy on Christmas Day. It was a Fines trait, this playful love of presents, for Percy was the same way. Paul withdrew the set of handkerchiefs. She'd chosen the finest quality linen and embroidered his initials upon each one. He examined them in silence.

Growing nervous, she said, "I hope you like the colors that I used. They're meant to match your outfits."

He ran a finger over the monogram on the top handkerchief.

Using gold silk thread, she'd sewn the *AF* in a bold, masculine script and set it within a diamond-shaped frame.

"Your handiwork is exquisite. I shall carry these with pride. Thank you, sweetheart."

The appreciation in his eyes made her feel adrift on a warm, blue sea.

"You're welcome," she whispered.

He deposited a small, black velvet box into her palm. "Your turn. It's a belated gift, actually."

With care, she lifted the lid, and … her breath stopped.

There, on a bed of white satin, lay a ring of unimaginable splendor. A flawless opal cabochon blazed at the center, flames of iridescent green, blue, and gold dancing upon its surface. Surrounding the opal was a circle of pearls, each one snowy and flawless.

Emotion clogged Charity's throat.

"Happy engagement," Paul said, "though I'm afraid it's too late for you now, Mrs. Fines. Would have gotten the ring sooner, but given that our engagement lasted a blink of an eye, and I had to look high and low for something that suited you, I hope I can be forgiven for being late."

She still couldn't find the words.

"And I have another confession to make," he went on. "The ring came from a competitor. No choice, I'm afraid. A first-rate opal is hard to find—never mind one brilliant enough to match your eyes."

A sound finally did escape her: a sob.

"Christ, you don't like it?" He frowned. "Well, there's no need for a leaky bucket, we can find you another ring—"

"I *love* it." She threw her arms around his neck, planting her face against his hard chest. His arms closed instantly around her as she wept, "It's the most b-beautiful ring I've ever s-seen. In the entire *world*."

"Then why the waterworks?"

"Because," she said between sniffles, "you thought *me* ... worthy of it."

A pause. He drew back, a notch between his brows. "Well, of course you are. You're worth a thousand such baubles. Why would you think otherwise?"

His incredulous tone almost started her tears again. She couldn't convey what the ring meant—to her, the weed, on whom adornment was wasted. For whom nothing but plainness and modesty would do. It was fantastical enough that this beautiful god-like man had given her his name; for him to give her this ring, to say that in his eyes she was worthy of this treasure ... she was overwhelmed.

"This is the most precious gift anyone has given me," she managed. "Thank you, Paul."

He gave her a tender smile. "You're welcome. Let's see it on, shall we?"

Taking her hand, he slid the ring onto her finger above her wedding band. The ring flashed fire and magic, too beautiful to be real. Charity knew that she would cherish it forever.

Her vision grew blurry again. She dabbed desperately at her eyes with the bed sheet. "I don't know what's wrong with me. I'm never a watering pot."

"It's a wedding night tradition, I'm told. The bride's prerogative after the shock wears off." His expression grew thoughtful, and, winding one of her loose waves around his finger, he said, "Speaking of shock, I was rather astounded myself when I saw this hair of yours in its full glory. Why in blazes do you hide such an asset? Other females pay their *friseurs* a pretty penny to achieve such perfection."

More praise. She didn't know how much more she could take.

"It's unmanageable ... and immodest," she tried to explain.

"Who told you that?"

"My father." Guilt stabbed her at how disloyal that sounded. She hastened to add, "He raised me on his own, after my mama died. It wasn't easy, what with the shop and all his responsibilities. Some fathers might have given up an infant daughter, but not mine." She'd been so lucky, having a papa who let her stay by his side. "He's always done his best by me, and for that I shall forever be grateful."

"He's the one who ought to be grateful to have a daughter like you." Sifting his hands through her hair, Paul said, "No more gunk and nun's knots. Your hair is beautiful, a part of you, and as your husband 'tis my privilege to see it in its natural state."

"I suppose ... I could wear a looser style." The simple twist and fall of her coiffure at the wedding ceremony *had* felt better. It was nice not to have the tautness at her temples and the itchy paste against her scalp.

"That's my girl," he said.

Tension lingered, however, and she knew that more than her hair was at issue. She didn't know how to address the mutual animosity that had sprung up between her father and new husband; she found it difficult to speak up for one without feeling as though she were betraying the other.

Awkwardly, she said, "Please don't think badly of Father. He's just worried about Sparkler's. And, of course, our wedding took him by surprise."

"There's an understatement," Paul said.

"He'll come around, you'll see. The two of you just need to spend time together." She pushed away her unease. Paul was so wonderful—her father had to see it eventually. "And when you help Father make Sparkler's a success, he'll be so pleased."

A shadow fell across Paul's face.

"I meant after the tournament," she said quickly. "Your boxing must come first, of course. I know how important winning the title is to you."

"It isn't that." He hesitated. "I just hope that I'll be able to help make the shop a success."

She looked at him in surprise. "Of course you will."

Over the years, she'd observed that Paul was a man who, once he set his mind and heart to a thing, did not falter. It was why he excelled at pugilism; it was why he loved Rosalind Drummond ... she shook away the thought. She wasn't going to ruin the night's happiness.

He cupped her cheek, the pad of his thumb following the slope of her cheekbone. "Such a loyal thing, aren't you?" he murmured. "I hope to God I don't disappoint."

"You couldn't," she said. "You won't."

Something drifted through his eyes like clouds over a clear sky. She wondered what he was thinking and would have asked, but his lips were suddenly on hers, banishing further thoughts from her head. When his tongue touched her lips, she opened to him immediately, hungry for the wordless intimacy, hungry again for his kiss.

Laying her back, he murmured, "Sore, sweeting?"

"No." She rocked her head against the pillows.

His eyes were heated. "I'll be gentle. And it'll be even better this time, I promise." He caught the tip of one breast, lightly pinching, and her insides melted like wax.

"Is that even possible?" she managed.

He gave her a rakish grin ... and proceeded to show her that it was.

Chapter Twenty-One

The morning after her wedding night, Charity woke at her usual hour just before sunrise. Seeing that Paul's long lashes rested against his lean cheeks, she just lay there admiring him. She loved how boyish he looked with his angelic features relaxed and his hair tousled. She had to restrain herself from brushing back his willful forelock. She didn't want to disturb him. When she tried to slip from the bed, however, his arm snaked around her waist.

"Where are you going?" His drowsy murmur filled her ear.

"To put a kettle on," she said breathlessly. "I'll make your breakfast."

"You've wed a slugabed and one who enjoys company. Now get over here, wench,"—he yanked her playfully against him—"and I'll show you what I want for breakfast."

His wandering hands made her giggle until he brought her bottom flush against his front. Then she wasn't laughing anymore. Clearly, he *was* awake ... a particular part of him fully alert. A hum began in her blood, and what progressed next, whilst still new to her, made a convincing case for lingering in bed.

Afterward, she dozed off and woke, disoriented, to find that it was nearly noon. Paul, freshly shaven and in his shirtsleeves, sauntered into the room with a tray, explaining that the maid from the village had already come and gone. Propping himself next to her on the bed, he began to feed her from the array of foods he'd brought: thickly buttered bread, crisp bacon, juicy slices of tomato. When she protested that she couldn't eat another bite, he handed her a cup of tea—milk and no sugar, the way she preferred—and polished off the food whilst she sipped her beverage with a dazed kind of joy.

What had she done to deserve such a husband?

The days passed with a surreal quality. Charity was used to being busy, but here at the cottage there were no tasks to complete, no chores to do. Nothing on the agenda but getting to know the man she'd loved from afar for so long.

It was remarkable to her, how at ease they were becoming with each other. Or rather, how at ease Paul was with himself—which, in turn, began eroding some of her natural awkwardness. He was undoubtedly a sensual creature and seemed to relish physical contact, touching her often and not just during lovemaking. They spent lazy hours curled up together on the parlor sofa. While she worked on her embroidery, he made a pillow of her lap, reading or napping. When they went to explore the outdoors, he kept a hand on her waist, his stance almost ... possessive, she thought wistfully.

If their lovemaking brought them physically closer, their talking fostered a growing intimacy of another kind. One night, as they lay facing one another in bed, they discussed the topic of their childhoods. She described growing up at Sparkler's, her desire to help her father, who worked so hard despite his ill health. She also admitted to Paul how much she'd missed having a mother and the silly dreams she'd secretly woven about Mary Sparkler someday returning. Surfacing, like a long-lost survivor of a shipwreck.

Paul returned her confidences, sharing his own past.

"I always knew Papa loved me," he said. "In retrospect, I think that made things worse."

She frowned, not understanding. "Worse?"

"Yes, because what did I do to deserve such devotion? Jeremiah Fines started with nothing and earned his successes and the admiration of all. I, on the other hand, was given everything—and look what I've accomplished," he said grimly. "I nearly destroyed my father's company, endangered Percy, and gambled away my accounts. I'm living off the dividends of my father's hard work. He was right: I am a disappointment."

"You're not a disappointment. Far from." She touched his taut jaw. "You've so many talents I don't know where to begin."

"You only say that because you've spent the last three days in bed with me."

"I'm being serious." She was getting to know him, the way he defaulted to wit when matters got difficult or unpleasant. "You've always protected Percy—she looks up to you ever so much, even now." Encouraged by the easing of the lines around his eyes, she said, "You're kind and clever, and people like to be around you. And you're the most honorable, most determined gentleman I've ever met."

"Sweeting, are you certain you have the right fellow?" he murmured.

"I know the man I married," she insisted. "For instance, look how well you've done with boxing: that's a culmination of hard work as well as talent. And when you win the tournament, everyone will see what a champion you are."

He studied her intently. "You won't mind being married to a prizefighter?"

She didn't mind his choice of profession, as long as he didn't get hurt. She wasn't keen, however, on the fact that his training would take him away from her so soon and for so long. She understood why he had to go ... but she would miss him. More so now, after these magical days together. She'd never known that she could feel this close to another. At times, she'd had to bite her lip to prevent imprudent words from spilling out, reminding herself that he didn't want messy emotions in their marriage.

She'd contented herself with learning as much as she could about Paul. As a result, she knew how important winning the championship was to him. She saw, perhaps more than he did, that boxing gave him purpose and a sense of self-worth. She prayed that he would emerge victorious—and was gripped with anxiety when she considered the alternative. If Paul lost ... how would he cope? His entire focus was on winning ...

For the most part, she managed to push her doubts aside. Her husband deserved her faith, so she would give it wholeheartedly.

Hiding her trepidation, she said, "I'll support you in whatever makes you happy."

"After the tournament, your father won't be able to get me out of the shop," he said.

She loved him all the more for keeping his promises to her. "The shop will be there when you return. As will I."

"Now that's a homecoming I'll look forward to." His eyes smiled into hers, and he curled his hand around her nape, drawing her mouth to his.

Over the past days and nights, she'd grown addicted to his kiss. To his masculine flavor, the bold sweep of his tongue. Her initial hesitancy about her wanton response had faded; she'd learned that he *liked* for her to participate in their lovemaking and, in fact, encouraged it with naughty (and rather stimulating) praise. So when he rolled her onto her back, she wound her arms around his neck, kissing him with the desire that flowed more and more freely within her.

Soon kissing wasn't enough.

They separated just long enough for him to drag the chemise over her head and toss his own dressing gown to the floor. Then he lay atop her once more, and she shivered at the hot, hard press of his member against her bare thigh. His lips wandered down her neck and over her bosom.

"I love kissing you here." His breath puffed against her erect nipple, making her shiver. "You've the prettiest tits. They have the pinkest, perkiest tips."

His approval thrilled her, especially since she'd always believed herself lacking in this area. "You don't think they're too small?" she said shyly.

"They're just right, darling. For instance, see how nicely they fit inside my mouth?"

Pleasure swirled in her veins as he mouthed her entire breast, then drew hard on the sensitive peak. He repeated the action on her other breast, and she whimpered, her fingers sliding into his thick, silky locks. He went back and forth until her blood pulsed with need. He peppered kisses over her ribcage, his lips burning down her belly. Before she could grasp the implication of this new direction, his hands clamped upon her thighs, spreading them, his mouth moving lower and ever closer to ...

Goodness, he can't mean to kiss me there!

A shocked moan broke from her as he did exactly that. His tongue delved into the most secret part of her, his grip on her legs preventing them from closing.

"Let me taste you, darling," he muttered. "I've been dying to know if your pussy is as sweet as the rest of you ..."

His hot breath and words fanned her flames. Her fingers burrowed into the bedclothes as he put his lips on the most intimate part of her body. Cheeks burning, she writhed in blissful agony as he licked and sucked, all the while praising her, telling her how delicious she was, how he'd never get enough of her honey, how he wanted to eat her forever.

Tension burgeoned in her. She could feel the tightening from her belly to her toes.

"Almost there, aren't you? Let's see if this will take you over," he growled.

The velvet flick of his tongue sent her hips bucking from the bed. He did it again and again, lashing her pearl with heated, wet strokes until she was whimpering, her fingers clutching his hair, holding him to the molten center of her being. Then it happened: the explosion that stole her breath, her very sanity.

"Yes," he groaned, "I can taste your sweet honey ..."

He continued to lick her until she lay limp, too sated to move. Only then did he enter her, filling her with a thick thrust that made her spent nerves flutter. She watched his face as he worked himself inside her; his cheekbones were flushed, his brows drawn in a look of pure pleasure. Exhilaration suffused her: *she* was giving him this. Eager for him to find satisfaction, she moved with him, urging him on.

He made a sound low in his throat, and all of a sudden, he pushed her knees back, spreading her legs wide. He drove into her, and her breath whooshed out as the altered angle allowed him to go deeper, harder. Upon impact, their bodies made a lewd, wet sound that made her blush and squirm with excitement.

"Alright, darling?" he rasped.

"Yes, oh yes, don't stop ..."

His nostrils flared. "Never. God, I *never* want to stop."

His chest heaved as he pounded into her. The weight of his bollocks smacked her sex, the heavy momentum making her gasp with delight. His jaw tautened, his smoldering eyes on her face. The strength and power of his rhythm sent her soaring into ecstasy once more. He joined her, groaning as he filled her with his jetting heat, with the sudden, dizzying knowledge that in this, at least, she could be the wife he wanted.

Chapter Twenty-Two

In the village a few days later, Paul watched with amusement as Charity bartered with a cheesemonger for a hunk of the local delicacy. Polite yet determined, his little wife went back and forth in earnest tones with the equally determined merchant. Paul found this practical streak of hers rather endearing; he, himself, never bothered to haggle over anything. And the ladies in his circle were equally blasé when it came to money: just one of Rosalind's hats had probably cost more than Charity's entire wardrobe combined.

Frowning, he caught himself. This was the first that he'd thought of his past love during the wedding trip; it made him feel oddly guilty. So he pushed the thought aside and focused on the pleasures of the present.

By Jove, there'd been many. Charity's passion surpassed his wildest dreams, and he'd never been a tame dreamer. They were getting on well outside the bedchamber, too—better than he'd even expected.

Of course, there were differences in their natures. She was careful with everything—for instance, saving their meal scraps for their village maid's pig farm—whilst he didn't give things like trash a second thought. She preferred quiet and shied away from attention whereas he liked the hustle and bustle of boisterous activity. Yesterday, he'd gone to join in a game of cricket with some local lads he'd met whilst she'd opted to stay in the cottage and work on her sewing.

He didn't mind their divergent ways because they always came back together in the end. What did bother him was when he felt a different kind of distance from her. She had a tendency to withdraw into her thoughts, and he couldn't read what was on her mind.

Was she worried about the shop, her father? Or perhaps she fretted over him going away to box or doubted his ability to help with Sparkler's or found him lacking in some way ...

Whenever he asked, she just smiled and said everything was fine.

Disquiet would cast a shadow over him. He had the vague, irrational sense that he'd done something wrong. That their present sunny idyll was too good to last ...

He shook off his doubts as she came toward him. She was such a fetching thing, he thought with a pang, a wood nymph hiding in plain clothing. For other than the stylish traveling dress compliments of Percy (Paul could hug his sister), Charity had only her own uninspiring gowns to wear. At least she'd left off the pomade: her hair gleamed beneath her old straw bonnet. Once they returned to London, he resolved to see her properly outfitted from head to toe.

He took her shopping basket and held the door open. "Got what you wanted?"

"Yes," she said, "and for two shillings less than what I was willing to pay."

Hiding a grin at the hint of smugness in her voice, he offered her his arm as they walked along the neat row of shops. "Where to next, Mrs. Fines?"

"I'm ready to head home if you are," she said.

He thought an afternoon session between the sheets quite the capital idea. "I like the way you think," he said huskily. "Your pleasure is my command."

She colored. "I was thinking of getting the cheese into a cool place. It'll melt in the sun."

"I'd like to melt in you, sweeting," he said for her ears only.

Though she ducked her head, he caught the sparkle in her eyes, and his blood rushed with anticipation. He was one lucky fellow, no doubt about it. He was about to hurry her along, when the next storefront caught his attention. The millinery that Mrs. Kent had mentioned. A notion came to him, so alluring that it put a rein on his lust.

He didn't have to wait until London to buy his wife a present.

"Let's take a look in here," he said.

"But I don't need any hats—"

Ignoring her protests, he led her inside.

The boutique's chic powder blue and gold interior belied its location in a country village. A few splendid specimens were set on pedestals so that the customer could see the hats from all angles. As Paul went to examine a white satin creation lined with pink fluted net, the proprietress emerged from the back. Her Parisien accent explained the *à la mode* establishment.

"*Bienvenue.* What may I assist *monsieur* and *madame* with today?"

"My wife needs a hat." Paul gestured at the white one. "I think this will do."

The milliner smiled. "*Monsieur* has an excellent eye."

Beside him, Charity said in an undertone, "Paul, I don't want it."

"Choose another then, sweeting," he said, smiling. "Any one you like. 'Tis my gift to you."

"I don't want any of them."

His smile faded at her somber expression. Why was she being difficult about this? He could see that her straw bonnet was worn at the edges, and there was a mended patch beneath the brim.

"Perhaps you need some time to view the merchandise?" the milliner suggested. "Ring if you need me." With French discretion, she disappeared behind the back curtain.

"What's the matter?" Paul said. "Don't you like any of the hats?"

"You don't need to waste money on frivolous things," Charity whispered. "We ought to save the funds for the future. For useful things—a house, for example."

Given their hasty marriage, there hadn't been time to find a place to live, and they couldn't reside in his bachelor apartments. Upon their return to London, they would be staying with his mama until they found a suitable place of their own. The fact that Charity questioned his ability to provide such a home nettled his pride.

"I'm not a pauper, you know," he said stiffly. "I can afford a few bits of frippery *and* a decent house. Besides I wouldn't call your hat situation frivolous—it's a downright emergency."

Her cheeks reddened. "There's nothing wrong with my bonnet. It's perfectly functional."

"So is a chamber pot, but I wouldn't wear it on my head."

"That's an absurd comparison." Though her voice was calm, her chin lifted a fraction. "I appreciate your gesture, truly I do. But I know you're recovering from losses, and there are better things to spend money on. If we could be rational for a moment—"

His temper flared at the reminder of his disgrace. Why did she bring that up when all he wanted to do was buy her a bloody hat? To pamper her, give her the things that she deserved? Any other lady would thank her husband prettily. But Charity questioned whether he was being *rational*?

At that instant, the milliner returned. Her smile dimmed as her gaze darted between the two of them. "Ah ... perhaps *monsieur* and *madame* need more time?"

"No," Paul and Charity said simultaneously.

He took one look at his wife's mutinous expression ... and grabbed the white satin hat off its stand. He shoved it at the milliner. "We'll take it."

"I don't want—" Charity began.

He picked up the next hat, a black leghorn trimmed with blond lace. "This one, too."

"Paul, you're being—"

He paused before a lilac toque studded with pearls. Raised an eyebrow at his wife.

Charity pinned her lips together.

After the transaction was completed, they rode back to the cottage in silence. Charity looked out the window, her profile turned from him. With bewildered anger, Paul tried to make sense of what had just happened: how had his intended act of generosity led to their first quarrel as a married couple? And why did he feel so bloody miserable at the moment?

By the time they got back, he still didn't have an answer.

He let her down from the carriage, and she headed for the cottage. He remained where he was, his insides roiling with restless energy. How he wished he had a boxing ring to go to, some way to work out his frustrations.

At the door, Charity turned to look back at him.

"Aren't you coming in?" she said.

"I'm going to go for a walk," he said abruptly. "Maybe find a few lads for a round of cricket."

"Oh ... alright then. Will you be back for supper?"

The quiver in her voice made him feel worse. He didn't know whether he wanted to apologize to her or shout at her ... mayhap both.

So he did the wiser thing.

"Don't wait up," he said gruffly and left.

Chapter Twenty-Three

The next morning, Charity awoke alone, with a dull, throbbing headache. She must have fallen asleep last night whilst waiting for Paul to return home. She'd tossed and turned, her anxious dreams shaped by their argument. Things had been going so well between them: why, oh why, had she gone and ruined things over a stupid *hat*? If she could do it over, she'd have kept quiet and let him buy her the whole millinery if he wanted. She'd even wear the dashed merchandise—the hideous lilac toque included.

But she hadn't kept quiet. Something about Paul brought out a latent willful streak in her nature. Perhaps it was his kindness and attention these days past: she'd never been as comfortable with anyone before. They seemed to be friends. And there was no doubting the physical intimacy between them. Up until yesterday, she'd even entertained the hope that he might be developing affection toward her.

But all that did not mean that he loved her. Or that he ever would.

After the incident at the milliner's, she couldn't blame him.

In retrospect, he'd only wanted to make her fashionable. Why had that garnered her resistance? Why had she been so stubborn about spending a little money?

Because you'll never be fashionable. You'll never be the lady he wanted. His Rosalind.

Her insides knotted at the wretched thought. And that wasn't even her only concern. Knowing his financial situation, she truly didn't want to add to his burdens. He had enough on his shoulders with the tournament, the shop ...

She left the bed, unable to stay there a minute longer without giving into tears. She dressed herself and drew back the curtains; the light of midday greeted her startled eyes. Good heavens, how late had she slept?

And where was her husband?

The door opened.

"Charity, are you up?"

She spun around to see Paul in the doorway. He was in yesterday's shirtsleeves, his jaw covered with dark gold bristle. Despite his disheveled state, he was the most gorgeous sight she'd ever seen.

"You're home," she whispered.

"Got in late." He rubbed the back of his neck. "Didn't want to wake you, so I camped out on the sofa. Thought I heard you rustling about just now."

She nodded—and then she was running toward him. To her everlasting relief, his arms opened to receive her. Held her tightly as she said in a suffocated voice, "I'm so sorry, it was all my fault—"

"Shh, sweeting. I was equally to blame."

"No, you weren't. You just wanted to buy me a present," she sniffled.

"And you just wanted me to be practical." He tilted her chin up, and the warmth in his azure eyes eased the painful tightness in her belly. "Let's let bygones be bygones, shall we?"

He was willing to forgive her—of course, she wanted to move on!

She eagerly nodded.

He kissed her on the forehead. "'Tis our last day before we return to London, so let's not waste it. Come along, I have a surprise for you."

"No more shopping," she said immediately ... and could have *kicked* herself. Why had she gone and reminded him of their disagreement?

Thankfully, he laughed. "Don't worry, my little nipcheese. This surprise won't cost a thing."

An hour later, Charity was beginning to doubt the value of the surprise even if it *was* free. Paul led the way on horseback through the local flora and fauna. The sun was blistering over-head as they passed clearing after clearing. She grew increasingly hot and tired but didn't want to complain. At this particular junc-ture, she'd ride through the Sahara to stay in her husband's good graces.

"We're almost there," he said. "It's up ahead, behind the trees."

To Charity's surprise, they arrived at a picturesque creek minutes later, a forest oasis hidden behind clustering trees. As Paul tied up the horses, she went to the edge of the bank and climbed atop a smooth boulder which provided a natural dock of sorts. Diamonds sparkled upon the water, bracken and sweet moss scenting the air. The velvety breeze was a welcome respite from the scorching blaze of the sun.

"How did you find this place?" she asked as Paul joined her on the rock.

"Lads down in the village mentioned some good spots for swimming," he said. "No current and the water is sweet from a spring."

Charity peered into the dark, clear depths below. "Isn't it too cold to swim in?"

"Only one way to find out."

She turned to look at him, her jaw slackening as he divested himself of his jacket and tossed it onto the mossy ground beyond. "You're not serious!"

In response, he sent his waistcoat and cravat on the same trajectory as his jacket.

"But—but anyone can see you," she said, aghast.

He yanked the shirt over his head, and at the sight of his muscled chest, she lost track of her next argument. The filtered rays of sun glinted off the sprinkling of bronze hair on his carved torso. The trail of hair narrowed as it descended past the taut bands of his belly and vanished into his waistband ...

"There's no one here but you, and I do believe"—he waggled his brows as he yanked off his boots—"you've seen it all before."

He stripped off the rest of his garments.

Her breath puffed from her lips. Her sex fluttered and dampened.

Oh my *goodness*.

No matter how many times she saw her husband naked, she'd never get over the thrill of it. He was so boldly male, so virile in every edge and line of his chiseled form. The sleek muscles of his thighs rippled as he came toward her, and her gaze drew unerringly to what jutted between.

She'd snuck glances at his phallus before, of course. She hadn't dared to do much more. Which was rather silly, come to think of it, given the other ways in which she was acquainted with this part of her husband's anatomy. Lifelong modesty was hard to overcome, however, and she'd thought it forward enough that she'd caressed his naked chest the last time they'd coupled. He'd seemed to like her touch, certainly.

The thought occurred to her: would he want her to touch him ... there?

With a pulse of heat, she wondered if he would fit within her hand. Even at rest, his member hung thick and heavy between his legs, and now, aroused, it pointed straight up from the patch of light brown hair, the broad tip almost skimming his navel. He sauntered up to her with no apparent embarrassment, his shaft and bollocks swaying with each step.

He ran a finger along the edge of her jaw. "Coming in with me?"

"I—I'll just watch," she said breathlessly.

Lips curved, he bent and took her mouth in a hard kiss ... and then turned and went dashing off the rock like a lunatic. His loud whoop echoed along with the loud splash. Peering over the edge, she saw nothing but waves of froth and concentric rings spreading over the surface. She clambered from the boulder onto the bank, her eyes anxiously on the water.

When his head emerged seconds later, she released a breath.

"It's glorious in here," he called, droplets flying as he shook the water from his eyes. "You must come in."

"You go ahead and enjoy it. I'll watch from here."

"For God's sake, at least dip your toes in."

"I don't want to get my dress wet."

"Then take off the damn dress." He swam in sure strokes toward her, stopping to tread water several feet away. "There's no one here to see. Besides, aren't you boiling in that rig?"

It *was* hot on the bank, and she'd been roasting the entire journey over. Perspiration adhered her skin to the layers of her unmentionables and trickled into equally unmentionable places. She felt sticky and itchy all over. She darted a glance around, saw nothing but birds and ruffling leaves. What harm would it do to take off a layer or two? She'd keep her chemise and drawers on.

She managed to remove the dress and front-lacing corset. Sitting on the edge of the bank, she dangled her feet in. Pure bliss.

Closing her eyes, she leaned back on her elbows. Cool water slid between her toes and lapped against her ankles. Then something gripped her calf.

Her scream was muffled by a giant splash.

A moment later she broke the surface of the cool water, sputtering. Paul held her in his arms, grinning from ear to ear.

"You cad, I can't swim!" She clutched his hard, slippery shoulders in a frantic grip.

"Better hold on tight then," he advised.

She had no choice but to cling tighter, wrapping her arms and legs around him as he took her toward the deep heart of the creek. His strong, easy strokes gradually eased some of her anxiety. Before she knew it, she was relaxing, enjoying the silky water against her skin.

"Let go and try to float. I won't let you drown," he said.

"Are you certain?"

His eyes crinkled at the corners. "Positive. I'm a lazy chap, and it would be an inconvenience to have to replace you." He kissed her, all the while coaxing her arms from his neck. "There now, lie back and breathe."

Slowly, she did. With the support of his hands beneath her back, she allowed her muscles to relax, her breath to come in natural surges. Before she knew it, she was doing it, floating as effortlessly as a leaf on the water's surface. *Marvelous.* When his hands eased away, she continued to drift on her own. She closed her eyes, weightless, surrendering to the gentle bobbing of the waves.

They stayed in the water for some time. He taught her a few elementary strokes so that she was able to paddle about with some semblance of direction. They laughed and played, yesterday's tension washed away. When she began to tire, he brought her safely to shore. He laid her down, the cushion of moss soft and warm beneath her back. Staring up at him, she saw the playful heat in his eyes and as ever she responded, her nipples rising against her damp shift, her thighs twitching as moisture gushed between them.

His slow, wicked smile sped up her pulse. His approval filled her with joy, especially now after their tiff. She felt an overwhelming urge to touch him, to be connected to him in any way possible. So she ran a hand through his hair; the flames in his eyes leapt higher. With hammering excitement, she followed a rivulet with her fingertip, tracing its path down his temple and jaw. His neck arched as her finger traversed that corded length.

The tiny stream trickled over his pectoral muscle, which turned rigid beneath her touch. She loved the smooth tautness of his skin, like satin wrapped over mahogany. The droplet caught in the fine whorl of his chest hair, adhering to one flat nipple.

Her friend's advice surfaced: *whatever feels good to you will feel good to him.*

Leveraging herself up on her elbows, she licked the water away.

His growl thrilled her.

Recalling how he'd ministered to her, she flicked his nipple again. It pebbled beneath her tongue. She suckled him, his groan inciting her to draw harder. She couldn't reach his other side, so she pushed him up and followed him so that they were both kneeling on the grass. She put her mouth on the neglected nipple. When his fingers dug into her scalp, she grazed him with her teeth.

He bit off a curse and yanked her mouth up to his.

Thrilled with her success, she returned his deep, tongue-ridden kiss. But instead of wrapping her arms around his neck, she let her hands wander. Over his granite-hard chest. The twitching bands of his abdomen. And finally ...

"Sweeting," he groaned against her lips.

Her pussy quivered as she held his pulsing rod in her hand. It was so thick that her fingers couldn't fit around its circumference, so long that the blushing brown tip nosed beyond her grasp. With great care, she curled her fingers, moved them up and down. The sensation—like dragging velvet over an iron poker—suspended her breath. When pearly moisture seeped from the burgeoned tip, she paused, not certain what to do.

"Don't stop, darling." His hand closed over hers, firming her grip on his phallus. "That's a tear of joy. My cock loves what you're doing, you see."

"Oh. Good," she said in a breathy voice.

He brought their linked hands up to the dripping dome of his cock, and his wetness smeared her palm. When he guided her hand down his shaft again, the slippery movement made him groan.

"Ah, love, that's *incredibly* good," he sighed.

It was so exciting, arousing and pleasing him with her touch. From his guiding hand, she learned the rhythm of a firm stroke, one that covered his cock from thick root to bulging tip. She must have gotten the hang of it because his hand left hers to cup her jaw. She pumped him as they kissed, open-mouthed and panting. Heat poured through her, her heart pounding with wild desire. Her other hand instinctively joined the fray, cupping the smooth weight of his stones ...

"Devil and damn," he gasped.

The next instant, he yanked her chemise over her head and flipped her onto her hands and knees. Before she could wonder at this startling position, his lips burned at the back of her neck, down her spine, the sensations so thrilling that she arched for more. She shuddered as he rained kisses over her bottom and further down still ... she cried out as his tongue delved into her sex.

"You have the sweetest cunny," he groaned. "I'll never get enough of it."

As he continued to eat her from behind, pleasure burned away her reserve, her limitations, freeing her from her own skin. She blurred into a creature of forest and stream, a wild thing who thrust her pussy against her lover's mouth, moaning an ancient summons. Soon his tongue left her, and she shivered when his manhood took its place. He entered with a powerful thrust. Her nails dug into the mossy carpet as he rammed his shaft inside her. Again and again, he surged, his cock so deep that his balls ground against her folds. She took every throbbing inch, loving it, loving him.

"I want to come with you," he growled at her ear. "Squeeze my prick, love. Take it from me."

Her cunny tightened in response. Ecstasy roared over her, and his primal shout startled the birds from the trees. At that moment, with his hot essence gushing inside her and bliss swirling in her veins, she grasped a sudden, incontrovertible truth.

I want him—all of him.

She wanted everything: his body, his heart ... a part of his soul that belonged only to her.

With his breath hot upon her neck, his sweaty, hard body covering her own, she knew that she could not settle for less.

All or nothing—an impractical bargain. But there it was.

He collapsed onto the ground, tucking her into his side. As she lay listening to his thundering heartbeat, her lips curved. She drifted off, dreaming that anything was possible ... even for her.

Chapter Twenty-Four

A summer storm interrupted the journey home. They were nearing London when the sky darkened and raindrops began pelting the carriage roof as thunder simultaneously rumbled in the distance.

Paul thought to himself, *All good things come to an end.*

His arm tightened around Charity, who was snuggled up against him, napping. Her long sable lashes lay against her cheek; she didn't stir. He smiled because he knew what had exhausted her so—and the recollection had the exact opposite effect on him. His body awakened as he saw her pretty rump turned up for him, heard again her sigh muffled against the forest floor. Sinking into his delicate, lush nymph from behind had no doubt been one of the most decadent thrills of his life.

They'd explored erotic terrain beyond his wildest expectations. It'd taken only three days for him to drink her sweet nectar at the source. Less than a week to know the bliss of her hands stroking him. His cock stiffened, though, by rights, that randy monster should have already gotten its fill. More than its fill, in truth. For despite his lusty adventures in the past, Paul couldn't remember anything like the past week:

with every taking, he'd only wanted more, his desire unending, at times even desperate ... as if he could never get enough ...

Apprehension needled his insides. If he was honest, he was no stranger to being out of control. Was this in the same vein as his old obsession for Rosalind? And his consequent compulsion for drink and gaming? Could that dark, self-destructive part of him be at work yet again?

He'd sworn to better manage himself. To keep himself in check. He'd vowed that moderation would be the ruling theme in his marriage—yet was it moderate to tup one's wife three, sometimes four—and aye, one time, *six*—times a day?

He bit back a groan. If he could have banged his head against the wall without waking Charity, he would have. Deuce take it, what had he been thinking?

He *hadn't* been thinking; that was, and had always been, the source of all his problems. He tried to calm the thudding in his chest. Alright, so he'd been somewhat ... immoderate in his dealings with Charity. This had only been their first week of marriage; he could chalk it up to novelty. The first bloom of passion. But once the intensity faded ... then what?

Could he be the kind of husband Charity wanted? The son-in-law Sparkler demanded?

What about his own dreams? He needed his concentration, his focus to win the championship. He couldn't let himself get distracted, no matter how sweet the diversion.

Charity burrowed deeper into him. His arm locked around her even as disquiet gnawed. The last week, while sublime, had not been without conflict. While they'd smoothed over the tiff at the hat shop, he wondered how long their happiness could continue. He knew that his feckless nature was bound to grate on her sensible nerves again and, truthfully, vice versa.

Nothing this good had ever lasted in his life.

Though it shamed him to be thinking of another with his wife tucked in his arms, he couldn't prevent his final meeting with Rosalind from surfacing.

They'd stood by the Serpentine, a stolen moment like so many they'd shared. He remembered the hammering ache in his chest, the frantic way he'd tried to memorize the details of her before he lost her forever.

"Kiss me, Paul," she'd whispered. "Give me a kiss I'll remember forever, even when you've forgotten me."

Fiercely, he'd said, "Never. I'll never forget you, Rosalind. I swear I'll love you forever."

Guilt pierced Paul for the vow he'd made—as if he'd somehow betrayed both Charity and Rosalind. Which was ridiculous. Rosalind was Countess Monteith, the mother of two young boys. Having moved on—and up—surely she didn't expect him to carry the torch for her indefinitely. She'd probably forgotten him. With a jolt, he discovered that his memory of her had also faded: he could no longer recall the exact shade of her hair or the precise timbre of her voice, the laugh which had enthralled him so.

Truly, his feelings were too confusing to examine in the light of his new circumstances. Confusing and damned disrespectful. Hadn't he promised Charity that his past would not interfere with their future? So why was he thinking about Rosalind at all?

Locking the memories away, he brushed his cheek against Charity's silky hair. His wife was a sensible woman. She'd understand—he'd been a different man back then. Aye, with each day that he spent with her, he was beginning to believe that he was changing for the better. Yet he couldn't quite shake off the sense that he was an imposter: that he was playacting at being a good husband and could forget his lines at any moment. As if he were about to bollix this up ...

"A penny for your thoughts." With sleep-soft eyes, Charity was watching him. She placed a fingertip between his brows. "Why are you frowning?"

He hesitated before saying, "Regret." It wasn't a lie. He

regretted so many things.

She stiffened against him. "About what?"

"That our wedding trip has to end," he said—also not a lie—"and that we must come back to the real world." He brought one of her hands to his lips, kissing the palm. "There's much to be done upon our return."

Her shoulders relaxed. She sat up. "Preparing for the tournament, you mean?"

"There's that, and we also have to find a place to live. We won't be staying with my mama forever, you know."

"I know," she said quickly.

"I won't leave for training for another week. I'd like to look at a few places before then, if it suits you." He tapped her on the nose. "Unlike the nursery rhyme, I don't intend to have my wife living in an old shoe."

"I wouldn't mind. As long as you lived there with me," she said.

The sweet, steadfast simplicity of her statement made him feel awestruck and, simultaneously, like more of a heel than ever. An apt metaphor, given the talk of footwear. Yet what else would one call a man who thought about his old paramour in his wife's presence?

"We're going to get properly situated," he said firmly. "I thought Bloomsbury might be a possibility."

"I'd like living near your mama," Charity said.

"Good thing, as we'll be with her for the interim. Which reminds me—we'll have to find you a proper lady's maid. Can't expect Mama's maid to take you on as well." He had a long way to go to prove himself a worthy husband, but by God, he would give her this. "We'll also have accounts set up for you at all the fashionable shops in Town."

"But I don't need—"

"You're my wife, Charity. Trust me to know what you need."

Let me be a good husband to you.

She bit her lip. He guessed that she was thinking about the millinery and whether or not to argue with him now. As he didn't want a repeat performance of their row either, he employed the most expedient strategy. He kissed her until she was pliant in his arms once more.

"See how easy it is when you give me my way?" he murmured.

"You can't settle every argument by kissing me," she said breathlessly.

"Let's try out that hypothesis," he suggested. "First thing back, I'm buying you a diamond tiara."

"Now you're being silly—"

His stratagem proved successful. In fact, their mutual distraction worked so well that he didn't realize that they'd arrived at Sparkler's townhouse until the groom knocked on the carriage door.

As Charity frantically shoved pins back in her hair, he straightened his cravat and looked out. The rain had stopped, but the sky remained gloomy and grey, the streets sloppy with puddles. The Sparkler residence was similarly uninspiring: a narrow, weather-beaten building with windows that peered at visitors like suspicious eyes.

Thank God they were just stopping by to collect a few of Charity's things for their stay at his mama's. At this hour, his father-in-law would be at the shop, so another bonus there.

"Ready, love?" he asked.

Cheeks still flushed, Charity nodded.

He stepped down first, reaching up for her. As her boots touched the ground, the door of the house swung open.

A woman—the housekeeper, he presumed—came running out, her cap askew and frizzy strands sticking out from beneath. "Oh, Miss Charity, thank God you're back!"

Charity tensed against him. "What's amiss, Mrs. Doppler?"

"It's your father," the woman said, twisting her apron. "He's in a bad way. Again."

Chapter Twenty-Five

"Are you certain he'll recover, Dr. Harrison?" Charity asked anxiously.

"Aye, he's lucky this time. But as you know, Mrs. Fines, this isn't the first instance your father has had a spell," the portly mustached man replied. "Yet he refuses to take my advice to work less and rest more."

"Nonsense," her papa argued weakly from the bed. He looked so grey and frail that Charity's heart lurched, and she rushed over to prevent him from getting up. "Have a shipment of silver plate coming in today," he said between labored breaths. "I must inspect it."

"Please, Father," she pleaded, "you must rest."

"For God's sake, Sparkler, don't push your luck." Dr. Harrison's brows lowered in a censorious manner as he set a small brown glass bottle on the bedside table. "Mrs. Fines, make sure your father takes a spoonful of medicine at noon and bedtime—it'll help him rest, which is what he needs if he wishes to recover."

"Don't need that snake oil," her father said, "or a damned quack."

Dr. Harrison's moustache bristled. Charity wanted to apologize, but she had to concentrate on keeping her struggling parent in bed. Through his worn sleep shirt, she could feel the fragility of her father's bones.

Before she could beg him once again to be still, her husband intervened. With a single hand, Paul pushed her father back into bed and held him there. Gently, but firmly.

"You're not helping anyone, sir," Paul said. "You'll be of no use at the shop in your present condition. You're certainly not helping yourself by committing suicide through overwork. Then there's Charity, who'll be heartbroken if you die. Since she hates shopping, I'll have to pitch in and get her a proper mourning wardrobe. Do you really wish to put everyone through all that trouble?"

Charity looked nervously at her papa.

"That's absurd!" Father sputtered. "The shop needs me. Who will tend to it if I don't?"

"Put that way, how can I refuse? I'd be honored to keep an eye on Sparkler's during your recovery." Paul frowned. "Well, *honored* is doing it a bit brown. As I've said before, I'm willing and able to do what is necessary."

"*You?* What could you possibly do?"

Charity winced at her father's scathing disdain. "Paul is offering to help—"

"He's done plenty already. Ruined you and the future of Sparkler's. Everything would be fine if you'd just married Garrity as I'd planned."

The muscle ticked along Paul's jaw. "She's my wife now, Sparkler, and you'd better get used to that."

"Please, Paul, my father doesn't mean—"

"I mean every word. You're a good-for-nothing *rake* ..."—her papa's words came out slurred—"and you'll never amount to more."

Though his color was high, Paul gave a sardonic bow. "Thank you for the vote of confidence."

"Bloody ... fop ..." Father's eyes closed, and a snore escaped him.

Charity sagged against Paul, whose frame quivered with tension.

"I put some laudanum in his tea earlier," Dr. Harrison said, "and next time I'd advise you to use an even stronger dose. Stubborn old goat."

"My father doesn't mean to be surly," Charity said quickly. "Please know that he—*we*, that is—truly appreciate your expertise, Dr. Harrison."

The doctor gave a gruff nod. "Ever since you were a girl, you've been the sensible one of this household. Now keep giving your father the medicine like I told you, and for God's sake, stay by his side and make sure he doesn't overexert himself for at least a fortnight. His heart can't handle it. You do understand what I'm saying, even if he doesn't?"

Fear seeped through Charity. "Yes, doctor. I'll take good care of him."

After Dr. Harrison departed, Paul took her in his arms.

"Don't worry, sweeting," he murmured. "Everything will be alright."

"But look at him, Paul." The pallor of her father's face made her throat burn. "He can't go on working the way he has, but Sparkler's means everything to him. He won't stop."

"We'll have to make him stop then."

"How?" she said in frustration.

"Once he knows that Sparkler's is in good hands, he'll be able to rest easier. And you will too, I hope. Leave everything to me."

"But the tournament. You're supposed to leave for training next week—"

"I'll make alternate arrangements with Traymore. I can train in London if I have to. Jackson's Saloon is as good a place as any," he said decisively.

She stared at him in wonder. He would do that ... for her?

She'd always believed that he was a hero; now she knew he was the *noblest* of men. Yet she couldn't allow him to risk his chance at winning—at achieving the one thing that mattered most to him—out of marital duty.

"No," she said, shaking her head. "The Championship is too important. You'll need your focus—"

"How well will I focus if I leave my wife in the middle of a crisis?" he chided. "You need to be by your father's side, sweeting, and you'll have your hands full when he wakes. Which reminds me: I'll let Mama know that we shan't be staying with her. It'll be easier for you to nurse him with us here."

Despite the terrible situation, Charity's heart swelled. He was the kindest, most generous of husbands. Yet the toughest, most virile. She loved him *so much*.

His softness. His hardness. All of him.

Lifting one of his hands, she kissed the callused knuckles. "No one has ever been so good to me," she said fervently. "Thank you, Paul."

"'Tis my pleasure to take care of my wife," he said in a husky tone. "Now kiss me properly before I toddle off and see what's what at the shop."

She did, and the warmth of their kiss banished some of her chill.

Paul arrived at Sparkler's just as a pair of customers was leaving. The ladies were dressed in fashionable gowns and chattering as they came down the pavement.

"Dreary place, isn't it?" the one with the yellow plume in her bonnet said.

"It had the feel of a warehouse," the other said with a shudder. "No style whatsoever."

Yellow Plume said with a laugh, "And that clerk? He belongs in a museum, not a jewelry shop."

"Well, we've had our misadventure, and it shan't bear repeating." Her friend sniffed. "Back to familiar waters?"

"Rundell's had a lovely diadem in the window," Yellow Plume agreed.

Paul bowed politely as they passed, ignoring their arch looks. Once their carriage rolled off, he stepped into Sparkler's and saw with dismay that the biddies were right. The shop looked as shabby as it had on his last visit—worse, in fact, for now several large boxes were stacked haphazardly upon the counters. The clerk, Mr. Jameson, worked at removing the contents. If the old man were in a race against a tortoise, Paul would give the reptile the edge.

"Good day, Mr. Fines." The clerk's face scrunched into a smile that displayed his plentiful wrinkles and not so plentiful teeth. "Wasn't expecting you. Honeymoon over already?"

He could say that again.

What in bloody hell had Paul gotten himself into? With a feeling of panic, he said, "Sparkler's held up. I'm here in his stead."

"That's mighty kind of you, sir. Could use a hand. Shipment of plate arrived just now and I was working on ..." Jameson frowned. "Wait a minute, what do you mean held up? How late is the master going to be?"

Paul gave the explanation.

"Mr. Sparkler will be out *indefinitely*? And Miss Char—I mean, Mrs. Fines—will be with him?" Jameson looked as if the rug —if there'd been one over the worn floorboards—had been pulled from beneath him. "But I'm just a *clerk*. How on earth will I manage the entire shop?"

"You won't." Paul rubbed the back of his neck. "I believe that pleasure is to be mine."

"You?" A notch worked between Jameson's grizzled brows.

Paul shared the other's disbelief. He hardly knew what he was doing here. Never mind the fact that he'd stopped off at Traymore's club directly before, informing the other of the altered plans for training. While the viscount hadn't been pleased, he'd grudgingly accepted Paul's decision.

"But you will make *absolutely* certain that you're ready to fight in five weeks?" Traymore had said. "I've got money on you, Fines, and more than that, my pride's on the line. I don't like backing a losing proposition."

"I won't lose," Paul had said firmly.

Now he had to wrestle down his growing doubts and trepidation. With the work to be done here, *would* he have time to train sufficiently? Would he be in top condition, be strong and fast enough to win?

Yet what choice did he have?

The shop's in terrible shape, old Sparkler even worse. There's no way I can leave Charity. Not now—not when she needs me the most.

For her sake, he would have to find a way to balance training with the demands of the store. If he had to, he would get his practice in before dawn and spar again after the shop closed. Whatever it took, he would do it.

And, hell, it might be worth the effort just to see Uriah Sparkler eat humble pie.

"Well, better you than me." Jameson blotted his forehead with a handkerchief. "Running this place is a young man's job, and I'm not as spry as I look."

Paul eyed the heap of boxes. He had to begin somewhere, and it was time to take matters into his own hands—literally.

He slung his jacket over a counter and rolled up his sleeves. With a sigh, he said, "Let's do something about this mess, shall we?"

Chapter Twenty-Six

As much as Charity loved her father, she had to admit that he was a difficult patient. She spent the next week in a state of frenzy—trying to keep him in bed, convince him to take his medicines, and coax him into eating more than a few bites of food, all his favorites that she'd had specially prepared. He complained about everything and demanded incessantly, "Take me to the shop." A few days ago, when he attempted to get up on his own, he grew faint and almost fell to the ground before she rushed over and caught him.

By week's end, she was exhausted from worry and lack of sleep.

As she fluffed his pillows to make them more comfortable, Father grumbled, "I'm going back to the shop tomorrow. I'm fit as a fiddle."

"Let's see how you feel tomorrow," Charity said.

"I'm telling you I'm *fine*. Which I won't be if that fribble has destroyed my life's work." His grey brows lowered in a glower. "By now, he could have frittered away the entire store. Or razed it to the ground on some drunken lark. That's what these feckless young bloods do, you know."

Her jaw clenched. She didn't like the way her father put Paul down. How he did so constantly. He seemed oblivious to all the efforts her husband was making, and his behavior was unappreciative to say the least.

Her patience fraying, she said, "That fribble happens to be your son-in-law and my husband. I'll thank you to speak of him more kindly. He's had to compromise his plans in order to oversee the shop during your illness."

"Plans, hah. Boxing isn't a plan—it's a waste of time," her father groused.

She knew that he was wrong. Paul was making such a sacrifice for her, for Sparkler's. Every morning for the past week, he'd been up and out of the house before she even awakened. He'd arranged for pre-dawn practices at Gentleman Jackson's Saloon, boxing for several hours before he went to tend to the shop. After working all day, he went to practice again. He didn't arrive home until late at night; he fell straight into bed, exhausted. And the next day it began all over again.

Her papa's gaze thinned. "And I'll thank you not to take such a tone with me, missy. What happened to the obedient girl I raised? Am I nothing to you now? Nothing but an old cripple not worthy of the simplest courtesy and respect?"

Charity's cheeks burned. "Of course I respect you, Father. I just wish you would give Paul a chance. If you did, you'd come to love him as I do. Or at least like him. He's a good, honorable man and—"

"*Love?* Did you just say you believe yourself in love with this *n'er-do-well?*"

She swallowed as a wild light came into her father's eyes. She hadn't meant to admit her love aloud; she hadn't told anybody yet, not even Paul. She'd wanted to wait until the right moment to confess her true feelings to him ... the right moment being when he might return the sentiment. After their magical week at the cottage in Chudleigh Crest, it had seemed possible that he might come to love her, at least a little. And now he'd selflessly placed her welfare and that of the shop before his own.

Since their return to London, however, they hadn't had much time to spend together, what with her nursing Father and Paul busy with his schedule. For the first time in their marriage, they'd also had to take separate rooms for the beds were too narrow to fit more than one occupant comfortably. It never rained but poured, and her monthly flux had arrived as well, putting an additional damper on their lovemaking.

Well, her courses were over now, and she planned to spend an evening alone with Paul when he returned home. Hopefully, the intimacy of their wedding trip would rekindle, giving her the courage to tell him the truth of her feelings.

Lifting her chin, she said, "Yes, Father, I love him."

She braced herself for her father's anger. His scorn, perhaps. So she wasn't prepared for the quiet resignation in his voice when he said, "I pity you, my daughter. That I do."

"Pity?" Her brow furrowed. "But why? I'm happy to love my husband."

"Aye. But does he love you?"

Her fingers pleated the edge of the sheet. "We're newly wedded. These things take time. And I ... I have kept my feelings to myself until now."

"At least I know some of the sense I ingrained in you remains." Her papa gripped her hand with sudden strength. "Heed me: if you're wise, you'll never let him know of your love."

"Why do you say that, Father?"

"Because it can only lead to pain." His grey eyes flickered with shadows. "Sparklers do not lie to themselves: they see their true reflections in the looking glass. Haven't I taught you that? Look at yourself, my daughter—and look at your husband. You must see the difference."

Her heart beat faster. An image materialized of herself, covered in spots, watching Paul as he was surrounded by pretty debutantes.

As he cast longing glances at the only one he'd wanted: raven-haired, violet-eyed Rosalind—the night to his sun. The one for whom he'd admitted that "sentiment lingered."

Just then, the gleam of her opal ring caught her eye, its fire renewing her strength.

"He thinks I'm beautiful," she said.

"Pretty words don't cost much, especially not for a silver-tongued rascal like him. Charity, my poor deluded child," her father said with such misery that her throat cinched, "all my life I've sought to protect you. To arm you with good sense and modesty so that you would know your place in the world."

"My place is with my husband. We made a vow to each other before God."

"Are you such an innocent that you don't realize that such vows are broken more oft than not? Your husband is a known philanderer. Do you actually think he'll change ... because of you?"

"He promised me." Her voice wavered.

Father shook his head. "He may have made promises now, but they shan't last. With his sort, they never do. Mark my words: he will tire of you and toss you aside as carelessly as he does last season's fashion."

No. Paul wouldn't. He couldn't.

"It pains me to say this, Charity, but"—her father let out a wheezing breath—"the truth is that whilst we Sparklers remain steadfast in everything we do, the same cannot be said of others. That is why we get left behind. Haven't you learned from my own suffering?"

"But Mama died. She didn't choose to leave." A voice, new and defiant, rose within her. *Your suffering doesn't have to be mine.*

"What does it matter? She's gone, isn't she?" His voice turned harsh. "She left me to raise you, an infant girl, on my own and with no one to count on but myself. It wasn't easy, and others in my shoes might have given you up to an orphanage or the workhouse. But I didn't abandon you—do you know why?"

Her breaths rapid, she shook her head.

"Because Sparklers stick together. We do our duty to each other. Hasn't it always been this way, you and me against the rest of them?"

Her defiant spark extinguished as memories crowded her: walking to and from the shop with her papa, taking hasty suppers together in the back room of Sparkler's. The hours they'd spent poring over the merchandise—and the triumph she'd felt when he had complimented her on the neatness of the displays. All her life, she'd yearned for his approval.

"I *am* trying to do what's right," she said, swallowing, "and so is Paul. He's worked tirelessly at the shop while you've been ill—doesn't that count for something?"

"He can't save Sparkler's." The starkness of Father's tone released a trickle of fear in her. The anger seemed to leave him, deflating him, and he slumped back against the pillows, his eyes closing. "We had one chance, and that was with Garrity. Well, that's gone now, and the only thing left to save is you. Your ... your heart." His voice cracked as he said, "Protect it, child, for I may not be long in this world to do it for you."

"You'll recover fully," she said, squeezing his hand, "and then you'll see that everything will turn out fine."

He didn't open his eyes. "I'm tired. Leave me to rest."

Blinking back sudden moisture, she tucked the coverlet over him and said, "Yes, Father."

She closed the door behind her, leaving it slightly ajar. From the thin crack, she kept watch over him. And worried ... about everything.

Chapter Twenty-Seven

Paul didn't return until after ten that evening. Charity rushed from the front parlor to greet him. He looked as handsome as always, though a bit worse for wear. Dirt smudged his left cheekbone, and dust dulled the shine of his boots.

"Hard day?" she asked.

Taking off his hat, he ran a hand through his tousled hair. "Sparkler's makes working the coal mines seem like child's play. Between that and a grueling session at Jackson's, I'm starved and in need of a bath." Removing his jacket, he sniffed at himself and grimaced. "And not necessarily in that order."

"You don't have to choose," she told him. "I had the tub readied, and supper's on a tray."

"Always said you were an angel." He leaned in to kiss her.

"Actually," she said a few breathless moments later, "you called me a mouse."

He grinned. "You're an angelic rodent. An adorable one who scurries about doing acts of kindness for mankind. And, in particular, me."

"I'm not sure I can handle such flattery," she said wryly as she headed for the stairwell. "Let's go upstairs before the water cools."

"See? Always with my best interests at heart—ergo, my angel."

His boots thumped behind her. When his hand clamped on her bottom and squeezed, she squeaked, nearly missing a step.

He steadied her, said with a catch of laughter, "And she makes the most darling sounds and has a very lovely tail, both attributes of our four-legged friend. Therefore, I give you Madam Guardian Mouse."

Her lips twitching, Charity continued up the stairs with him close behind. They entered the snug guest chamber where Paul was staying, and his presence dwarfed the space further. Besides the narrow bed, there was only a tiny desk and cabinet. The tub had to be squeezed in between the foot of the bed and the hearth. At least the fire was built, warming the room and imbuing it with a cozy glow.

Paul snagged a chunk of mutton from the supper tray and popped it into his mouth. As he chewed, he loosened his cravat and disrobed with a casual grace that she could never aspire to. He was so comfortable in his own skin—and what a skin it was. The layers fell to the ground as he carelessly shed them.

Oh my.

Her mouth watered a little as the firelight licked the taut ridges of his manly form. His hard-paved chest and torso looked deliciously out of place against the faded floral wallpaper. The sleek muscles of his thighs flexed, his male equipment swaying as he lowered himself into the tub.

With a tingle, she recalled how his rampant instrument had moved inside her, filling her so completely that there'd been no room for thought or worry. No room for anything but him and the glorious pleasure they shared.

She hoped for such intimacy tonight.

"Ah, that's better," he sighed, leaning back. Although he was too big to fit entirely in the tub—he had to bend his knees—he looked like a king in repose.

She smiled and, out of habit, went to pick up the heap of

clothes he'd left on the floor. As her father's home was not large enough to accommodate Paul's valet, Mr. Bromley came for daily visits to dress Paul and pick up soiled garments. She folded the dirty clothes into a neat pile ... and noticed a stain on the lapel of the waistcoat.

Inspecting the jade jacquard, she rubbed at the spot. "Oh dear. Ink can be terribly difficult to remove from fabric as fine as this."

"Don't worry your head over it," Paul said from the tub. "Just have it tossed in the rag bin."

She looked at him in surprise. "But it's a beautiful waistcoat. Not to mention costly."

"It's last year's fashion." He yawned, stretching his arms. "Bromley was going to dispose of it anyway."

He will tire of you and toss you aside as carelessly as he does last season's fashion.

Her grip tightened on the waistcoat. "There's no need for such wastefulness. I'll get the stain out. If I can't, I'm certain I can reuse the fabric."

"Suit yourself, sweeting." He gave her a lazy smile. "Now would you mind coming over here and helping me bathe?"

Her pulse unsteady, she chided herself for being silly and went over. Perching on the stool next to the tub, she poured a handful of his soap—an aromatic blend of lemon and sandalwood specially formulated by his valet—and lathered it into his hair. Paul moaned as she massaged his scalp with deep strokes. The way, she knew, that he liked it.

"By Jove, you've got the magic touch. Don't know how I got along without you." His eyes were closed, his head resting against the towel she'd placed on the edge of the tub.

She worked at the tight muscles along his neck, the pleasure of his words, of touching him, slowly dispelling some of her anxiety.

It's just an old waistcoat. Don't overreact.

Letting out a breath, she said, "You're stiff."

"I'll say." Though his eyes remained shut, his lips took on a wicked curve. "It's a problem I seem to develop whenever I'm around you."

His flirtatiousness filled her with relief. She *loved* it when he bantered with her in this manner. Especially now that she understood the naughty innuendos. Her fingers dug deeper into his tight muscles and he groaned, water sloshing against the tub's edge. She worked at his neck and shoulders, reveling in her ability to give him pleasure.

"How was your training?" she asked.

"They're toughening me up." He lifted his left hand from the water, and she gasped at his bruised and swollen knuckles.

"Does it hurt? I'll get the salve—"

"Don't fuss, sweeting. It just stings a little. Can't be a prize-fighter with soft hands."

She couldn't shake off the sudden fear. If practice resulted in such injuries, what would happen in a real fight? "Will you be safe in the ring? Are you certain this tournament is a good idea?" she blurted.

"You know this is what I want." She caught the edge to his voice. "I'll be fine. Don't worry, alright? Let's change the subject. Ask me about the shop, for instance."

Afraid to press him further, she swallowed and said, "How is the shop?"

"We're making progress." His voice warmed with satisfaction. "Cleaned up the display cases. New carpets came in today as well."

"That sounds lovely." But what she felt was more worry. Hesitating, searching for words that wouldn't sound ungrateful or managing, she said, "You're not changing things too much, are you? Father's quite particular and set in his habits, you see, and—"

"He'll approve, don't fret," Paul said, yawning again. "My greatest triumph has been to cure Jameson of the tendency to salivate like a butcher's dog over every customer. Surprisingly, he's proving the adage false: old canines *can* learn new tricks, and we're reaping the rewards. He's doubled his sales in the past few days."

As changes to the shop went, that didn't sound too outlandish, Charity thought. And if Paul's new approach improved the profits, then surely her papa would approve.

"It isn't Mr. Jameson's fault. Father trains the clerks to be attentive to the patrons," she said. "His motto has always been, *The customer always comes first.*"

"That strategy may work well amongst certain classes, but not the one you want patronizing Sparkler's. Trust me, you must fight fire with fire. Or, in this case, snobbery with snobbery."

"I don't understand."

"If you kowtow to the *ton*, they assume you're beneath their notice. If, on the other hand, you act as though you're doing *them* the favor by giving them the privilege to shop, they'll be tripping over themselves to buy up the merchandise."

"So if you treat someone badly, they'll want your goods *more*? That doesn't make any sense," Charity said with a frown.

Paul snorted. "Since when do logic and the upper class mix?"

She rinsed the soap from his hair, contemplating his words. The times she'd entered a fashionable establishment—usually with Percy—she *had* noticed that the clerks seemed, well, uppity. Their noses had been elevated to such high altitudes that it was a marvel they didn't bleed. She'd found their attitude intimidating and hadn't wished to return.

Of course, she was not of the upper class and didn't understand their sophisticated ways. And she couldn't deny that the snobbier the shop, the better they seemed to be doing.

Could it be that her father had it wrong all this time?

She was about to question Paul about it further, but seeing the relaxed lines of his face, she decided not to bother him and fetched the kettle from the fire, adding hot water to his sigh of satisfaction. She poured out more soap and ran her hands over his chest. His eyes grew heavy-lidded as she skimmed the hard contours, searching out knots and rubbing them until they loosened.

The task eased some of her earlier worry. He was so strong, so quick and powerful—surely he could take care himself in any fight. She must trust in his judgment.

Resolved, she concentrated on soaping and massaging his bent legs. Beneath the water, she worked on his calves and large feet, rubbing the arches as he murmured with pleasure. Through the patches of foam on the water's surface, she could see the shape of his cock lying against his thigh, and a wicked impulse stole over her. Her palms itched to touch him there again. To run her fingers along that thick length, to explore every inch of him from the fat tip to the heavy sac beneath.

With great daring, she reached between his legs and wrapped her hand around his member. Even at rest, the girth of his cock exceeded her grip. She glided her hand along his length, and to her delight, the column stiffened, burgeoning within her fist. Her pussy dampened, fluttered.

He mumbled something, and her gaze flew to his face.

She blinked.

He was ... asleep. Eyes closed, he was slumped against the edge of the tub, his chest rising and falling in steady surges.

The memory of another time crept like frost over her insides. *He doesn't even know you're here.* She removed her hand, surprised to find it was shaking.

Swallowing, she said, "Paul. Wake up."

She had to repeat it before his lashes slowly lifted.

"Did I drift off?" He yawned.

"I'll help you towel off so you can get to bed," she said quietly.

By the time she tidied up after the bath, he'd fallen asleep again. She stood by the bed and watched him as he slept, his face as beautiful as an angel's. She brushed a damp, gilded curl off his forehead. When her touch failed to rouse him, she lingered a few moments longer before she doused the lamps and left unnoticed.

Chapter Twenty-Eight

Three days later, in the gloom before dawn, Paul made his choices from the scanty pickings on the sideboard and plunked his plate on the dining table. The grimly drab parlor seemed to reflect his own foul mood, which he could pretty much blame on his host. He bloody hated Uriah Sparkler. Yes, *hated*. There was no disguising the matter. His father-in-law's animosity was like a slow-acting poison, trickling into and tainting every aspect of his life.

He'd compromised his training to help the bastard, and what did he get for his troubles? Nothing but hostility. Sparkler took jabs at him at every opportunity; just yesterday, he'd ripped Paul's hide for wasting water on daily *baths*, for crying aloud. For Charity's sake, Paul had gritted his teeth and walked on. He didn't know how much longer he could maintain the moral high ground—not his preferred real estate. He despised every second living under the skinflint's roof. The miserly lack of heat and good food ... not to mention the separate sleeping quarters.

He hadn't plowed his wife for ages. Alright, perhaps it had only been ten days, but *still* ... it was like Siberia compared to the balmy tropics of their wedding trip. It seemed his life had gone topsy-turvy: for the first time ever, he was working *too* hard and not having *enough* sex. How could anyone live in this fashion?

He hadn't even been able to frig himself for fear of the maid discovering soiled sheets and his father-in-law somehow learning about it. His thinking verged on paranoia, he knew, but Uriah Sparkler seemed to be watching his every step, waiting for the moment he made a mistake. It was unnerving—not to mention dampening to the amorous spirit.

Paul pushed the thought aside; he didn't want to mull over Sparkler any more than necessary. Better to think of more pleasant things—like how to get back the Charity from his honeymoon. His sweet, hot bride who had been so eager to discover the intimacies of lovemaking with him. Her courses should be over by now. There was no reason they couldn't resume where they'd left off.

In fact, he thought as he chewed on rubbery eggs, perhaps he could arrange for them to get away for the night. Now that her father was on the mend, surely she could spare an evening for her husband. Paul could get them a room at an inn, she could wear that negligee for him again so he could take it off. With his teeth ....

Even as his cock perked up at the notion, the niggling unease returned. Would she be so abandoned with him again? Had the bliss of their wedding trip been a temporary state? After all, nothing that good could last forever. Somehow, he always managed to squander any fortune that fell into his lap. He wasn't oblivious to the unfolding events. Since their return to London, his wife had grown increasingly distant, withdrawn, more like the Charity of old. The one he'd made the mistake of not noticing.

The parlor door opened, and the object of his musings appeared. His pulse quickened, with desire and ... dismay. Not because her hair was once again bound in a knot or even because she was wearing one of her colorless, shapeless gowns. He couldn't give a damn about her appearance because he saw the true Charity now, the beauty that shone through everything else.

No, his anxiety was due to the expression in her moss-green

eyes: the guardedness that hadn't been there during their wedding trip. That coolness that raised the hairs on his nape.

He rose automatically to greet her; she curtsied.

Like a pair of damned wooden marionettes.

She smiled, yet the tentativeness of her expression didn't escape him. "Good morning," she said. "You're off to an early start."

"I've been up early every day since we returned."

His response was sharper than he intended, and her shoulders stiffened as she turned to the sideboard. Damnit, she should understand that he didn't mean anything by it. She, of all people, should know how exhausted he was trying to balance boxing with saving her father's shop. He was toiling his bleeding arse off.

The embers of resentment he'd kept tamped down began to smolder. For all his hard work, what did he get in return? A father-in-law who treated him like dirt. A wife who was growing more distant toward him each day.

"Have you started interviewing for a lady's maid?" he said curtly.

Her lips pinned together. An expression of the old Charity. "No."

"Why not?"

"I've had my hands full. Vanity," she said primly and, he thought, pointedly, "is the least of my worries."

Enough of this madness. He stalked over to join her at the sideboard, which she was inspecting as if there were a grand buffet there instead of the paltry dishes of overcooked eggs, gristly sausage, and toast not fit for birds.

"Did you sleep well?"

She looked both startled and relieved at his non sequitur. "Yes, thank you. And you?"

"Poorly," he said.

"I'm sorry to hear it. Is the bed uncomfortable? I could have—"

She let out a squeak, most likely because he'd hauled her up onto the sideboard. There was plenty of room given the paucity of food offerings. He wedged himself boldly between her thighs and leaned in.

"The bed isn't the problem," he told her. "The lack of you in it is."

"Oh." The syllable fluttered from her lips. Relief flooded him as he saw desire reflected in the brilliant facets of her eyes. "Oh Paul, I—I've missed you, too," she whispered.

He kissed her. Their mouths met hotly and eagerly, and there were teeth as well as tongues, but he didn't give a bloody damn. It felt so *good*, a return to Eden. Primal need rushed through him: to reassert his claim, to remind his forgetful little wife of just how much she needed him.

"I'm bloody randy for you." He nipped her ear, loving her shiver, and wanting even more from her. Needing her to feel the dark edge of passion, to respond with the wantonness he knew resided within her. "You little tease," he murmured in her ear, "we haven't fucked in days."

Her pupils dilated, her breath coming quicker at his naughty word. "But we can't ..."—she gasped when he plucked away her modest fichu, bearing the milky skin of her décolletage—"anyone could come in ..."

"Then you'll have to be very quiet, won't you?" He slid his hand inside her bodice, managed to make his way to one perfect breast. His finger and thumb worked her hard nipple mercilessly as she bit her lips, clearly trying to muffle those sweet sounds she made whilst in the throes. "Don't worry. I won't torture you too much."

"T-torture?"

"Hmm." He yanked her skirts up, exposing her slim white thighs to his greedy gaze. He reached for her sex and nearly groaned to find her ready, so plump and lush. He drove his middle finger in to the knuckle. "What a hungry little pussy you have. Has it missed me?"

Her eyes were glazed over, her cheeks flushed. The slick clench of her cunny was driving him wild. Yet she clearly hadn't learned her lesson, for she whimpered, "We mustn't here. It isn't decent—"

Her words faded to a moan as he thrust into her again, two fingers this time, curling to find the secret spot high inside her. His thumb rolled her pearl. Her neck arched, her lips parting on a soundless cry.

"You're my wife. I'll have you wherever and whenever I want, decency be damned," he growled. "Now I repeat—has your pussy missed me?"

He fingered her harder, deeper, determined to have the answer from her.

"Yes." Her eyes were dazed with pleasure.

"Yes, what?" he challenged her. "Give me the words."

"Yes, my pussy has missed you," she whispered.

Triumph and lust made him want to pound his chest.

"There's my good little wife," he said.

He unbuttoned his fall, freed his cock. He was as hard as rock, moisture oozing from the tip. He tormented them both by rubbing the engorged dome up and down her dewy lips before hilting himself in a forceful thrust. His hand grasping her nape, he pounded into her, their panted breaths in rhythm with the rattling dishes. His bollocks pulsed with fire, his pent-up seed climbing. He gritted his teeth. God help him, she'd better be close because he was going to blow any second—

Footsteps pierced his haze of lust. He had only an instant to yank out of Charity, shove himself back in his trousers. She jumped off the sideboard whilst his fingers fumbled with his buttons. The parlor door slammed open and Sparkler demanded, "What is the meaning of this?"

Paul couldn't speak, could barely control his breaths. Now he understood the expression *dog-drawn*: he gnashed his teeth against the physical pain of frustration. Mere seconds he'd been from ecstasy, from shooting so hotly inside his wife ...

"Father, wh-what are you doing up?" Charity stammered.

She might have asked her own husband the same thing, Paul thought with an inward groan. His cock throbbed like a second heartbeat against his belly. He'd never been harder, randier, more in need of release.

"Trying to protect my good name." Sparkler hobbled in, slapping a newspaper down on the dining table. "How much longer are you going to drag my daughter through the mud, Fines?"

What was the bastard going on about now? Paul went over, making sure his jacket was drawn over his groin and trying not to wince as his erection chafed with each step. He grabbed the paper: *The First Stare*, a notorious scandal sheet. He skimmed through the contents ... and anger overtook arousal. With each sentence, his pulse pounded more violently.

Goddamn Parkington. The bastard still wasn't satisfied with the pound of flesh he'd exacted. He'd dug up dirt faster than a grave robber and must have bribed servants to get all the sordid details.

The sheets crumpled in Paul's fist. "Where did you get this?"

"Someone left it on our doorstep. The maid brought it up with my breakfast tray," Sparkler snapped. "Not that I had any appetite left after reading about who my daughter has married. Have you no shame at all? Just how many females did you fornicate with at that iniquitous house party where you compromised my Charity?"

Shame crawled over Paul's skin. Charity's soft intake of breath made his stomach churn.

"*Five*, this article says." Sparkler shot him a triumphant glare. "Do you deny it?"

Paul was aware of his shallow breathing, of the fierce desire to lie and wipe that smug look off his father-in-law's face.

"Paul?" Charity's trembling voice gutted him.

Because he couldn't lie ... not to her.

"It happened before you and I met at the party," he said gruffly. "They meant nothing, Charity. It was just ..."

Her face paled. She swiped her palms against her skirts—skirts that he'd just tossed up. He wanted to punch a wall. *Devil take it.* If only he could explain how different it was, his careless fucking and what they shared ... Yet the accusation in her eyes dried up any words he might have uttered. In truth, there were no excuses: he had been indiscriminate, a rake in the worst sense of the word.

"Now do you see who you married, daughter?" Sparkler demanded.

Her silence said everything.

"Charity, that was the past. Things are different now. I made a vow to you," Paul said tightly.

She wet her lips, but before she could reply Sparkler butted in.

"I'm going to the shop today," he announced. "I don't trust you with that any more than I do with my girl."

"You can't, Father!"

Charity spoke up—of course she would, where her bloody papa was concerned, Paul thought with a flare of bitterness. Just once, why didn't she stand up for *him*? He might be a detestable rake, but he'd never lied about who he was. And he hadn't a done thing since he'd met her to warrant her judgment.

"I can and I will," Sparkler said.

"But Dr. Harrison said—"

"That quack will say anything for coin. I'm fit to walk, I'm fit to work." Sparkler weaved toward the door. "I'm leaving this instant."

Charity chased after him, leaving Paul no choice but to follow.

At the shop, things went from bad to worse.

Sparkler took one look around the refurbished room and

bellowed, "What is the meaning of this? What have you done to my place of business?"

"I should think it obvious that I've improved it," Paul said evenly.

He'd made strategic changes to drag the place into the nineteenth century. Stylish new fixtures, including a brass chandelier, relieved the gloom. Cameo blue silk revived the tired walls, and indigo carpets strategically covered the worn patches on the floorboards. Next to one of the display cabinets freshly lined with velvet, Jameson stood as unmoving as a statue in his crisp new uniform.

"*Who gave you the authority?*"

"Please, calm yourself." Charity tugged on her father's sleeve. "Paul was only trying to help."

Anger and disbelief scalded Paul. *Trying to help?* Like he was a *child* getting in the way of adults at work?

"You gave it," he clipped out, "when you asked me to look after the shop during your illness."

"I didn't *ask* you to do anything." Spittle flew from Sparkler's lips as he faced Charity, shook her hand off his arm. "This is your fault, you faithless girl. You drugged me with that medicine when I should have been here. You're in cahoots with this fop and together you've destroyed my life's work!"

Charity's bottom lip quivered, and Paul's grip on his temper slipped. "Do not take that tone with her. She's done nothing," he snapped.

"I'll speak to my daughter however I wish!"

"She's my *wife*." Paul extended a hand, palm up. "Charity, come over here."

Her gaze darted between him and her father ... and she hesitated. Her uncertainty obliterated his self-control. He couldn't think through the miasma of resentment and confusion. How had this happened? Somehow he'd managed to snatch defeat from the jaws of victory. Somehow—despite doing his best, doing the *right bloody thing*—he was coming up a failure yet again.

His hand curled and dropped to his side. "Charity, you can see the changes are for the better." He sounded eerily calm. Rational, though his inner voice was shouting, *Goddamnit, side with me just once. I have the right of it. You must know that I do.*

"I ... the shop does look more stylish." She bit her lip, said tentatively, "Father don't you agree that the showroom looks more spacious with the lights and mirrors? And the new cabinets do display the merchandise nicely, don't they?"

At least she noticed that much, Paul thought bitterly. *All that deuced work ... for naught.*

"Style." Sparkler spat the word like an epithet. "That's all that matters to a fashionable buck like him. Remember what I told you: he doesn't give a damn about substance! Wouldn't know good quality if it slapped him in the face. Out with the old and in with the new, that's all these top-of-the-trees toffs know. Soon he'll tire of this and be onto the next whim that catches his fancy."

Charity paled.

Paul's hands balled.

"And what I want to know," Sparkler said, directing his venom toward Paul, "is where you got the funds to make these so-called improvements."

"The money was my own," Paul said through his teeth. "I didn't take a penny from you—even if there was a penny to take from your empty coffers." Though Sparkler kept the ledgers locked up, it didn't take a genius to see that the establishment hadn't seen a profit in years.

Blinking rapidly, Charity said, "Father, Paul has done the best he could."

Paul's fury mounted at her beseeching tone, as if she had to beg her stubborn ass of a father for forgiveness on *his* behalf. *He'd* done Sparkler the favor, not the other way around! What the bloody hell was the matter with her?

"Throwing away good money," Sparkler sneered. "That's one talent you do have."

Paul was *done* with this madness.

"Consider my duty discharged. I'm washing my hands of this miserable sinkhole," Paul ground out. "If you wish to flounder in your miserable ways, so be it. I'm not staying here a minute longer. Charity, are you coming?"

Her grey-green eyes pleaded with him. "Can't we talk this over? It's just a misunderstanding. Father doesn't mean to be unreasonable—"

"I'm *unreasonable*, you ungrateful chit?" Sparkler said through wheezing breaths.

"That's not what I meant. You must remain calm, Father. If we could all go home, talk about this in private—"

Sparkler jabbed a shaking finger at Paul. "That n'er-do-well is not to step foot in my house ever again!"

"Excellent. Because I wouldn't dirty my boots entering that hovel," Paul snarled.

Gasping, Sparkler said, "Get out! Get out of my shop!"

Paul stormed toward the door, yanked it open. Sunlight and the empty walk beckoned—anywhere was better than where he was. Without turning, every muscle poised for flight, he bit out, "Charity, are you coming?"

"If you would just wait. I have to see to Father—"

He didn't wait to hear the rest. His boots hit the pavement, the voices fading behind.

Chapter Twenty-Nine

Shaking the sweat from his eyes, Paul swung at his opponent, fueled by a savage need for blood. When the other man knocked away the punch, Paul drove in again, a barrage of jabs and crosses that pushed his strapping rival back toward the ropes. Paul kept at it, even leaving himself exposed to the other's powerful fists because the pain felt good, cleansing.

He barely heard the hoots and shouts rising from around the ring as he traded shot for shot.

Bloody Sparkler can take his shop and shove it up his arse. His blow struck his adversary's shoulder, and the impact sizzled up his arm. *Don't have to apologize to him or anybody.*

The hook snapped his head back. Lights blinked in his vision.

When he could see again, he was staring up at the ceiling of the Saloon.

Cheers went up from the other students who had gathered to watch the practice match. Paul's sparring partner, who happened to be the proprietor of the establishment and his teacher, helped him to his feet.

"By Jove," Gentleman Jackson said, "well done."

Stripping off his gloves, Paul gave the brawny pugilist a courteous bow, his head spinning as he did so. "Thank you, sir. As usual, your right hook was undefeatable."

"Not if you'd had your usual concentration," Jackson said.

"Sir?"

The other's dark brows lifted. "You've got a devilish blend of my power and Mendoza's defenses. What you lacked today was focus. Anything troubling you, Fines?"

Paul's face heated. Was it that obvious?

"Nothing I can't handle, sir," he muttered.

"You'll need a clear head in the tournament. You'll be taking on prizefighters like Jem Barnes, men who fight to win—and they don't care what happens to their rivals. A moment's loss of focus can cost you more than the match," Jackson said.

Paul knew about Barnes. The infamous Champion had three titles ... and three badly injured opponents to accompany each of his wins. One unlucky fellow had lost the sight in his left eye as a result of Barnes' powerful cross.

Recalling Charity's concern about his safety, Paul felt a pang. Then anger emerged, covering up any remorse. She should trust in his abilities—in *him*. She should take her husband's side and not her damned father's. She should ...

"Brilliant advice, Jackson." Traymore's brusque tones cut in.

In his forties, Viscount Traymore was a gentleman's gentleman who preferred sporting above all else. With his shaggy brown hair and alert manner, he reminded Paul of a foxhound. The viscount dressed like a Corinthian, was a founding member of the Fancy, and, according to rumor, had never met a bet he didn't like. Luckily, he had the wealth to support his pursuits.

"Perhaps you can convince Fines to take up my offer," Traymore went on. "I've proposed that he stay at my country seat where he can train without the distractions of the everyday. He needs to be in prime form to win the tournament."

"An idea worth considering, Fines, if it would clear your head," Jackson said.

Suddenly, the idea appealed to Paul. When he'd turned down the invitation before, he'd had his reasons. He'd felt obligated to help with the shop, had wanted to shelter Charity from any woes. His jaw tightened. Clearly, his presence at Sparkler's was not welcomed, and Charity had chosen to stay with her father. Had chosen him over her own husband.

That, he realized, was what stung the most.

He'd compromised his training, his *dreams*, for her, and she'd paid him back with a lack of faith. So what was keeping him from going off to pursue his goal now?

Absolutely bloody *nothing*.

"Give me a night to sleep on it," he said.

"Tournament starts up in a month," Traymore said doggedly. "Haven't got time to waste."

"I'll let you know," Paul said firmly.

How would Charity react if he left? Would she support his endeavor? Would she ask him to stay? Or mayhap, he thought with smoldering anger, she'd *want* him gone so that she could focus on pleasing her ass of a father.

"Whatever you decide, I predict success for you, Fines," Jackson said. "In fact, I have your triumph at the exhibition to thank for the recent increase in enrollment." He nodded to a trio of plump lordlets who were ogling the weighing machine, a contraption made up of a plank suspended by ropes. "Everyone wants to be The Fighting British Male."

"But there can only be one Fancy Champion," Traymore said. "And that'll be you, Fines, if you would just prioritize your training."

"I'd best go attend to my new pupils," the Gentleman said with a sigh. The lordlets were giggling as they took turns riding on what they thought was a swing. "God help them if they break my weighing machine," he muttered as he strode off.

"Send a note around to my club first thing," Traymore said. "I hope you'll make the right decision, Fines."

Paul hoped so, too.

After taking leave of Traymore, he lingered a while longer. The Saloon had always been a home away from home for him, and he welcomed this small respite. Bellinger and Sands, companions from his rakehell days, caught him up on the latest *on dit*. The pair proposed a night out on the Town.

Knowing what a night out with the fellows entailed—wine, wagers, and wenches—Paul had the presence of mind to decline. He exited the boxing studio, his mind occupied with possible next steps. As annoyed as he was with Charity, he had to speak to her; it was the mature, husbandly thing to do. But he'd be damned before he went to the shop or her father's house to fetch her. Perhaps he'd send round a note ...

Caught up in his thoughts, he didn't hear the voice at first. It drifted over him, an echo from his past. He halted in confusion ... and heard those familiar, silky tones again.

"A penny for your thoughts, darling."

A carriage pulled up next to him. A lady looked out the open window. His heart began to thump as he beheld a perfect oval face framed by ringlets as dark as midnight. Exotic violet eyes smoldered into his.

No, it can't be ...

"You do remember me, don't you?" Her pink lips held a tempestuous curve, and he had the jarring memory of thinking that he'd do anything for the favor of that smile. "Because I certainly haven't forgotten you, my love."

"Rosalind?" he said blankly. "Why aren't you in Scotland?"

"Oh, Paul. You haven't changed," she said with her light, intoxicating laugh. "You're *exactly* as I remembered."

"But what ... what are you doing here?"

"I came to talk to you."

"Why?" He couldn't think, so dazed that he might have been half-seas over.

"'Tis a matter best discussed in private." She signaled one of her liveried footmen, who jumped from his perch and opened the door. "Come for a ride, darling."

Paul took in the sumptuous red velvet interior, the plush cushions, the sensuous fall of Rosalind's silk skirts.

"I'm married," he blurted.

"I know." Her lashes lowered, and the droplet that tracked down her cheek wracked him with guilt. "But you made a promise to me as well. You do remember what you said to me, don't you? That last day by the Serpentine?"

He stared at her beautiful, upturned face. This woman who had haunted him for so long. He couldn't form a coherent response.

"All I'm asking for is a few minutes of your time. Surely you can give me that much?"

He didn't move. "Rosalind, I'm not certain—"

"Please, Paul." Her peerless gaze glimmered. "For old time's sake? After the promises you made, you owe me this, at least."

Remorse weighted his chest. He *did* owe her this, he thought miserably. And seeing the looks of passersby, he knew this wasn't the place to dredge up old wounds. The last thing he needed was to set more tongues wagging.

"I have a short while only," he said.

Her brilliant smile flashed like the sun after the rain. "This shan't take long. I promise."

Chapter Thirty

The next morning, the tinkling of the bell jarred Charity from her glum state, and she sat up straighter on the stool behind the counter. Mr. Jameson had gone out to fetch some supplies, leaving her to tend the shop on her own for a few minutes. She'd assured the clerk that she was up to the task. She'd volunteered to be here today; it was the only way she could persuade her father to rest the morning before coming to work in the afternoon.

She discreetly dabbed her eyes with a handkerchief as a customer entered and browsed through the displays. The lady wore a flower-laden bonnet that obscured her face, a trio of large footmen trailing in her wake.

Hold it together. No waterworks in front of customers.

Yet Charity couldn't stop the worry wringing her insides. Paul hadn't come home last night, and she didn't know where he was. She told herself that he must have gone to stay with his family, Mrs. Fines or Percy. But the fact that he hadn't bothered to let her know of his whereabouts ramped up her anxiety.

How angry was he at her father? At her?

Remorse gnawed at her. She'd known Father was in the wrong,

but she hadn't known how to stop him. She never had. And she'd been so worried about his health that she hadn't left with Paul ... she'd been so torn and confused at the time! The ugly revelations in the scandal sheet had hurt; though the pain remained, she told herself, *What's done is done.* She knew the man he'd been before they'd married. He'd promised to change, and as far as she knew, he'd kept his vows to her.

The past was over; it was time to move forward. She needed to explain to Paul that she *was* grateful for all that he'd done, the compromises he'd made for her. Only she wasn't certain how to do so. Loyalty made it difficult for her to say, *Please, please forgive my father. He doesn't mean to be difficult.*

But surely she could beg forgiveness for herself? Paul *would* forgive her, wouldn't he? He wouldn't toss her aside over a disagreement, the way her father kept insisting he would.

He walked out, just as I predicted, Father had said. *It's off to another lark for him—or to another fancy piece. Good riddance, I say.*

"Is that you, Miss Sparkler?"

Charity gave a start. The customer had approached the counter, regarding her with a quizzical smile. In the next instant, she recognized the auburn curls and petite, striking features.

"Mrs. Stone." Hastily, Charity hopped off her stool. "I beg your pardon. I didn't recognize you from afar."

"It's quite alright. You seem preoccupied." Astute hazel eyes studied her. "Is something amiss?"

The other's direct manner summoned an alarming heat to Charity's eyes. She blinked quickly and forced a smile. "Just wool-gathering, I'm afraid. Are you, um, shopping today?" That was an asinine thing to say. Why else would the actress be here? "I mean, is there anything I can assist you with?"

Mrs. Stone hesitated, her gaze circling the shop. "Are there no clerks at present?"

Flushing, Charity realized how incompetent she must appear,

first staring off into space and now babbling and on the verge of tears.

She drew her shoulders back. In a polite, brisk voice, she said, "I'm the only one here at the moment. I'd be happy to show you whatever you'd like."

"In that case, I'd like to see the silver vinaigrette. The one with the grapevine motif."

Charity fetched the item from the case. "It's a lovely piece, as you can see," she said, holding it out to the other, "made by one of our most popular artisans. The silverwork is sturdy yet exceedingly intricate. If you look closely, you can see the veins on the leaves."

"Indeed. Quite lovely."

"And if you like the vinaigrette, there's a chatelaine that would suit it most admirably."

A smile hovered on the actress' mouth. "I suppose I'll have a look at that, too."

A while later, Charity was quite pleased with herself as she wrapped up the other's purchases. She handed over the package, and as she did so, the lady's gaze caught on her hand.

"That's a pretty ring," Mrs. Stone said. "Opal, is it?"

Charity's heart gave a painful squeeze. "Thank you, yes. But it's not our stock. My husband gave it to me."

"You are recently wed?"

Charity began to nod ... and, to her mortification, a tear escaped.

"Oh, f-forgive me. I think I have something in my eye ..." She fumbled in her skirt pocket—where was her blasted handkerchief?

"Here, take mine. And then take a nice, deep breath."

Charity accepted the handkerchief, blotted her eyes. She tried to calm her fitful respiration.

"And another breath ... doesn't that feel better? Breathing calms the nerves. 'Tis what I do before a big performance," Mrs. Stone said.

After a few more breaths, Charity was able to say, "I'm fine. And ever so sorry. I don't know what came over me."

"There's no shame in tears, my dear. Marital woes?"

Charity's lips quivered again. Was the reason so obvious?

"I've been married myself," the lady said wryly, "and I recall those early days. Full of fire and passion—that desperate, terrifying, wonderful feeling of being alive."

Charity felt her jaw slacken. Not because this veritable stranger was talking about passion, but because the words resonated within her. She did feel alive—terrifyingly so. She loved Paul with all her heart and soul ... but what if he never returned her love? What if he tired of her? What if he was tiring of her *at that very moment*? What if yesterday's conflict had damaged their fledging marriage irreparably?

"I've frightened you." Clearly misinterpreting Charity's reaction, Mrs. Stone said, "Forgive me. Being in theatre, I tend to forget that passion is not a topic of everyday conversation. That not everyone believes, as I do, that life is too short to be lived for anything but happiness. You see, I—"

The tinkling bell cut the actress short. Jameson entered with parcels in hand. "Good day, ladies," he said on his way to the back room.

After returning his greeting, Charity prompted, "You were saying, Mrs. Stone?"

But the other woman's gaze had flitted to the door, her demeanor suddenly restless. "I'm afraid I must go. An appointment I just remembered."

"Oh. Well, it was a pleasure to see you," Charity said. "Do come again."

"I would like that." The wistful smile transformed Mrs. Stone's face into one of unforgettable beauty. With a graceful inclination of her head, she made her exit, her footmen flanking her.

Too late, Charity realized that she hadn't returned the other's handkerchief. She looked down at the fine linen, her finger tracing

Marietta Stone's initials, exquisitely rendered in silver thread. As she did so, the actress' words raced through her head. *Life is too short* ... and suddenly she knew what she had to do.

"I'm so glad you came to call, Charity."

Percy was glowing in a sunny frock that hinted at the slight rounding of her figure. The two were sitting on a settee in Percy's study, a spacious room that Mr. Hunt had dedicated to his wife's sole use. It was a feminine version of his own office, furnished with daintier furniture and done up in pretty shades of ivory and primrose. Eyeing the shelves stuffed with books and piles of parchment and paraphernalia occupying every surface, Charity thought love might not have been Mr. Hunt's only motivation for giving Percy a space of her own: the study kept the clutter from spilling over into the rest of the house.

Mr. Hunt had a keen sense of self-preservation. More importantly, he seemed to accept his wife's quirks, the same way Percy accepted his. Charity's heart clenched. Her own marriage had yet to achieve such a harmonious balance, but she wasn't giving up.

"How is Mr. Sparkler faring?" Percy asked.

"He's fine now. Back at the shop, against the physician's advice."

"Well, I'm relieved to hear of his recovery. But you, my dear, are looking rather peaked." Percy studied her with concerned eyes. "Is anything amiss?"

Of course her bosom friend would sense her turmoil.

Charity's hands knotted in her lap. "Have ... have you seen Paul?"

"Not recently." Percy frowned, and Charity's heart sank. "Don't you know where he is?"

Charity shook her head, her voice cracking as she admitted, "Oh Percy, I think ... I think I've driven him away!"

Percy gave her hand a comforting squeeze. "Tell me everything, dear."

After providing a halting description of the past week and a half, Charity concluded in tones of misery, "I understand why Paul is angry at me. I should have left with him or at least pleaded harder for him to stay. 'Tis all my fault—"

"It's *not* your fault. As much as it may pain you to hear this, your father is to blame," Percy said bluntly. "He's had it in for Paul from the start. While I can understand his reservations given my brother's reputation and the fiasco with Parkington, I cannot see why he won't at least give Paul a chance now that you're married. And from the sounds of it, my brother has never worked harder in his life."

"Father is worried for me. It's been him and me up until now, and he doesn't want to see me hurt," Charity said in a small voice.

"Then he'd be wise to stop creating trouble with your husband," Percy said tartly, "and putting you in the middle. If anything, there's your fault, dear: you try to please where there's no pleasing. And often at the cost of your own happiness. You've been that way ever since I've known you."

Charity bit her lip. Was that true? Was she overly accommodating ... too biddable? Did she fail to take into account her own feelings?

"But Paul has to bear some blame as well," Percy went on. "He ought to have at least sent you a note."

"I think he must be quite angry with me."

I should have thanked him for looking after the shop. For putting up with my stubborn papa. I should have told him how proud I am of him: for balancing Sparkler's with his training, for being the strongest and best man I know.

"It'll blow over. As Mr. Hunt says, one must develop sea legs being married to a Fines." Percy gave her a reassuring grin. "Paul may bluster about, but the storm will calm just as quickly as it started, you'll see."

Charity blew her nose. "I hope you're right."

"I know I am. And I also know that you're the perfect match for my brother: a true port to his tempest. After how steadfast you've been—from Spitalfields on through the business with Parkington—how can he doubt you?"

With a rush of guilt, Charity delivered the truth. "Actually, Paul doesn't know about Spitalfields."

"You haven't told him?" Percy exclaimed. "Why ever not?"

She herself didn't know why she hadn't confessed; at this point, what harm could it do? Most likely, Paul would be apologetic. Yet she held onto the secret like a soiled undergarment she didn't want anyone else to see. Perhaps that was it: she couldn't bring herself to air the ugly past, didn't want her husband to remember how little he'd thought of her ... and how much he'd loved another.

But that was going to change. Because Mrs. Stone was right: life was too short to be lived with regret. If Charity wanted her husband's love, then she would have to ask for it. She couldn't hide her feelings any longer. She would have to take the ultimate risk: she would declare her love for him and ask for his in return.

"I'm probably the last one who ought to be giving marital advice," Percy said, "but the one thing I have learned is that honesty is the best policy. Whenever Mr. Hunt and I keep something from one another, we invariably end up fighting over it."

"You and Mr. Hunt fight?" Charity said in surprise.

Percy's blue eyes shone with amusement. "Of course we do, dear. We're married."

"But you seem so"—Charity tried to describe the powerful connection she witnessed between the pair—"*blissful* together."

"That is the result of what happens *after* we fight." Clearing her throat, Percy said in an unusually delicate manner, "And from your blush, may I infer that you know the sort of, um, marital bliss I'm referring to?"

Charity was determined to turn a fresh page and be more truthful. So she said simply, "Yes, I do."

"I'm ever so glad. As much as I hate to ask since this involves my brother,"—Percy wrinkled her pert nose—"I am assuming that he lives up to expectations in that regard?"

"He does." Sudden humor bubbled up, and Charity said slyly, "He lives *up* indeed."

Percy's eyes rounded. "Charity Fines, did you just make a warm jest?"

"Well, yes ... I suppose I did."

"How very wicked of you! I am impressed," Percy said gleefully.

"Paul's influence, I'm afraid." Her smile fading, Charity said, "And henceforth I shall strive to be more honest with him. About everything."

"In that case, I say we put our heads together and locate my brother so that the two of you can patch things up in the time-honored tradition."

Anticipation fluttered in Charity's breast. "I suppose we should start at your mama's?"

"Capital idea. At this time of day, there's bound to be some of Lisbett's apricot buns and as I'm eating for two,"—Percy grinned and patted her belly—"I'll have the excuse to claim twice my share."

Chapter Thirty-One

Paul came awake ... and wished he hadn't. Hades' own hammer pounded at his temples. When he tried to sit up, he fell back with a queasy groan.

Bloody fucking hell.

A few seconds later, he tried again, cautiously cracking one eye open. Once his vision focused and the room stopped spinning, he saw pink velvet drapes, a vanity cluttered with colorful perfume bottles, a secretaire stacked with hatboxes ... and his insides turned to ice.

Bloody fucking *hell*—where was he? What had he done?

He bolted upright in panic. The bedchamber wavered before his eyes, and he pushed himself from the bed, stumbling against the vanity. Bottles rattled, and one rolled off the surface, shattering against the ground.

Heart thudding, he heard approaching footsteps.

The door swung open ... and Thomas Bellinger poked his head in.

"Surprised to see you up, old chap. By Jove, we went on the mop last night, didn't we?" Though Bellinger's eyes were red-rimmed, his freckled face creased in a grin. "I haven't been that top-heavy for ages. Just like the old times."

Memory returned. Yesterday, after the torturous episode with Rosalind, Paul had sought out Bellinger. He'd intended to visit Oblivion, and no one knew the way there better than his friend. Along with a crowd of the old cronies, he and Bellinger had gone for a night on the town. His gut roiled as he recalled how much alcohol he'd imbibed. He'd broken his vow of abstinence ... yet as far as he could recall, that was the only vow he'd broken.

"Where are we?" he said hoarsely.

"Don't remember? Well, you were drunker than a wheelbarrow, so I can't blame you," Bellinger said, chuckling. "The other fellows wanted to end the night at a Covent Garden Nunnery. Lovely fresh recruits plucked from the countryside, don't you know."

At the mention of prostitutes, Paul's belly lurched again.

Bellinger waggled his brows. "But the drink must have affected your brain for you transformed before our very eyes."

"What do you mean?"

"You turned from our adored rake, the one all of us fellows have aspired to be at some point or another and became the deuced *Prince of Virtue*!" Bellinger slapped his thigh, hooting with laughter. "Refused to go to a bawdy house because you're leg-shackled. Went on and on about *vows*. You had the others roaring." He had to catch his breath before sputtering, "Ain't *ever* going to live this one down, Fines!"

"Glad I could provide the evening's entertainment." Scrubbing his neck, Paul muttered, "How'd I get here? Where *is* here?"

"My sister's room in my father's house. She and the rest of the family are off visiting our ever ailing great-aunt in Yorkshire." Bellinger yawned. "Since the place was empty and more spacious than my apartments, I brought us here."

Paul's chest loosened. He realized that he'd begun to breathe again.

"Well, what's next on our agenda, eh? Have a shave and off to the club?"

"What time is it?" Paul said.

Bellinger blinked as if he'd been asked to solve a complicated maths problem. "Buggered if I know. Late afternoon, maybe. What does it matter?"

Paul refrained from rolling his eyes. Mostly because his head hurt like murder when he moved any part of it. "It matters because I have business to attend to."

"Back at Gentleman Jackson's, you mean?" Scratching his head, Bellinger said with a grimace, "Not sure the old skull can handle getting thrashed about at present."

"I'm in no mood to box." Paul went to the window, parted the drapes. Tried to get his bearings and decide what he should do next. He wondered if Charity was worried about him ...

"Ah, I see," the other said in a knowing manner. "Perhaps you have an intimate *tête-à-tête* with a certain Scottish countess, eh?"

Paul's head whipped—*Ouch, devil take it!*—in Bellinger's direction. "Why do you say that?"

"Easy there, old boy." Bellinger held up his hands. "It don't take a genius to surmise you've got the former Miss Drummond on your mind. Hell of a shocker, I'm sure, with her showing up in the carriage like that."

"Goddamnit. Were you *spying* on me?"

"Spying implies premeditation, and I never plan ahead," Bellinger said defensively. "I happened to see the two of you from the window of the Saloon; fair Rosalind always did catch a man's eye. In fact, a bunch of fellows stopped practicing to get a closer look."

Bleeding perfect. Just what Paul needed: a roomful of young bloods with their noses pressed up to the glass, eager to report and embellish everything that they thought they saw.

"Nothing happened," Paul snarled. "For God's sake, I'm *married*."

His friend shrugged. "So is she. Hasn't changed much though, has she?"

Indeed, she hadn't. What had surprised him more, however, was the fact that *he* had. So much so that when she'd taken him on that carriage ride and proposed that they now enjoy the freedoms that their respective marriages permitted, he'd felt nothing. No, nothing wasn't it.

He'd felt disgusted. At himself.

For ever believing that he'd loved Rosalind and for acting like a bloody fool because of it. Had he truly been so shallow that he hadn't seen past her beauty to her true character? The fact that he'd spent years nursing a delusion—that he'd nearly destroyed his life and his family's fortunes because of it—made him feel nauseous. It wasn't that he judged Rosalind for pursuing extramarital activities; wives carried on *affaires* all the time.

Just not the kind of wife he wanted for himself.

At the thought of Charity, his gut balled. He knew he was making a mull of things with her. His marriage was like a runaway carriage, and the reins were slipping from his grasp. His exchange with Rosalind only heightened his sense of an impending Doomsday. Although he'd turned down her proposition as gently as he could, she'd broken into tears.

Feeling awkward and guilty, he'd passed her his handkerchief. Her shimmering gaze and pretty protestations had made him even more uncomfortable.

"You're a liar, Paul Fines," she'd said finally, blotting her eyes, "and a fool. Do you know how many gentlemen would give their eyeteeth to have a dalliance with me?"

Not knowing how to answer, he'd said, "I'm sorry if I've disappointed you."

"Who do you think you're fooling, masquerading as a virtuous husband?"

"I'm not masquerading as anything." Yet his heart had begun

to thud, his inner voice sneering, *You're an imposter and everyone can see it.*

"You'll tire of your little mouse soon enough."

"Don't call her that," he'd said between his teeth.

Rosalind had given a silvery laugh, tossed back her dark curls. Had he truly found her affectations pleasing at one time? Looking closer, he'd perceived the faint lines that hardened her beauty—and the streak of vanity that threatened to destroy it entirely.

"Charity Sparkler ... ironic name, isn't it?" Malice had given Rosalind's voice a grating edge. "I can barely recall what she looks like, save for those unfortunate spots. You told me once how you pitied her—how your sister *made* you dance with her."

Self-loathing had scorched his gut. Had he said such a cruel thing? He probably had, the bastard that he'd been. In that moment, he'd truly despised himself: bloody careless and blind, the scoundrel that Uriah Sparkler accused him of being.

"She's changed," he'd bit out, "and, more importantly, so have I."

"A leopard never changes his spots," Rosalind had drawled. "You are as you always were. The only difference is that now you've got delusions of nobility." She'd run a finger along his jaw. "How I miss the man who knew exactly what he was ... and wasn't. The Paul I knew would have recognized the simple truth: you're meant to be a lover, not a husband. Good for fun but not much else."

He rubbed his temples now, trying to blot out the unpleasantness, trying to think. Trying to fend off the urge to do something easier ... like down a bottle of whiskey. But, no, he wasn't going to add insult to injury and get drunk again. He had that much control at least.

"I have to see Charity," he said at last.

Bellinger blinked. "What for?"

"She's my wife, man." Paul glared at him.

"Huh. Well, I'm a bachelor, so what do I know?" Bellinger

gave him a once over. "For what it's worth, however, I wouldn't suggest going to your lady in your current condition."

"Why? What's the matter with me?" *Besides the fact that I'm a worthless bastard.*

Bellinger cocked a brow and answered with a question. "How do *I* look?"

Paul ran a cursory glance over his friend's rumpled clothes and disheveled appearance. "Like something the cat dragged in ..."— his nose caught a whiff and he grimaced—"from the Thames. Right." He dragged his hands through his own hair. "That bad off, am I?"

"Worse," Bellinger said cheerfully. "*I* didn't get into fisticuffs with those lads from Oxford."

Paul looked at his hands—bruising splotched the knuckles. He touched his jaw and grimaced at the swelling. No wonder his entire head was throbbing.

"Hell," he muttered. "I can't let her see me like this."

"Wait until the morning to serenade her," Bellinger advised. "After a good night's sleep, you'll have your angelic countenance back. You might consider sweetening her up with a poesy, too; I reckon you'll need all the help you can get."

Paul reckoned that for once Bellinger was right. "When did you get to be so clever?"

Bellinger grinned. "How do you think I've maintained my bachelorhood until now? Takes brains to evade the parson's mousetrap, y'know."

And even more brains, Paul thought glumly, to figure out how to make the contraption of marriage work. But he'd have to find a way—because this time around he couldn't face the consequences of failure.

Chapter Thirty-Two

Charity returned to the shop at half-past four. Although the visit to Mrs. Fines' house had yielded no information about Paul's whereabouts, she nonetheless felt reassured by the conversations with her friend and mama-in-law. She took heart from the fact that a couple as blissfully happy as Percy and Mr. Hunt had their share of marital ups and downs. And Mrs. Fines had revealed that, as newlyweds, she and her beloved Jeremiah had fought like *cats and dogs*.

Charity was struck by a revelation: she didn't have much experience with arguing. She'd learned over the years, particularly with her father, to simply hold her tongue. But maybe continually sweeping things under the carpet wasn't such a good idea. Maybe doing so made arguments, when they happened, even worse.

At times like these, Charity missed having a mama more than ever, that source of infinite feminine wisdom to bolster her through difficult times.

She had Father, of course. But he wasn't exactly sympathetic to the plight of her marriage.

"Waste of time," he grumbled when she explained where she'd

been. "Chasing after that scoundrel when the shop needs you. When I need you."

Guilt immediately prickled her, yet it was accompanied by another feeling: burgeoning resentment. And for once, she lost the desire to hide it.

"I'm doing my best," she said, lifting her chin. "It isn't easy to be a daughter and a wife. But I'm married now, and I must give my husband his proper due."

Her father's jaw slackened. "*His* due? You dare talk to me—the one who raised you—in this disrespectful manner?"

"I'm grateful for everything you've done for me. Truly I am. But I must also be allowed to make my own decisions." She inhaled, allowing her lungs to expand more freely. "I'm not a little girl any longer."

"I wish to God that you were."

Her papa's gruff tone caught her by surprise; he was not a sentimental sort.

"Everyone's got to grow up," she said softly, "and I'll always be your daughter."

"But I can't protect you anymore." The lines on his forehead deepened, and his somber grey gaze held hers. "You don't know the world like I do, Charity, how it treats people like you and me. People who aren't beautiful, whose only weapons are diligence and modesty." His hand fumbled for hers. "People like us get *hurt*, don't you understand?"

Before Charity could reply, the bell chimed. An exquisitely turned out woman entered the shop, her profile shaded by a dashing bonnet of green straw. Her promenade dress clung to the peaks and valleys of her flawless figure, the flounces swaying sensuously with each step. As she glided toward them, her face came into the light.

Charity's lungs constricted. She knew that face. The unforgettable violet eyes, the dramatic black curls, the smoother than cream skin. Rosalind Drummond—nay, Lady Monteith ... what was she doing here?

"How can I be of service today?" Her father went forward eagerly.

Rosalind waved a delicate blush-colored glove in his direction, the way one might swat away an annoying insect. "I'm not here for you. 'Tis Mrs. Fines"—perfect pink lips pulled into a hard smile—"with whom I wish to have a word."

Charity stepped from behind the counter. "Yes?"

"You do know who I am?" One raven brow arched.

Recalling her manners, Charity dipped in a quick curtsy. "Yes, of course. Good afternoon, Countess Monteith." From the corner of her eye, she saw her father's puzzled expression. What did a titled lady want with her? Though Charity didn't know herself, dread percolated through her. "How may I help you?"

Haughty eyes swept over her. "My, you *have* changed."

You haven't. You're as beautiful as you ever were, Charity thought with a sinking feeling. And Paul was bound to think so.

"Are you looking for P—I mean, Mr. Fines?" she said quietly. "If so, he isn't here—"

Rosalind gave a casual wave of her hand. "Oh, I've seen him already. I make it a point to visit with my oldest and dearest friends when I'm in town."

The gleam in the other woman's eyes shredded Charity's heart. It was a physical pain, the slicing of her deepest self by a surgeon's precise blade. She couldn't speak for fear of what might come out: the cry of an injured animal—a pathetic, soul-deep sound.

"Actually, that is why I'm here. I believe I have something that belongs to you." With a smirk, Rosalind removed a handkerchief from her reticule. "He left this at our ... meeting. Such exquisite embroidery work—yours, I believe?"

Charity had no choice but to take the dangling handkerchief. Paul's initials branded her palm.

"Men will be men," Rosalind said with a lilting laugh. "They always forget ordinary things, don't they? Leave them so carelessly behind."

"That is *enough*, you trollop!" Her father spoke up, and even through the veil of numbness, Charity could hear the anger in his voice. "Shame on you for flaunting your sins. Title or no, we Sparklers don't cater to the likes of you—get out of my shop!"

Still smiling, Rosalind sauntered toward the door. "I shouldn't blame myself if I were you. 'Tis a miracle you managed to land him in the first place. But then again, his weak spot was always pity. He used to laugh about it with me, the way his sister made him stand up with you for all those dances."

The barb struck the center of Charity's being. She pressed a hand against her mouth to prevent a choked sound from escaping.

"Well, I wouldn't worry about it," Rosalind said. "I tire easily of novelty, you see, so you'll have your merchandise back soon."

The bell announced her departure, then ... silence.

"Have a seat, daughter."

Charity remained standing, her body and mind frozen.

"Charity?"

Feeling a tug on her arm, she looked at her father. Saw the anguish mirrored on his plain, weathered face as he said hoarsely, "This is what I wanted to protect you from. The ugly world. It's no place for us."

"Father?" she whispered.

He placed a tentative hand on her shoulder. It was a rare show of affection, an offer of comfort in a time of grief. An ache began to spread in her throat.

"I'll go make us a pot of tea. Keep your chin up like I taught you, and you'll get through this." He gave her another awkward pat. "Be glad you learned this lesson sooner as opposed to later, my girl."

Watching her father hobble off, Charity thought numbly, *Soon has come and gone. It's already far too late.*

Chapter Thirty-Three

The next morning, the doorbell rang, and Charity knew it was Paul. Apparently, so did her unexpected visitors, for Percy and Helena said as one, "We must be off now."

She managed to keep her mask of calm in place. She'd worn it for the past half-hour while her guests had delivered the bad news. Knowing that Charity did not read the gossip columns, Percy and Helena had come to inform her of the sordid business before she heard about it from less well-intentioned sources. They'd tried to soften the blow.

Percy had insisted that the article in *The Times* about a rekindled flame between *Mr. F.* and *Lady M.* was nothing more than slander. Helena had stated her belief that it was likely all some sort of misunderstanding, a chance meeting blown out of proportion.

Charity had listened ... and felt nothing.

Because she already knew that it was all true. Paul was in love with Rosalind; he'd always been. He'd only married Charity out of obligation. And whatever she'd believed to be developing between them since had been a figment of her imagination. Or physical lust, at the very best.

What finally deadened her heart was this: he'd lied to her.

Broken his vow of fidelity to her. And while she might be plain and insignificant and not the wife of his choosing, she did not deserve that.

Paul came into the room, his gaze searching out hers. With an odd sense of detachment, she observed that for once he did not appear to be his impeccable self. It was as if his godly veneer had been stripped from him, leaving behind a mortal man who'd clearly been engaged in worldly activities. A purpling bruise marred one side of his jaw, and dark shadows hung beneath his eyes. His hair was unruly beyond what fashion dictated, as if he'd run his fingers repeatedly through the gilded waves. Even his cravat lacked its usual finesse.

He stopped short at the sight of Percy and Helena, who were standing, ready to flee.

"Good morning." He did a perfunctory bow. "Have I interrupted a *tête-à-tête?*"

"You know very well why we're here." Percy scowled at him. "Dash it all, what is going on Paul? Why are the papers filled with this nonsense about you and—"

"Hush, dear." Taking Percy's arm, Helena pulled her toward the door. "I think we'd best leave the two to sort this out for themselves. See you both soon, I hope?"

"Thank you, my lady," Charity said.

"Your servant," Paul said curtly.

Then she and Paul were alone. The sea of silence and tension would once have intimidated her, but now she felt a strange calm. In this shabby parlor of this shabby house, she was where she belonged. She no longer had to hide who and what she was. There was a bittersweet freedom in that, a power in her knotted hair and unattractive dress.

Why should I try to please him? He doesn't want me anyway.

He took a step toward her, then stopped as if he didn't know quite what to do. Clearing his throat, he said, "Charity, you know it's not true."

Oh God, how much time had she spent deceiving herself, weaving futile dreams about their future? "Actually, I don't know that," she said coolly, without inflection.

He flinched but said, "I gave you my word—"

"And I was fool enough to believe it. I know." She kept her gaze and voice level. "But I don't, not anymore."

"You ... you don't mean that."

Why did he sound so stricken? When she was the one who had to bear the brunt of his betrayal, his lies? Anger was an ice floe through her veins, numbing her against remorse, chilling her words.

"My father was right: you *are* selfish and irresponsible and incapable of keeping your vows. No pretty words can change that fact."

His eyes blazed. "That is bloody unfair! I have kept my vows—"

"Have you?" Her brows rose. "So you weren't foxed last evening and that isn't the souvenir of a drunken brawl on your jaw?"

His chest heaved, his high cheekbones stained with color. "That is different! Goddamnit, last night was the first time I've had a drink since ... since ..."

"Since you made that promise never to drink again?"

"Yes! I mean *no*." His hands curled into fists at his sides. "I can explain, if you'd just listen to me—"

"I am *tired* of listening to you." Her voice shook with sudden violence, and she had to take a breath before saying more calmly, "I'm tired of being disappointed. And I see now that is what this marriage will amount to: disappointment for you ... and for me."

"I never said I was disappointed!"

She shrugged. "Your actions speak louder than words. So loudly, in fact,"—she gestured to the newspaper that lay on the coffee table, the one that Percy and Helena had come to warn her about—"that it seems the whole Town knows about it."

Pain spurted in her chest, and it took every ounce of self-possession to staunch the flow. While she had been trying to chase him down in order to apologize for her behavior, he had been out *cavorting* with Rosalind. Out pursuing his Daphne, the beauty who would forevermore be his fantasy. No, more than fantasy for she was flesh and blood. The image of Rosalind in Paul's arms made Charity's breath catch with agony: two exquisite people who fit perfectly together.

"It's not true. None of it is. And if you'd just give me a minute to explain—" Paul took another step toward her, a hand stretched out, but she cut him off.

"Were you or were you not with Lady Monteith?"

"I ... was. But not like that." His hand fell to his side as he grated out, "Nothing happened! 'Pon my honor, I swear it."

Charity couldn't take any more of his lies. Her insides were so cold, cracking like a sheet of ice. The rage was like nothing she'd known before, bone-deep, a wintry blast that swept away everything but the instinct to lash out. To erect a wall of ice between herself and the source of her torment.

"The way you swore never to drink again?" she said. "The way you swore to help my father? Or, perhaps, you mean the way you promised never to let Rosalind interfere with our marriage?" She gave him a withering look. "I'm tired of listening to your explanations. My father was right: you have no honor, no shame, and I won't believe another word you say, not ever again."

Paul's chest burned with an agony worse than any he'd felt before. It was worse than the disillusionment of Rosalind, worse even than his father's harshest criticism. Because he could have expected those things—but not this. Not from Charity, his port in the storm. Too late, he realized that her faith in him had become a beacon, and now that light was gone. Extinguished. He could see no sign of understanding in her cold, opaque eyes.

He was abandoned, adrift.

Alone.

Panic cinched his throat. *What do you expect, you fool? You've shamed her in front of everyone, and she'll never forgive you. You've ruined everything—like you always knew you would.*

Yet for some reason, words continued spilling from his mouth. "I'm sorry I've caused you embarrassment, but this article—engineered by Parkington, I'm sure—is pure defamation. Yes, I did see Rosalind. She approached me, asked me to ... to speak with her."

Mouth pinched, Charity said nothing.

"I went because I ..."—he wracked his brain for the reason—"I felt I owed it to her. Yes, that's it. Because for so long I thought myself in love with her, you see ..."

Charity's cheeks grew even more bloodless, and he could have bitten his tongue off then and there. *Stupid, stupid thing to say! You just told your wife that you thought yourself in love with another woman, you moron.*

"But I'm not," he said quickly, "and so I turned her down."

"You're not in love with her." He'd never heard Charity's voice so cold and unforgiving. She chilled him to the core, and the instinct to escape the squall took hold of him, but he soldiered on even as she said with scathing disbelief, "When did this happen?"

Confusion whipped at him. "I just ... realized it. That she wasn't who I thought she was. Or what I wanted." That was part of it, but there was more, more that he himself did not truly understand. Yet with a strained breath, he took the biggest risk of his life and said, "And that perhaps I ... I was developing feelings for you."

"How kind of you."

He recoiled at her indifference. Here he was trying to pry his heart open ... and she was *mocking* him? Who *was* this Charity? The uncertainty chilled him to the marrow, as did the icy fingers of self-doubt. He'd started to think that he might be falling in love with her, but did he know his wife at all? Had he misjudged his feelings yet again? He'd been wrong about Rosalind, certainly.

Rosalind's words mocked him. *You're meant to be a lover, not a husband. Good for fun but not much else.*

Anger suddenly erupted. He hadn't done anything wrong, so why was he constantly apologizing to Charity? Why did he always end up the one groveling, the one who got blamed for everything? Devil take it, he was *sick and tired* of being judged as worthless!

"I can see that your mind is made up," he said in a tone that matched hers, "and that there's no use discussing matters further."

Her lips pressed in a line, which enraged him further. "I agree."

"Forget what I said about my feelings for you," he said acidly. "I'm sure I was wrong."

"I didn't take any stock in what you said—in anything you say, in point of fact." She spoke through her teeth. "Why would I? You're as fickle as the weather."

"And you're as stubborn as a rock," he bit out. "A real chip off the old boulder."

"Do *not* bring my father into this."

"He does it himself by sticking his bleeding nose into our business at every turn." Seething, Paul gave his pent-up frustration full reign. "He treats me worse than dirt and you like his goddamned slave. Yet you welcome every lash, cower to his every demand— what the hell is the matter with you? Haven't you any backbone?"

"My father loves me, wants the best for me," she said in a shaking voice.

"Telling yourself something doesn't make it true."

She looked as if he'd slapped her. Remorse pierced his rage but was wiped out in the next instant by her calm, clear tones. "You wish to know the truth? You don't even know what love *is*. The only one you care about is yourself."

"I gave up my bloody training for you!" he roared.

"I didn't ask you to. Nor did I ask for those stupid hats or a lady's maid or accounts at all those snobbish shops. Those were *your* desires, not mine." Her chin angled up. "You want me to be someone I'm not."

It was so far from the truth, such a twisting of his intentions that his vision actually turned red. He couldn't think; his lungs burned, his chest heaving as if he'd gone twenty rounds.

Yet she had a final blow to deliver.

"Marrying you was the biggest mistake of my life. I want you to leave," she said.

"Good," he shouted over the pounding in his ears, "because I'm going. I'm going to focus on the tournament like I should have in the first place instead of wasting my time with that sinkhole of a shop—and you!"

"Go do your stupid boxing. Or go to hell for all I care," she snapped.

Rage darkened his vision. In that moment, she represented every failure he'd ever had in his life—and he couldn't get away fast enough. He turned and stalked out without another word.

Chapter Thirty-Four

"I'll be off now." Mr. Jameson poked his head through the curtain of the back room.

Bent over a ledger, her father gave the clerk an absent wave.

Charity said quickly, "Thank you for staying so late. I'll walk you out, Mr. Jameson."

As they headed to the front of the shop, the clerk said in an undertone, "Has your father seen a physician of late? He doesn't yet seem his old self."

Charity shook her head in frustration. "He refuses to see Dr. Harrison. And he's not eating or sleeping well. His worry about the shop's future keeps him up all hours."

"Any news from Mr. Fines?" Jameson said hopefully.

An arrow shot through Charity's heart. Paul had been gone over a month. He hadn't written, and even if she wanted to send him a letter, she wouldn't know where to address it. The Fancy tournament had begun, the roving matches moving from county to county. The locations of the matches were kept secret until the last moment as prizefighting was not strictly legal and frowned upon by local magistrates. According to the papers, the bouts were attended by thousands, and the wagering that took place added up to hundreds of thousands of pounds.

At any rate, what would she write to Paul? While her anger had faded, her hurt had not. She could not bring herself to apologize, even though she regretted her part in their quarrel. She'd acted badly. With deep shame, she recalled how viciously she'd lashed out, wanting him to feel the same pain that she had over his betrayal.

Yet *had* he dallied with Rosalind?

Whenever she faced that question—and it was often—she experienced a volatile mixture of anger, bitterness, and longing. Paul had denied an *affaire* with his former flame; could she believe him at his word? She tried to take a logical approach. She pitted the precious memories of Chudleigh Crest against the ugly encounter with Rosalind, trying to decide which had been real.

Magic versus reality: what was the more likely truth?

As the days went on, her hope dwindled.

"No," she said quietly. "No news."

Jameson patted her arm. "I'm sure he's just busy. He's stunned everyone, coming out of the blue and winning all those fights." Excitement sparked in the old man's rheumy gaze. "According to the papers, he's got a real shot at becoming Champion now. One more match and he'll make the final fight two weeks from now."

She forced a smile. "Yes, he's done very well."

He's free now to pursue his true dreams. Why would he ever come back?

"He'd have done well here too, given half a chance. But not my place to say." Jameson pulled on his cap, tipped the brim. "Good night to you, Mrs. Fines, and see you in the morning."

Charity watched from the doorway until the clerk's hunched figure disappeared down the street. The balmy night air felt good, an escape from the stifling confines of the shop. At half-past nine, the other shopkeepers had closed their establishments. The street was dark and empty save for a stray hawker's barrow in the distance.

She and her father had been at Sparkler's more than twelve hours already; her muscles ached with fatigue, and she was ready to go home. Though the thought of what awaited her there—an empty house, a cold bed—didn't exactly lift her spirits. Strange how she'd never noticed how dreary her existence was until Paul had come along. For a short time, he'd lit her world up.

The ever present heat pushed behind her eyes. Chiding herself for the umpteenth time not to be so dashed maudlin, she closed the door, preparing to lock up. When she searched her skirt pockets, however, she couldn't find the key. Perfect. Now she was a feather wit *and* a watering pot. If only she had looks as well, she could be debutante of the year.

As she headed to the back room to retrieve the key, she heard the door bell jingle behind her. With a smile fixed on her face, she turned, saying, "I'm afraid we're closed ..."

Her sentence sputtered out. Her brain tried to assimilate the sight of three large brutes—menacing in black greatcoats—standing inside the shop. *Cutthroats?* Before she could scream, one of them grabbed her, his thick leather glove smothering her cry.

"Button yer 'ole if ye know what's good for ye," he said. "Where's the old man?"

She struggled frantically, shouted a muffled warning to her father. Panic thumped in her chest as her papa emerged from the back. Dear God, what would they do to him—

The sight of the pistol in his hands delivered another shock.

Father ... with a *firearm*?

"What do you want?" her father demanded.

One of the villains stepped forward, a hulking man with dark whiskers. The leader? "Don't bugger yourself more than you already 'ave, Sparkler. Put the bleedin' piece down. We've just come fer a chat."

"Garrity sent you?" her father said.

Charity's breath puffed against the suffocating leather. Mr. Garrity? What did he have to do with these ruffians?

"Mr. Garrity 'asn't 'eard from you," Dark Whiskers said, shaking his head and making a *tsking* noise. "And our employer, 'e don't like those who welsh on their debts. That's why me and the boys are 'ere—to apply a bit o' persuasion, see?"

The other two laughed, the pitiless sound sending chills down Charity's spine.

"Let my daughter go." Her father sounded weak and faint. The gun shook within his frail grip. "She's got nothing to with this."

"I wouldn't agree." Dark Whiskers crossed over to her. When his beefy hand reached toward her, she shrank back, but his accomplice held her in place. She yelped as the leader yanked at her topknot. Her hair tumbled down, and, shaking, she could do nothing as he fingered a long wavy strand of her hair.

"Pretty little piece." His leering grin made her skin crawl. "And a valuable bargaining chip, eh?"

"I'm warning you, *let her go*. Do it or I'll ... I'll shoot!"

The pistol wavered madly in her papa's hand, and Charity was overtaken by a fresh wave of fear. To her knowledge, he had never shot a gun—had never even gone hunting. What if he accidentally injured himself?

The leader must have been thinking the same thing, for his beady eyes narrowed. "Put the bloody pistol down before you shoot yourself or your precious daughter. We 'aven't come to 'urt you—but we will if you don't stop wavin' that damn thing."

"What do you want?" Father said in a trembling voice.

"To collect what's owed. Where's the blunt?"

"I ... I don't have it. Not yet." A thin line of perspiration trickled over her father's pale brow. "But I will have it soon, if Garrity would only—"

"Our employer's been more than patient wif you. Seein' as 'ow you've already failed to keep up your end o' the bargain once before,"—the brute cast a knowing glance at Charity, confirming

her sudden terrible suspicion of what that bargain had been—
"you're lucky 'e gave you a second chance. But time's up, Sparkler:
Mr. Garrity wants 'is thirty thousand quid."

Charity's breath halted. Her papa owed *thirty thousand pounds*
to Mr. Garrity?

Alarmingly ashen, Father stammered, "I've got f-five thousand.
I'll get him the rest soon, I promise—"

"Mr. Garrity's tired o' waitin'. 'Is instruction was to collect."
The leader motioned to the other cutthroats. "C'mon, lads, start
loadin' up. Ev'rything we can fit in the wagon. Start wif the jewelry
first."

Charity was thrown aside. As she caught herself against a
counter, her previous captor removed a cudgel from his greatcoat.
He stepped over to a display case of necklaces and, without hesitation, brought the iron head down. Glass shattered, the shards
tinkling onto velvet. He reached in, scooped out the contents, and
dumped them into a sack. His fellow cutthroats did the same,
methodically ransacking the shop.

"No, stop. Stop I say! Not my shop!"

Before Charity's stunned eyes, her father went running into
the fray, tackling the leader. The ruffian grunted, hauling him up
by the throat, shaking him with such force that the pistol flew
from his hands. Her papa dangled as if from a noose, his feet
jerking.

"Leave my father be!" She lunged forward, and a fiery pain
seared across her scalp.

One of the cutthroats had caught her by her hair. His vicious
grip tightened, and he laughed as she struggled as helplessly as a
mouse pinned by the tail. "'Tis men's work, little hussy. Stay out
o' it."

She ignored the pain, trying to tear free. Trying to get to her
father whose eyes were bulging and glazed, his hands clutching his
chest.

"Stop, he's ill!" she cried. "You're hurting him!"

Her papa made a loud gasping noise ... and slumped in his captor's grip.

"What in bloody hell?" The man released him.

Father crumpled to the ground. Didn't move.

"Father!" The hold on her loosened, and Charity scrambled to her papa's side. Cradling his head in her lap, she placed a shaking hand on his neck. His pulse fluttered as lightly as a moth's wings.

His eyes opened. "Daughter?"

"Yes, Father, I'm here," she choked out.

"S-sorry ..."

"No, save your strength. We'll call for Dr. Harrison—"

"Too ... late." With obvious effort, he raised a hand to her cheek. "My poor Charity ... who will take care of you now?"

"I'll be fine, Father. So will you. We'll be together, the two of us, like we've always been."

"Something ... need to tell you ..."

His hand fell, his head rolling to the side. Desperately, she patted his chest, trying to find a beat, a sign. But there was ... nothing.

"No," she whispered.

"I didn't do it." The leader's shaken voice came from above her. "Wasn't my fault. Daft bugger came runnin' at me, just holding 'im back I was—"

Her head whipped up. "You're a *murderer*!"

"Ain't gettin' paid eno' for murder," one of the others muttered. "I'm gettin' out of 'ere."

Two of them rushed from the shop. The leader took another look at her face and backed away with his hands held up, repeating, "I didn't kill nobody."

"Get out!" she cried.

He ran off.

It was just her and her father again. The two of them ... together in the shop. She clung to his hand as the chill came to claim them both.

Chapter Thirty-Five

"We'll have your things packed," Percy said, "and you'll come stay with me."

Charity concentrated on snipping the black grosgrain ribbon. She wound it around a sprig of fresh rosemary, tied a neat bow, and added the mourning memento to the pile on the coffee table. She raised her eyes to her circle of female friends, all wearing dark gowns and concerned expressions.

She forced a smile. "There's no need. I'm fine."

Mrs. Fines said quietly, "It isn't good to be alone after a loss, my dear. You need company. And rest—you haven't slept more than a few hours these days past."

Charity paused to look around the parlor, which was draped in black. She'd kept vigil here, staying at her father's side until the church service earlier this afternoon. The funeral had been an intimate gathering, with no more than a dozen in attendance. Percy, Mrs. Fines, Helena, and Marianne had accompanied her back to the house afterward.

Her throat thickened, but she did not cry. Grief seemed to absorb her tears. She felt dry, hollow as a husk. Her head ached, and her insides buzzed with numb, restless energy. Picking up the sewing shears, she resumed cutting lengths of the ribbon.

"I appreciate your concern, truly I do," she said, her eyes on her task, "but I wish to stay here."

"Will you eat something at least?" From across the coffee table, Helena held out a plate of sandwiches. "All you've had today is tea."

Even though she had no appetite, Charity saw the worry on all the ladies' faces. So she put down the scissors and took the plate. The sandwich tasted like sawdust.

"We should ring for some hot milk as well," Mrs. Fines said.

"Given the occasion, I think something stronger is warranted." This came from Marianne, who removed a silver flask from her jet-encrusted reticule. She tipped amber liquid into a tea cup and handed it to Charity.

Charity sniffed the contents. "What *is* this?"

"Cognac," Marianne said.

"I don't think—"

"Drink up."

Grimacing, Charity held her breath and downed the contents. Fire blazed down her throat. An instant later, the burn mellowed and warmed insides that she hadn't realized were cold.

"Better?" Marianne asked.

"Yes," Charity said.

"On to details then. First off,"—at Marianne's uncharacteristic hesitation, Charity instinctively braced—"does anyone know how to get a hold of Mr. Fines?"

"Mr. Hunt is searching for him," Percy said. "He thinks my brother might be in Yorkshire."

Charity's head jerked up. Her friend hadn't mentioned this.

"You have enough to contend with," Percy told her, "and before you argue, yes, Paul does need to know about what happened. He cares about you so very much."

"Percy is right. The nonsense in the past must be put aside, my dear. At a time like this, you need your husband, and I'm certain my son needs you, too," Mrs. Fines said stoutly.

Charity wasn't as certain. Paul was likely doing just fine without her. She twisted the ring on her finger; in the gloom of the parlor, the opal appeared milky white, its fire dimmed.

Over the past three days, she'd spent a great deal of time in sober contemplation. Why hadn't her father told her about the enormity of his debt? Why had he kept his burdens to himself at the cost of his health ... his life? Through the veil of grief, she'd come to see the truth: she was her father's daughter. She could see now how pride and fear had blinded him, much as it had blinded her.

From seeing what was real.

Because her marriage had been real and worth fighting for, no matter what Paul had done. And thinking back on his protestations of innocence, she'd begun to believe she'd made a grave mistake. In not believing in him—in not at least listening to what he had to say. And now it was too late.

Just like it was too late for her papa.

Her fingers reached instinctively for her silver locket. But it wasn't there. She'd placed it in the casket so her father wouldn't have to be alone.

Her temples throbbed. Her thoughts blurred. With a disorienting pang, she wondered if she'd wound her topknot too tightly as Paul had used to tease her for doing.

His voice drifted back her, "Why do you hide yourself?"

The truth hammered in her head. *Because I'm so afraid. So afraid you'll see me as I truly am ... and I'll be alone.*

But wasn't she already alone?

The doorbell rang.

"Who would call at this time, with a mourning wreath on the door?" Mrs. Fines muttered.

There was the sound of voices, footsteps, and then the parlor door opened.

Mrs. Doppler came in first, her arms barring the entryway. "Mrs. Fines," the housekeeper said between short breaths. "I told the gent you weren't taking callers, but he wouldn't—"

Charity gasped as Mr. Garrity emerged in the doorway. Pushing the hapless housekeeper aside, he walked into the room. His somber outfit matched his onyx eyes.

"I came to pay my respects," he said, bowing.

Charity was on her feet in an instant. "How *dare* you come into my father's house," she said in a shaking voice.

"You'd better leave, Mr. Garrity, before we have you thrown out." Glaring at him, Percy rose to stand beside Charity. "You are not welcome here."

"I won't stay long. I merely came to offer my condolences." His smile had a razor's edge. "And to settle the matter of your father's debt to me."

"Have you no shame, sir?" Mrs. Fines said. "This is a time of mourning."

"Business waits for nothing, madam." Pulling a packet from his pocket, Garrity held it out to Charity. "Inside you'll find the details of our business arrangement. Your father borrowed quite a sum from me in the last year."

Charity snatched the paper from him. Her jaw dropped as she scanned the contents. "At the rate of *sixty* percent?"

"He was lucky to get money from anyone, given Sparkler's falling profits. I took a risk on him. But like a fool, he thought to reverse his and the shop's fortunes by investing the blunt. Mining ventures and the like." Garrity smoothed a wrinkle from his gloves. "Pardon the pun, but he kept digging himself into a bigger and bigger hole. Not my business, however. Now if your father had kept up his end of the bargain"—his black gaze flicked over her, making her shiver not with cold but rage—"I'd have made things easier for him. Family ties and all."

"You're despicable," she said, her hands curling.

Garrity's eyes thinned. "And you're in debt. Thirty thousand pounds, to be precise."

The staggering figure elicited murmurs from Helena and Marianne. Percy, whom Charity had already filled in on the calamitous news, said belligerently, "That's an impossible sum to come up with at short notice."

"I'll grant you a month," Garrity said, "and consider that my parting gift to your father. But hear me well: if I don't have my thirty thousand pounds within that time, I will take the shop, this house, and everything else in your possession until the debt is paid." He bowed. "Good day, ladies."

Charity stood frozen as he exited.

"The snake!" Percy exclaimed. "When Mr. Hunt returns, I shall have him pay that slimy bounder a visit."

"Perhaps if Harteford and Hunt put their heads together," Helena ventured, "they might be able to arrange a loan of some sort ..."

"No." In a dull voice, Charity said, "That is an enormous sum, one that I'll never be able to pay back. I'll not involve anyone else in this."

Silence descended. Charity knew the others were contemplating the facts just as she was. She'd already lost her father and her husband. Now she would lose the shop, her home, what remained of her world as she knew it ...

She heard the others talking, mulling over possible solutions, and all of it seemed to come from a great distance. She grew lightheaded, a strange, crazed feeling spreading over her, as if she might burst from her skin. As if she *wanted* to. Being mad suddenly seemed preferable to holding onto her sanity, to containing the emotions pushing at her tightly stitched seams. What a relief it would be to just unravel ...

"Oh, you poor dear," Percy said in distraught tones. "Come, sit down—"

The doorbell rang again.

Marianne's brows shot up. "Good heavens, what *now*?"

They didn't have long to wait. Mrs. Doppler appeared moments later, her hands nervously twisting her apron. "Pardon, Mrs. Fines, but there's a lady to see you. I wouldn't have let her in, but she says ... that is, she claims ..."

"Step aside, if you please," the new voice commanded.

The housekeeper shrank back, and a lady outfitted in a navy frock swept in. In her buffle-headed state, it took Charity a second to recognize her.

"Mrs. Stone?" she said, blinking. "What ... what are you doing here?"

"My dearest Charity." The actress' eyes blazed. "I am here because I am your mother."

Chapter Thirty-Six

Charity stared at the actress. "Pardon?"

"It is the truth," Mrs. Stone said. "After all these years, I am free at last to come to you. My precious daughter, how I have longed for this moment."

"Holy Mother of God," Percy breathed.

"You're l-lying," Charity stammered.

"No, 'twas your father who lied to you, may God have pity on his soul." Mrs. Stone's chin lifted. "I am not dead as you can see."

A ringing started in Charity's ears. The actress' voice came at her as if strained through tin, setting bright sparks off in her head. Her senses wavered as reality began to fray.

"Charity, you'd better sit down."

Was that Percy's voice? Marianne's? She couldn't tell, could only stare at the woman who professed to be her mother and who had come back from the dead.

"But why?" she blurted. "Why did you leave us? Where have you been?"

Pain flashed across the actress' face, and Charity saw with disorienting acuity her own nose, her chin in the other's petite features ...

"I had to leave, my dear. I had no other choice." The navy plumes on Mrs. Stone's hat trembled. "If I hadn't, I would have perished ... my soul's essence drained from me."

Charity's heart thumped with dizzying force.

"I always wanted to be an actress. But against my will, my father arranged for me to wed Uriah. I knew from the start that our marriage was destined to be a tragedy." The other's voice vibrated with emotion. "Our happiness, what little we had of it, did not last for long. A year in, I gave birth to you—when I was but a girl myself—and my life turned suffocating. I was left alone, with no one to help me. I couldn't sleep, couldn't eat. The walls closed around me."

"I ... I suffocated you," Charity said numbly.

"No—no, my dear girl, not you. My *life*. With Uriah, who never understood me ..." Mrs. Stone's hands fisted. "At first, he was drawn to my passionate nature, but then he grew to fear it—my power, my ambition. He tried to control me, to clip my wings, to make me feel that I was less than I was."

"So you just ... left?"

"My only regret was that I did not have the strength to take you with me. I barely had the means to take care of myself; how could I support a babe working as a fledging actress?" The other woman expelled a breath. "Despite what transpired between Uriah and me, I have *always* loved you. Not a moment has passed when I haven't thought of you."

"When *you* haven't thought of *me*?" The gust of fury propelled Charity out of her own body. It was as if she were watching the scene from above, the words coming out of lips that she could not feel. "Do you know how many hours I've spent thinking of *you*? How badly I've longed for a mother all these years?"

"I have longed for you, too," the other said, her voice pleading. "That is why I have been following you in secret for years. From afar, I've watched you grow into the beautiful woman you are.

When I received the Hartefords' invitation, I knew the time had come for us to meet again."

Mrs. Stone took a step toward her; Charity backed away.

"My precious daughter, I have done you a grievous wrong. But I am here for you now, in your time of need, and I will do everything in my power to make it up to you. Can you forgive me?"

Eyes bright, the actress held out her arms.

"Get away from me," Charity whispered.

Her temples pounded. Pain gripped her scalp, and her head felt on the verge of exploding. *So much pressure.* She stumbled, the back of her knees colliding with the coffee table. Objects rattled, splashed. Her gaze fell on the shears. The next instant they were in her hands. Cool silver. Glinting promise of relief.

"Charity, what are you—"

"Don't—"

She couldn't bear the agony for an instant more. As voices erupted around her, she shut her eyes. Took aim and lifted the blades.

When she was finished, she looked down to see pieces of herself lying on the floor. Her old brown locks ... gone. No longer a part of her. Her head felt light, weightless.

She looked up to a ring of pale faces.

Mrs. Stone was the first to break the silence.

"Oh, my darling girl ..." she said in a choked voice.

"Get out," Charity said flatly. "I never want to see you again."

"A toast," Viscount Traymore said, "to the future Champion!"

As the crowd crammed into the smoky tavern cheered, Paul held up his foaming tankard at the head of the table.

"My thanks, lads." He shouted to be heard over the whistling and foot stomping. "Here's hoping the next fight goes as smoothly as the last!"

The ovation shook the low rafters, followed by more toasts and drunken congratulations. Paul took many slaps on the back, but none of the ale, and no one questioned him. Probably they chalked it up to one of the many eccentricities and superstitions that populated the sport. Ross Anderson, the fellow Paul had beaten in eight rounds this afternoon, boasted a dark hedge of a beard for apparently the fellow feared shaving off his luck.

Well, poor sod could take a razor to those bristles tonight. Because with this last win, Paul had ousted the other from the tournament and now found himself in contention for the title. Jem Barnes would be his final opponent. As fierce as that prizefighter was—Barnes' last challenger had had to be carried from the ring—Paul could not wait for the final battle, a mere ten days away.

He had focus, momentum, and he knew he could win it all.

The past weeks of ruthless physical training and stringent living had built up more than his musculature. The ascetic existence had, surprisingly, given him a measure of peace. For the first time in his life, Paul's head was clear. As he'd won rout after rout, gritting out the rough moments and never giving up, he'd begun to gain true confidence in himself. He was not destined to be a worthless failure. He wasn't destined to be anything.

He was responsible for creating his own future, and when it came to the ring, he was doing a damned good job of it. When it came to his marriage, however, he had a long way to go. His chest tightened.

If only Charity could have been there to see me win …

"'Ere you go, luvie. Nothin' but the best for the man o' the hour." Winking, a buxom serving wench plunked a platter of roasted meat in front of him. "And if there's anythin' else you'd care to sample," she cooed, leaning over and showing him what was on the menu, "you just let me know."

"Thank you, I have what I need," he said.

With a good-natured pout, she went to ply her charms on

Stickley, his bottle man, whose craggy face lit up with interest. Paul continued to mull over his untouched ale. The celebration around him only made him feel more alone. Because he wasn't interested in drinking or flirting or the general carrying on.

What he wanted was ... Charity.

He missed her gentle voice, her sly humor, the way her soft, sweet body fit perfectly with his. How could he have allowed his past to wreak havoc on his future? 'Twas a damnable thing, but it took his leaving to make him realize the value of what he'd left behind.

Though Charity's accusations had cut him to the core, he saw now that she hadn't been wrong. Not entirely, at any rate. While he had been innocent of wrongdoing where Rosalind was concerned, he *had* been guilty of carelessness. Cowardice. Once again, he'd run away from difficulties rather than facing them head on. He'd given up on his marriage before it had had time to fully flourish ... as, deep in his soul, he knew that it could.

Hell, after their wedding trip, they'd been halfway there already.

Determination charged through him, dispelling the bleakness. He was going to make things right with Charity. If he could best the fiercest fighters in England, then he surely could win over his sweet slip of a wife. He didn't care what it took; he would do whatever was necessary to regain her trust and get their marriage back on track ... even if it meant trying to make peace with her blasted father. He grimaced at the thought.

First thing on the morrow, he was returning to London. He had ten days before his final fight at Banstead Downs; he'd use the time to straighten out his marriage. God willing, his wife would be by his side when he took Barnes down in the championship round. Resolved, Paul went to take his leave of the party's host, who had a tankard in hand and a trollop on his lap.

"To bed so early? But there are plenty of festivities yet to come," Viscount Traymore protested.

"I'm returning to London in the morning. Business to attend to," Paul said.

The viscount frowned and rose so quickly that the trollop would have tumbled to the ground had Paul not caught her and set her on her feet.

"The final round is in ten days," Traymore said. "You ought to be training, keeping your focus. Any business can wait."

"It's waited long enough." *Too long.* Paul's throat constricted, and he had to clear it to say, "Don't concern yourself. I'll see you at Banstead."

"But the championship is too important to ..."

Paul lost track of the other's words, his attention caught by the tawny head ducking to fit through the tavern doorway. Even from this distance, he could see the jagged slash on the man's face. What the hell was *Hunt* doing here?

A sudden premonition made him push through the crowd, meeting the other halfway.

"Why are you here? Is something wrong?" Paul said tersely.

"You're a bloody difficult sod to find, you know that?" was his brother-in-law's reply.

"Is it Charity—is she alright?"

At Hunt's stark expression, dread paralyzed Paul.

"She's fine for now," the other man said. "Let's talk in private."

Chapter Thirty-Seven

Five days later, Percy stood in a corner of Sparkler's with Marianne and Helena, the three of them observing the afternoon crowd milling in the shop.

"Look at all those patrons," Percy said. "The merchandise is flying off the shelves. Business has never looked better."

Marianne arched a brow. "The same could be said of the proprietress herself. She should have taken shears to her hair years ago."

"She makes a lovely gamine," Helena agreed.

All three of them regarded Charity, who was standing by a case of gentlemen's accoutrements. Charity's hair was now a shiny, tousled crop as short as a boy's. With all that excess hair gone, her elfin face took on a bold, unforgettable focus. Her eyes shone with the same mysterious fire as her opal ring, her only adornment. She wore a smart black gown with a white lace collar, and the severity of the dress displayed her slender, vulnerable femininity to perfection.

Percy thought her friend made the perfect gothic heroine.

Apparently, so did the circle of bucks who were vying for Charity's attention. As soon as Charity set a toothpick case or a snuff box on the display cloth, one of them eagerly snatched it up. Seemingly oblivious to the attention, she kept her focus solely on the task of the sale. She completed transactions with a polite, inscrutable expression which seemed to drive her customers into a purchasing frenzy.

"Dearest, our little Charity makes Caro Lamb look *matronly*," Marianne drawled. "At this rate, the shop won't be able to keep its shelves stocked."

Percy knew her friend's transformation wasn't just due to the outward changes: something essential had altered in *Charity* herself. It was as if Charity had been a powder keg, and her fuse had finally been lit. Those shears had removed more than a topknot: they'd blasted away years of fear and self-denial, and the true Charity had emerged from the ashes.

Percy's heart ached as she thought of her friend's suffering, of the pain of being abandoned by one's own mama. She didn't blame Charity one bit for sending Mrs. Stone away.

"I almost fainted when Charity picked up those scissors," Percy said with a shudder, "and I'm ever so relieved she only meant to cut her hair. But do you think she is truly, well ... alright?"

"She lost her father, inherited a thirty thousand pound debt, and discovered her mama is not only alive, but an actress," Marianne said. "Given all that, I think she's doing fine."

"Poor thing," Helena murmured, "and so brave as well. I can't believe she's kept working through all of this."

After Charity had cut off her hair and dispensed with Mrs. Stone, she'd declared with a fierce light in her eyes that she was *not* losing Sparkler's to Garrity or anyone else. The shop was hers and she was going to see to its survival, no matter what. She'd worked tirelessly ever since.

Percy bit her lip. "Yes, but thirty thousand pounds ..."

She didn't have to finish because she knew the others were thinking the same thing. It was a nigh impossible task to raise such an amount, even with sales being as brisk as they were. Yet Charity remained hell-bent on the task, and none of them had the heart to dissuade her.

"Well, we must help her any way we can," Helena said.

"Your social connections have helped already," Percy said. For the past week, the Hartefords had attended *ton* events sporting Sparkler's merchandise. "There's no better advertisement than word of mouth."

Helena touched the fine cameo brooch pinned to her maroon riding jacket. "The goods speak for themselves—they only lacked discoverability. And Harteford helped as much as I." With a sly smile, she said, "I never thought to see him carrying a snuff box."

"Darling, your husband does whatever you ask him to," Marianne said dryly.

Helena's lashes lowered in a demure manner, yet a grin tucked into her cheeks.

"And you've helped as well, Marianne," Percy said. "You've given Charity dash."

"'Twas nothing." Marianne waved a hand. "Madame Rousseau and Signore Antonio merely allowed Charity's natural beauty to shine through. The truth is, Percy, you've done more than anyone."

"I couldn't let Charity do *everything* on her own," Percy said.

In an effort to lessen the weight on her friend's shoulders, Percy had brought on two new clerks, as well as an employee of Gavin's former club. William McLeod, an ex-soldier with a fierce demeanor and soft heart, had proven quite handy at preventing sticky fingers and providing general protection for the shop. After Garrity's brutes, Percy wasn't going to let her friend take any chances. At present, McLeod was posted at the door, watching the crowd like a hawk.

"I'm worried about Charity," Percy admitted. "Do you know I haven't seen her cry since Mr. Sparkler's passing?"

"Grief strikes everyone differently. Charity is obviously channeling hers into work; once the shock wears off, however, her emotions will undoubtedly catch up to her. She will need us then more than ever," Marianne said. "In the meanwhile, Percy, you must take care not to overdo. Truly, I don't know where you find the energy in your condition. I'm exhausted from the moment I wake up."

"Queasy in the morning?" Percy said with sympathy.

"'Tis absolute hell. I don't remember it being this bad with my first child."

"Don't pay Marianne any mind. She enjoys having Mr. Kent wait on her hand and foot," Helena teased.

"Ambrose spoils me whether I'm increasing or not," her friend said with a faint smile. "Just as a husband should. Speaking of which, what is the latest news on your brother, Percy?"

"A missive from Gavin arrived three days ago. He found Paul near Ripon, and they're headed back."

Gavin's note had been characteristically to the point: *Be home with Fines soon. Bed's cold without you, buttercup.*

Percy felt a pang. Gavin had left directly after the funeral, and she missed him too.

"When do you think Mr. Hunt and Mr. Fines will arrive?" Helena asked.

"By tomorrow, I hope. I can't stand the thought of Charity going through this without Paul by her side." In an undertone, Percy added, "They seemed so *happy* after their wedding trip. I cannot for a second believe that my brother would be so idiotic as to lust after Rosalind now that he has Charity. And I know for a fact that he would never *ever* break his vows."

"I'm sure they just need to sort things out between them," Helena said. "Being married is an adjustment. Early on, Harteford and I had our share of ups and downs."

"Mostly up, on Harteford's part." Marianne's lips curved. "And, speaking of the devil, there he is."

Nicholas came toward them. He bowed before pressing a kiss to Helena's temple.

"Any new news from Hunt and Fines?" he asked.

Percy shook her head.

"Knowing Hunt, they'll arrive soon," he said in reassuring tones. He turned to his wife. "I left the warehouse early and thought I'd see if you were ready to go home."

"Yes, I think Charity's got everything in hand." Helena smiled up at him. "It's still light out. Perhaps we could take the boys to the park?"

"Hmm." Nicholas sounded noncommittal. "I had other plans, actually."

"What plans?"

"I'll explain them to you on the ride home."

Helena's cheeks turned rosy. "Oh. Well. Um, we'll see you both later then?" Though she was addressing Percy and Marianne, she had eyes only for her husband. After another quick bow, Nicholas steered her toward the door, his hand splayed possessively on the small of her back.

"Those two will never cease being newlyweds," Marianne said with affection in her voice. "Which reminds me: Ambrose will be arriving home at any moment so I must be off as well. Shall I drop you off, dear?"

Percy shook her head. "I'll stay. Charity might need me."

"She appears to have plenty of company." Marianne aimed a pointed glance over at Charity and the ever growing throng of male customers. McLeod had taken a protective stance, hovering behind her.

"Charity needs her husband," Percy said firmly.

And, dash it all, Paul, where are you?

Chapter Thirty-Eight

"Tapping out a jig won't make the horses go any faster," Hunt commented. "Watching you is giving *me* the bleeding jitters."

Scowling, Paul stilled his foot. He'd eat his boot before admitting nerves to his brother-in-law. "I don't have jitters."

Hunt's raised brow was patently skeptical.

"I don't," Paul insisted.

"Looking forward to groveling then, are you?"

"I won't need to grovel." *Damnit, will I?* Sweat trickling beneath his collar, Paul said, "My wife is a reasonable woman. We merely need to talk matters through."

"Your wife might have changed since you saw her last," was the other's cryptic reply.

"What the bloody hell is that supposed to mean?"

"Grief alters a person. I know this from experience and so do you." Hunt shrugged. "All I'm saying is prepare yourself."

Paul narrowed his eyes. "I can't tell if you're trying to help or terrify me."

"Sometimes they're one and the same." Hunt's mouth twisted

into what might have been a smile. "Let's just say I sympathize with your situation, Fines. Been there myself."

"You have?"

Hunt gave a brief jerk of his chin. "Almost lost Percy once. So I know what it's like to be buggered by one's own stupidity. Doesn't exactly put a fellow in a good frame of mind, does it?"

"I haven't bollixed up my marriage." *Please, God, let that be true.* "I don't know what Percy told you ..."

"Know about Lady Monteith," Hunt said smugly.

Jaw set, Paul said, "Then you know that *nothing happened*. I didn't do a damn thing, yet Charity wouldn't believe me. She wouldn't even listen."

Of everything, her lack of faith had hurt the most.

"Are you telling me that *you* wouldn't be up in the boughs if the tables were turned?" Hunt quirked an eyebrow. "If she'd been alone with some sod from her past and everyone was flapping their lips about it, what would you do?"

I'd rip the bloody sod's head off. Charity is mine. She belongs to me.

"Females got as much pride as males—they just show it differently," Hunt said. "Me, when I'm angry, I like to punch things."

"Me, too." Paul wouldn't mind starting with his brother-in-law's face.

"Percy, when she's annoyed, might ignore me instead, see? Give me the cold shoulder." With a gleam in his eye, Hunt added, "Not that the chit can resist me for long."

"Is there a point to this," Paul said, "other than your apparently irresistible charm?"

"My point is that tempers flare. Wives and husbands say things they don't mean. You learn to get over it."

"So I'm supposed to just *get over* the fact that Charity accused me of being unfaithful? When I didn't even touch Rosalind?"

Hunt gave him an assessing look. "Why didn't you?"

"I beg your pardon?" Paul said indignantly.

"According to Percy, you've been carrying the torch for this high-kick trollop for years. And yet you turned down the chance to tumble her?"

"You really want to talk about this?" Paul said in disbelief.

Hunt leaned back, stretched out his long booted legs. "Ain't much else to do."

Lovely. A heart-to-heart with his former nemesis. But maybe it wasn't such a bad idea to get things off his chest—to vent some of his lingering frustration before he saw Charity. Maybe if he got it out now, things would go more smoothly with her.

"When I met Rosalind again, things were, I don't know ... different," he muttered.

"Aged like a prune, did she?"

"No, she was still beautiful. I just didn't feel the same way about her. Didn't love her like I used to or maybe I ..." He found it hard to admit the truth aloud.

"Maybe you never loved her at all?"

"How pathetic is that?" he said grimly. "After I nearly destroyed myself and my family over losing her."

"You were just a lad. Lads tend to think with their bollocks," Hunt said.

Had it been a simple matter of lust?

"When she married another, I became so ... low." Paul dragged a hand through his hair. "And the oddest thing was, 'twas as if I'd known all along that it was going to happen. That I was going to lose her. That I would fail in this as I had ..." He swallowed. *Everything else in my life.*

A moment passed.

"We find what we're looking for, Fines."

Paul frowned. "Pardon?"

"Let me put it this way. Once, I believed that I was a brute," Hunt said matter-of-factly. "So I associated with brutes. That led me to do brutish things, and in the end I became what I believed: a bloody cutthroat. See?"

Paul chewed on the possibility. "So because I thought I was a failure ... I was drawn to a failing proposition with Rosalind?"

"You tell me."

It made an odd, albeit twisted, kind of sense.

Paul released a breath, eyed his brother-in-law. "So you're not a brute after all?"

"Didn't say that. But I ain't half as bad as I believed," Hunt said. "Love changed me."

Paul stared at the scarred former cutthroat. This menacing fellow, who'd survived and thrived in the London underworld, was talking about *love*?

Looking not in the least bit discomfited, Hunt said, "I like being the kind of cove a woman like Percy could love. Like that I'm about to be a father, too. Respectability ain't all fun and games, but it beats the cutthroat business any day of the week."

Heart pounding, Paul thought of the qualities that had always drawn him to Charity: her sweetness, steadfast loyalty, the way she'd believed in him from the start. In her presence, he didn't feel like a failure ... he felt like the man he wanted to be.

A man of honor and worth.

A man worthy of a wife like Charity.

He blurted, "I love her."

God. He did. So bloody much. Why hadn't he realized it sooner?

"We men can be sods about love," Hunt said, not without sympathy. "Or so Percy says."

"What if Charity doesn't love me back?" Paul said suddenly.

He'd given her so many reasons *not* to love him. Self-loathing swirled like acid in his gut. He'd made her an object of ridicule and gossip—not once, but *twice*. He'd left her, wasn't with her now when she needed him the most. His throat closed as he thought about how much she must be grieving, how alone she must feel.

"You do whatever it takes to win her love and devil take the rest."

Paul's shoulders bunched. His plan exactly.

He slanted a look at his brother-in-law. "I was under the impression that we weren't on the best of terms. Why are you helping me—for Percy's sake?"

"Aye, I want Percy happy." Hunt crossed his burly arms. "But I've also come to see that you ain't a bad sort. Not every man can pick himself up from the gutter and keep on fighting."

Paul's brows shot up. "Do I detect a hint of respect?"

"More like self-interest." A grin chased across Hunt's harsh features. "Been following your fights, Fines, and you've won me a pretty penny."

"You bet on me to win?" Paul said in disbelief.

"Aye."

The notion that *Hunt* saw him as a winner astonished him. "But *why*?"

"A Fines is a Fines." Hunt's lips twitched. "Being married to one, I know you're a stubborn lot who don't like to lose."

By seven o'clock, Charity cleared the shop of its last customer and sent the clerks home. Percy and Mr. McLeod remained to help with the last of the tasks.

"Can't it wait until tomorrow?" Percy said. "For heaven's sake, you've been working since dawn, Charity."

"I'm not tired."

She wasn't. Despite little sleep and low appetite, a strange energy buzzed through her veins. It was as if she was peering through a tunnel and all she could see was the goal at the end: saving her father's shop. Seeing Percy hide a yawn and rub at her lower back, however, filled Charity with remorse.

"Oh Percy, you've done far too much for a lady in your condition," she said. "You're going home right this instant."

"I'm not leaving you here alone," her friend protested.

"I'm not alone. Mr. McLeod is here, and he'll help me close up, won't he?"

Charity tipped her head at the stoic ex-soldier. His blunt features and brawny build made his an intimidating presence, but she'd come to know him as a gentle giant. He didn't speak much, and in his silence she sensed a certain kinship. As if he, too, had his reasons for remaining solely focused on the tasks at hand.

He gave a grave nod of his dark, shaggy head. "I'll see you home safe, Mrs. Fines."

"But—"

"No fussing, Percy. Go home." Charity steered her friend outside to the waiting carriage. "What would Mr. Hunt say if you didn't take care of yourself and the babe?"

Percy lingered even as the groom unfolded the steps. "Promise me you shan't stay much longer."

"Go, mother hen. I'll be perfectly fine."

After seeing Percy off, Charity returned inside and locked the door behind her. "Let's start with restocking," she said decisively. "There are boxes of merchandise yet to sort through, and I want everything we have out on the floor."

McLeod followed her, his habitual limp barely slowing his stride. They entered the cramped back room which served as an office and a storage space. Boxes lined the shelves, which covered two walls from floor to ceiling. McLeod fetched a ladder, propping it against the highest shelf. When he placed a large boot on the bottom rung, the rickety contraption gave a protesting creak.

"Wait," Charity said. "I had better go up."

McLeod shook his head. "It isn't safe."

"Safer for me than you." She tested the first step with her entire weight; no creaking. Being slight had its advantages. "I'll hand the boxes down to you."

Climbing onto the fourth rung, she was able to reach the top shelf. She removed a box and carefully handed it down to McLeod's outstretched hands.

"Do you have it, Mr. McLeod?"

"Will," he said as he took the box.

She passed him another. "Pardon?"

His gaze—a velvety brown—met hers. "You can call me Will. Most everyone does."

"Whatever you prefer." She continued unloading the shelf until there was one last carton remaining. It dangled like the farthest apple on a branch. Holding on to the ladder with one hand, she stretched her other hand toward it. Almost there ...

"Have a care, Mrs. Fines—"

Will's warning came too late. Just as her fingers grasped the corner of the box, she lost her balance and her grip on the ladder. Crying out, she tumbled backward through the air.

Paul unlocked the door to Sparkler's—and heard a piercing scream.

"Charity!" he shouted.

He raced toward the back, shoved aside the curtain. Heart hammering, his gaze locked on Charity ... lying in the arms of a stranger. A tall, dark-haired man was cradling her against his chest, murmuring her name. Two facts struck like lightning.

First, Charity was unharmed.

Second, whoever that stranger was, he was a *dead man*.

Paul's vision darkened at the edges, and he heard himself roar, "*Unhand my wife*" the instant before he charged.

Chapter Thirty-Nine

One moment, Charity was falling to her doom ... the next she landed safely. As she tried to catch her breath to thank Will, *Paul* tore into the room. Before she could recover her equilibrium, he snatched her up, set her in a chair, and went charging back at Will.

She jumped to her feet. "What are you doing?"

Neither man heard her. They were too busy exchanging blows. Despite Will's bulkier build, Paul had the clear advantage, his fists striking with lethal speed and force, backing the other into a wall.

"Stop it!" Charity dashed toward them. "Paul, stop hitting Will!"

"*Will?*" Paul's head jerked back as if he'd been punched.

Wrong thing to say, apparently. Paul glowered at her, and her breath caught at the blue flames leaping in his eyes. His momentary distraction cost him, however, and Will plowed his fist directly into Paul's gut. She cried out, but Paul only grunted and gave as good as he got, landing a right cross that snapped Will's head back.

Enough was enough.

Charity grabbed the first thing she could lay her hands on—a teapot—and sent it flying against a wall. The resounding *smash* filled the room.

"Bloody hell, stop!" she shouted. "Or I'll summon the damned magistrates!"

Paul stopped mid-punch. Will did likewise. They both stared at her.

"Did you just curse?" Paul said.

"Twice," Will said.

"I'll do more than that if you don't stop acting like two idiots," Charity said through her teeth. "What in heaven's name are you doing here, Paul? And why are you attacking Will?"

Paul scowled. He didn't release his hold on the other's lapel.

"He had his hands on you. On my bloody *wife*," he snarled in Will's face.

Paul was ... jealous? Over her?

Despite her irritation, Charity felt a betraying thrill. She quickly shoved away the feeling.

"He caught me when I fell off the ladder," she said coldly.

"Someone had to be around to do the job," Will added in hostile tones.

His face reddening, Paul gave the man another shake. "Who the devil are you, anyway?"

"Mrs. Hunt hired me to guard Sparkler's."

"*Percy* hired you?" Paul's gaze shot to Charity.

She dipped her chin in affirmation.

"In case Garrity's men came back. Mrs. Fines is a lone female, vulnerable,"—Will aimed another dirty look at Paul—"and Mrs. Hunt wanted me to keep an eye on her and the shop."

Paul released his grip on Will's jacket. The two stood, toe to toe, glaring at each other. They were a hair's breadth from another brawl: two males raring to scrap over their perceived territory.

Which was ridiculous.

Restraining the urge to roll her eyes, Charity said, "Thank you for your help, Will, and in particular for saving me from a fall just now." She smiled at him. "But I'm fine and it's getting late, so I think it's best you go."

Will didn't break his eye contact with Paul. "Are you certain that's a good idea?"

Paul growled, "She's *my* wife. I'll take care of her."

"Like you were doing the past few weeks?" Will said.

For heaven's sake. She could see the ominous twitching of Paul's jaw.

"Please go, Will," she said. "I'll see you tomorrow."

Moments passed. The guard inclined his dark head. "You can count on that, Mrs. Fines."

Will left, the tension he took with him replaced by another, far stronger, that pulsed in the air as her gaze locked with Paul's. Her throat cinched. She didn't know what to say. Since her father's death, a mantle of numbness had shrouded her, and she had gotten used to its protection.

Now Paul was here. After all these weeks. He and she remained a few feet apart, and he looked as uncertain as she felt.

"I ... how are you?" he said.

She didn't know how to respond to the mundane opening. Settled for, "Fine."

"You look different," he said. "Your hair ... it suits you. Lovely and unique."

At his tentative smile, a droplet of sensation trickled down her spine.

"It was time for a change," she said.

His eyes widened slightly, and he blurted, "I came as quickly as I could. Once I heard ... I'm sorry about your father. I know how much you loved him."

She gave a tight nod.

"I'm sorry about other things as well. I should have been here with you, through all of this." He ran a hand over his mouth. "Instead I ran away like a coward at the first sign of trouble between us."

The warning prickle centered in her chest, like pins and needles greeting an awakening limb.

He took a step toward her. "There's so much I want to say to you—I don't even know where to begin. But I think I must start with Rosalind."

Yes, feeling was returning because the mention of that name made Charity's belly tighten into knots.

His hands fisted at his sides, Paul said, "Rosalind wanted to have an affair."

The knots twisted painfully.

"I turned her down," he said. "I know you have no reason to believe me, but I swear on my mother's name that nothing happened."

Charity swallowed. She knew how much Paul loved his mama, and he wouldn't make such a vow if it weren't true. Hope budded, pushing through the layer of frost.

"Why?" she said through dry lips. "When you have loved Rosalind for so long—"

"I thought what I felt for her was love, but it turns out I was wrong." He came closer, close enough for his familiar masculine scent to feed her famished senses. "I was infatuated, yes, but I was an imbecile to mistake that for love. And an even greater fool for nurturing that delusion. And while I have to ask forgiveness for those and so many other things, you are to blame as well, sweeting."

His endearment caused a shift within her, like a slow crack spreading through ice.

"For what?" she managed.

"For not showing me sooner what love truly is. You've been there this whole time, Charity, and I never saw you. Why did you hide from me?" His handsome face looked so *fierce*. "How could I have missed such a treasure otherwise?"

Powerful torrents raged against her barriers, yet she said, "You had eyes only for Rosalind. I don't blame you. She's as beautiful now as she ever was."

"Hold up ... how do you know what she looks like now?"

Charity's pulse skipped.

His brow furrowed. "Have you *seen* Rosalind?"

Unable to bring herself to lie, Charity took a breath and told him about Rosalind's visit to the shop.

"The lying *bitch*."

The vehemence of his tone stunned her. But not as much as being suddenly swept off her feet and brought to the nearest chair. He sat, cradling her on his lap, his hand on the nape of her neck so that she had no choice but to meet his desperate, burning gaze.

"I owe you an explanation, my love, and I need you to listen. Parts of it aren't pretty, and I'm sure to bumble through the others as I haven't worked it all out myself. But I'd like to talk it through with you—as I ought to have done instead of leaving." His tone was firm, yet his eyes beseeched her. "Can you give me the chance? Save judgment until I've finished?"

She gave a small nod.

"When Rosalind approached me, it was after the blow up with your father," he said tautly. "I was furious at him ... and at you. I'd worked so hard to make things right, you see, and—I don't wish to speak ill of the dead or to cause you further pain—but Sparkler seemed hell-bent on pinning me as a failure. He never even gave me a chance."

It *was* painful to hear. It was also the truth.

"As for you,"—his shoulders hitched in a self-deprecating manner—"I wanted you to take my side. To stand with me against your father, which I understand now was an unreasonable expectation. An untenable position to put you in."

His honesty made her heart beat faster.

"When I've mulled it over—and, it seems, I've spent the length of our separation mulling—I see now that anger was but a small part of what I was feeling." He paused a fraction. "Mostly, I was afraid."

"Afraid?" she ventured.

Beneath her skirts, his muscular thighs grew rigid, his arms tightening around her. "I have failed at so many things. I've been irresponsible, aimless, and lacking in good sense. Everything good in my life I've somehow managed to destroy or put at risk." His jaw clenched. "Deep down, I believed the same would happen to the *best* thing in my life: you."

Now she couldn't speak even if she wanted to. Emotion clogged her throat.

"Charity, that week in Chudleigh Crest—it was magical for me," he said hoarsely. "I've never been that happy, that purely content. Yet I was still battling that secret fear: something was going to go wrong. *I* would make a mistake, and you would see me for who I am. My flaws, my failures."

"You're *not* a failure." The jammed words burst from her. "I've never thought that about you. My father was wrong, and I'm sorry I didn't defend you as I ought to have. Those terrible things I said —I was angry because of Rosalind. Fearful that you'd chosen her over me again—"

"*Never*, sweetheart." His hands were so strong, and yet they trembled as they cupped her face. "You are my *wife*. I love you."

A tear escaped her. A tear of joy.

He tenderly thumbed it away. "I was an idiot not to realize it sooner. Because of my past, I thought of love as a storm, tumultuous, unpredictable, a wild happenstance over which I had little control. I never thought that love could be simple and good. Like sunshine, you've quietly lit my every day. Your mere presence makes everything brighter, more beautiful. Sweetheart, you've brought me a peace that I didn't even know was possible."

Tears were falling now in earnest. She couldn't stop them. Grief, sorrow, happiness ... all that she'd held back these past weeks was washing through her.

"Love, I can't keep up," he said huskily as he wiped her cheeks with a handkerchief. "Did I say something wrong? I'm rambling like a nervous schoolboy."

She managed to say, "Y-you won't tire of something as o-ordinary as sunshine?"

"*Ordinary?* I'm making a hash of this if that's what you think. Charity, my angel, my love," he said on a note of desperation, "without you, I am *lost*. A shipwreck of a man. You're my guiding star."

His eyes finally convinced her. In all the years she'd studied his gaze, she'd never seen it so clear and intense, kindling with the depth of his emotion. She saw herself reflected in his eyes ... and the image was beautiful.

"That's a lot of metaphors," she said, sniffling.

"I can come up with more. Dozens," he said earnestly. "I'll write odes to your jewel-bright eyes, your sylph-like form, your honey-sweet kisses—"

"Stop, please," she said, between tears and laughter. "I never wanted a poet for a husband."

Paul's eyes searched hers, his gorgeous face etched with determination. "Whatever you want, I can be that man. I can earn your love. I'll take care of you and won't run away again. If you give me another chance, I swear I'll be the husband you deserve."

Her heart swelled. She placed her hand on his taut jaw.

"You are," she said. "And I am as much to blame for our separation as you are."

"Charity," he said hoarsely.

"I love you—I always have." The truth popped like a cork, releasing a feeling of heady liberation. "I just never thought that you would love me back."

"I do. More than life itself. I'll do whatever it takes to convince you of it," he said with such passionate fervor that she gave a watery laugh.

"You don't need to move mountains," she whispered. "There is, however, one thing you could do ..."

"Anything. Name it."

"Perhaps after you finish talking, you could ... kiss me?"

His eyes blazed brighter than the heavens. Then his lips claimed hers, and it was a kiss sweeter, more passionate than all her dreams combined.

When he lifted his head, they were both breathless.

"I've got so much to make up to you, and I want to start tonight." With a trace of vulnerability that made her love him even more, he cleared his throat and said, "May I come home with you, Mrs. Fines?"

She gave him a tremulous smile and the answer that lived in her heart.

"Always," she said.

Chapter Forty

They returned to the Sparkler residence. Against Charity's blushing protests, Paul swept her into his arms and carried her up to her room, stopping only to ask the astonished housekeeper to send up a bath and food. He'd meant what he said: he was determined to take care of Charity, his precious wife who somehow loved him despite his mistakes and foolish actions.

When the bath arrived, he helped her to undress. The sight of her lithe, naked body instantly made him harder than granite, but he tended to her with gentle hands, his intent to soothe rather than arouse. He'd left her for nearly six weeks, hadn't been there for her when she needed him most. He wasn't going to compound his errors by pouncing on her like a lout.

Even if his cock was nudging against his smalls.

He ought to be grateful—and he was, he *so* was—for the fact that she let him touch her at all. His chest warmed at how trustingly she gave herself over to his care. He was damned fortunate to have a forgiving wife, one who didn't hold a grudge. Her sweetness made him want to protect her, to know every single thing about her, to be one with her body and soul.

He wanted her so much and in so many ways, he didn't even know where to begin. Bundling her into her robe, he set her on the narrow bed. He stood, gently toweling off her curls—her adorably *cropped* curls—and decided to start there.

"Your hair is entirely enchanting," he said, "but may I ask what prompted this change?"

Her bosom rose on a breath, and she told him. From Hunt, he'd already known about Garrity and the astronomical debt. But this was the first he'd heard of Mrs. Stone being Charity's *mother*.

"She had the gall to come into my father's house, the earth still fresh on his grave, and ask for *forgiveness*? After she abandoned us ... she expected me to take her calling card, welcome her with open arms?" Charity's voice shook. "I *never* want to see her again."

"And you shan't have to," he said. "My poor darling, how have you borne this all?"

"I don't think I have, really," Charity said in halting tones. "'Tis as if I've just been going through the motions these weeks past. I didn't even know what I was doing when I cut my hair. All of it—Father's death, the debt, Mrs. Stone—hit me at once, and suddenly my life just seemed like a ... a *sham*. I'd lived under the weight of pretenses for so long that I couldn't bear it a moment longer and *had* to be rid of it." She bit her lip. "Sounds mad, doesn't it?"

"No, love," he said. "You've survived a test of fire and risen like a phoenix from the flames. I'm so proud of you—of your strength and courage. My only regret is that I wasn't by your side." The mattress creaked as he sat next to her, linking his fight-toughened fingers with her infinitely daintier ones. "But I vow that I will be here for you from now on. I'll set up a meeting with Garrity and negotiate terms. Trust me in this?"

"I trust you," she said softly.

Joy lifted his heart. He placed a fervent kiss on her tender palm. "Thank you for believing in me, sweeting. For making *me* believe that I can be a better man."

"You are perfect as you are," she said.

"Perfect … despite my flaws?" he said hoarsely.

"Perfectly imperfect." Her mouth tipped up at the corners. "We are a pair, it seems."

He brushed his knuckles against her downy jaw. "Not in this. You, my sweet, are goodness itself. Your only flaw is in your judgment—mainly when it comes to your choice of husband."

"That's not true." She exhaled. "I've been a coward. I, too, have a confession to make."

The seriousness of her tone gave him pause. "Go on."

"I've been in love with you since the day we first met."

"But our first meeting was years ago." He frowned, thinking back. "When you and Percy were in finishing school together."

"The exact date was the 29th of September, 1813," came Charity's startling reply. "You were home from Eton for Michaelmas. You wore a new checkered waistcoat of which you were inordinately proud. Until you got a spot of goose grease on it, that is."

He couldn't summon more than a fuzzy recollection. "You remember all that?" he said in surprise.

"I remember every time we met. Every time Percy made you ask me to dance, every passing conversation," she said quietly. "Once, when I had those terrible spots and was standing alone at a ball, you came up and quoted Wordsworth to me."

A sudden memory unfurled of Charity, a shy violet in a field of wallflowers.

"*She Walks in Beauty*," he said with dawning recognition.

She gave him a tremulous smile. "I memorized the entire collection."

He couldn't believe what she was saying. "I had no idea. You said *nothing* …"

"How could I? You were so beyond my reach." She gazed at their linked hands. "In truth, I idolized you, placed you on a pedestal worthy of your namesake."

Bewilderment made him bereft of words. All this time ... he'd been so stupidly blind ...

"There's more." Peering up at him through her lashes, she said, "It has to do with Spitalfields. I was there."

He jolted. "What?"

"Percy wanted to check in on you, but she was worried that Mr. Hunt would follow her there. So I offered to go instead."

"You were there?" His head spun, his gut churning with sudden shame. "Then you saw me. In that despicable state ..." Another memory exploded—sudden knowledge that made him jerk as if he'd been pummeled in the gut. "Did ... did something happen between us?"

She gave a small nod. "We kissed. And, um, a bit more."

"Holy hell, why didn't you *say* anything?"

"I was afraid. I knew you would regret what had happened and insist on doing the honorable thing. I didn't want you to have to marry me out of obligation."

Stunned, he stared at her, and then another thought occurred. "Does Percy know about this?" Because if his sister was in on this conspiracy, so help him God ...

Charity shook her head quickly. "Not that anything happened between us. And I made her swear not to tell a soul that I'd gone to you."

Paul rubbed his neck. He couldn't think clearly. Didn't know who he was more furious at—her or himself. "Devil take it, I ruined you and didn't even know it. Do you know what kind of bastard that makes me?"

"A blissfully ignorant one?"

He glared at her. "This is no laughing matter."

"I know." She gave him a little smile. "Now that we're married, we can let bygones be bygones, can't we?"

"Christ, Charity—"

She placed her fingers on his lips, silencing him. "Now it's your turn to listen, Paul. I *was* wrong to deceive you, and I do apologize, with all my heart. But I want you to understand why I did it."

He stilled.

"It's true that I didn't want you to feel obligated, but the greater truth is that I acted out of fear. I didn't feel worthy of you. I was certain you'd reject me."

Before he could argue, she said, "My father always told me I wasn't much to look at, that I was small and plain." Her voice cracked a little. "He told me to keep my head down and act sensibly, because that was all a girl like me could do."

"That's utter rubbish." Paul couldn't keep the anger out of his voice. "Your father didn't know the first thing about you—"

"I understand now that he was trying to protect me because *he* had been hurt. By my mother. Grievously, I think, and because he never aired the wound, it festered all these years." Charity let out a breath. "And while I don't agree with my father's methods, I believe he was doing his best. The point is, knowing all this, can you see how I might believe myself too plain, too invisible to warrant your attention?"

He did see, though it pained him greatly. Worse yet was the fact that he might have added to her misperceptions. Cupping her small face, he said, "As long as you know that it's not true. That you are, in fact, precious and unique, every facet of you beautiful beyond compare."

"I feel that way," she whispered, "because of you."

"And I feel worthy ... because of you," he said in wonder.

Love *was* magic.

"I shan't hide myself any longer," she said.

"I wouldn't allow it. You, my sweet, were meant to shine." The last word came out rather breathless because of the adoration he saw in her eyes ... and the way her fingers were working nimbly at his cravat. Through the sudden haze of lust, he remembered he'd spent the day traveling. "Sweeting, I haven't yet bathed ..."

She tossed aside the neckcloth. Her eyes were as brilliant as her opal ring, and her mouth took on an undeniably erotic curve. And he knew this moment would blaze in his memory forever: the instant his wife fully transformed from a sweet, shyly passionate girl ... to a wanton nymph brimming with sensual power.

The woman she was meant to be.

"I don't give a damn," she said.

His breath stuttered, his cock turning harder than rock.

Chapter Forty-One

She was loved, cherished, and it filled her with a heady sense of power.

Her husband, that godly creature, watched her with heavy-lidded eyes, and she didn't mistake the obvious bulge in his trousers. He desired her, thought her beautiful beyond compare. His love flowed through her, hot and emboldening, and she couldn't wait to show him how much she loved him back.

She was done with hiding.

Done.

She popped the buttons of his waistcoat one by one. "I've missed you, Paul." Even her voice sounded different, sultry and sparkling with passion.

"Not as much as I've missed you, my darling."

She loved the rasp in his voice, the way his throat worked when she tore off his waistcoat. She did the same to his shirt and cravat, tossing them to the floor.

She wasn't in the mood to be tidy.

"What did you miss about me?" she said.

"Everything. God, Charity,"—he groaned as she ran her hands over the chiseled perfection of his chest—"every blessed thing."

"You've gotten bigger." He'd always been lean and solid; now, after weeks of prizefighting, his muscles rippled beneath her touch. She flattened her hand over the hard board of his stomach, following the delicious path of hair. He released a sharp breath when she palmed his crotch and squeezed. "Harder, too."

The next instant, she was dragged onto his lap, facing him and straddling his thighs.

"And you, lovely wife, have grown into a tease," he growled.

She shivered when he nipped her neck and licked away the small hurt. His hands braced her hips, the touch branding even through the layer of her robe. She was tempted to let him do the rest as he'd always done ... but not as tempted as she was by another notion. When he loosened the tie to her dressing gown, she clamped her hand over his.

"No. This time," she said, "I want to please you."

His nostrils flared, his eyes blazing sapphires. "By Jove, you already do. I've been deprived of you for weeks. Any more of your teasing, little nymph, and I'll go off like a firecracker."

She *liked* that notion.

"I suppose you'll have to try to hold on, then." As if she'd let him. "Now be a good husband and lean back against the headboard."

Though his eyes narrowed, she could see the flush of lust on his high cheekbones. "Are you ordering me about, you saucy wench?"

"Just this once." Gazing at him with all the love she felt, she said, "Please?"

"You're not a nymph, you're a siren. Impossible to deny," he muttered.

He did as she asked, his corded arms propping up against the wood and his thighs splayed in a wickedly masculine pose. She took a moment to admire him: a god in the flesh, his powerful chest heaving with desire, his eyes dark with need. And he was all *hers*.

On her knees, she moved into the lee of his legs, and leaning forward, pressed a kiss to his bristly jaw. She licked her way down, over the bump of his throat, which leapt beneath her lips. She tasted him, salty and masculine, and became even hungrier. Ravenous for him. Reaching one nipple, she circled the flat disc her tongue; hearing his harsh breath, she suckled him. Gave him a gentle bite.

"Christ, woman, do you want to drive me mad?"

She licked his other nipple, peered up at him. "Do you think I can?"

He groaned when she peppered his hard abdomen with kisses. "Hell, Charity, you can do whatever you put your mind to. You're the most strong-willed chit I've ever met."

Smiling, she found the buttons of his trousers. She released the fall and gave a deft downward tug on his smalls. His cock sprang into her hands like a racehorse leaving the gate. The virile pole quivered, its tip damp and glistening. Dreamily, she bent and rubbed her cheek against him. Iron wrapped in heated silk.

"Sweeting," he said, his voice strained, "what are you doing?"

She looked up at him, and his adoring gaze gave her the confidence to do anything.

"Exploring," she said. "I thought I'd try being less sensible and more impetuous. For instance, what do you think of this?"

She eased his skin back, placed a soft kiss on the vulnerable dome.

He bit out a curse. "Perfect—if your intent is to torture me."

As if to confirm this fact, a tear welled up in the eye of his cockhead. The pearly bead looked so lovely that she licked it. The salty, virile taste of him made her hum.

"Delicious," she murmured.

"Plenty more where that came from." Despite the raspy humor in his voice, he cupped her cheeks, his rough palms tender against her skin. "Love, I don't want you to do anything you're not comfortable with."

"Alright," she agreed.

She fitted her mouth over the tip, sucking gently.

"*Holy fuck.*"

His primal response thrilled her. His back bowed, his hips thrusting upward with animal force. Instinct guided her to relax her jaw so that she could accommodate more of his potent shaft. She loved the feel of him filling her mouth. Of him filling her anywhere. Warmth flooded her pussy as she tried to cram more of him past her lips. Her hands caressed what she could not fit.

He groaned her name, his fingers threading through her curls, guiding her in a bobbing motion. "Hell, that's good. So bloody *deep*. Sweeting, you're killing me ..."

Could she truly slay her god with pleasure?

She'd certainly *try*.

Breathing through her nose, she allowed her throat to grow even more lax, and he slid in farther. He shouted out when his tip nudged a barrier so deep that she came up gasping for air. But she went down again, breathless from the challenge of it, the indescribable intimacy of pleasuring her husband in this wicked fashion.

She was attuned to everything that seemed to heighten his bliss. His eyes shut when she touched his bollocks, squeezing the velvety weights gently as she sucked. He let out a string of curses when she got him so deep that the hairs of his groin tickled her nose. His pleasure fed her own. Heat sparkled over her skin, and her core was melting, trickling between her legs. She was desperate for more of him, wanted to touch him everywhere, needed to have every last inch of him to herself ...

He pulled her from his cock, the wet *pop* tearing a guttural sound from his chest. Before she could protest, he hauled her onto his lap, and her spine arched at the slow, stretching penetration. Her head fell back, her lashes fluttering as his cock drilled up into her drenched passage.

"Look at me," he ordered.

Her gaze flew to his, and she was enveloped in smoldering midnight.

"I want to see your beautiful eyes while I take you." His hands framed her hips, steering her motion. "While you ride my cock, my sweet wife."

Placing steadying hands on his shoulders, she rose up on her knees and then sank down, moaning as she impaled herself on his throbbing manhood. His touch, his earthy commands—everything he did made her blood run hotter. *Take me deeper.* She did and his cock grazed her pearl with each pass, sending a jolt of pleasure down her legs. *Harder.* He yanked her down, skin slapping skin, and she ground against him, a desperate ride, as wild for him as he was for her.

When he captured her nipple in his mouth, sucking hard, she cried out. White stars exploded before her eyes, and her body clenched as cataclysmic tremors overtook her. He pumped into her spasming flesh, groaning, and just as she floated upward from the earth-rendering climax, his fingers dug into her bottom.

"Everything I've ever wanted," he breathed. "I love you, Charity."

Her heart burst just as he did, his seed shooting so hotly into her womb that her world shook once more. Words flew from her lips, caught fire in his kiss. They burned together, the little death forging them into one body, their love binding them into one soul.

Chapter Forty-Two

The next afternoon, Charity sat hand in hand with Paul. They were in the drawing room of the Hunts' town-house, where the Hunts, Hartefords, and Mrs. Fines had gathered. The Kents had sent their regrets: their daughter was abed with a head cold, and they'd stayed at home to nurse her.

"First off, I want to thank you all for taking care of Charity in my absence," Paul said.

"Someone had to." His mother aimed a stern look at him over her spectacles. "Now that you're a married man, you have responsibilities. You can't go harrying off to this fight or that."

Charity went still, uncertain at how her husband would respond to the criticism. He squeezed her hand.

"I know, Mama," he said calmly.

Hunt made a clearing sound in his throat. "But you'll still be competing in the final fight three days from now, won't you, Fines? Got a few wagers on that one." When Percy nudged him with her elbow, he raised his brows as if to say, *What did I do?*

Charity spoke up. "Of course he'll be fighting. He's made it this far and can't stop now."

"Are you sure you don't mind, my dear?" Mrs. Fines said.

"Not at all." Charity brushed away her husband's ever unruly forelock and smiled into his eyes. "I rather like the idea of being married to the best prizefighter in all of England."

"Do you now?" Paul murmured. "In that case, I shall have to win. Seeing as I'd do anything for you, sweeting."

Feminine sighs rose up in the room as he leaned in to kiss her.

"Far be it for me to interrupt the lovebirds," came Harteford's dry voice, "but I believe we have a debt to discuss?"

"Yes, of course." Blushing, Charity tried to focus her whirling senses. The thought of looming disaster dispelled some of her giddiness. "First off, sales at Sparkler's have improved tremendously, thanks to all of you. I want you to know that you have my deepest gratitude."

"Unfortunately, it was too little too late," Paul said bluntly. "Sparkler's has been in trouble for years. Despite your help and my wife's extraordinary business *savoir-faire*, we're still short."

Paul had spent the morning poring over the store's ledgers, and she'd watched as his expression grew grimmer with each page. She, herself, was finally beginning to accept reality. Thirty thousand pounds was too vast a sum to accumulate in a month—or even years.

Her chest tightened. There was no way they could meet Garrity's deadline in two weeks. Which meant ... she was going to lose Sparkler's.

Her father's legacy.

"How far off the mark are you?" Hunt asked.

"Sparkler had five thousand saved, and Charity's sales have added another thousand to that. I've got another few from holdings and prize money, but even with that we've only a third of what's owed," Paul said matter-of-factly.

Glances chased around the room.

Harteford spoke first. "Hunt and I have talked, and we want to do what we can. We can offer at least some part—"

"I can't accept it," Charity said firmly.

"Not even a loan?" Percy asked.

"I won't be able to pay it back. I can't allow you to throw good money after bad," Charity said. "Besides, Mr. Garrity was quite clear that he wants all or nothing: anything less than thirty thousand will be unacceptable to him."

"Mayhap I can get him to change his mind," Paul said. "I'm meeting him tonight."

"Is it safe, Paul? To negotiate with such a man?" Mrs. Fines' brow furrowed.

"I'll have his back," Hunt said.

"As will I," Harteford said.

Charity placed a hand on Paul's arm. "You'll be careful, won't you?"

"I'm going to make this right for you, sweeting." Determination glittered in his eyes. "Trust me, there's nothing to fear. I've dealt with cutthroats before."

Mr. Hunt snorted.

Garrity's lair turned out to be a surprisingly well-appointed building only several blocks from Sparkler's. Located a stone's throw from the Bank of England and the Royal Exchange, it was ideally situated for a money lender. Paul guessed that the elegant Palladian structure might have once belonged to a family of the *ton*; with the flourishing of commerce in the area, the fashionable world had departed in droves to avoid the taint of trade.

"Doing well for himself, I gather," Nicholas commented as they mounted the front steps.

"At a rate of sixty percent, are you surprised?" Hunt said. "Clearly, we're in the wrong business."

Paul rang the bell. When the door opened, he handed the butler his card.

"Good evening, sir. Mr. Garrity has been expecting you." The servant cast an appraising eye over Paul's companions. "He did not mention guests."

"The Marquess of Harteford and Mr. Hunt are my friends," Paul said, "and we don't relish being made to cool our heels on the front steps."

The butler bowed low. "Of course. Follow me, if you please."

The three were ushered through a paneled foyer and into a hallway papered in silk. Midway down, the butler stopped at an open door and announced them. Paul went in first. The study was outfitted to impress. Portraits of the aristocracy—including, if he wasn't mistaken, several by Georgian society painter Benjamin West—graced the walls. To Paul, they seemed like trophies of war: pounds of painted flesh collected as payment.

The study smacked of wealth and a certain smug opulence. Much like the man who uncoiled from a studded wingchair to greet them. Garrity was dressed in formal black, his ruby cravat pin glinting like a drop of blood.

"You're on time, Mr. Fines," he said.

His host's tone was as chilling as Paul remembered. Ignoring the bait, he said, "You'll recollect meeting Lord Harteford and Mr. Hunt?"

"They were present at our last encounter." Garrity's mouth thinned. "Distasteful business."

"No less so than what we have to discuss this evening," Paul said.

"On the contrary, this I'll enjoy." Garrity waved them to the seats next to the roaring fire. "Reaping the fruits of my labor, so to speak."

"You'll have your harvest," Paul said, "but I wish to discuss the schedule of delivery."

"I gave your wife the schedule. A generous one, I might add. You have a fortnight remaining to come up with my money."

"That's not enough time, and you know it." From his jacket pocket, Paul removed the thick bundle of banknotes Charity had given him—everything that she and Uriah had saved. He placed the money on the coffee table between him and Garrity. "That's six thousand pounds to start. In a few days, I'll add more."

Garrity didn't even look at the money. "Thirty thousand, Fines. That's what I'm owed, and that's what I'll accept."

"I can't get you thirty thousand quid in two weeks. Either we negotiate payment installments or we discuss a reduction of—"

"I don't negotiate, Mr. Fines."

"Why the bloody hell not?" Hunt cut in. "Never met a money lender who didn't want to get paid. You give Fines a chance, and you'll get your blunt back, every last penny. He's a man of his word."

Paul's brows rose at the compliment. His brother-in-law sounded almost ... sincere.

"If you don't, you get a failing business and a mediocre property that don't near add up to thirty thousand quid. Why would you be willing to take that loss?" Hunt's tawny eyes narrowed in suspicion.

"Perhaps Mr. Garrity is motivated by something other than money," Harteford said.

Something flickered in Garrity's onyx eyes. Rage.

The realization struck Paul. "This is because of Charity. Because she married me instead of you?"

"She was *mine*." Frost edged Garrity's words. "I selected her from a field of candidates. I invested time and energy into developing a relationship with Uriah Sparkler. We had a bargain, he and I—and you ruined it."

If Garrity had expressed any sorrow over losing Charity, Paul might have pitied him. Because Paul knew what a jewel she was—and shuddered to think that he might have lost her. What he saw in the money lender was not sentiment, however, but pride.

A child enraged by the loss of a coveted toy.

"By developing a relationship, you mean snaring Sparkler in your money lending scheme," Paul shot back. "You targeted him, didn't you? Wanted him indebted so that you could strike your nefarious bargain."

Garrity's knuckles were white against the arm of his chair. "He needed funds, and I provided it. He was lucky because no other lender would have done it." Seeming to catch himself, he leaned back, his grip relaxing. "Thus, I am owed, and I will collect my due."

Anger seared Paul's chest. "Charity was never a piece of collateral to be bartered."

"Everything is collateral." Garrity's smile made his expression even more sinister. "If you realized that, instead of being a sentimental fool, you'd be a far better negotiator. And that is why you're here—to discuss terms?"

Don't rile him further. For Charity's sake, you need to save the shop.

Paul gave a terse nod.

"I don't discuss my business in public." Garrity flicked a glance at the other men.

"Fines?" Harteford quirked a brow.

"Wait for me in the carriage," Paul said. "I'll be there shortly."

The two left, and Paul and Garrity faced each other across the coffee table.

"We're alone as you wished. Now what will it take for you to reconsider the terms of repayment?" Paul said evenly.

"You are persistent. Not surprising, given what I've heard about you. Fight like that, too, don't you—fists flying, never backing down."

Paul's eyes narrowed. He didn't understand the smugness in Garrity's tone but had a certainty he soon would. "What's your point?"

"I've been following your matches."

"Meaning what? You're a fan?" Paul said sardonically.

Garrity made a sound that might have been a laugh. "I

wouldn't say that. But like any gentleman, I enjoy my wagers—and, more specifically, winning. You've added to my pockets."

"Glad to be of service. Would you care to return the favor and subtract that amount from Sparkler's bill?"

"I never mix business with pleasure." The reptilian gleam in Garrity's eyes raised the hairs on Paul's nape. "Unless, of course, it's a guarantee that the former will lead to the latter."

"I'm not following."

"The Championship round takes place three days from now, doesn't it?"

The question was rhetorical. Clearly, Garrity had his sights on the match; the question was what did the money lender want?

Shoulders tensing, Paul said, "What about it?"

"I'm considering placing a wager on the outcome. Being conservative by nature, I'd like to pick a winner. One that is foolproof, so to speak."

"I'll do my damnedest to win," Paul said, his brow furrowing, "but I can't guarantee that—"

"Of course not. No one can guarantee a win." Garrity flicked a speck from his sleeve. "It is, however, possible to guarantee a loss, is it not?"

The meaning belted Paul in the stomach. "You want me to deliberately *lose* the fight?"

"It's not as simple as that. I want you not only to lose, but to do it"—Garrity leaned forward in his chair—"in a *spectacular* fashion."

"The hell you say." Paul was on his feet before he knew it, glaring down at the snake. "What kind of a gentleman do you take me for?"

Garrity smiled thinly. "A desperate one."

"Not desperate enough to besmirch my honor, my name as a gentleman and a fighter." Paul's chest burned with outrage.

"Perhaps I misunderstood, then. I thought you wanted to save your wife's little shop." Garrity reclined in his chair. "Or perhaps your dreams are more important than hers?"

The bastard's words struck painfully close to home. Paul's anger morphed into a conflict more potent than any he'd experienced before. Was that what he was doing ... putting himself before Charity? Being selfish yet again?

It was true that prizefighting had given him purpose, an identity, and a sense of his own worth. It had paved his way to redemption. All along, he'd believed that winning that final match would give him the future he wanted.

But then he flashed to Charity. His gut twisted at the thought of her losing her legacy on top of everything else. His wife had suffered too much already, and he hadn't been there to support her in her time of need. *He hadn't been there*—and he'd sworn to her, to *himself* that he would be henceforth.

He'd told her he loved her.

Mere words, if they weren't backed by actions.

All his life, he'd wanted to be a man of honor and worth: here was his chance. Because the exchange of his dream for Charity's was the one thing he could give her, true proof of the depth of his feeling for her. And compared to what she'd given him—her glowing, steadfast love, which hadn't faltered through all these years— his was a paltry gift indeed.

She, not the championship, was his true future.

His throat thickened.

"Well?" Garrity said.

"Define spectacular," Paul said flatly.

"Twenty rounds. You take five here and there, to give an appearance of a true fight. But you let Jem Barnes take the rest."

Paul's muscles bunched. "Barnes has the most powerful uppercut in the tournament. If I give him an advantage, what's to prevent him from knocking me out before the twenty rounds are up?"

The rules of prizefighting were simple: fight until you

couldn't. Certain maneuvers—such as hitting below the belt—were prohibited, but everything else from eye gouging to kicking was considered fair play. The rounds that made up a match ended when a fighter was knocked or thrown off his feet. He had to rise and make it to the scratch line within half a minute in order for the next round to begin. This would go on until a fighter either couldn't get up again or his second declared him beaten.

It made for a long—and often savage—battle. Paul loved the primal rush of it. His main strategy, which had proved a winning one, involved maneuvers that exhausted his opponent. He'd wear his adversary out, then go in strong. On average, his matches had lasted less than ten rounds, and due to his defense tactics, he'd managed to escape any major injuries ... thus far.

Garrity's proposition could see him seriously harmed—or worse.

Paul's nape grew cold as he recalled seeing one of Barnes' opponents carried out of the ring, bloody and unmoving. That bout had only lasted six rounds. Surviving twenty with Barnes would take a miracle.

"You'll have to find a way to take a beating and still get up." Garrity's mouth curled. "The odds of a man lasting that long against Barnes are low—which will make my bet pay off in spades. All in all, a bargain for us both."

Easy for the bastard to say. He wouldn't be the one getting pummeled into dust.

For a minute, Paul considered turning down the offer. Instead, he could wager what money he had on *himself* to be the winner. His competitive spirit rallied at the thought.

But it would be far from a sure thing. A ruthless and savage brawler, Barnes was favored to win. Paul believed he could take the match from the other—but he didn't know it with a certainty. His hands balled in frustration.

He couldn't risk Charity's happiness for the sake of his own pride.

Losing a match meant nothing if he could erase the worry from her beautiful eyes. All he had to do was somehow survive Barnes' murderous blows ...

"I'll take your offer," he said grimly, "but it stays between us."

Knowing Charity, she would never allow him to lose for her, which meant ... she must never know.

"Done. 'Tis not a fact I'd care to share with the bookmakers." Smirking, Garrity held out a manicured hand.

Their hands met in an unshakeable grip, the devil's bargain struck.

Chapter Forty-Three

When Paul returned home, Charity was waiting for him. Bundled up in a flannel wrapper, her shiny curls framing her piquant little face, she ushered him into the parlor where a fire was merrily burning. She fussed over him in the wifely manner he adored, helping him with his jacket and boots. A cup of soothing tea and a collation of meats and cheeses had already been arranged on the nearby table.

Only when he was comfortably settled did she perch next to him on the settee and ask, "How did things go?"

He gave a rehearsed version of events to her—the same he'd given Nicholas and Hunt. While he hated lying, Paul knew that his wife and his friends would try to dissuade him from his plan, and he could not allow that to happen. One fight and they would be free of Garrity once and for all. One fight for a lifetime of happiness with Charity.

A risk he'd take a thousand times over.

"Mr. Garrity took the six thousand pounds as a down payment? He'll allow us to pay the rest off in installments?" Charity blinked at him. "Truly?"

"He also agreed to a more reasonable percentage," Paul said, "so we will be done with the loan soon. Not bad for a night's work, eh?"

Her brow puckered as he'd known it would. "But *why* would Garrity do that? He's never been reasonable before."

"He knows he won't get his thirty thousand," Paul said smoothly, "and, in the end, he realized something was better than nothing. With our current agreement, he will get his capital back —and a healthy amount of interest besides."

His breath held as she searched his face.

Then she threw her arms around his neck. "I don't know what to say ..."

He inhaled the clean fragrance of her hair, his arms closing around her slim back.

"You don't have to say anything," he said huskily.

"But I do." Her head tipped back, and her radiant gaze stole his breath. Until this moment, he hadn't realized how much he'd yearned to have her look at him this way again: as if he were offering her the moon and stars—which he would, if she asked.

Because there was *nothing* he wouldn't do for her.

He told himself he'd survive the match with Jem Barnes. Even as coldness seeped into him as he thought of the other's lethal style of brawling, he told himself he'd find a way. Somehow he'd make it through so that he could hold Charity this way forever.

Her palm curved around his jaw. "You came back for me. You saved my father's legacy, even though he gave you little reason to do so. You, Apollo Fines, are my hero."

The brightness of her love fought back the shadows. What would come would come. In this moment, he wanted to savor being with his wife.

"I like the sound of that," he murmured.

"I have something else you'll like." Rising, she stood in front of him and tugged on the belt of her robe. The thick flannel fell away, leaving nothing but ... Charity. His nubile nymph, her delicate skin spangled with blushes and her gaze shining with passion.

He sucked in a breath. Darted a look at the closed door, which the maid or housekeeper could open at any moment. "Sweetheart, let's go upstairs—"

"I love you," she said. "With all my heart and soul."

Servants be damned.

Desire crashed over him, a burning need to affirm life in the face of looming danger. He took her up in his arms. He sensed her surprise when he carried her past the settee to the adjacent scrolled bench. The backless frame had front and back posts that curled inward on both ends, and the cushion was just sufficient to fit Charity's petite length. He spread her there like a feast, lowering to his knees beside her.

He loved how sensitive she was, responding to his mere look as if it were a touch: beneath his possessive gaze, her pink nipples hardened, jutting toward him. The soft dip of her belly quivered. And farther down ... his nostrils flared at the decadent sight of her dewy thatch.

Some of her boldness slipped, her arms crossing over her chest.

He halted that movement—circling her wrists and bringing them above her head. Gently, he folded her hands around the posts of the bench.

"Keep them there," he ordered huskily. "You're exquisite, love. Let me look my fill."

Her bosom rose and fell in a sharp wave. But she didn't move. Love and trust lit her face like a beacon and nearly undid him.

He flattened his palm against her throat, ran it in a straight path down between her small, heaving breasts, her delicate rib cage, her silken navel. He cupped her sex—just held her there, relishing her lushness, the way she arched to his touch.

"Mine," he said. "All of this. All of you."

"Yes," she whispered.

He slid a finger inside her, his pulse erratic as slick muscles clamped around him, pulling him deeper. He obliged, frigging her steadily.

"You're drenched," he breathed, "So sweet and tight. Do you want more?"

Her hips pleaded as much as her words. "Yes. Oh, please, *yes*."

He drove in with two fingers, slapping his palm against the peak of her pleasure. With each thrust, she grew wetter, hotter, her cream dripping over his palm. She writhed against the cushion, her knuckles white against the mahogany, and he bent to take her nipple into his mouth, sucking hard as he gave her pearl another sharp smack. Her hips jerked, her pussy squeezing him with ecstatic force. Her grip on the bench loosened as her cry of release soared with the joy of a Bach hymn, striking fervor in his heart, in his turgid, throbbing cock.

In the next heartbeat, he flipped her over, bending her over the width of the bench. Too far gone to deal with his boots and trousers, he ripped down his fall and fisted his cock, groaning as he rubbed it along her dripping slit. Then he gripped her hips and slammed into her from behind. His back bowed as her tight cunny embraced him, milking him and taking him to the balls.

"Christ, I love fucking you." He bucked, hard and deep. "I'll never get enough."

Her hips shoved back to meet his thrusts. She twisted her head to look at him, her eyes full of fire and love. "Good, because I love having you inside me. Fucking me ..."—her eyes squeezed shut as he rammed his shaft home—"loving me."

"I'll always love you," he said savagely. "To my dying breath."

Her head dropped, a dreamy smile on her lips as she gave herself over to their lovemaking. He wanted to make this last, to draw out her passion, but the sight of her milky bottom, reddened from his pounding began to unravel his self-control. His vision darkened as he watched his cock spreading her swollen lips, felt the hips beneath his palms vibrate as his bollocks spanked her sex again and again.

Too much.

His climax roared over him. Heat rushed from his balls, gushed with shuddering intensity up his shaft. Groaning, he emptied himself inside her, gave her everything he was as if this were the very last time.

When he could catch his breath, he gathered her in his arms and held her tight. His eyes were damp. Because now that he'd found heaven, he never wanted to let her go.

Chapter Forty-Four

"I do wish you'd let me go with you," Charity said.

Paul nodded at his valet, who exited the bedchamber with the traveling cases. Paul was leaving for Banstead Downs, a three hour drive south of London. The match was tomorrow afternoon, and his plan was to get there a day early to rest and prepare for his fight against Barnes.

He cupped his wife's shoulders and placed a kiss on the tip of her little nose.

"We've been through this before," he said. "I can't afford a distraction."

"But I won't get in your way, I promise—"

"No, love," he said gently but firmly. As much as he hated to be parted from her, he could not allow her to witness what was certain to be a bloodbath. Shaping his lips into a smile, he said, "It's considered bad luck to have one's woman watching the fight. I'll lose my focus worrying about you amongst that rough and tumble lot. Trust me, the place will be teeming with ruffians, ready to riot and pillage at a moment's notice." This part, at least, was true. "A fight is no place for a lady, and you know it."

She huffed out a breath. "Fine. Banish me from the most important event of your life."

Her expression was the closest to a pout that he'd ever seen from her, and his smile deepened into a true grin. "At least you won't be the only one. Hunt says Percy's been sulking ever since he forbade her from going with him."

"One can't blame Mr. Hunt for being protective," Charity muttered, her eyes on his lapel. "Percy is in a delicate condition and mustn't take such risks."

"Precisely. Now are you going to blame me for having husbandly concerns about your welfare?"

"It's not the same. I'm not ..." She turned a charming shade of pink.

And well she should. Given the frequency of their beddings, such an outcome was more than possible. His chest expanded as he thought of Charity, plump with his child. He'd never thought of himself as a fatherly sort, but to have a little girl with eyes like her mama's ... or a boy he could teach to box and ride ...

Conviction flowed through him.

He would survive the damned fight. He'd come back to Charity.

And then they could really start their lives together.

"We have been busy, haven't we?" he murmured. He drew her close, inhaled once more the heavenly scent that was hers alone. "I have to be off, sweeting. Be a good wife now, and give me a kiss for luck."

Her lips were sweet and passionate, everything he could want. In the end, he had to break the kiss. If he didn't, he feared he wouldn't have the courage to leave her.

"Good luck," she said, her voice tremulous. "Be careful, my darling."

He ran a hand over her silky curls, cupping her nape.

"Never forget how much I love you," he said.

He brushed his lips against her forehead and left.

Charity awoke with jarring swiftness, clutching the sheets, her chest rising and falling with quick, shallow breaths. Rubbing her hands over her damp face, she told herself she'd just had a bad dream. She couldn't recall the specifics of the nightmare, but tendrils of fear snaked through her still.

You're overwrought. Paul will be fine. He'll win today, come home safe and sound.

Yet a shiver coursed over her nape.

Chiding herself for being silly, she got out of bed and lit the lamp. It was still dark, at least an hour before dawn. Restless energy buzzed through her, and she knew she needed something to occupy herself. After performing her ablutions and donning an old gown, she headed to the guest bedchamber.

She set down her lamp, perusing the cramped space. Paul had been using it as a dressing room, and his personal items littered every surface. Shaking her head, Charity picked a rumpled cravat off the floor. She paused, bringing it to her nose. Paul's woodsy scent both soothed her and made her miss him more.

As she sorted his belongings, she realized that Paul was right. They did need to find a home of their own soon. He needed more space, and though they managed to fit themselves in her bed—cuddled like two spoons in a drawer or with her nestled atop of him—a larger bed would give them more room to sleep ... and play. With a wistful smile, she retrieved a pair of cufflinks from the coverlet where he'd tossed them.

Yes, it was time to move on. If they weren't ready to purchase a property of their own, they could rent a flat or cottage for the time being. A place to call their own and to start their new lives together. The thought of leaving her father's house no longer filled her with grief.

I'm sorry you were hurt, Father, and I wish that you could have found happiness. That you were here now to witness mine, she thought with a pang. *To know that we Sparklers* are *deserving of love.*

When Paul returned, she would tell him she wanted to sell this house and begin afresh.

The thought of their future filled her with anticipation.

With cufflinks in hand, she searched for the large leather case that housed his accoutrements. He had brought his compact *nécessaire* to Banstead, so she was certain he'd left the heftier storage case behind. She'd seen it yesterday on the desk, but now all that lay on the surface were some assorted bottles and grooming implements.

Her brow furrowed. *Odd. It has to be in here somewhere.*

Given the close quarters, there were limited places the case could be. She searched the small cupboard to no avail. She thought for a moment ... and crouched to look beneath the bed. *Voilà.* She dragged the case out, torn between amusement and exasperation. Knowing her husband's habits, he'd probably kicked it aside without a thought.

She lugged the box onto the mattress. Opening the lid, she lifted out the top tray full of stick pins ... and her heart seized. Her mind couldn't make sense of what was before her. With trembling hands, she lifted out the familiar stack of banknotes. She counted them, twice, found the entire sum that she'd given Paul. The amount that he'd told her Garrity had accepted as down payment.

Why did Paul lie to me?

Agitation filled her, the formless panic from her dream now taking on the shape of very real questions. She paced, her mind racing. Why had Paul lied? If he hadn't given Garrity the money, how had he negotiated to get Sparkler's back? What had he used as leverage ... and why wouldn't he tell her the truth?

Fear spurred her heart into a gallop. Clutching the banknotes, she rushed from the chamber. She called for the carriage, grabbed her reticule, and hurried out.

"Mr. Garrity is not at home." The butler looked down his nose at her. "Even if he were, I'm certain he wouldn't take uninvited callers at this early hour."

Charity drew herself up. "This is a matter of utmost importance. Where can I find him?"

"I'm not at liberty to say."

She dangled a purse from her fingers, letting the coins within jingle. "Would this change your mind?"

She'd read the butler correctly. His gaze darted around before he held out his hand. Untying the drawstring, she placed a single guinea in his palm.

"Mr. Garrity left for Banstead Downs at dawn," the servant said, confirming her fears. "Got a wager on the match. A surefire win, he said."

Charity forced herself to sound calm. "Which fighter is he betting on?"

The butler arched his brow, his hand outstretched.

She gave him another coin.

"The master says Jem Barnes will take the match, and it'll be a fight for the ages," he said.

"For the ages? Why?" she said in a wavering voice.

When the other did not reply, she shoved the entire coin purse at him.

"Mr. Garrity predicts a bloodbath, and he's never wrong about these things." The money disappeared into the servant's jacket. With a hint of wistfulness in his voice, he added, "Wish I could be there. Like a bit of carnage myself."

The door shut behind him.

Charity stood frozen on the steps, the truth hammering in her chest.

Paul's bargaining chip with Garrity had been the final match. He was going to *deliberately lose* the championship as payment for the shop's debts. He was going to let himself get beaten, likely *injured*, all for ... for her.

Like hell he will.

Even as her love for her husband swelled to infinite proportions, fierce determination surged through her. She turned and dashed down the steps. Because she knew what she had to do, and she only hoped she was not too late.

Charity arrived at the pristine Italianate villa in St. John's Wood a short while later. She'd never had occasion to visit the elegant and rather scandalous neighborhood just northwest of London. Despite its bucolic setting of gardens and cottages, the area was home to the mistresses of the rich, famous artists, and generally anyone who had the money and inclination to live life away from prying eyes.

Charity rang the bell.

The door opened and the large footman said, "Yes, miss? How may I help you?"

Taking a breath, Charity said, "Tell Mrs. Stone that her daughter is here and wishes a word."

The man didn't blink an eye. "Right this way," he said.

He led Charity into a drawing room done up in dramatic shades of emerald and gold. She declined the footman's offer of refreshments and stood by the window as she waited. The peaceful view of the garden did nothing to calm her inner tumult.

Moments later, Mrs. Stone came in. She was *en dishabille*, striking in her red silk dressing gown patterned with chinoiserie. With her hair down and face free of cosmetic, she looked younger, more vulnerable than her usual sophisticated self. The hope shining in her hazel eyes pierced Charity to the quick. Anger spurted, thick and dark as crude.

How could you leave me, mother?

"Charity, my dear," she said, "what a lovely surprise—"

"This isn't a social call. I have come for a reason. To ..."—swallowing, Charity forced out the words—"to ask for your help."

"Anything," Mrs. Stone said. "Anything at all."

"I want you to know that even if you help me, it changes nothing between us," Charity said as her heart thudded. "I can never forgive you for what you've done."

The light faded from the actress' eyes. "I know. That makes two of us." Exhaling, she said, "How can I be of service to you, my dear?"

Chapter Forty-Five

Though the match had not yet begun, the roar of the rabble was already deafening, even inside the carriage where Paul waited. The mob at Banstead Downs was larger than any he'd seen at his previous fights. Beside the carriage, the ring was being set up: four stakes roping off the eight-foot square where the final battle would be held. On the opposite side of the ring stood Barnes' carriage. It gleamed, enormous and black, the crimson drapes pulled shut.

Surrounding the ring were men—mostly drunk and getting drunker—as far as the eye could see. Like a swarm of termites, the crowd had taken over the dusty field. Traymore had estimated that upwards of ten thousand spectators would show, and an exponentially larger amount of blunt would change hands.

Glancing out into the throng, Paul could make out the bookmakers: like pebbles landing in a pond, they were surrounded by ever growing circles. Men shouted and waved their caps to have their wagers taken. The sight made bile rise in Paul's throat. Sods who were betting on him didn't stand a chance. All because of that bastard Garrity.

Paul's fists clenched. What he wouldn't give to have a chance at a fair fight. To face Barnes on his own terms.

As if sensing his tension, Fogg, his knee man, said, "Touch o' the nerves is perfectly normal. That's a right proper crowd. Weren't 'alf as many 'ere at the Mendoza-Owens match last year."

"That's on account o' Mendoza and Owens bein' old codgers past their prime." Snorting, Stickley readied the bottles of water and oranges that he would use to refresh Paul during the fight. "Trust me, you've got nothin' to worry 'bout, sir. Forget the crowd. Just fight like you've practiced an' you'll make mincemeat out o' Barnes. He ain't nothin' but a brawler, and a true boxer like yourself wins every time."

Paul's gut curled. He gave a tight nod.

"Barnes is a brute," Fogg agreed, "so remember to keep your guard up. 'E likes to come in 'igh, and 'e's rung more than a few bells with that uppercut o' his."

Paul hoped his skull was hard enough to survive Barnes' summons.

The carriage door opened, letting in a swell of noise as well as Lord Traymore.

The viscount's face was red and glistening with excitement. "Now that's a crowd!" he said. "'Pon my honor, the Fancy's never had such a turnout. Those coves outside are raring for a good fight. Which you're more than ready to deliver, eh Fines?"

"I'll do what I can," Paul said. *To stay alive.*

"Barnes doesn't stand a chance. I can't wait to see the looks at White's when I collect," Traymore crowed. "Bets against me took up several pages in the betting book."

Paul walled off the tide of guilt and shame. A fixed fight was ungentlemanly in the extreme, yet what options did he have? This was fun and games for men like Traymore. Losing a few thousand pounds meant nothing to him but injured pride.

Charity's legacy and future were depending on Paul. She was

his wife, the only woman he'd ever loved, and he would sacrifice anything to make things right for her.

Even his honor.

Even his ... life.

His fingers closed around the belt that Charity had sewn for him. It was the current fashion for prizefighters to wear a colored scarf around the waist, and she had fashioned his in rich blue and gold stripes. *The colors of Apollo,* she'd said.

His chest throbbed. He had to make it back to her. He had to.

A sudden hush filtered into the cabin as if the air had been sucked out. A roar followed that shook the glass panes, and Paul looked out the window.

Jem Barnes had descended from his carriage. A showman, the prizefighter had emerged without his shirt, his huge, hirsute chest bared to the adoring hordes. He was a hulk of a man, over six feet tall and with at least three stone on Paul—all of that weight in muscle. Barnes raised his ham-sized fists, punching the air, and the throng went mad.

"He's all brute strength and no skill. You can take him, Fines," Traymore said.

It didn't matter what he *could* do; his hands were literally bound.

Paul's jaw clenched. "Let's do it, then," he said tersely.

Traymore opened the door to the blast of the crowd.

The conveyance pulled to a halt. Heart pounding, Charity spotted the ring in the distance. She was too far away to make out the fighters' faces, but, squinting, she caught the splash of blue at the leaner man's waist. *Paul.* Her hands gripped the carriage door as she saw the Goliath towering over him. In the next instant, the giant brute charged Paul, picking him up and *tossing* him across the ring.

Charity's lungs seized. The crowd cheered as Paul struggled to his feet.

"Why aren't we moving?" Charity cried.

Mrs. Stone opened the window. "What's happening, Jim?" she called up.

"Can't get any closer," the driver shouted back. "Too many carriages and people in the way."

"Perhaps if we wait a bit—Charity, what are you doing?" Mrs. Stone exclaimed.

Charity's borrowed Hessians touched the ground. "I'm going to find my husband."

"Being dressed like a gentleman only protects you from being accosted, not from being trampled." In the blink of an eye, the other—perfectly convincing as a blond Corinthian—joined her on the ground. The actress' voice dropped to a startlingly masculine octave. "The boys and I are going with you."

The "boys" referred to the trio of burly footmen who clambered down from the carriage to flank their mistress. Apparently, the three served as guards for the famous actress who'd faced her own riotous audiences. With their muscular frames, Charity had to admit that they would come in handy today.

"We'll lead the way, miss," one of the large men said.

Another of the footmen elbowed him. "Fat good 'er costume will do if you keep callin' 'er *miss*," he said. "It'll be *lad* or *sir* from 'ere on in."

Charity's hands went to her head and lip. Both the hat and moustache—compliments of Mrs. Stone—were in place.

"Let's go," she said urgently.

"Don't forget to disguise your voice," Mrs. Stone said.

Charity nodded, and the three footmen formed a protective triangle around her and Mrs. Stone. Together, they cut a swath through the thick crowd. Shouts and shoves greeted their progress, but the guards managed to keep a forward, if slow, momentum. Anxiety surged in Charity as the mob closed around her. Given her small stature, she couldn't see the stage, couldn't see anything beyond the sea of bodies. Overhead, the sun blazed; the stench of unwashed skin and pungent spirits assailed her. Perspiration trickled beneath her cravat, and dots floated before her eyes.

A hand closed around her arm. Mrs. Stone gave her a sharp look. "Can you do this?"

"Yes." Charity fought off crushing panic as they inched forward. "I must get to Paul."

"You're a strong woman, my dear, and should never be under-estimated." Mrs. Stone paused. "You may not want to hear it, but in this you take after me."

The other was right—Charity *didn't* want to hear it.

"Uriah feared my strength, you know," the actress said in conversational tones. "He sought to douse my fire, and my greatest fear was that he'd try to do the same to you."

Then why did you abandon me? Charity kept her mouth shut.

"I begged him to let me see you, but he refused. Threatened to poison you with lies about me if I tried to make contact and—"

"I don't want to talk about this," Charity said flatly. "Why aren't we moving any faster?"

Mrs. Stone sighed. "At any rate, I'm gratified that you came to me for help today."

"I had no choice," Charity shot back. "You were the only one I could go to."

"What about your bosom chum, that troublemaking blond chit ... your husband's sister?"

The other knew of her friendship with Percy?

Her surprise must have shown, for Mrs. Stone said, "As I've mentioned, I've been observing you from afar. Watching you grow and blossom. Wishing ... that I could be there."

The surrounding hubbub grew quiet compared to the havoc within Charity. She could hear the poignant regret in Mrs. Stone's words ... yet the other had no right to march back into her life and say such things! As they inched forward through the masses, her throat worked around words she wasn't ready to give.

Instead, she said, "Percy is expecting, and I'd never risk her well-being." Then she blurted, "She is *loyal*, you see, and even if she were as large as a house, she'd insist on accompanying me. She'd never abandon me in a time of need."

Pain rippled across Mrs. Stone's face, and Charity felt a shameful satisfaction.

"Rome wasn't built in a day." The actress gave a curt nod. "You should know that we're getting close to the ring."

Charity blinked. Standing on her toes, she craned her neck—and got a glimpse of Paul. Her heart slammed against her ribcage. Even from a few dozen yards away, she could see the blood: so *much* of it, scarlet streaks down his face and chest. He dodged a blow, disappearing from her line of vision. She jumped up and down, desperate for another look.

"Can you see Paul?" she cried. "Dear God, is he losing?"

"Your voice," Mrs. Stone hissed.

"Er, I mean, what in blazes is happening?" Charity said in her gruffest tone.

"Bloody Fines is gettin' killed, that's what's happening." The slurred voice belonged to the scruffy fellow a few paces to her right. Bleary-eyed and scowling, the man was clearly jug-bitten. "'Ad a month's wages on the cove, and there'll be trouble an' strife to greet me at 'ome all right. Married to a bloody 'arpy on the best o' days. Tonight? She'll tear my bloody 'ead off."

Panicked, Charity said, "How badly is Fines losing?"

"Bugger's down five rounds to eight. But the last three rounds, 'tis been a massacre. Barnes got 'im against the ropes an' punched the tickin' out o' 'im." The man took a swig from his flask, adding sourly, "Should've known better than to bet on the dark 'orse."

"Fines is a *winner*," Charity said fiercely.

"Bastard'll be lucky to make it out alive." The other belched. "Not that I give a damn, after what 'e's cost me."

Before Charity could snap back a rejoinder, a collective gasp filled the air.

"What happened?" she cried, just remembering to keep her tone low.

One of Mrs. Stone's footmen turned to look at her. "Fines just got knocked off 'is feet. 'E's got thirty seconds to make it to the scratch line or 'e's lost the match."

Fear paralyzed her. *Please God, don't let Paul be hurt...*

"Bastard just got up again!" A voice rang out from the crowd. "That's the lad! Fight's not over yet!"

"Can't we get any closer?" Charity shouted to the footman in front.

"Doin' our best, m—I mean, sir." Sweat dripped down the man's face. "Crowd's packed so thick there's 'ardly room to breathe, let alone move."

Charity searched wildly for any route to ringside. As her gaze swept the yards separating her from Paul, it latched upon a figure standing halfway between them. A man garbed in elegant, unrelieved black, surrounded by a circle of henchmen. Her teeth gnashed.

She grabbed the leading footman's arm, pointed to her target. "Get me over there!"

The guard nodded. Moments later, she reached Garrity.

His cold black gaze slitted when he recognized her. He waved his cutthroats aside. "Mrs. Fines," he said with disdain. "How unconventional you are today."

"And how dastardly *you* are," she snapped. "What did you do to Paul?"

"I don't know what you mean."

She detected the smugness in his tone. "You're forcing him to lose," she said with ferocity. "He's working off my father's debt by deliberately losing this fight—"

Garrity grabbed her by the arm, his gaze darting around them. "Continue talking that way," he hissed in an undertone, "and you'll have a riot on your hands. And, trust me, it'll be your husband's head they're after first."

Charity swallowed but stood her ground. "Why are you doing this?"

"You've heard the expression *an eye for eye*? He took what was mine."

"You don't even know me. You couldn't possibly care that I married someone else!"

"I don't give a damn about you," Garrity said icily, "but about the fact that Fines had the audacity to steal from under my nose. I never forget a wrong."

"I was never yours to begin with. Release Paul from this devil's bargain!"

"What's done can't be undone," Garrity said.

"We'll see about that," Charity said.

She prodded one of Mrs. Stone's footmen. "Hoist me up."

The fellow blinked. In the next heartbeat, she was seated upon his massive shoulders. From this height, she witnessed Barnes' fist slamming into Paul's jaw. Pain splintered her chest as Paul sagged against the ropes, his face battered and bleeding, one eye swollen shut. The audience stomped and jeered.

Desperation gave her strength. In a gruff voice, she declared, "Apollo Fines is going to win!"

Boos and raucous calls greeted her.

"Get off the sauce!"

"Cove doesn't stand a chance. In fact, 'e can barely stand at all!"

"Who'll put their money where their mouth is?" she shouted back. "Who'll take my wager? I've got quid that says Fines takes the match!"

A murmur spread through the crowd. She knew what they were thinking—a lordlet plump in the pockets but thin in the attic. A pigeon ripe for the plucking. A few yards from the ring, a hand shot up in the air, waving a betting ledger.

A bookmaker.

"Let the lad pass!" he shouted. "Get him over here!"

The audience, obviously wanting to see a pompous greenling get his just deserts, parted to allow her passage. But they blocked the footmen and Mrs. Stone, who called out, "Be careful!"

Charity jerked her chin and wriggled through the space between the bodies.

Have to get to Paul ... almost there ...

Hands grabbed her just before she reached the ring.

The bookmaker was short and fat, his waistcoat bulging at the seams. His might have been an avuncular air had he not been flanked by brutish cutthroats and an assistant whose job seemed to be to function as a desk. The latter was bent over, an open book on his back and a pot of ink in one of his outstretched hands.

The bookmaker held a quill over the page.

"What is the amount you wish to wager, sir?" he said silkily.

"Er, six thousand pounds," Charity said in her best male voice.

The man didn't blink. "Be very certain: once a bet is recorded, there's no going back." A drop of ink dripped from the tip of his pen and splattered onto the page. "And I'll require the full amount now."

Her gaze darted to the ring. The fighters were resting between rounds, and she could see the sweaty, quivering muscles of Paul's back as he sat on his knee man's leg. Suddenly, he bent over, retching.

Withdrawing the packet of banknotes, she shoved it at the bookmaker.

"I'm certain," she said.

The bookmaker took his time counting the notes before scribbling in his ledger. "Odds are twelve to one if you win." The corners of his mouth curled as he held out the quill. "Sign here."

She committed herself to the line.

Receipt in hand, she plunged forward. She squeezed between

bodies and pushed her way through to the ring. Just as she neared Paul's corner, hands grabbed her.

"No closer," the guard said.

Desperately, she watched as Paul remained with his head between his knees. Was it too late? Could he get his strength back?

"Paul," she shouted frantically.

He didn't turn.

She gave up any pretense of sounding like a male. Raising her voice, she cried, "Paul, it's me, Charity! You have to win, do you hear me? Our future is riding on it!"

Chapter Forty-Six

Paul's entire universe was made of pain. His head pounded, and he couldn't see through his left eye, which was swollen shut. His guts continued to spasm, even after he'd puked them up. All of this was the consequence of allowing himself to be used as a human punching bag. He gargled some water, tried to eat the slice of orange Fogg held to his mouth. The fruit's acid scorched his cut lip.

And damn, if he wasn't hearing things on top of it all. He could have sworn ...

"Paul, it's Charity! Behind you! Look at me!"

He bolted upright. Staggered to his feet. Spinning around, he saw ... the blow to his stomach was worse than any Barnes had delivered.

"What are you doing here?" he yelled.

"I came to see you win!" his wife shouted back. She was struggling, held back by one of the guards hired to protect the ring.

The sight of a man's hands on her sent a fresh sizzle through Paul's blood. He started forward, a growl in his throat. It took both Fogg and Stickley to restrain him.

"Don't be daft!" the latter said. "You'll forfeit if you leave the ring now."

"Paul, you have to *win*, do you hear me?" Charity's small face bobbed in the crowd. "Damn Garrity—I bet our future on it, all six thousand pounds! I need you to win, my love—I know you can do it!"

Paul reeled as if he'd been punched. Everything she had ... she'd bet on him.

Because she loves me.

"Win and we'll be free, my darling!" Her cries were drowned out by the eager mob, who roared to see more bloodshed. "I believe in you, Apollo Fines!"

She believes in me.

"Fifteen seconds," Stickley warned.

"Fix my eye," Paul said tersely. "Can't fight if I can't see."

The bottleman produced a razor, wielded it with methodical precision. A tiny, swift cut released the blood from Paul's eyelid. Stickley applied clotting powder and gave him a shove toward the chalked line in the middle of the ring. He stumbled there with a second to spare.

He had no more time to think. His waiting opponent loomed over him.

"Ready for more of a pounding?" Barnes sneered, cracking his blood-splattered knuckles.

Wearily, Paul eyed his adversary. The Goliath gleamed, a tower of sweat-covered muscles, bloodlust flaring in his eyes. In comparison, Paul hurt from head to toe, his strength sapped. But Charity's voice, her spirit, recharged him. Energy buzzed through his throbbing muscles. A shot of clarity burned away the exhausted fog.

She believes in me. I can't let her down. I have to win.

He knew Barnes' weaknesses. The man was all brawn and no brains. He had powerful fists but lacked movement and speed. An overconfident brawler through and through. Paul flashed to his own training, all the mornings he'd risen before dawn to hit a bag, run the country hills. *A true boxer always beats a brawler.* All Paul had to do was use the other's strength to his own advantage.

I can do this.

"Yes, I'm ready," Paul said, gritting his teeth. "I'm ready to pound you into the ground."

With a snarl, Barnes took the first swipe.

Paul dodged, air whipping the place where his head had been a second earlier. With lightning speed, he went in low, his fist connecting with Barnes' midsection. It was like punching a boulder, and pain jolted through his arm. He ignored it, following through with alternating jabs, finding the chinks in the other's defenses. Ducking blows, he drove the other backward into the ropes. A right cross to the jaw finished the job, and with a stunned look, Barnes dropped to the ground.

"Round to Fines!" one of the umpires shouted.

Barnes was back on his feet within seconds. Swiping sweat from his eyes, he charged like an enraged bull. Paul sidestepped, and the other flew past him, bouncing off the ropes.

"You bloody flea! I'm going to squash you!" Barnes roared.

Paul replied with a beckoning gesture aimed at tempting the beast. Barnes came at him again, swinging fists that would have felled trees. Paul kept on the balls of his feet, executing defensive maneuvers that seemed to madden the other who swung harder, faster, sweat pouring down his face. Paul kept the dance going, and Barnes wasted more and more of his strength.

Soon, Barnes' punches slowed, lost momentum. At this moment, Paul struck, delivering quick, pounding blows to the torso that knocked Barnes down again.

Paul won this round and the next. They were neck-to-neck, eight rounds apiece.

But Barnes would not stay down.

Barnes came at him with a right hook. Paul's arm came up to block the blow, and the instant he realized his mistake—that he'd been taken by a feint—was an instant too late. Barnes' uppercut caught him squarely in the chin.

Black lines waved across Paul's vision; he teetered on his feet.

He swayed away from the incoming attack, the power behind that cross whooshing air against his face. He shook his head to clear it, blocked another attack. Barnes clinched him, aiming punishing blows to his kidneys.

"The match is mine, you worthless git," the other shouted.

Sudden fire blazed through Paul. With his last reserve of strength, he wrestled free of Barnes' hold, plowing his fist into the other's gut as he did so.

"I. Am. Not. Worthless," he spat, bouncing on his feet.

By now, the crowd was deafening; Paul blocked it out. His concentration opened the portals to another realm, one governed by clarity, stillness. Charity's scent, her touch flitted through him like a charge. The sweet science flowed through his being, and he gave himself over to its transcendence. His muscles hummed with power, his every movement directed by instinct. He floated, his feet barely touching the ground before he took flight again, dodging and twisting. His fists hit their mark with the deadly swiftness of a bee's sting.

Two jabs to the face.

He heard the cracking of bone.

Right cross.

Blood flew.

Bob, block, hook him by the neck.

Barnes weaved, unsteady on his feet, and Paul closed in, locking his arm around the bigger man's neck. He held Barnes in position as he rammed his fist into the other's face. Over and again, until the other sagged to his knees, no longer struggling.

Paul released him.

Gravity did the rest.

Barnes slumped to the ground, moaning.

Lungs burning, sweat pouring down his face, Paul waited for

the count. Barnes' second crouched next to the fallen fighter, prodding to no avail.

"Time's up. Jem Barnes is defeated!" one of the umpires shouted.

The other umpire grabbed Paul's arm and held it up. "The winner of the match—and of the Fancy tournament—is Apollo Fines!"

Pandemonium exploded.

Paul noticed none of it.

He shoved through the throng that surged forward to congratulate him. He hopped the rope, his gaze roving wildly.

"Charity!" he shouted into the mob. "Charity—where are you?"

"Here!"

He spotted her waving at him, her small face a shining beacon in the crowd. He tore past bodies to get to her. The instant he gathered her in his arms, the world disappeared, and all he saw was the love in her eyes.

"I won," he said hoarsely.

"I knew you would," she said.

His hand shook with the force of his emotions as he stroked her cheek. "A great hulking brawler like Barnes couldn't take me down. But you, my sweet nymph, you slay me with a look. With a smile. A touch." He thumbed away her tears. "Distance may separate us, but I'll always feel your power in me. I love you. More than anything."

"And I love you, my Apollo," she whispered.

"Before I kiss you," he said, "do you mind if I do something?"

She smiled up at him. "Anything."

With a swift tug, he removed her fake mustache. She yelped.

"I'll kiss it better," he promised.

He was a man who kept his vows.

With the sweetest of sighs, his wife melted into his arms.

Chapter Forty-Seven

The next hour flew by.

Charity watched on proudly as Paul accepted congratulations from members of the Fancy. They presented him with a handsome silver cup and an equally handsome purse of five thousand pounds—to be split with Lord Traymore, who grinned from ear to ear as he accepted slaps on the back from his friends.

Afterward, Charity had her own transaction to complete. The none-too-pleased bookmaker marched her to his carriage and counted out her money. Her winnings plus her initial stake added up to seventy-eight thousand pounds.

A *fortune.*

Dazed, she didn't know what she found more fantastic: the fact that the bookmaker shoved the stack of banknotes at her ... or that her winnings scarcely made a dent in the pile of money she glimpsed in his trunk.

Mrs. Stone, her retinue, and Paul were waiting for Charity outside by the ring—or what remained of it. The stakes had been pulled, the chalk wiped. The only evidence remaining of the match was four divots and dark splotches on the dusty ground.

Charity shuddered at the stains. She looked up at her husband's smiling face: his left eye had swollen up again, an assortment of bruises decorating his cheeks and jaw. Wrapping her arms around his waist, she planted her face against his chest.

"It's not as bad as it looks," he murmured into her hair.

"That's good," she said, her voice muffled, "because it looks terrible. I brought some salve."

"A barrel or two should cover it," he said, a smile in his voice.

"You've both accomplished quite a bit today, and I daresay it's time to go home," Mrs. Stone remarked.

Raising her head, Charity looked over at the actress, who'd switched back to feminine garb. The gold tassels on her walking dress *à la militaire* swayed and gleamed in the rays of the setting sun.

"All's well that ends well," Mrs. Stone said. "Now that the excitement's over, I should be off. I'll leave you two lovebirds to celebrate."

Charity exhaled. "Before you go, there's something I wish to say."

"Indeed?" The other's timbre was neutral; the only thing that betrayed unease was a slight stiffening of her shoulders. "I think you made yourself quite clear earlier. You needn't worry, my dear. I know today changes nothing between us."

"I can never forget the past," Charity said.

"I understand. It was foolish of me to expect otherwise."

"What you did to me—and to Father—was abhorrent."

"Without a doubt, I have sinned against you. Against Uriah?" Mrs. Stone shrugged. "We'll have to agree to disagree."

Charity swallowed. "I don't think of you as my mother."

"Why would you?" Mrs. Stone's mouth twisted. "I haven't been one, have I?"

"But mayhap ..."—Charity released a breath and the words rushed out with it—"mayhap one day we could grow to be friends."

Marietta Stone blinked. Then her eyes shut, and when she opened them, a single tear trickled down her cheek. "I should like that above all things," she whispered.

"Ah, Mr. Fines." A sinister voice dispelled the tender moment. "Just who I was looking for."

Charity spun to see Garrity approaching. His cadre of cutthroats followed in his wake.

Paul pushed her and Mrs. Stone behind him. Mrs. Stone's footmen joined him, forming a wall against the oncoming threat. But there was no doubting Garrity's advantage: he had at least a dozen men to their four.

"This business concerns Mr. Fines only," Garrity said. "The rest of you are free to leave."

Charity peered from behind Paul's shoulder. "I'm not leaving my husband."

"And I'm not leaving my daughter," Mrs. Stone said.

"How touching," Garrity said with contempt.

"I think so," came a new voice.

Relief spread through Charity at the arrival of Mr. Hunt and his footmen.

"Bloody ripper of a fight, Fines." He cuffed Paul on the arm, a grin on his scarred face.

Paul winced, rubbing his limb. "Christ, watch it, will you?"

"Harteford sends his congratulations, too," Mr. Hunt said. "He'll be right along. Broken axel."

"Fines, this is between you and me," Garrity said between his teeth.

"Fines is family. What involves my family involves me," Mr. Hunt said.

"You failed to keep your end of the bargain, Fines," Garrity snarled. "That's twice now you've ruined my plans. Today you will render payment—in one fashion or another."

Alarm shot through Charity at the menacing words, at the way the men all tensed, some of them reaching to their pockets for weapons.

Quickly, she called out, "How much do we owe you?"

"What are you doing? Stay back," Paul hissed.

"How much?" she repeated.

Garrity pinned her with an icy gaze. "Your father owed me thirty thousand pounds. I bet another five thousand that your husband would lose the match."

"Thirty-five thousand and we're free and clear?"

"You've exhausted my patience. I'm collecting on my debt *now*." Garrity signaled his men, who advanced with eager menace.

Paul and the others readied to meet them.

"Wait!" Charity withdrew a sheaf of banknotes from her jacket, waved it like a flag. "I have your money here!"

Garrity held up a hand; his men fell back.

"Bring it here," he said.

"Charity," Paul grated out.

"Let me go. I know what I'm doing, my love." She gave him a reassuring smile; emotions warred on his face before he slowly lowered his arm.

She slipped by and went to face Garrity. Counting out the money, she handed it over.

He, of course, recounted it. "There's forty thousand here," he said curtly.

"The extra is for your trouble. I wish to wipe the slate clean between us."

His mouth curled. "You think money will accomplish this?"

"My father should not have bartered with my future when it wasn't his to decide. You should not have sent your brutes to collect." Her gaze steady, she said, "So, yes, I would say that we are even. Please take this money: after all, it is what you wanted."

His gaze roved over her. After a moment, he pocketed the sum.

He leaned toward her and said softly, "Not *everything* I wanted."

Charity blinked.

With a curt bow, he left, his men following behind him.

The next instant, Paul seized her into his arms.

"What did Garrity say to you?" he demanded.

"Nothing of import." Peering up at his beautiful, battered, and scowling face, she risked a smile. "Can we please go home now? I'm feeling a bit peaked."

"My wife goes to a boxing match dressed like a lad, wagers her future, confronts a cutthroat—and *now* she's peaked," Paul muttered.

But in the next instant, he swept her up and strode toward their carriage.

Laughter rang behind them.

Blushing, she protested, "Put me down. Your injuries—you must ache all over."

"In one place, especially." His kiss brimmed with laughter and love, the sweetness of their future. Against her lips, he murmured, "But I can depend on you to ease me, can't I, my steadfast darling?"

"Yes," she said.

She spent the ride home demonstrating that she was indeed capable of that ... and more.

Epilogue

The main problem with house parties, Paul decided, was that they deprived one of sleep. With doors opening and closing all night long as various guests sought out their sport for the evening, a fellow could scarcely get in a wink. And that wasn't accounting for the female company present in his own bed. Between the pair of them, he hadn't gotten much rest at all.

Then again, he thought, his lips curving, the lack of sleep had been worth it.

He pressed a kiss to the top of his daughter's downy blond head, tucked securely in the crook of his right arm. Miss Prudence Anna Fines' rosebud mouth puckered in reflex, but she did not awaken ... *thank God.*

Despite her angelic appearance, the four-month-old imp was more than capable of raising hell and had proved that again last night. At wit's end, the beleaguered nurse had come knocking on the door, bearing the inconsolable infant. The instant Pru had nestled into her papa's arms, however, she'd calmed instantly, cooing and batting her impossibly long eyelashes at him.

In this way, Pru took after her mama.

Smiling, Paul turned his head to the other side, his chest

swelling even further. Charity lay sleeping within the cove of his other arm. Her short, silky curls tumbled over his shoulder, and her bosom rose and fell in deep, even movements. As always, the sight of his wife released quiet joy, a bone-deep contentment within him.

Thanks to her, the past year had been the happiest of his life.

After winning the title, he'd retired from prizefighting. Since Charity had bet all her savings on him and won, they'd found themselves rich, even after paying off Garrity. Thus, they'd had the luxury of making decisions based on their hearts' desires and what they most wanted from their future together.

They'd bought a house, close to his mama's.

They'd made a precious child.

Paul had opened up his boxing club, and Charity had decided to close Sparkler's.

When she'd first told him of her plans to sell the shop, Paul had been stunned.

"Are you certain, sweeting?" he'd said. "I thought that keeping the shop and preserving your father's legacy was what you wanted."

"So did I, at first. Now I realize that it isn't the shop itself that I want, but a home. And the true legacy that I want to pass on is love." Her hand resting on her burgeoned belly, she'd smiled at him. "Now that I have both those things, I don't need the shop."

She'd given Mr. Jameson a generous pension and closed the doors of Sparkler's for good. Since then, Paul had witnessed his wife blossom even more. Liberated from the cares that had weighed her down since she was a little girl, she took to life with a renewed vigor. She'd always been efficient; now she was free to be efficient doing the things she truly wished to do.

Their home was a masterpiece of comfort and organization. Her beautiful embroidery added graceful touches to every room. And she'd even found the time to start a new business.

The belt she'd designed for him to wear during the championship fight had become all the rage amongst the *ton*. Every fashionable buck in London wanted one. Charity had teamed up with Madame Rousseau, and even with the latter's team of seamstresses, they could barely keep up with the demand.

Smiling, Paul looked at his sleeping spouse. Life with her was never boring. She was, without a doubt, a force of nature to be reckoned with.

Taking care not to wake her, he rose with their daughter in his arms. He placed Pru in the bassinet in the sitting room and returned to the bedchamber, closing the door softly behind him. He climbed into bed, trying not to disturb Charity, and yet she stirred. Her lashes lifted, and he found himself mesmerized as ever by those jeweled depths.

"Did I drift off? Is Pru asleep?" Charity murmured.

"Yes." Unable to resist, he nuzzled her ear. She smelled of everything clean and good. Everything he could ever want. "I put her down, and hopefully she'll stay that way for a bit."

"Like her papa, she never stays down for long," his wife said with a yawn.

"Funny you should mention that." Catching his wife's hand, he brought it against his morning cockstand.

"I was referring to you in the boxing ring," she said with a muffled laugh.

But her hand eased up and down, her touch so perfect.

Lying on his side, he gave himself over to the pleasure of a morning frig from his wife. He was, undoubtedly, the most fortunate man alive. Lust unfurled in his belly as he watched her small hands take charge of his eager equipment. She knew just how to touch him, fisting his shaft with one hand whilst cupping his balls with the other. And that expression on her face, so sweetly lusty ... for that alone, his cock wept a tear of joy.

He leaned over and claimed her mouth. Their kiss was drowsy and passionate, and they rolled sensuously over the sheets, tangling tongues and limbs and shedding robes along the way. He nibbled her ear, her neck, made his way to her breasts. He was fascinated and aroused by the changes pregnancy had wrought in his little nymph. Her tits had grown plumper, her nipples more sensitive. When he licked those perky tips, she shivered.

When he suckled a drop of liquid sweetness from her, she moaned.

He indulged himself, playing with her breasts while she clearly had some ideas of her own. Her hands found his prick again, and his hips jerked in helpless pleasure at her caresses. It was too good, too fast and too soon ...

"Sweeting, I won't last if you keep that up," he murmured.

She looked at him with steady, loving eyes. "I want to kiss you. Here," she said throatily, swirling the damp tip of his cock with her thumb. "May I please?"

Devil and damn. His temperature shot up another ten degrees; he was lucky he didn't just explode then and there.

"There's nothing that would please me more," he said. "Only ..."

"Yes?"

"I want to taste you, too."

Her brow furrowed adorably. "I suppose we could ... take turns?"

"And here I thought you were the efficient one," he chided her.

"What do you mean ...?"

She didn't get a chance to finish for he lifted her, maneuvering her into the position that he had in mind. Now she lay atop him, her lips poised above his quivering cock ... and her sweet pussy above his watering mouth. A winning proposition from all angles.

"This is so ... wicked," his wife breathed against his prick.

"I knew you'd like it," he said.

Then he wrapped his hands around her slim thighs, groaning as he indulged himself. It became a decadent game of pleasure, a sensual follow-the-leader. When he licked her slit, she tongued his cock from root to tip. When he tickled her love-knot, she suckled his sensitive cockhead. When he plunged his tongue inside her hole, she took him to the balls. And on it went, until they were straining against one another, breathing hard, bound by the hot, frenzied intimacy ...

As his climax raged near, he had just enough presence of mind to try to dislodge her, to gasp out, "Sweetheart, I'm too close—"

She didn't budge. Kept right on sucking him, and from the way her hips wriggled, she expected him to do the same.

Luckiest. Man. *Alive.*

With a lusty sigh, he dove back in.

They came together, a deep shuddering ecstasy that rocked his body and soul.

Afterward, he gathered her in his arms. She lay with her head on his chest, their limbs entwined and heartbeats mingling. The moment was so beautiful that Paul wanted to stay that way forever.

Forever lasted approximately two minutes.

A cry came from the sitting room.

Charity sighed. "We'd better get Pru before she wakes everyone in the house."

"Everyone's up anyway." Paul slung an arm over his eyes as his wife left the bed. "I'm pretty certain I heard my niece raising havoc about an hour ago." He took some consolation in the fact that at least Hunt wasn't getting any sleep either. "And at this rate, the Kents' little boy won't be far behind."

"Since everyone's up, we might as well go down and visit," Charity said. "Your mama and Marietta are probably lying in wait already. You know how they love to dote on Pru. With those two for grandmamas, Pru could end up a spoiled little hoyden if we're not careful."

"A bit of indulgence never hurt anyone," he said. "After all, you let me have my way with you quite often—and I turned out fine, didn't I?"

Paul grinned when Charity made a face at him. As she dressed, he lay back and admired the view. He'd never tire of the pleasure of simply seeing his wife each and every day. For as long as he lived, he knew he'd never take that privilege for granted.

"Are you going to leer at me all day, or are you getting up?" she said.

"Leer," he said.

He smiled when she tried to look annoyed and failed. Rising, he sauntered over, cupped her nape, and kissed her until she went limp against him once more.

"What was that for?" she said breathlessly.

"For being you," he told her. "My sunshine, my heart, and my home."

Her radiant smile spoke louder than words. Her hand slipped into his, and together they went to fetch their daughter. To greet the love and mayhem of their happily forever after.

Thank you for spending time with Paul and Charity! I hope you loved this angsty tale of a rake and wallflower finding each other—and themselves—in their journey to happily ever after. I had so much fun with these two and with the familiar characters who popped in to support them :-)

As this series comes to a close, I find myself both saddened to bid farewell to old friends ... and excited to greet new ones! My next series, Heart of Enquiry, is a spin-off of Mayhem in Mayfair and features the spirited and unconventional Kent family first introduced in *Her Protector's Pleasure*. In the prequel novella, *The Widow Vanishes*, you'll see some familiar faces from the Mayhem in Mayfair series and The Duke Who Knew Too Much tells the love story of determined spinster Emma Kent and the wicked, tortured Duke of Strathaven.

Thanks for hanging out in the Callawayverse. Here's to many more adventures together!

#1 National Bestselling Regency Romance

He's a rake accused of murder. She's the spinster accusing him. Enemies make the hottest lovers.

"This book is FIRE…Alaric & Emma make you believe that the passion and relationship is as real as the book in your hand." - *Regency and Romance*

Until the next time…hugs and happy reading,

Grace Callaway

Acknowledgments

To my readers and fans: thank you for your support of Mayhem in Mayfair. I hope you've enjoyed spending time in this world as much as I have enjoyed creating it. Your encouragement has literally helped me to follow my dreams. Heartfelt appreciation to you all!

To my writing posse: Tina, best of friends and writing partners—I'm loving our weekly work/hanging out sessions! Thank you for being a support and an inspiration. Virna, brilliant writer and friend—thank you for your honesty, help with my work, and your friendship. Diane Pershing, developmental editor extraordinaire—this book is better because of you. And to Brian, who manages to be the perfect spouse and perfect editor ... a monumental feat!

To the team that supports my work: Carrie, you make my books beautiful, and you're such a joy to work with. Melissa, thank you for keeping my newsletter (and me) on track. John, thank goodness you're a technical whiz ... so I don't have to be!

To my family, immediate and extended: hugs and kisses for supporting me in this wild, wacky, and wonderful journey. Love to you all!

Last, but not least, this book is dedicated to Brian ... because I *did* want a poet for a husband. Love you, baby.

About the Author

USA Today & International Bestselling Author Grace Callaway writes hot and heart-melting historical romance filled with mystery and adventure. Her debut novel was a Romance Writers of America Golden Heart® Finalist and a #1 National Regency Bestseller, and her subsequent novels have topped national and international bestselling lists. She has won the Daphne du Maurier Award for Excellence in Mystery and Suspense, the Maggie Award for Excellence, the Golden Leaf, and the Passionate Plume Award, and her books have been shortlisted for numerous other honors. She holds a doctorate in clinical psychology from the University of Michigan and lives with her family in a valley by the ocean. When she's not writing, she enjoys dancing, checking out cafes with her rescue pup, and going on adapted adventures with her special son.

Keep up with Grace's latest news!

Newsletter: gracecallaway.com/newsletter

facebook.com/GraceCallawayBooks

bookbub.com/authors/grace-callaway

instagram.com/gracecallawaybooks

amazon.com/author/gracecallaway